THE LONELY STRONGHOLD

MRS. BAILLIE REYNOLDS

By MRS. BAILLIE REYNOLDS

A CASTLE TO LET

THE DAUGHTER PAYS

THE COST OF A PROMISE

A DOUBTFUL CHARACTER

A MAKE-SHIFT MARRIAGE

OUT OF THE NIGHT

GIRL FROM NOWHERE

THE NOTORIOUS MISS LISLE

GEORGE H. DORAN COMPANY
NEW YORK

THE
LONELY STRONGHOLD

BY

MRS. BAILLIE REYNOLDS

AUTHOR OF "A CASTLE TO LET," ETC.

NEW YORK
GEORGE H. DORAN COMPANY

PRINTED IN THE UNITED STATES OF AMERICA

CONTENTS

CHAPTER   PAGE

I   THE PALATINE BANK 9

II   OLWEN AT HOME 21

III   "WHAT IS A PELE EXACTLY?" 30

IV   HER FIRST OFFER 40

V   TRAVELLER'S JOY 49

VI   COMMENCING ACQUAINTANCE 60

VII   THE DARK TOWER 67

VIII   THE FIRST DAY 79

IX   INDIAN MAGIC 89

X   A QUEER HOUSEHOLD 100

XI   MISS LILY MARTIN 108

XII   A CONFIDENCE: AND SOME SPYING 117

XIII   NINIAN'S DEFENCE 128

XIV   A FRESH START 137

XV   A COLD WALK 144

XVI   A LITTLE FRICTION 153

XVII   BALMAYNE'S WARNING 162

XVIII   VISITORS 173

XIX   A DISCOVERY 185

XX   THE PHILTRE 194

XXI   BY THE LOUGHSIDE 203

XXII   THE MILE-CASTLE 211

XXIII   WHAT THE DAWN BROUGHT 220

XXIV   THE FINAL WARNING 233

v

CHAPTER		PAGE
XXV	THE UNEXPECTED	242
XXVI	NINIAN'S TWIN	244
XXVII	THE FINAL INSULT	265
XXVIII	ESCAPE	277
XXIX	BRAMFORTH AGAIN	288
XXX	THE INCREDIBLE TRUTH	299
XXXI	THE CHANGED WORLD	308
XXXII	ONE TWIN RETURNS	320
XXXIII	THE BULL-DROP	330
XXXIV	THE MILE-CASTLE AGAIN	340
XXXV	'TWIXT CUP AND LIP	355
XXXVI	IN THE DARK	363
XXXVII	VINDICATED	369

THE LONELY STRONGHOLD

THE
LONELY STRONGHOLD

CHAPTER I

THE PALATINE BANK

THE sleet drove spitefully against the dirty windows of the stuffy room behind the Palatine Bank in the High Street of Bramforth.

The air was close, without being warm; a smell of tea and toasted bread lingered upon it. The clock struck, and the girls who sat upon their high stools, cramped over columns of figures, straightened their backs with long sighs of relief.

"Snakes! What weather!" muttered Miss Hand as she pushed back her stool until it almost overbalanced in her efforts to gaze at the December night without.

"With my usual luck, came without a gamp this morning," grumbled Miss Turner, collecting loose sheets with a dexterity born of long practice.

"And you've got a mile to walk when you get off the tram," exclaimed Miss Donkin sympathetically.

Mrs. Barnes, who presided, seated not at a desk but at a central table, wiped her pen, looking across the room with knitted brows.

"It has struck, Miss Innes," said she.

The click of the typewriter went on nevertheless, and the operator replied without desisting from her work. "Let me get to the foot of this page, please."

There began the rustle and murmur of the girls leaving their places, in what was described by the bank managers as "The ladies' room." Mabel Hirst, a pretty girl with dark eyes, ran to the fire and held her chil-blained hands to its warmth. "Oh, my goody," said she, "when will old Storky start in on that 'chauffage centrale' which he is always gassing about?"

"At the coming of the coquecigrues, I should think," said the voice of Miss Innes, who now ceased her clicking, rose from her chair, and raised her arms above her head, breathing a long "A-ah!" of relief.

"Not that I think it would be much improvement," she went on. "It probably wouldn't work. Nothing *does* work in this old town; and as long as we have the fire there is at least one place where you can go and thaw now and then."

An electric bell rang twice.

"Hallo, Barney, old Storky wants you," said Mabel Hirst. "Beg him to accept my compliments, and ask if he ever gives compensation for chilblains."

"Tell him it's my birthday to-morrow!"

"Say you think my work during this past quarter merits a rise!"

"Suggest he gives us a Christmas treat—stalls for the panto!"

The chorus was practically simultaneous, and Mrs. Barnes put her hands over her ears. "I'm far more likely to ask permission to increase the fines for talking," was her parting shaft, as she vanished in obedience to the summons.

"You look a bit fagged, Innes," remarked Mabel Hirst, as the typist approached the fire, and knelt down so that the flames shone upon her small, intense face.

"Oh, it's not fag so much as disgust," she replied, in a

voice of individual quality. "I don't think I can stick
this any longer. I didn't take a secretarial training in
order to type out rows of figures all day long. I am
bored, dears—bored stiff! All my powers are wasting
their sweetness on the desert air—or rather the town
lack of air! The desert would be all right. I shouldn't
a scrap mind blushing unseen if I had plenty of space
to blush in! Ouf! I feel as if I should choke!"

She stared at the fire with firmly folded lips, every
line of her slender person seeming to breathe the resentment she felt.

"It's pretty bad," agreed Miss Turner, who was lacing
up her boots. "Suppose nobody's got a raincloak they'll
be saint enough to lend?"

"Yes," replied Miss Innes, "you shall have mine. I
brought a gamp, and I haven't far to walk. But look
here—mind you bring it back."

"Course I will. To-morrow without fail, moddum.
Oh, this sleet! It really is something chronic."

The dressing-room opened out of the office, but in
the absence of Barney the connecting door stood wide,
against all rules, and the girls went in and out, warming their boots before putting them on, commenting on
the frozen water-pipes and kindred grievances, after the
manner of their kind all the world over.

In the midst of it, the superintendent returned.

"Hallo! What did the old bird want? Give you
the sack, or tell you to bestow it on any of us?"

"I'm sure it was about a Christmas tree for the young
ladies, in recognition of the fine work they have put
in——"

"Not quite that, but the next best thing," replied
Barney, in a cheerful tone. "In view of the coming
heavy work in the New Year, you and I are to have an

extra day for Christmas—the 24th to the 28th! What d'you think of that ?"

There was a whoop of joy, and the babel of voices broke out anew.

"If only he would give us the day before instead of after," sighed one malcontent. "If we had Christmas Eve now——"

"My dear, you know that's impossible at a bank. Take your extra day and give thanks for it. It's more than the men are getting," was the rejoinder of Mrs. Barnes.

"Three whole days !" echoed Blanche Turner. "I shall have forgotten you all by the time we reassemble. Think of that! Shan't know you by sight!"

"I can easily believe that! Having spent your holiday entirely at the 'movies,' your sight will have given out," jeered Miss Donkin. "Then you'll lose your job, my girl."

"I shall go to Leeds, to my aunt !"

"And I to Driffield."

"And I home."

The chatter waxed louder and louder, as gradually girl after girl got ready. Then they began to depart, drifting out by twos and threes through a side door into an alley giving upon the High Street.

Miss Innes was last. She stood alone before the little looking-glass fitting her hat dexterously upon her gleaming hair, her eyes mechanically assisting at the process, but really far away with her busy thoughts. She had not anticipated such a violent downpour as greeted her when she emerged into the street; and as she crossed, to await a tram, she half regretted her loan of her cloak to Miss Turner. She was lucky enough to get a place in the first car that passed. Ten minutes' journey brought her to the residential suburb of the ugly town, and as she descended into the road the rain poured down upon her with such vehemence that she took shelter under a tree for a minute, in order to get her breath and decide what to do.

Struck by a happy idea, she turned into a road close by, and made her way to a detached house, standing inside a wall with two carriage gates. In the comparative shelter of the porch she halted and rang the bell.

The middle-aged servant who admitted her said with a smile that Mrs. Holroyd and Miss Gracie were in the dining-room.

Miss Innes wiped the rain from her face, placed her dripping umbrella in the stand, and opened the door of a hot, over-furnished, but comfortable room, in which a stout, rather shapeless lady and a good-humoured girl who would be a duplicate of her mother in twenty years' time, sat at a huge dining-table strewn with paper, string and parcels.

"Olwen!" cried Gracie, jumping up with a pleased cry of greeting.

"Why, how do you do? We're downright pleased to see you. I was saying to Gracie, it was only yesterday, that Ollie never takes advantage of our invitation to drop in upon us any night on her way back from the bank. So here we are as usual! Busy with the Christmas packing! But it's almost done now, and as I say to Gracie, when it's done, it's done for a year, that's one good thing."

Olwen kissed the jolly lady. "I feel a regular beggar," said she. "I have come in now for the sordid reason that I want to borrow something. And you pay the penalty for being the kindest people I know."

"My dear! Anything we can lend you!—"

Olwen explained that her raincoat had been borrowed,

and that the storm was so severe that she feared to reach the Vicarage wet through without one. "If Gracie will lend me hers I can leave it as I go down to-morrow morning," said she.

"Well, of course! But now you're here, won't you stay the evening? Pa'll be in, and Ben, for supper before so very long, and we'll clear up this mess in no time. Now do, child! Think how pleased Ben'll be to find you here!"

"You are always so kind, but I can't, really. To begin with, I always feel so soiled in my office frock. Gracie will know what I mean! And, to go on with, this evening is my only time for any little Christmas work that I have in hand. To-morrow night we shall almost certainly be working overtime, as they are giving us girls an extra day off, and so you see I simply must get back."

"An extra day's holiday? Well, that is a bit of luck, any way. Now sit down while Gracie gets you a bit of cake and a glass of port, for you look perished. And tell me how the dear vicar is."

"Thanks. Grandfather is wonderfully well."

"That's right, that's right! I daresay he finds Mr. Witherly a great help in the parish—so active and energetic! Dear, dear, what a good thing he bore up so well at the time of your dear grandmother's death. I said to Gracie, I remember, 'My dear, this will mean the break-up of our vicar.' But, after all, it was not. He bore it nobly, like the Christian he is."

"Aunt Maud and Aunt Ada take care he shall feel it as little as possible," replied Olwen. "You see, grandmamma had been ailing so long before her death."

"Yes, that's true enough," sighed Mrs. Holroyd. "It's a trial, Ollie, as you will find when you get into years, to be taken off your feet, so that you hinder the ones

you have always been used to help. I must say I am
thankful I can still get about."

"Get about indeed! Walk me off my legs!" put in
Gracie dryly.

It was good to hear her mother's fat, contented laugh.

"Oh, well, it's your merry heart goes all the day,"
said she, "and look what a happy woman I've always
been, with your father ready to cut off his head and
serve it up in a dish if he'd 'a' thought I wanted it; and
such good children as I've had; my girls so well married,
my boys so well started, and now me left with Ben, my
eldest, and Gracie, my youngest, and the grandchildren
now and then! Now, it was different with your poor
grandma! One trouble after another! Your poor dear
mother's unlucky marriage and sad death! Your Uncle
Charles's misfortune, your Uncle Horace's sad end! Oh,
she had her troubles, poor, dear lady, and no doubt she
was glad to be at rest at last!"

Olwen listened with an indulgent smile on her expressive face. Once long ago she had determined to
count the "poors," the "dears" and "I-said-to-Gracies"
in Mrs. Holroyd's talk; but had soon abandoned the
enterprise as hopeless. "Did you know that Aunt Ethel
and her whole family are coming for Christmas?" she
asked.

"No, my dear, is that so? . . . Well, of course, not
but what there is plenty of room in that great Vicarage
for all . . . but let me see, how many children are there?
Five, it must be!"

"Five and a nurse," said Olwen, smiling.

"Well, but dearie, that is a great expense for the
vicar."

"It is Uncle George who bears it, not grandfather.
They bring two of their own maids to help ours, and I

think everybody enjoys it. Frank and Marjorie are getting quite grown up now."

"Well, I call that a very nice arrangement, a good old-fashioned way to keep Christmas. Most sensible! I daresay your Aunt Ethel knew the vicar would be feeling his loneliness this year, didn't she now?" Mrs. Holroyd expatiated for long on the subject. She was still talking when the front door was heard, and Gracie, with a sly glance at Olwen, said:

"There's Ben, I do believe."

Olwen had been so comfortable in the easy chair drawn up to the great fire that she had stayed longer than she intended. Ben Holroyd was the reason why she did not oftener avail herself of his mother's unaffected kindness. The Holroyds were not aristocratic. In fact, when Mrs. Holroyd said "packing up," her accent came perilously near to the "paacking oop" of the lower orders in Bramforth. They were genuine and hospitable, and the girl's life was starved; not so starved, however, that she was as yet ready to take Ben as a way out.

He now entered the room, a short, stocky man of five-and-thirty, even now redder in the face than was strictly becoming, and probably to grow more so as years went on. He had a ragged dark moustache and uneasy eyes, which seemed always apologising. The good-humoured simplicity which made one pardon his mother's lack of breeding was wholly absent in him. He had fixed his heart upon Olwen Innes, who was a very poor match from a pecuniary point of view, but whom he knew to be above him socially.

Gracie and Olwen had together received their education at the Bramforth High School for Girls, wherein Olwen had always been the show pupil and Gracie at the bottom of her class. Day by day the two had gone and returned together, with their satchels and lunch

packets, and there subsisted between them a real friendship. Had it not been for poor Ben, the friendship would
have been closer, as Gracie more than suspected.

His face, as he came in, showed his delight. He sat
down by Olwen, and at his mother's instigation earnestly
sought to make her reconsider her decision and stay the
evening. She was resolute in her refusal, and Mrs.
Holroyd, her heart sore for her boy's disappointment,
bethought her of the bit of information incautiously let
drop before he came in.

"Never mind, Bennie, we'll do better," said she cheerfully. "Ollie says the bank is giving her an extra day's
holiday. Now, why can't you and she and Gracie find
somebody to make a fourth, and take the train to Leeds
day after Boxing Day? Lunch there, and go to a mattin-
nay, mother standing treat. Eh? How's that?"

Ben and Gracie thought this a brilliant suggestion.
Olwen did not see how to decline it. A matinée at Leeds,
where an excellent company was then performing,
was a treat she seldom obtained. Mrs. Holroyd, proud
of her success, ordered Ben to the telephone forthwith to
engage seats. After a little more talk, Olwen took her
departure, but, as she had foreboded, Ben thought it
necessary to escort her home. She resisted as firmly as
was possible without rudeness, but was obliged at last
to give in.

Warmly wrapped in Gracie's raincoat, she found herself out in the storm, her hand linked to Ben's sturdy
arm, while he held one umbrella over the two of them.

"Mind the mud, Miss Olwen. The Council ought to
have mended this road last summer, as I told my father."

"Yes, indeed, what is the use of a father in such an
exalted position if he can't get the road mended outside
his own house?" laughed Olwen, hoping to keep the talk

on this prosaic subject. Inwardly her thoughts ran somewhat thus:

. . . Would it be possible? Would even this be better than her present life? . . . Always had she been surrounded by the hosts of the Philistines, she who was born, she was very certain, upon the sea-coast of Bohemia!
. . . It was merely existence, not life, in the shabby Vicarage, with the two parochial aunts, the weary old grandfather and the periodical inrushes of the Whitefield clan! Her Aunt Ethel had married George Whitefield, a man of no more exalted origin than Ben Holroyd. A mill-owner, but a very wealthy one. The Holroyds were only comfortable——

Could it be that she was so utterly contemptible that she was loath to swallow poor Ben merely because the pill was insufficiently gilded? . . . Well, it did make a difference. Aunt Ethel lived in a palace. She had hot-houses and motor-cars, her boy had been to the University. Marriage with Ben would mean a semi-detached villa in a suburb of Bramforth. Dear Mrs. Holroyd would present, and consequently would expect to choose, the Brussels carpet and rep curtains, and to lay the best quality cork lino plentifully over halls and passage ways. . . .

"You can't think how pleased I am that the bank has given you an extra day," Ben was saying when she began to listen. "It doesn't seem right to me for the likes of you to be working there. Why, Flora Donkin, the butcher's daughter, is in your room, isn't she?"

"Certainly she is, and a very good sort. So neat, I love copying out her figures."

"But it's not the place for you," repeated Ben more fervently. "You ought to have a home of your own, and someone to take care of you all the time."

The moment for the inevitable cold water had arrived, and she was forced to throw it. A declaration at this moment would be more than she could bear. "Dear me, how Early Victorian you are!" she laughed. "We girls of the twentieth century don't want people to look after us. We want to live our own lives, don't you know?"

He was silent, swallowing down mortification. He had got quite near that time! Then: "Gracie doesn't want to do that kind of thing," he muttered sulkily.

"Gracie's vocation is very plain. She has a mother who can't do without her. I have no home ties. I can go where I like and do what I like."

"And what you like is the baank?"

She laughed. "Oh, the bank's all right!" she told him lightly. Not for worlds would she have divulged to him her deep dissatisfaction with things as they were. She could not tell him that she had secretly sent an advertisement to the papers only a day or two previously —an advertisement to which she was at the moment feverishly awaiting replies. Aloud she went on: "Gracie and I are great friends, but we are not a bit alike, you know. She is the fine domestic type of woman, but that is just what I'm not. My father, as you know, was the reverse of domestic. I take after him."

Ben felt very uncomfortable. Madoc Innes, Olwen's father, was what Ben would have described as a "bad hat." He felt any allusion to this discreditable parent to be in the nature of an indelicacy. He knew that Olwen was capricious and perverse, but he held the steadfast belief of many a good man, that she would after marriage turn automatically into just the woman he would have her be.

Something in her made special appeal to him, and had always done so, even in the days when she wore short skirts and long black stockings, and her remarkable hair had streamed in the wind, all shaded from dun colour to old gold.   The thought of her scapegrace father was the one point upon which he was uncertain.   Olwen had accomplished her intention.   They reached the Vicarage with no further attempt at love-making on his part.

CHAPTER II

THE large family of the Reverend James Wilson had been brought up on the fringes of Dartmoor. His income there was, however, of so inadequate a nature, in view of his domestic requirements, that when the question of education demanded heroic measures, he accepted the living of Gratfield, a very large town in the industrial Midlands—a post for which both his temperament and his habit of life hitherto made him singularly ill-fitted.

Of his seven children, four were girls. They were fine creatures, with white limbs, blonde hair, complexion of cream and roses. Their natures were placidly bovine, except during that brief period in which a girl's own sense of her own beauty and the power it bestows kindles in her a fictitious vivacity, and nature, for her own purposes, lends a charm which is incredibly fugitive.

The young ladies made quite a sensation upon their arrival in Gratfield. Not long before, Madoc Innes, a clever young Welsh journalist, had bought the *Gratfield Courier* and settled in the place. He was handsome on a small scale, and passed for rich—drove good horses, smoked expensive cigars, and was much in demand in a society where such young men are rare.

The sight of Clara Wilson at a ball set his Celtic blood on fire. Her Juno-like loveliness made so powerful an appeal to his senses that the limits of her mind or the faults of her disposition did not enter the question. She was stupid, and she was essentially Philistine, but he shut his eyes to it until too late. They were married, and he committed his first enormity by the purchase of a little old Elizabethan farm up on the moor outside Gratfield, planning to drive to his work each day.

Clara detested the place. She had had as much of moors and heather in her childhood as would last her all her life. What she desired was shops and fine clothes, plenty of company, the chance to show off and be admired. For these things she had married, and not for love of Madoc, with whose tastes she had no sympathy, and whose disposition she would have disliked had she ever given a thought to the subject.

After the blind fashion of a man in love, the young husband felt that he had not won his wife's devotion long before he consciously admitted anything of the kind. He began by spoiling her outrageously, giving her all she craved, in the vain hope that gifts might propitiate her and incline her to a more favourable—one might say a more interested—attitude towards himself.

Unhappily, a year or two after the marriage his rising fortunes underwent a sharp change.

Being a Welshman, he was a violent partisan, and his knowledge of the temper and prejudices of the North was very imperfect. He attacked a certain public character, and found himself up against a stone wall of implacable hostility. A costly libel action left him a ruined man. He being thus deprived of what had been his sole asset in his wife's eyes, their lack of unity became at once nakedly apparent.

He had plenty of courage and belief in himself. He took his wife and baby girl to London, where he got work on a big "daily," and hoped for better things.

Clara, however, had no forgiveness for him. She had married with one object, that of being well off; and her failure was more sharply accentuated in her eyes by the fact that Ethel, her next sister, had made a conquest of

George Whitefield, only son and heir of the richest mill-owner in Gratfield.

Hopelessly out of sympathy, the Innes pair drifted wider and wider apart. The discovery of his wife's indifference warped Madoc's unstable temperament. Miserable at home, he consoled himself elsewhere. They ran continually into debt, there was even an execution in the house. Scenes grew frequent and even violent. At last, when Olwen was about seven years old, her father disappeared completely, leaving behind an envelope, addressed to his wife, containing a hundred pounds in bank-notes.

Clara, her beauty gone, broken in health, soured in temper, returned, with her little daughter, to her father's rectory.

She came at an unlucky turn in the family fortunes.

It had long been apparent that twenty years of sloth in a tiny parish, in a mild and balmy climate, had permanently unfitted the Rev. James Wilson for strenuous work and the rushing life of a big town. After a struggle, hopeless from the first, against his constitutional inertia, and the growing dissatisfaction of his parishioners, he was stricken down by severe illness. His return to health was seriously retarded by the sad climax of Clara's marriage, and the failure of his sons to do anything to lighten his burden of undone work and unpaid bills.

At this point his old college offered him the living of St. Agnes, Bramforth, about fifty miles further north. It was a depressing district, semi-suburban, semi-industrial, with an 1850 church, pew-rented, and a fluctuating congregation. The income was, however, as good as that of his present cure, and the work less than half. About twelve months after the flight of Madoc Innes, and fifteen years before that Christmas when Olwen decided that the bank was intolerable, the family migrated to Bramforth, and Mr. Wilson, with the assistance of a curate, thankfully lapsed into the stagnation which suited him.

Olwen's mother was at this time an invalid. Three years later a prominent surgeon diagnosed serious internal trouble. She underwent an operation, failed to rally from the shock, and died a few days later.

The two younger Miss Wilsons, Maud and Ada, did not marry. Perhaps they looked too high, for while in Gratfield they had not been without admirers. They were, however, still single, and had borne with fine unselfishness their share in the strain on the meagre family resources involved by the necessity of supporting Clara and Clara's child.

Olwen's memory of her father was vivid. In fact, she often thought that the first seven years of her life had left a mark far deeper than those that followed. She was always striving, in an unformed, eager way, to arrive at the truth concerning the breach between her parents. Her mother remained in her memory as mostly fretful and complaining, uncertain in temper, dissatisfied and uncontrolled. She knew now that Mrs. Innes was a deeply wronged woman; yet she could not escape the bias of mind produced by the fact that she herself owed every hour of happiness as a child to her father. She remembered him as invariably sweet-tempered and gay—as a constant companion, more like a contemporary—liable as herself to incur the sudden and capricious wrath of the mistress of the house.

His upbringing had been cosmopolitan, his parents having lived much abroad. To adapt himself to the Wilson standpoint had been from the first impossible. The laborious etiquette of the provinces was a matter of which he could never grasp the importance. That his wife's happiness should depend upon such things as card-cases, "At Home" days, late dinner, or a "drawing-room suite" was to him unthinkable.

Olwen remembered best of all their habit of escaping together. They went to remote corners of Hampstead Heath or Battersea Park, or, if he were in funds, to the Thames, where they took a boat. They spent long days in make-believe, with a packet of picnic lunch, and a few pence for their omnibus ride home through the magic dusk of London. His faculty for story-telling was endless, and one romance, especially dear, went on in sections from week to week, and was entitled: "Story of the Dandy Lion and his four friends, the Pale Policeman, the Cheery Churchwarden, the Sad Sweep, and the Tremendous Tramp." An illustration of this group of friends was one of her few mementoes of her vanished boon companion.

From him, too, she heard the tales of the Mabinogion, the "Romance of Kiluch and Olwen"—whence came her own name, so severely condemned by the Wilson family —the "Romance of Enid and Geraint," and so on.

This all made it hard for her to apportion the blame between the sundered pair. At the Vicarage, of course, all the guilt was heaped on Madoc Innes. She supposed this to be in fact just. His temperament may have been charming but his principles were apparently all wrong. She saw only part. Yet as she grew older she found herself concentrating more and more upon her mother's share in the débacle.

That Clara Innes was unable either to sympathise with or to understand her husband was the result presumably of her limitations, and these, one would suppose, she could not help. Not until Olwen read her "Pilgrim's Progress" and learned, with a sudden shock, that Ignorance was thrust down into hell, did it occur to her that

Ignorance is a crime, since it is a thing one may remedy if one chooses.

Grumbling, one grants, is not a sin. To fail in sympathy to your husband is hardly a sin. To make his home uncomfortable is not a sin, that is, not of the sort called deadly. But to be unfaithful to your wife is a direct breach of a commandment. Therefore, in the Wilson code, Clara was innocent and her husband criminal. To his other crimes he added wife desertion, which is a matter for the police courts. Clara had never done anything in her life which could conceivably have landed her in the police court. It was all very puzzling. When Olwen had spent time, as she often did, in considering the subject, she usually found that she ended by wishing that her father had taken her with him when he fled. She felt sure they could have been happy together.

In her heart she knew herself for her father's daughter, and from the Wilson point of view wholly alien. It was typical of them that they should so dislike her name, for no reason but because they had never heard it before. The name of Gwendolen, just as Welsh, and more high-falutin in sound, was quite popular in Bramforth, because Gwendolen was in fairly common use. Olwen was different, and she was usually called "Ollie" in hopes that the casual acquaintance might suppose her baptismal name to be Olive, a name which, mysteriously enough, was under no ban.

Her defaulting father had made no sign, and sent no message upon the occasion of his wife's death. It was tacitly assumed that he was either dead or had gone to some remote quarter of the globe, where he was living most probably under an alias.

For nearly three years now Olwen had been self-supporting. At first her post at the bank had possessed that elfin charm with which most novelties are gilded

when one is in one's teens. Life itself is then a romance,
the mere act of coming out into the streets on a fine
morning may be the beginning of endless adventure.

Now the monotony had killed the novelty. Her father's
restless blood stirred and demanded relief. She felt
almost desperate as she let herself into the Vicarage and
pushed her streaming umbrella into the untidy receptacle.

A lowered jet of gas burned dimly in the hall. Yet by
its light she could descry a letter upon the hall table,
addressed "Miss O. Innes, St. Agnes Vicarage, Bramforth."

An answer to her advertisement at last! A way of
escape from the bank or its alternative, Ben and the
linoleumed villa!

Snatching it up, she hurried away to her own room,
to enjoy the excitement of reading it.

On the threshold of that sanctuary she paused. It was
in a state of upheaval. There was no bedding on the
bedstead, no carpet on the floor. Instantly she remembered that her room was being cleaned for the reception
of Marjorie Whitefield, and that she herself was to "double
up" with Aunt Maud during the period of invasion.

Ashamed of her own feeling of acute distaste, she
turned and went slowly along the passage.

Aunt Maud was washing her hands for supper, and
the subdued kindness with which she welcomed her niece
and showed her how she had taken things out of drawers
and bestowed them as well as she could during the girl's
absence, made Olwen vexed at her own irritation.

Aunt Maud was very fond of "Ollie." She turned
wistfully to the only young creature left remaining in
the shabby old Vicarage. She lingered now, to explain
in detail every point in her successful "packing of them
all in." It was her part to superintend the housework

while her elder sister did the catering, an arrangement which, on the whole, worked well.

Olwen strove with courage and some success to make her interest seem real. The way in which a certain hole in the dining-room carpet had been triumphed over, and the report that the re-enamelling of the bath was a com-plete success, were things of deep importance to Aunt Maud, and it would have been brutal to snub her.

When at last she went downstairs, there were but five minutes before the supper bell, but curiosity would no longer be denied. Olwen sat down on the bed with the letter in her hand, enjoying the delights of speculation before opening it. It was addressed in a very pretty hand, and bore the postmark of a part of England noted for fine scenery.

"Suppose," thought Olwen, whose suppositions leaned always to the romantic, "that I hold my destiny in my hand at this moment?"

Excuse enough, in all conscience, for some dallying with the anticipation!

However, at last the envelope was broken and the letter lay under her eyes:

"Dulley Vicarage.

"Mrs. Jones, having seen Miss O. Innes's advt., thinks the post she can offer might be suitable. She is in want of a lady to live in the house and help in the training of her children, five in number.

"A servant is kept, but Miss I. would be asked to make herself generally useful. Her secretarial training would be very useful to Mr. Jones in copying out his sermons and conducting his correspondence. If Miss I. has a typewriter of her own, Mrs. Jones would have no objection to her bringing it with her. She would be treated in all respects as one of the family, and Mrs. Jones would give a pound a month pocket money, as to her own daughter."

For a moment Olwen gripped the letter in her young fist as if she wished its writer were there instead. Then her sense of humour triumphed. Bursting into hearty laughter, she crushed the impertinence into a ball and tossed it into the fender.

"Well," she mused, "I think that is the limit! And there is my sole reply to an advertisement which cost me five shillings!"

Fiercely she brushed the thick mane of dun-coloured hair that shaded to gold, "And I thought my destiny lay in that envelope!" she whispered quite fiercely. Her eyes seemed to blaze. They were pale grey eyes, made beautiful by noticeably fine lashes, which, with her eye-brows, were too dark for such fair hair. She was not going to be discouraged. She would write to London, to a first-class agency, and pay whatever fee they demanded. To go to London would be to escape from Ben.

She laughed and sighed both at once. Aunt Maud would have liked her to marry Ben—poor Aunt Maud, who knew nothing of the discontent which had grown up within the daughter of Madoc Innes. She had feared it in Ollie's early girlhood—had watched for signs of it. But by degrees she had reached the comforting conviction that Olwen inherited from her Wilson relatives too good a strain of steady devotion to duty to be troubled by her father's vagabond instincts.

She loved Olwen, and confided in her. Olwen loved her, but never reciprocated the confidences. Aunt Maud might have inferred much from the circumstance, but she belonged to a type which does not draw inferences.

CHAPTER III

"WHAT IS A PELE EXACTLY?"

"OLLIE has changed a good deal during these last three years," remarked Mrs. Whitefield, as she reclined in the least uncomfortable of the Vicarage drawing-room chairs, beside a huge and glowing fire such as seldom burned in the little-used grate.

Aunt Ada, opposite, was knitting, with fingers knobby with rheumatism. "We think we see a great likeness to poor Mamma in her at times," she remarked, with that softening of the voice in which she always spoke of her niece, and which vaguely stirred Ethel's resentment.

"Likeness to Mamma?" she repeated scornfully, "why, she is as like Madoc Innes as two peas in a pod! See the way her eyes wrinkle when she laughs—and that mouthful of little short teeth—and the small-boned type, so Welsh, you know. When we took Lord Fishguard's place in Glamorgan last summer we were always meeting people who reminded me of Madoc! And she is just the same. Yet she seems fairly steady, you say?"

"She is the best girl in the world," put in Aunt Maud fervently. "Week after week she hands over nearly half her earnings to Ada and me; and she gives every satisfaction at the bank. You know Mrs. Barnes only took her post there because she was left a widow on very small means. She is a friend of the Otleys, and she told them that Ollie is highly thought of at the Palatine."

"Well, it is to her credit that she should earn her living, but in my opinion a private post would be more suitable," said the rich man's wife reflectively. "It's not a nice

30

thing for the family, you know, having her in business in
the very town where you reside—trudging out to work in
all weathers. I wonder if George could get her a better
berth. A good many of our friends keep a private secretary, and it is quite what George calls a soft job."

Though older than either of her maiden sisters, Mrs.
Whitefield looked years younger. Her golden hair was
not tinged with grey, and her faint suggestion of three
chins suited her Juno type. Aunt Ada, with sparse, fading hair, brushed flat, pale face and spectacles, might
have been her mother.

It was the afternoon of Christmas Day, and the young
people were upstairs, planning a charade to be performed
next evening. The Whitefield children had been born at
what their mother described as easy intervals. Hugh and
Marjorie were in their late teens, Lionel fourteen, and
the two youngest still young enough to be in the nursery.

"She is rather pretty, you know," went on the lady,
still considering her niece. "Though I don't know that I
admire any type so mixed. Her mother's hair and eyes,
with her father's dark skin and eyelashes, make rather a
curious effect. Pity she can't marry, poor girl, but I
don't suppose that's likely."

"She might marry to-morrow if she liked, as I happen
to know," burst out Aunt Maud, who could not bear to
hear Ollie patronized.

"Indeed? Anybody worth having?" was the somewhat
surprised rejoinder.

"That depends on what you mean. In my opinion, not
nearly good enough for her, but well enough off to marry
and make her comfortable, and his family would welcome
her with open arms."

"Bless me! Then why does she go fagging on at the
bank like this? Doesn't the young man object?"

"She hasn't given him the right to object," sighed Aunt

Maud, "and I don't think she will; at least, I should have said so a couple of days ago, but she told me yesterday that she is going out with him—that is, with his family—the day after to-morrow."

"Oh!" Mrs. Whitefield was half interested, half envious. "George and I would give her a handsome present," said she, speaking as though this fact, if known, should weigh heavy in the result. "I suppose I must be pricking up my ears about Marjorie soon," she added. "She hasn't inherited the Wilson beauty, but she'll be worth picking up, as George says."

"So far as I have observed," said Ada suddenly, "a girl needs only two things in order to get married. I don't mean a girl with money. Marjorie will get married in any case, she needs no internal charm. But for a poor girl, there are two essential things——"

"And they are—— ?"

"A pair of fine eyes and an empty mind. The fine eyes may now and then be dispensed with; but emptiness of mind is indispensable."

"Really, Ada, you musn't talk like that, even to me! It sounds so embittered. It is sheer nonsense to say men like stupidity."

"Not stupidity—emptiness. A man wants a woman into whose vacant mind he can pour the image of himself. Jane Austen describes the pose as intelligent ignorance; but I don't think the intelligence matters much so long as the ignorance is there."

"You are suggesting," said Ethel superciliously, "that Clara and I had vacant minds, and that you and Maud are single because you were more intelligent."

"Yes," said Ada bluntly, "I think it's true. I was every bit as handsome as you, but George would never have married me, because I had ideas of my own. So had Maud. Ideas get in the way. Life is far easier for a woman who has none. In that case, almost any man will do."

"Which makes one afraid for Ollie's happiness," said Maud softly. "She is just a mass of ideas—has a really original mind."

As she spoke, voices were heard, and Hugh, Marjorie and Olwen entered the room together. Marjorie, big and bouncing, with the hockey stride, a purplish complexion, and red patches where her eyebrows should have been, looked beside Olwen like a coloured supplement in an illustrated paper beside a Cosway miniature.

They came to obtain permission for Hugh and Marjorie to join the theatre party next day.

"The Holroyds," said Mrs. Whitefield vaguely, "the people who spoke to us after church this morning, do you mean? Ah, yes. Who are they, Ada? All right?"

"What do you mean by all right? They are friends of ours."

"Well, but you know how careful one has to be now-adays. In our position we must pick and choose, I can tell you. If you are in with one lot, you must be out with the other. There are so many jumped-up, common rich folks about. You should see some of the boys' parents at Oakstone (the big public school in the Midlands where her boys were educated) rolling up in their motors, all furs and diamonds, and then hear them talk! Yet you have to conform to the standard they set. Hugh used to tell me he would rather I didn't go to Oakstone at all than come without the car."

There was a slight pause after this exposition of Mrs. Whitefield's social views; then Aunt Ada said incisively:

"The Holroyds are good people, but they are nothing great socially—just mill-owners, like George."

Ethel's colour rose, but she was not abashed. "How much money have they, that's the point," said she.

"Money talks. Have they enough to make people forget the mills? George has, you see."

Olwen was shaken with a gust of contempt such as her father might have felt. She spoke swiftly. " Everyone forgets to be snobbish in talking to Mrs. Holroyd, because she is sincere and generous and kind," she cried impetuously. "But, if mill-owning is a thing to be forgotten, don't on any account let Hugh and Marjorie run the risk of contamination. The awful truth must be confessed, the Holroyds don't keep a car."

Mrs. Whitefield laughed sleepily as she gazed at her niece's heightened colour. She saw something unusual, something compelling about Olwen. Married to a man with means, she might go far.

"Why, Ollie, we'll take them on your recommendation. I didn't know they were intimate friends."

"Gracie is my best and oldest friend."

" And what about the son? Is he, too, a diamond in a plain setting?"

"There are four sons," was the quick retort. "You saw the eldest this morning."

Her aunt smiled at the adroit evasion, and said she had no objection to the proposed expedition.

When the young people had left the room there was a short silence among the sisters. Presently Mrs. Whitefield remarked, "Well, Maud, judging by that ebullition, she means to have him, doesn't she?"

Maud made a gesture of helplessness. "She ought to have a future," said she quite passionately, "only we are so helpless——"

"And being in this bank is so against her. No young man in a good position hereabouts would marry a girl who, as all his friends must know, is merely a bank clerk."

"Why don't you invite her to Mount Prospect for six months and give her a chance, Ethel?" asked Ada sharply.

"She wouldn't come," was the placid response. "I can't picture Madoc Innes's daughter taking six months' holiday to find herself a husband, can you?"

"It's a case of these ideas Ada was talking of just now," said Maud. "I fear they will get in her matrimonial way, poor child."

"And after all, the men she would meet at your house are only Ben Holroyd over again," chimed in Ada, who was really on the warpath that day.

Mrs. Whitefield, however, prided herself upon making all allowance for the inevitable souring of her maiden sisters. "I don't think I should care in any case to make myself responsible for marrying that man's daughter to any friend of mine," said she, quite good-temperedly. "What's bred in the bone, you know. She might develop very undesirable traits. Think of poor Clara, with her large, fair beauty, and this little spitfire, her father's own daughter if ever a girl was!"

This was too true to be contradicted.

Olwen awoke, upon the day that followed Boxing Day, with a feeling much like that of Pippa on her holiday morning. The world, which had for the past two days displayed closed shutters, was now awake again, and going on its way as usual. The mill hooters had rung at six, everywhere the toilers were thronging back to work once more. Yet she still lay luxuriously in half Aunt Maud's bed, with a whole holiday before her, and a matinée into the bargain.

As she put on her prettiest blouse, in honour of the day's excursion, she heard the postman's knock; and when she took her place at table, a letter in an unknown hand lay upon her plate. Another reply to her advertisement!

Hugh and Marjorie were discussing the rival merits of two actresses who were to appear that afternoon. The vicar was behind his paper, nobody's eyes were upon her.

After the sharp disappointment of the other answer, she had no superstitious feeling about this one, but she opened it forthwith.

The enclosure was in a slanting, spidery hand, and the address was plainly stamped upon the top of the sheet.

> "Guysewyke Pele,
> "Caryngston,
> "Northumberland.

"Miss O. Innes, Dear Madam,——

"I have seen your advt. in last week's paper, and write, in case you may not as yet have engaged yourself, to tell you that I am in want of a young lady as companion and secretary. I live in a very remote spot, and am not as young as I was. You would have no menial duties. Your salary would be £5 a month, and I would pay your railway fares. I suppose you can give me references. I am a widow, my late husband was first cousin to the present Lord Caryngston, to whom I can refer you if necessary.

"Should you think this suitable, please come as soon as you can. Even should you not desire such a post as a permanency, you might like to come for two or three months, until you find something else. Would next week be too soon?

> " Faithfully yours,
> "CHARLOTTE GUYSE."

Olwen looked doubtful as she laid the letter down. To be companion to a solitary elderly lady in the wilds of Northumberland was not at all what she desired. Her training would rust in such a place, she would be hopelessly bored. There was a postscript to the letter which she did not at first see, since it was written overpage.

"There is a valuable library here which requires cataloguing."

This modified her intentions. The writer perhaps really only wanted temporary assistance. When the catalogue was complete, she might be able to come away again. By that time she would have found out how she liked the post. She would not feel herself permanently cast away in the wilds. . . . And it was a way out. Until the offer of release lay before her she had not realized how strong was her craving for some change.

It sounded like what Mr. Whitefield would call "a soft job." If she found herself with a good deal of spare time it might be possible to indulge her secret ambition, which was to become a journalist like her father. If she could remain at the Pele for a twelvemonth, which did not sound impossible, she might be able during that time to lay by enough money to take her to London and give her a start.

Breakfast was over before she had come out of her dream. Shaking herself free of fancies, she ran off to help Aunt Maud with the beds, thrusting the letter out of sight for a while, though her mind ran upon the plan, and played about the thought of the future.

She started upon the day's expedition with an odd feeling of reinforcement against Ben. He was no longer the sole alternative to the bank. There was a *tertium quid,* should she decide to avail herself thereof.

Ben and Gracie awaited them with a simple eagerness which took no pains to hide itself. Mr. Witherly, the new curate, proved to be the sixth member of the party. Ben had ordered a motor to take them to the station, and had not, as Olwen had feared he might, attired himself in a frock coat. He wore a lounge suit which she thought was new, and looked better than she had ever seen him.

But it need not come to that! Every time she caught the deprecating glance of his uneasy eye she fortified herself with the assurance of the existence of the *tertium quid*.

Ben was well known on the line, where he travelled daily to and fro. The guard was attentive, they had an empty compartment, and travelled luxuriously first class; a pleasure in itself to the young bank clerk.

On reaching Leeds, they went and lunched at the Café Luxe, to the accompaniment of a good band. Afterwards, as they sat at coffee in the lounge, Ben as close as he dared sit to Olwen, she asked him suddenly,

"Did you ever hear of a place in Northumberland called Caryngston ?"

"Yes, it's a small market town, out on the moors, miles from anywhere."

"No railway ?"

"Not to Caryngston. You go on a branch line to a place called Picton Bars, I think. It is between the Roman Wall and the Cheviots."

"It sounds remote! Have you heard of a family thereabouts called Guyse ?"

"Lord Carnygston's family name is Guyse. I fancy there are several of them in that part."

"Living at a place called Guysewyke Pele ?"

"I've heard Guysewyke Pele spoken of several times. It is supposed to be the finest Pele remaining, next to the one at Chipchase."

"What is a Pele exactly ? I thought it was a watch-tower ?"

"That's more or less right, but it was a fortress, too. When the borderers went raiding, the women and children and cattle were driven into the Pele and shut up there. The ground floor was used as a stable, and the larger Peles had a well inside, so that the inmates could hold out for some time."

"Have you seen one?"

"Yes. Quite a small one though. It is in the church-yard at Corbridge-on-the-Tyne. The parson lived there in raiding times. It is quite interesting. You like such things, don't you?"

"Love them. I hate places like Leeds and Bramforth, where the present day has stamped out and obliterated every trace of former ages."

"But you wouldn't like to live in a very lonely place, would you?"

She laughed. "I am trying to make up my mind."

He went quite pale. "To make up your mind?" he stammered, with such a stricken look that her heart re-proached her.

"Oh, only an invitation to go and stay in those parts," she replied hurriedly. "I don't fancy I should like it for long."

"Ben," said Gracie, "we ought to be on the move. This thing begins at half-past two, you know."

They rose, and went to find taxi-cabs.

CHAPTER IV

BEN was badly shaken.

So long as Olwen was in Bramforth and he knew where she went and the people who were her friends, there did not seem to be so much need of haste. If she were going away, however, he had no intention of allowing her to vanish from his sight without arriving at an understanding. He was not a quick-witted man. Often as his beloved had sheered off, leading him away from the point, he yet was not certain that this was intentional. Girls very often, or so he was told, did not know their own minds until a man had actually spoken the fatal words.

He meant that Miss Innes should hear them, and he carried out his purpose with a ruthlessness which left no room for evasion.

The day at the theatre closed, as, according to Mrs. Holroyd's programme, with a supper at their house. It was a merry, noisy party, and after the meal, Gracie took Hugh and Marjorie to the morning room to hear the new gramophone. Olwen and Ben remained in the drawing-room, and after a while, Mrs. Holroyd, having been warned by her son, melted away, leaving the two *tête-à-tête*. The gramophone was playing "Tales from Hoffmann," and Olwen, feeling a little tired and dreamy, leaned back in a big chair, looking very young and small. Ben, standing before the mantelpiece, asked her gravely whether she was thinking of leaving the "Baank."

"You would approve of such a course, would you not?" she asked mischievously.

40

"I've never thought it suitable. But what have you in mind instead?"

"I have been there three years, and I want a change," said Olwen.

"Yes, I daresay. You are young. I suppose you don't feel in any hurry to settle down once for all?"

"Settle down once for all? Oh, I could never do that!"

"Never?" echoed Ben, in a voice faint from astonishment.

"I'm not domestic! I've told you so before. I want to go all over the world and try everything. If I thought I had to spend my life in Bramforth, I should go crazy, I believe."

He was silent, turning over this speech, so subversive of all moral order, in his keen, though narrow intelligence.

"Bramforth's not much of a place," he remarked, "I'm not set on it myself. But a man—or a woman, if you come to that—must stay in one place if they have their living to earn."

"Oh, no, not at all. I might be a newspaper correspondent, and travel from place to place. Splendid fun to write one's experiences!"

Ben shook his head. "All that's beyond me. When I've been all day at the Mills I like to come back to my own fireside, and I should like the same woman always there. If she was there I shouldn't mind where the house stood."

"Quite wonderful, isn't it, how different people's ideals are," said she conversationally.

"Are ours different? Perhaps not so much as you think." He turned so as to face her. "Miss Innes, you can't have been unconscious of the fact that I love you and want you for my wife."

There was a simple directness in this which Olwen liked better than she had ever liked anything in Ben before. It reminded her of his mother. She grew crimson, and gave a little gasp, for she had not expected quite such an onslaught.

"Oh!" her voice was horribly wobbly, "I—I have wondered if—it has seemed so—but I thought it must be my fancy. You see, it was so unlikely, we are not suited to each other in the least."

"Likely or unlikely, it's true, and it has been true for years. I know you pretty well, and I don't agree that we aren't suited. Anyway, I have told you at last. What are you going to say?"

She gave a sound like a sob. Ben was leaning nearer. Before she could speak again he was on his knees, his arms folded on the arm of her chair. "What are you going to say, *darling?*" he muttered, huskily.

She saw that she must be swift and definite. "I must say 'No,'" she uttered, fear of some untimely demonstration on his part rushing in to banish her nervousness. "I hate to seem so blunt, but it is No, and when you have time to think it over you will see that I am right. You want a good, affectionate girl, who would love to sweep up the hearth and bring your slippers and sit at home and do the mending. And I—I couldn't be happy—like that! No, I couldn't! Ben, it is no use, indeed, indeed! You know I am sincere. If I thought it possible that I could ever settle down to—to that, I would tell you in a minute. But I can't! I am Madoc Innes's daughter, one of the wild ones. I'm not a fireside woman. I'm not the woman for you."

He was silent for a long moment, and his face changed sadly. "I had not really very much hope," he said at last, "but one never knows. I was determined that you should understand what I feel. . . . But I don't think you quite realise that if you married me you would be far more your own mistress than you are now. You needn't

live in Bramforth if you don't like. You needn't
sweep up your own hearth or do your own mending. I
could give you servants to do that. You could travel. It
—it would be my greatest happiness to let you do as you
liked. If—if you could have brought yourself. . . . You
could make pretty well anything you chose out of me."

He broke off. She had shaken her head, slowly and
miserably. The motion caused the ripples of her hair to
shine like the tarnished gold of an old Florentine frame.
It came to the man's mind that he had always wanted so
desperately to see that hair once more free as he used to
see it in her girlhood; and that now he never would.

"Dear good Ben," she was saying, "I like you too well
to marry you and make you unhappy ever after. I have
a devil in me, I really have, and nothing would rouse it so
completely as to find myself tied for life to a man I did
not love. Oh, Ben, I hate, I *hate* saying No to you!
Please take it; please don't make me say it again!"

He got to his feet, drew out a handkerchief, and passed
it over his agitated countenance. "I won't," he then said
firmly. "That is, not at present. But I won't go so far
as to say that I consider it quite all over. There's no
other man so far?"

"Oh, no, no!"

"Then, as long as that is so, I take it that you might
change your mind."

She tried earnestly to prevent his indulging any such
false hopes. But as the idea seemed to make it easier for
him not to importune her further, she gave in after a
while, only uttering a fervent wish that he might find just
the right girl before long.

A pang shot through her as she went to find her kind
hostess, and timidly tell her that she thought they ought
to be going. Mrs. Holroyd looked from the girl to her
son. Her eyes filled, her sweet-tempered mouth quivered.

Olwen's vivid fancy leapt up to picture what her reception would have been had she given Ben the right to place her in those kind arms. How delighted they would all have been! How completely a daughter of the house she would have become! With her uncanny intuition she knew that she could have made herself just such a woman as they all desired—had she loved Ben she *would* have become such an one—have lived her monotonous life and died her peaceful death among the Holroyds and their kind, with only an occasional pang! . . . But she was not fool enough to give way now; though that picture also rose before her mind's eye. She could conjure up Ben's face should she suddenly surrender; could fancy him embracing her publicly, before his family, herself strained to his stout form, recipient of his kisses. . . .

Her involuntary shudder was the measure of her repugnance. With an air of shamefaced apology she took her leave, feeling, as she and her cousins walked home, that this had made it impossible for her to stay in Bramforth— that the Border Pele and the cataloguing of the library must be her way out.

Before she slept she wrote a letter to Mrs. Guyse, saying that the post was not quite such as the advertiser had contemplated, but that she was not yet suited, and would like further details. She knew nothing of nursing, and could not take a post where she would have the care of an invalid.

She decided to say nothing to her aunts until she received a reply to this; and for two days she sat in the bank and worked her typewriter, feeling as if her life had suddenly become a dream. She made jokes, ate surreptitious sweets, cooked cocoa, and chattered as usual. Her whole mind was meanwhile fixed upon the breaking of the news at home and the handing in of her notice at the Palatine.

Mrs. Guyse's reply was that her health was not very strong, but that she did not call herself an invalid, and that in any case she had an old and trusted servant who waited upon her. She renewed her suggestion that Miss Innes should come experimentally. She was directed to travel by train to Picton Bars, whence Mrs. Guyse would arrange that a fly should bring her on to Caryngston, at which place she would be met.

The mere fact that the Pele was evidently difficult of access acted as a lure to Olwen. She choked, she pined for adventure, for wild country, for something as unlike Bramforth as could be had. However elderly and dull this Mrs. Guyse, she came of good family, and must have some friends, who would be of the right kind.

That evening she took her courage in her hands and broke the matter to her aunts.

"Am I a beast?" she asked piteously. "I feel like a deserter leaving you two, who have made such sacrifices for me, and going off. But, oh, my dears, the world is so big and life is so short! I simply must try my wings! I don't feel as if I could hold on here any longer."

She spoke with her arms round Aunt Maud, who said nothing, but began to cry quietly. Aunt Ada made no pause in her endless knitting, but turned the heel of her sock before replying in a calm voice.

"There's no need to apologise, Ollie. I approve of the idea, and had thoughts of suggesting that you should give up your daily work and seek a resident post. This does not seem quite what one would have chosen, but if it is clear that you go to see how you like it, no great harm can be done. If you catalogue the books ably, Mrs. Guyse can give you a good reference, which will be more valuable in seeking another post than any reference from the Palatine."

Olwen sat incredulous. "Aunt Ada! You really advise me to go?"

"If you *want* to go, I agree with everything that Ada says," gulped Aunt Maud; "but, oh, my darling, I do hope it isn't because you are not h-happy—because you want something you can't have—because you c-care for——"

"I want heaps of things I can't have," broke in her niece hastily. "I want to go round the world and see its wonders! I want to go and work in London at the heart of things. But most of all I think I want fresh air. I almost forget what the far horizon looks like! Except for you two and Gracie Holroyd, there's not a creature in Bramforth that I shall regret leaving. I just want to be off!"

· "Then you will go quite soon?"

"If I give in my notice tomorrow I could travel on the 8th or 9th. I shan't want many grand clothes up there, I suppose. I wonder how one does one's shopping in a place like that?"

"The present Aunt Ethel gave you will come in useful," said Aunt Maud, wiping her eyes, and beginning to feel interested.

"Why, so it will! I never thought of that! I am always inclined to turn up my nose at Marjorie's cast-offs, but that motor-coat ought to be the very thing for the Cheviots in January."

"There's a difference," observed Aunt Ada, "between cast-offs and outgrowns. It's lucky for you that Marjorie is such a giantess. She only wore that coat about a dozen times, her mother told me."

They entered into all the intricacies of the girl's wardrobe, making valuable suggestions as to various garments which could be "done up." They were as eager as though she were their own child. Aunt Maud produced a bit of lace, Aunt Ada an amethyst pendant. The guilty feeling began to fade away.

Sincerely as Olwen was attached to these two, her youth prevented her from appreciating their wonderful unselfishness. Impatience of their limitations had often vexed her. She had not insight to value their renunciations.

When Faber wrote his lines on unselfishness:

"Oh, could I live my whole life through for others
With no ends of my own——"

he was probably unaware of the many educated women in England whose daily life is a repetition of his formula. Ada and Maud Wilson had no ends of their own. Their nearest relatives would have been astounded to learn that they had any personal interests to turn them aside from their quite obvious duty of running a household on insufficient means, doing their best to counteract the ill effects of an old man's parochial neglect, and showing hospitality to the various members of the family who simply claimed it as a right. Their father's death would throw them on the world practically unprovided for. Nobody deplored this. Nobody tried to alter it. Nobody gave it a thought.

When their best-loved niece had run off to rummage in her drawers, for a couple of frocks to be looked over, and have their claims to restoration considered, the two sisters fell silent.

They did not look at one another, for they were not demonstrative women; but they understood each other.

"There is nobody else in Bramforth," said Ada, as though in reply to something said by Maud. "If she stays here she will marry Ben Holroyd, simply because she will find that she has to. . . . I feel the child is made for better things."

Maud gave a long sigh, charged with the wasted regrets

of her vanished youth. "Oh, Ada! Was not that perhaps the mistake we made? We demanded more than we could get. Are you so certain that she does not like Ben? You don't think she is going off because he has not spoken?"

"I think she is going because the indirect pressure of her friendship with his sister, and the fact that there is nobody else, is pushing her," replied Ada decisively.

Maud said no more. Her own tragedy had been the long waiting for the beloved to speak—the vain waiting, while other men came forward.

She felt that, whether Ben had spoken, or whether he had not, it was best that Ollie should go away.

CHAPTER V

THE 8th of January dawned still and cold. A black frost was on the ground, and in the sky the yellowish greyness which usually precedes a heavy snowfall.

It was, however, perfectly fine and dry at Bramforth when Olwen set out upon her northward journey. At Newcastle she had to change, and later on must change again, for the little local line which would carry her to Picton Bars.

The lonely station stands high upon the fells, and the snow had begun to fall when she alighted upon the small, dreary platform.

A fly sent by Askwith, landlord of the Seven Spears at Caryngston, was duly in waiting, and when she and her baggage were safely bestowed they started off, up a hill so steep that the driver did not mount his box until they had gone a mile and a half. The Seven Spears was the curious name of the hostelry to which Mrs. Guyse in her last letter had directed her new secretary, with the information that at this point upon her journey she would be met.

By the time they had gained a wide, exposed plateau, the snow was falling with surprising and increasing rapidity. The great flakes were like lumps of wool, and the whole face of the country was white in half an hour. As they breasted the hill they encountered a keen icy wind from the north, against which the horses could make but slow progress. The train had been warmed, but the interior of the fly was very chilly. It seemed to Olwen that

49

in all the miles they travelled they never passed a single human habitation. How far they went she could not tell, but she was blue with cold, and very hungry by the time they reached the outskirts of a small town or a large village. The grey stone cottages were huddled in true Northumbrian fashion one against the other, right upon the road, with no intervening garden plots as in southern counties. Owing to the storm, nobody was in the streets; and against all walls which faced the north the snow had already drifted deeply. Darkness was closing in as they reached the market square, white and empty in the pitiless weather.

Olwen felt a little nervous at the thought that the last, and presumably the wildest, stage of her journey still lay before her. She had hardly realised that England contained a place so remote as Guysewyke.

The inn stood on the north side of the square, facing south. A wooden porch projected above the door, and wooden benches were ranged below the windows.

As the horses stopped before the entrance, a middle-aged woman, in felt slippers, drying her hands upon a large print apron, came and stood in the light of the doorway.

"Is it the yoong leddy for t' Pele?" she asked in a hearty voice, which was strangely comfortable in the circumstances.

"Yes," said Olwen as she jumped out eagerly. "Are you Mrs. Askwith? What dreadful weather you have here! It was quite fine at Bramforth this morning!"

"To think o' that! Coom away, Missie, and Saam'll put trooks doon in't baack kitchen. There's a canny bit o' snaw doon already, and we'll have more'n enoof, coom morrning. Bad time o' year to be travelling, and you sooch a bit lassie!"

The last words were tinged with wonder as Miss Innes walked into the passage, which was papered in imitation blocks of grey granite, divided into oblongs by bands of bright blue.

Olwen laughed. "I think it's fun—quite an adventure, you know," she replied gaily. "Is there anybody here to meet me 'from Guysewyke?"

"Ow ay, there be," said the hostess; and as she spoke she pushed open a door leading into the bar parlour, whence issued loud laughter and a whiff of mingled tobacco smoke, leather gaiters, beer, sawdust and hot humanity.

Olwen caught sight of several men on benches, three farmers round a central table, and the host, in a green baize apron, with a tankard in each hand.

The face of the farmer seated facing her was clearly visible for a few moments—a long dark face, with a pronounced chin, a slight black moustache, and eyes as green as jade. He seemed just to have said something to amuse his companions, and was himself smiling, showing two rows of teeth as perfect as those of an animal. He looked, she thought, like a picture of *Der Freischütz,* the demon huntsman.

In her hasty survey she saw nobody who looked like Mrs. Guyse's servant, but somebody must have been there, for the landlady called out:

"She've coom! Yoong lass've coom!" before banging the door and shutting in the noise and warm odours.

She turned to the other side of the central passage and ushered the girl into a second parlour, where a fire burned, but dully. Striking a match, the woman lit a paraffin lamp, and disclosed the typical, square, small-windowed inn sitting-room, with the usual rag hearthrug, china dogs on the mantelpiece, stuffed gamecock in a glass case, and corner cupboard with treasures of old cut glass and lustre ware. The panelled walls had been painted in a vile yellowish imitation of the real oak which the paint in all probability masked.

Kneeling down with a pair of bellows, the landlady quickly blew the sluggish fire into a leaping blaze, upon which she placed a huge log. Then rising and dusting her knees with one hand, she looked doubtfully at her guest.

"Ye'll no get to t' Pele to-night, loov," said she not unkindly. "It's drifting very hard oop on t' fell already. Muster Nin won't risk it in the dark."

Then, in reply to Olwen's "Oh!" of consternation she added, "Well, well, you'll hear what he says himself."

She paused and listened to a new burst of wild merriment, which was plainly audible from the bar. Her lips twisted into an indulgent smile.

"That's him. Troost him to set 'em all off!"

Her eyes wandered to the somewhat forlorn little figure of Olwen, who, doubtful as to whether she was to continue her travels or no, was standing by the table, cold, hungry and uncertain. "Bad time o' year for t' Pele," she remarked, as if puzzled. "Soommer's best, oop yander." Her expression was odd, and it seemed as if she was minded to say more, but instead she turned suddenly, marched out into the passage, half opened the bar door, and called loudly:

"Muster Nin! Coom you here! Didn't you hear me tell you yoong lass've coom?"

"All right, Deb, keep your hair on," said a voice from within; there was the sound of a chair being pushed back, and the young farmer with black hair and green eyes emerged, a pipe in his mouth, a tumbler of hot drink in his hand.

His eyes and those of the stranger girl met momentarily; and she was conscious of two very distinct impressions: first, of his real, though suppressed, anxiety to see her, and secondly, of his disappointment. She could not have explained how she knew this; but in some way she received the impression of his having expected something very different.

"Hallo!" he said, looking her up and down as she stood in cold dignity by the parlour table. "You Miss Innes—eh? How-de-do?"

She bowed. "You are——?"

"My name's Guyse. I drove down this morning to do some business in the town and bring you back. Didn't foresee this weather. Afraid it's no use hoping to get to the Pele to-night. What do you think, Deb?"

Deb's opinion, quite frankly and decidedly, was that it would be a fool's trick to attempt the journey. Madam would never expect them.

The Demon Huntsman, pipe in mouth, studied the silent girl with half-shut eyes. "Think you can make her comfortable here, Deb?" he asked at length.

"Ow ay, Muster Nin. I'll be going oop now and kindle a fire in her room. What time would you like supper—eh?"

"That's for the lady to say."

"You really think," began Olwen, summoning her courage, "that we had better not try to go on? You are not speaking on my account? I am not timid or nervous."

He grinned. "Dessay not. I am though."

"And you are sure that Mrs. Guyse will understand and approve?"

Both Mrs. Askwith and he were very sure of that.

"Then, if I am to stay here, might I beg for a cup of tea? I'm so cold and hungry."

"Tea?" The good woman was overcome with remorse that she had not thought of this. Off she went to prepare it forthwith, and Miss Innes and the young man were left together.

Slowly she laid down her muff and gloves, unfastened

Marjorie's motor coat in which she had travelled, and laid
it aside, disclosing her slim little person in a dark blue
suit.   Then she sat down in a big chair of the kind known
as a porter's chair, and held her stiff hands to the comforting warmth of the fire.

Her escort had moved round to the fireside, and was
sitting on a corner of the table, swinging one leg, and
smoking away with a total disregard of her permission.

His eyes were on her, and after a while he took out his
pipe, and chuckled, displaying his clean white teeth.
"Mean to say you've been a bank clerk for three years?"
he asked teasingly.

Olwen almost jumped, so much did this familiarity
astonish her.

"Why not?" she countered stiffly.

"You look to me as if you were straight from boarding
school, as if you had spent your days walking out in a
crocodile, with a mistress behind to see that you didn't
give the glad eye to anybody along the sea front."

Olwen was roused.   She must give this offensive young
cad something to remember.   "You were never more mistaken in your life," said she coolly.   "I am quite able to
take care of myself, and people are rarely rude to me
twice."

"Rude?" he laughed, not the least abashed.   "I should
think not!   Fancy cheeking a kitten at the age of six
weeks!"

"Your habits with regard to kittens or anyone else,"
she snapped, "are of no interest to me.   Pray don't let
me keep you from your—er—associates in the next room."

He laughed out, his head thrown back.   "Fuff-fuff!   I
do love to hear a kitten swear!"

Olwen tilted her chin to a very haughty angle.   "Mrs.
Guyse has provided me with an unusual kind of escort,"

she said. "May I ask who you are? Do you live near Guysewyke Pele?"

"No, I don't. I live inside it. I'm the son of the house, and I hope you and I are going to have fine times together. You looked such a mouse that I thought you had no spunk in you; but you've got a spirit of your own, all right, all right."

Olwen rose, and gathered up her coat, with the intention of asking Mrs. Askwith to let her see her room. As she made for the door, it was opened by an apple-cheeked damsel who carried a tea-tray. This she set down upon the table, giving young Guyse what he would have called the glad eye as she did so.

"Hallo, Flossie," said he, taking up his glass, "I drink to your very good health. You see before you, Flossie, no less a person than the Queen of Sheba. Make your very lowest courtesy. Her Majesty is travelling incog., and I've got into hot water by failing to recognise her. Look out for yourself, my girl, or you'll get the set-down of your life."

Flossie began to titter, and young Guyse, rising, said, "Ta-ta, kitten!" and walked back into the bar parlour. As the door closed behind him there sounded an outburst of laughter, and Olwen wondered if it were caused by some remark he had made about herself. Her cheeks were warm with indignation. This creature—this tavern wit—was to be her house mate at the Pele! . . . Why, Ben Holroyd was an aristocrat compared with this!

"Mr. Ninian's full of his nonsense, ain't he?" said Flossie cheerfully. "Known me from a baaby, he has. Me moother she says it's a fair wonder how he do keep up his spirits in that lonely plaace. There, Miss, your tea's ready, and should I carry your things oopstairs?"

Olwen sank down with relief to sip hot tea and eat excellent hot teacake. She was almost ready to cry at the prospect before her, but the refreshment and the warmth revived her somewhat. It was not yet twelve hours since she left the Vicarage; she could not yet accept defeat! But she felt uneasy.

Mrs. Guyse had made no mention of her son. She had conveyed the impression that she lived alone. Was it wildly possible that her real escort had been delayed by the snow and this unspeakable young man was masquerading? That might account for the merriment in the bar, but it seemed impossible that the Askwiths should be conniving at such a trick. Her gloomy meditations were broken into by the entrance of Deb, who came to know if she had enjoyed her tea. She thanked her politely, and asked whether there were such a thing as a telegraph office within reach, as she was anxious to send a message to her people to explain that the weather had delayed her.

Mrs. Askwith approved of this idea. "You caan't tell, you might be snowed oop here, and days before you get to t' Pele," was her disquieting opinion. Then, not pausing to consult her guest, she once more pushed open the bar door and shouted for "Muster Nin."

She explained to him that the young lady wished to send a telegram, and he replied, "That's easy enough, if the snow hasn't broken down the wires, and I don't think it will have yet." Advancing into the parlour, he peeped in, a mocking devil in his eyes. "If your Majesty will condescend to allow her slave to hold an umbrella over her, we will at once fare forth across the market-place," said he.

He did not wait for a reply, but took up her fur coat from the chair where still it lay, and held it for her to put on. She was taken by surprise, and did so almost mechanically.

"Now, Deb, the big umbrella," said he, "and I can manage so that this midget shan't be blown away."

They emerged into the porch. As the wind was behind the house, they were here comparatively in shelter, and the snow seemed a mere sprinkling. "Now," said he, as he set the umbrella firmly on his shoulder so as to shield their backs, "cling to me for all you're worth, little 'un, and I'll have you across in a brace of shakes."

It was not a moment for standing on one's dignity. The readiness with which he had come from the warm room to do her a service mollified her somewhat, and she tucked her hand into his arm as directed.

As soon as they were beyond the shelter of the house, the blast drove them on furiously. She had the sensation of being attached to a live wire, so elastic yet so complete was young Guyse's resistance to the storm.

Soon the snow was over their boots, and she was jumping along in a fashion which could not but provoke them both to mirth. She was gasping for breath when they reached the opposite side of the market-place, and stood before the chemist's shop, which was also the post office. The chemist, with a sack over his head, was busy sweeping the drifts from his doorstep. The colour was high in Olwen's cheeks, and her eyes were starry as she made a dash for the comparative light and warmth of the shop within.

The postmaster came to attend them, read Olwen's message slowly and laboriously aloud, and discussed the storm with great fluency in a dialect which Olwen could only partly understand. They discussed the chance of getting to the Pele next day, and Olwen found that her escort had no intention at all of remaining weather-bound.

"This fall is going to stop soon after midnight," he said, "the wind will drop, and then we'll have out Askwith's sleigh and go up there in no time."

On their return journey they met the wind, and young Guyse thought it better not to hoist the umbrella. As the gust shrieked in their faces the girl recalled the prosaic, everyday aspect which the residential district of Bramforth had worn that morning. Everything grey, everything dull, everything just as it always had been and always would be! . . . And now she was fighting the elements, the icy blast from the Cheviots like knives upon her face, ankle deep in snow, and clinging close to a young ruffian whom, an hour ago, she had never seen.

As they fought their way on, the white surrounding expanse of snow was broken by an approaching figure. There was a moon behind the snow-clouds, so that the night was not quite black, and she could see that it was a man in an oilskin coat and a cap with flaps tied down over his ears, who was moving towards them.

Young Guyse evidently had no wish to encounter the traveller. He flung his arm round Olwen and turned her in a slightly different direction. His attempt at evasion was thwarted by a shout from the man.

"Hi, Guyse! Guyse! Is that you?"

Guyse wheeled sulkily. "Hallo!" ungraciously, "what do you want?"

"Have you got . . . knife in pocket . . . with hook for clearing horse's hoof?"

The speaker was out of breath, but his voice was that of an educated man. Olwen saw that he had a short, pointed, fair beard, to which the moisture clung in drops.

Her escort most reluctantly felt in his pockets, and while he did so she knew herself the object of keen scrutiny on the part of the other.

"Thanks, I'm sure"—as the knife was produced—"I'm afraid I have kept this—er—lady standing. What shall I do with the knife, to return it?"

"Leave it with Askwith. I shall be at the Seven Spears till morning." With these words he dragged the girl away, ignoring the other's shout of thanks and good night.

"Who was that?" cried Olwen in his ear.

"That? The doctor. Fellow called Balmayne. Confounded busybody! Always spying!"

"Spying!"

"On me. Why can't he mind his own business? Out there in the snow just to get a look at you, I suppose."

"What nonsense!"

"Like to have been introduced to you, wouldn't he? No fear!"

As he spoke, they reached their haven, the lee of the storm, and she heard his words clearly. She disengaged herself from him, no longer in need of his support, which he nevertheless seemed disinclined to withdraw. The doctor, she thought, might well have felt curious as to who she was—careering across the market-place with young Guyse's arm round her waist!

CHAPTER VI

DEB having, as a matter of course, laid supper for two in the now warm and cosy parlour, Olwen could not object. Reflection showed it as hardly possible that this egregious young man was anybody but the person he claimed to be. She had agreed to go to his mother for a month, and she could not well say: "I have decided not to come any further, as I have taken a strong dislike to your son."

Thus no course was open to her but to endure his society, and do her poor best to mend his manners.

On their return from the post she found a room upstairs had been prepared for her; and as there was a good fire there, she did not go down again until Flossie knocked at her door and said that supper was ready.

The parlour was empty when she entered it; and she seated herself once more in the porter's chair, to await her companion, her feet extended to the warmth of the wood-fire.

Her feet, like the rest of her, were small. They were also perhaps exceptionally slender. She had her vanities, like other girls of her age, and she could not help thinking they looked rather nice in their buckled shoes as she turned them this way and that in the flickering light. The door being ajar, she was unaware of the entrance of Mr. Guyse until she heard a chuckle, and, glancing up, saw him close beside her, his black head sleek and silky like a seal's, his large hands red with cold water. She drew back her feet and straightened herself in the chair

with a "caught-in-the-act" haste which she instantly regretted, for his laughter increased as, pointing to her feet,
he said, in tones of what was apparently meant for complimentary chaff:

"Now that's too bad! You might have given me a
minute longer before ringing down the curtain. You're
a hard-hearted little midget."

"Your repeated allusions to my size begin to be irritat-
ing, Mr. Guyse," said she, rising as she spoke and taking
her place at table. "What is there for supper? It
smells very good."

"Before we uncover, tell me what you'll drink? Old
Dan's got some tolerable port."

"Thanks. I never take wine."

"Holy Moses! Never take wine!" He mimicked her
sedate accent. "Well, you are! I should have thought
——— Is it hot spirits and water, then?"

"Water, please."

"Water, please! On a night like this, I'll trouble you!
Comes of being brought up in a vicarage."

"To that I plead guilty. It had become a habit before
I was old enough to object."

He flashed a look at her, as of appreciation, and un-
covered the rump-steak. "Can your Majesty get her royal
teeth into this?"

"Indeed she can! I really am like the Queen of Sheba
in two respects. I have come from a far country—you
can hardly judge how remote—and I have no more spirit
left in me."

"Fate preserve me, then, when you are bucked up," he
grinned, "if this is a specimen of one of your off days.
This will do you good. Deb's steak and fried potatoes
are not to be sneezed at, even by travelling royalties."

"She has provided spinach too," said Olwen, uncovering the vegetable dish. "Where does she get that, I wonder?"

"Ah! that's one of her secrets. They're just nothing but turnip-tops put through a sieve. Good fake, aren't they?"

"Excellent! Quite an idea!" She began to put questions concerning the Askwiths and the little town of Caryngston, not caring in the least whether or no the young man might be bored. She thought he was, for his mind appeared to be elsewhere. He seemed to wish not to be supposed to be watching her; yet the rays of his odd, gem-like eyes met hers every time she ventured a glance at him. At last he burst out suddenly:

"You sent that wire to a parson called Wilson. He's not your father?"

"No. As you know, my name is Innes. He is my grandfather."

"Both parents dead?"

She hesitated; then, to avoid further questioning, said: "Yes."

"So that's why you have to support yourself?"

"I don't know. I think I should have chosen to be independent in any case."

"Hallo, hallo! A suffragette?"

"If you mean a woman who wants a vote, yes indeed."

He was intensely amused. "The vote! A shrimp like you! Three of you would go to one elector. Oh gee, I forgot! No references to size permitted. But, you know, you look as if you were cut out for a man's waistcoat pocket."

She made a little sound of disgust. "Men are all alike," said she in scorn. "You are the second man who has told me that within a fortnight."

"Oh, indeed!" He looked oddly alert and angry. She

thought he gave the impression of a dog who has pricked his ears. "I wonder who the other fellow was?"

"Your curiosity borders on impertinence, sir."

"If that's the kind of little thing you throw off when you're on half-time, I wonder what will happen to me when the machine is running full power? What may I say? What *does* one·say to a girl, if one mayn't chaff and one mayn't pay compliments?"

"You might try treating a girl like a rational human being for a change, and try how that works."

"Oh, moonshine! Mighty interesting you'd find that! Would you like to know something about steers? Or split-oak fencing? Or rotation crops?"

"I believe all those things might be interesting, but I am bound to own that as yet I know nothing about them. We might talk of books perhaps?"

"Books? We're so likely to read the same kind, aren't we? How about Bennett's theory of chemical manures? Eh? Or would you prefer Plato for a start?" ·

"Plato with all my heart," said she composedly. "Do you read him in the original, or translated?"

He looked up and laughed as if pleased that she had scored a point. "That's a good bluff," he said, with appreciation. "You'll get on, you will."

"But you don't answer my question. Can you read Plato in Greek?"

"No, I can't."

"Then we're quits. I never got beyond Xenophon. But I am rather keen on Plato when translated. Meanwhile, for a change, let me ask you one or two questions. Of whom does the family at the Pele consist? Your mother did not mention you. She said she was a widow, and I presumed that she lived alone."

"She doesn't. I live there too. If you'd known that, you wouldn't have come, would you?"

"No, I shouldn't," she answered simply and naturally; and could see at once that this was not the reply he had expected. He leaned back in his chair and stared without speaking.

"You might ring the bell," she suggested. With a start he rose and did as she asked.

When Deb appeared to change the plates, he put his elbows on the table and glanced up, a mocking gleam under his lids. "Deb, this young lady knows all about Plato. What d'you think of that?"

"Plato? What's that, Master Nin? Some kind of a silver polish! I haven't seen it advertised!"

His shout caused her to pause in the process of removing the dishes, and give him a smart slap across the shoulders. "You dare to laugh at me!" said she, beaming. "Oh, you're a rascal, if ever one was born in the north. There's Shino, and all these havering new fancies, and I nobbut thought Plato was another of 'em."

"Deb, you're priceless! I want to kiss you for that! Hang it, a man must kiss somebody, and Flossie says she's too old to be kissed any more!"

"Away with your nonsense, Master Nin! What do you suppose yoong lass thinks of 'e?" said Deb, somewhat tartly, escaping with her tray, while Olwen, with down-turned lip, sat silent in her place crumbling bread and trying not to laugh. The lamplight gilded those tendrils of hair, so dear to Ben—like the bits that escape from the coif of a Ghirlandajo Madonna. It also accentuated the curves at the corners of her mouth, where a dimple lurked betrayingly.

Deb brought back an apple-pie, and a little brown ewer filled with thick cream. She placed the dish before Olwen, who cut a piece for her *vis-à-vis* in complete silence.

"No more questions to ask me?" he demanded at length.

His voice sounded a little defiant, as if he resented her unspoken disapproval.

"I don't think so; yes, perhaps I have.   Tell me something of your mother.   What are her tastes, her habits, her opinions?"

"She has none.   Absolutely none.   That's why she ought to have a companion.   You must tell her what to like, what to do, what to read, and so on.   Perhaps I had better warn you that you won't find her very expansive. She has no use for me, which I dare say won't surprise you."

A pause.   The polite protest for which he evidently waited did not come.   "What does she do all day?" asked Olwen, after thought.

"Feeds her poultry.   That's about all.   There's another member of the household of whom I ought to tell you something—rather an important person—Sunia, my mother's ayah."

"Ayah!   Mrs. Guyse has lived in India, then?"

"No; as a matter of fact, my mother never was in India. My father had a young sister, who married and went out there.   She was left a widow very young and came back to England, bringing this woman with her.   I was a child at the time, and Sunia has been with us ever since, because—well, because she can't bear to part from me, I believe.   Rum taste, eh?"

This hint was no more successful in evoking a disclaimer than its predecessors had been.   Olwen had revenge to take for his impudence, and she preserved a steady silence.   After a somewhat lengthy pause, she inquired:

"Am I the first companion that your mother has tried?"

He lowered his gaze, which was fixed on her, to his plate.

"No," he said, "she had another. Not recently, though."

He did not change colour, but something in his voice sounded like embarrassment. She guessed, with a quick leap of her mind to a conclusion, that her predecessor had probably welcomed the "glad eye" in a manner she could not imitate, and it was possible that complications had ensued. For herself, she had no fears in this connection. A very few days would suffice to show the Demon Huntsman his place; and most probably her attraction—had he felt it, which, judging from his manner, seemed unlikely—would vanish when he found that in good earnest she declined to be romped with, flirted with, or teased.

Very soon after supper she excused herself on the plea of fatigue, and thought she detected relief in the alacrity with which he lighted her bedroom candle and set open the door.

CHAPTER VII

THE morning broke with a clear sky, proving that, whatever his shortcomings, Ninian Guyse was a good weather-prophet. Exactly what he predicted had happened. About midnight the wind dropped, the snow ceased, and now the frost gripped the ground like iron, and the village lay surrounded by radiant whiteness, reflecting the first sunbeam on its crystalline surface.

Flossie awoke Miss Innes just as day was breaking, to say that "Muster Nin" begged that she would be quick, as he meant to drive her to the Pele in Mr. Askwith's sleigh as soon as they had breakfasted. No heavy luggage could be taken, but that could be sent for as soon as the roads permitted.

There was an exhilaration in the air which made Olwen feel optimistic, in spite of the biting cold which nipped her as soon as she crept out from the warmth of her bed. Dressing with no unnecessary delay, she hastened down to the parlour, whence came an appetising odour of frizzled "rashers."

Young Guyse was standing before the fire, apparently making himself agreeable to Flossie in the way she understood, while she set the teapot and the dishes of hot cake on the table.

He greeted Miss Innes with an odd mixture of bravado and nervousness, as though anxious to conciliate, conscious that he had somehow failed to do so, yet in his heart convinced that the swaggering male attitude must be the right one to adopt towards any young woman.

Her greeting was as frosty as the morning, and it seemed to depress him, for he sat down to table, accepted his cup of tea from her in silence, and ate for some time without speaking.

"Sorry," he remarked at length, apropos of nothing, "sorry we didn't hit it off better last night."

"Oh, pray don't trouble; what *does* it matter?" said she cheerfully.

He frowned impatiently. "We've got to live in the same house," he growled, with a shake of the shoulders expressing the irritation of the man wholly unaccustomed to snubs.

"Yes, but I am to be your mother's companion, not yours," she returned with a dry little smile.

His green eyes had a resentful light. "You've taken a regular grudge against me, I do believe," he muttered, "and I only meant to rag you a bit. Women can't take a joke."

"You see, women of my class are not accustomed to be ragged by strangers," she explained with a condescending kindness. "It seems that you did not know that. However, as I understand you to be apologising, we will say no more about it."

He stared at her more openly than he had done hitherto —glared at her might be nearer the truth. The sun sent a shaft of light in at the plant-blocked window, and showed her thick black brows and lashes, and their piquant contrast to her fair head. "If I hadn't your own word for it that you are a bank clerk," said he, "I should have taken you for a schoolmarm. You've given me a bad mark. Hadn't you better set me an imposition? I might write out 'Keep off the grass' fifty times, don't you think?"

She smiled patiently. "Don't be absurd, please, but tell me how long it ought to take us to reach the Pele."

"About two hours"—snappishly. "Afraid you won't like it when you get there."

"I'm determined to like it if I can. I hate to fail."

"So do I," he flung back. "I'm not used to it either."

"Indeed!" She could not resist the temptation to say that, with an air of innocent surprise, considering him with an appraising glance that the most conceited of men, could not have thought flattering. "If I hadn't your own word for it that you are a gentleman, I should have taken you for a—well, for something else," she remarked; and then, as he started and crimsoned, she let her laughter have its way. "What's sauce for the goose is sauce for the gander, sir," she said.

Suddenly he, too, laughed. "That's one to you," he conceded in a sort of unwilling admiration. "Well, I suppose it's up to me to make you revise your impressions, isn't it?"

"Impressions of you? Oh, why? I'm not sure that I have any," she replied briskly, pushing back her chair and rising. "I must be off and make ready for our start," said she.

This time he accepted the rebuff as final and made no answer. Olwen departed to make her arrangements, as it seemed likely that she might have to wait some days for the arrival of her trunk. She went to the back kitchen, where her luggage was, and asked Flossie to help her unlock a box and take out a change of linen and an evening frock. While they were thus busy Deb came in and sent Flossie away, saying that she would help Miss Innes herself. She provided a big cardboard box to hold the extra things, and while Olwen was packing them she said gruffly:

"You only coom for a visit oop t' Pele, loov, or is there talk of your bid ng there longer? You may think I taake a liberty, but 'tis no idle curiosity in me."

Olwen looked at the hard-featured, honest face and
answered at once, explaining that she was on a month's
trial, and was to stay on if she suited.

Deb listened gravely. "I'm not one to make mischief,"
said she, "and I shouldn't open me mooth, only I can
see that you coom of a good home and a good breed.
They're queer folk oop t' Pele, what with the nigger
woman and all. Madam, she's a poor creature, and
Muster Nin's a bit wild, as you see. Go careful, loov,
and you'll be all right, but keep Muster Nin in his
plaace."

Olwen was a little pale. "Thank you, Mrs. Askwith; it is kind of you to warn me. I have to earn my
living, and I suppose I should find drawbacks everywhere
of some kind. The—the Guyses are all *right*, are they
not? There is nothing against them, I mean?"

Mrs. Askwith's "No" came after a slight hesitation.
She repeated it after reflection. "No, nothing against
them. They are of the old gentry, and near kin to his
lordship, poor though they be. You're not to be thinkin'
over mooch of what I've said, loov. Only, go canny
while you're there. If the Indian takes against you,
you'll not be stopping very long."

Olwen sighed. "I'm afraid Mr. Guyse has taken
against me, as you say, already," she replied; and as she
recalled Nin's assertion of the ayah's devotion to himself, she thought she stood small chance of favour in
that direction. "Well," she concluded, "it can't be helped.
I must try and stay if I can. You will laugh if you see
me back here at the end of my month."

"Or before," said Deb, with an admiring glance at
the resolute little face. "You've got a home of your own,
loov?" she asked anxiously.

"Oh, yes, indeed. I shall not stay if things are unpleasant," was the quick reply; and the assurance seemed

to console the good woman. Nin began to shout for Miss Innes, and they had to break off talk and hasten to the door, where the sleigh stood waiting.

Olwen took a cordial leave of the Askwiths, who all assembled to see the departure. Just as she was being tucked warmly in under a fur robe Dr. Balmayne was seen crossing the square.

"Here's the doctor, come to return your knife," said she to young Guyse, who was taking his place beside her.

"Damn him!" said the young man quietly, checking his horse unwillingly as the other hurried up.

Seen by daylight, Balmayne was a good-looking man, youngish, with keen blue eyes and closely clipped fair beard. He gave back the knife and said a few words about the violence of the storm, his eyes fixed with interest upon the young lady in the motor veil of such a particularly charming shade of blue. As Ninian was evidently determined not to introduce him, he turned pointedly to her and addressed her direct. "You will have a cold drive," he said.

She bowed and would have replied, but Nin whipped up the horse and it sprang forward. "Sorry can't stop. Deloraine will take cold," he cried as they rushed off.

Balmayne was left standing by the porch of the Seven Spears.

Olwen sat silent, her mouth a little compressed, while they sped out of the town and took a winding moorland road. The snow was quite hard, the motion of sleighing, which was new to her, very pleasant. The bare, heaving country rose grandly on all sides. Caryngston disappeared beneath them incredibly soon. They were off together into the unknown, and her mind was working uneasily about the memory of Deb's words of caution.

Presently her driver turned with a short laugh. "Another specimen of my beastly manners, eh? I'm not going to be pushed into introducing you to that chap just because he comes cadging for it. He can ask 'em at the Seven Spears who you are and what's your business if he's so anxious to know."

She made no reply, not knowing what to say.

"Too angry to speak ?" he demanded pleasantly.

"Angry—why should I be angry ?"

"Because I wouldn't introduce that chap to you."

"Whether or no you will introduce me to your friends must be a matter for you and Mrs. Guyse to decide. It can have nothing to do with me."

"Tosh! I do seem to have put you on your high horse."

She was determined not to go on wrangling with him, and she held her tongue. When at last she spoke, after some interval, it was to ask him a question about the country they were passing through. He pointed out a few landmarks to her, but without much interest; and they drove mostly in silence until they came in sight of a square stone tower standing up on the skyline, grey among the whiteness of the setting.

"That's the Pele," said he. "Ever seen one before ?"

"Never; but I have been told that Guysewyke is fine— that there is only one better along the border."

"Who told you that ?"

"Oh, a friend at Bramforth."

"Well, the difference between ours and everybody else's is that we live in ours and nobody else does anything so lunatic. Our reason is an excellent one. It is simply that we can't afford to live anywhere else. The Guyse who first built this had an eye to a military situation, as you will understand when we get closer."

As they drew swiftly nearer, it could be seen that they were also approaching the westward edge of the high plateau across which they were driving. Beyond the Pele there seemed to be a drop of many hundred feet in the level of the country, and they went as though making straight for the verge, until they came, on the very brink, to a gateway with stone sideposts of square, rough-hewn blocks, surmounted by two panthers holding the Guyse shield under their paws.

Ninian checked his horse, alighted and opened the gate. They passed through upon what seemed at first like a narrow bridge, bordered on either hand by a low parapet of stone, with a precipice beneath on both sides. As he fastened the gate behind them, Olwen looked about her, and could hardly believe her eyes.

The whole western edge of the plateau they had just left was a steep, almost precipitous cliff. A couple of hundred yards from its verge there arose out of the valley below a small conical hill, connected with the high land behind only by a narrow natural causeway, which was but just wide enough to carry the approach. Upon this isolated hill, forming an impregnable stronghold, the Pele was perched. No wonder that it had withstood the onslaughts of the ages.

The summit of the hill had been levelled and cut square. Round it, like a crown, a quadrangular fortress wall had been built, enclosing a courtyard. At the western end of the causeway, where it met the fortress wall, was a small tower, or gatehouse, with an arch passing beneath. The gate was open; one saw through into what was in summer-time a circumscribed bit of garden ground. The Pele itself occupied the northwestern quarter of the enclosure.

Under the gatehouse arch, a sturdy short man with the black hair, high cheekbones and small, twinkling dark eyes of his Pictish origin, was busily shovelling away the drifts. He had worked diligently, and succeeded in making the passage clear, so that the sleigh, with the lady in it, could enter the quadrangle.

He greeted his master with an outburst of dialect too broad for the stranger to understand. Evidently some damage to property had been the result of the storm, for he pointed along the river valley, above which the stronghold towered. His tidings seemed to vex Ninian.

The girl was so occupied in observing the remarkable surroundings in which she found herself that all anxiety concerning her own reception or comfort faded from her mind. Seen from within, the fortress wall showed itself as on two sides, little more than a shell. On the eastern side, where the gatehouse was, there were still roofed and habitable quarters, in which, as she learned later, Ezra Baxter and his wife dwelt, the remainder serving as stables.

The Baxters, with the ayah, formed the entire staff at Guysewyke. Against the western wall, south of the Pele itself, was a small stone one-storey erection which had been built within the last fifty years as a kitchen. Along the south side were outhouses, fenced off by a trellis from the garden, and here, she guessed, madam kept her fowls.

Guyse, who had been collecting her things while Ezra talked, now turned towards the tower. "All right," he said to his man, "I'll come down with you as soon as I've had my dinner. Come along, Miss Innes."

The low doorway of the Pele Tower was rudely arched, Saxon fashion, with two long stones inclined towards each other at an angle, like a V upside down. The door itself, of grey oak with big black nails and iron ring, dated evidently from many centuries back. Guyse pushed it open, shouting for Sunia at the top of his voice.

Olwen found herself in a strange, almost terrifying place.

It was not unlike a cellar, the walls being of huge

ashlar blocks of stone, and the small windows deeply splayed within, narrowing to something not much larger than a loophole. The roof was of stone, arched in what is known as a barrel vault. Evidently, in feudal times, the whole ground floor of the tower had been one chamber. Now a screen, or wall of black oak panelling, divided it in two, the northern half, through which they had entered, being a vestibule, the inner half, partly visible through an open door, seemed to be better lighted, and showed a glimpse of a table set for dinner.

On the hall floor were thick rugs; an iron stove, though its effect was not æsthetic, made the place pleasantly warm, and there was a gate-leg table, covered with an untidy collection of whips, gloves, clothes-brushes, and so on.

There was a slight rattling of the curtains which covered the door by which they had entered, and a woman emerged, without noise.

She was small and withered, and wore a dull crimson saree over her head and draped about her shoulders. Below it appeared a thick wadded jacket and petticoat. Her eyes were like clear, deep coffee, and her skin like the same coffee with cream added.

"Sunia, this is Miss Innes," said the master of the house, in a tone which to Olwen suggested apology. It was as though he said, "This is all—hardly worth the trouble of fetching!" "How is my mother? Ready to see her?" he went on hurriedly.

"Madam well," said a soft, clear little voice. "She like see Missee Eenis. I take her up, then you have your deener. You hungry, my sahib—eh?"

"Hungry? As a wolf! Nearly ate Miss Innes on the way up. Some storm last night—what? Bad enough in Caryngston. Here, Ezra tells me, it was prime. Miss

Innes wanted to come up last night in the dark, but I wasn't taking any risks."

"Poor Missee have a dreadful journey," murmured the ayah, her melting eyes on Olwen, who stood by the fire, her foot held to the blaze. "You come with me—yes?" she said, in the accents of one coaxing a shy child. Olwen met her gaze and smiled, with a quick sensation of liking, as she followed her guide to the curtain by the door. She found that the wall was double, and in its thickness a corkscrew stair twisted upward. On the next floor, although passages branched right and left, they did not pause, but ascended higher. On the second floor they went a little way along the narrow and icy cold stone passage, and the ayah, knocking, ushered her into a sitting-room. It was quite small, occupying only a fourth of the floor space, or being half as big as the vestibule. A good-sized casement window had been inserted, the stone walls had been plastered and hung with a light flowery paper. Near the fireplace, in an arm-chair, was seated a middle-aged woman, spare in figure, with faded fair hair and melancholy eyes. She rose as the girl entered, and said, with a little laugh of embarrassment, "Oh, here you are! How do you do?"

Olwen responded as cordially as she could, expressing her regret that Mrs. Guyse should have been put to the trouble and expense which the delay at the inn involved. "There was no snow at all when I left home," said she, "or I would not have started."

"The snow is often very bad here," said Mrs. Guyse languidly. "Quite a different climate. We did not expect you to come on last night, but I hope Mrs. Askwith made you comfortable; and then, you had my son to cheer you up. Very amusing, isn't he?"

There was something peculiar in the tone in which this was said, almost as though Ninian's mother were sneering. Olwen replied quite conventionally that Mr. Guyse had been very kind. She felt that her answer was listened for, not only by the lady but the ayah also; but neither seemed able to make much of it.

"It's dull for my son and me here in winter-time," went on Mrs. Guyse. "I hope you will brighten us up."

"I want very much to be useful," replied the girl, "and it will be a pleasure to catalogue the library."

"To catalogue the library?" echoed the lady, with an air of blank surprise.

"You said that was one of the things you wished me to do," began the girl, puzzled.

"Dear me, yes, of course. My memory grows bad. You don't look very big or strong."

"I'm not big, but I think I am very strong. For three years I have gone to work in all weathers, and only once in all that time been absent on account of illness."

"Well, we shall see. In the meantime, we had better have dinner as soon as you are ready. Ayah will show you your room."

"Up more stairs, Missee," said the Hindu softly. On the top floor were likewise four rooms, but not exactly the same size. This floor was probably an addition to the more ancient lower part. They came first to a kind of landing, or ante-room, small but adequately lighted. Beyond was a larger room, facing to the west and south, and just now full of sunshine. The walls were not plastered, but covered up to within a couple of feet of the rafters, with tapestry hangings, above which point the naked stone was visible.

There was a black oak bedstead, its canopy upheld by the four evangelists, quaintly carved. Two or three oak chests stood round the walls. There was a small table with a still smaller mirror upon it; and a camp washingstand looked like a new importation. The cold made the girl flinch, but she comforted herself with the thought that cold is a thing to which one becomes accustomed. In fact, as she gazed around, her main preoccupation was the wonder as to how the articles of furniture had been conveyed into the room up the twisting stair by which she had ascended.

CHAPTER VIII

THE ayah, who had set down the guest's things, closed the door behind her without a sound. As the girl removed her hat she was rapidly opening the bag and taking from it such things as she needed. Then, placing a chair before the tiny mirror, she invited Olwen to be seated, with a mute gesture of obeisance.

Hardly realising what was required of her the girl sat down. Kneeling before her, her new attendant swiftly unlaced her thick boots and held the little feet in her hands with a caressing touch, as though she would have chafed warmth into them.

"Too much cold," she muttered, relinquishing them as if unwillingly and putting on the buckled shoes. Then, rising before the girl had recovered from her astonishment, she took a linen wrapper which hung upon a chair, passed it over the young lady's shoulders, pulled out her hairpins, and let loose the rippling cascade of hair.

"You are very kind, but, please, I don't expect you to wait on me; I do all these things for myself," expostulated Olwen in some embarrassment.

"Missee, let ole ayah brush her hair—so long since me had pretty memsahib to dress," murmured the cooing voice. The brush passed through with a motion firm yet gentle; it tingled, as though there were hypnotism in the touch. It seemed to leave the mass burnished and gleaming with a new beauty. In a very few minutes all was deftly coiled once more, following the usual style in

79

which its owner dressed it, but done twice as well as she could ever accomplish.

Hot water was in readiness, and having washed her hands the visitor, feeling strangely refreshed, was ready to follow her silent-footed guide down that weird winding stair. When they reached the front door they did not emerge into the hall, but walked on, in the thickness of the wall, to a small, tapestry-hung doorway which opened into the dining-room.

In this room two large windows had been cut; one was semicircular and set just under the arch of the barrel vault at the south end. It was too high to afford a view, but the sun streamed down through it. On the west wall an oriel had been built out, and this commanded a fine prospect of the river valley below and the rising ground beyond.

As Olwen entered she came upon the mother and son unawares, and the last words of what they were saying were clearly audible to her. Mrs. Guyse had made some remark which ended with "all the easier to manage," and Ninian, before he realised the visitor's presence, replied with some bitterness, "I'm not so sure."

As they became conscious of her they fell silent. Nothing in the words themselves, but something in the silence, suggested that they had been talking of her.

They sat down to table, the ayah waiting upon them. Under the high window in the south wall was a hatch, communicating with the adjacent kitchen, and through this the dishes were passed by Mrs. Baxter. The food was abundant and very well cooked and served.

Both the Guyses seemed distressed that their guest drank only water; and after cheese had been served Sunia reappeared with a tray of coffee, which seemed to be an innovation from the manner in which Mrs. Guyse received it.

"Do Missee good. Missee must drink something,". murmured the Hindu in explanatory fashion.

Olwen was prompt in polite protest, but Ninian re-marked that it was a jolly good scheme, and he couldn't think why they didn't always have it. When the ayah had left the room he said to his mother, "She seems to have taken to Miss Innes."

"Yes. A very good thing. She's so troublesome with her likes and dislikes," said Mrs. Guyse peevishly. She rose from the table and stood in an irresolute fashion, glancing first at Olwen, then at her son with much the expression a dog wears when he is wondering whether his master will take him for a walk.

"What are you going to do, Nin ?" she asked.

"Got to go over to Lachanrigg with Ezra. The bliz-zard has broken down the new fencing, and we'll have all the ground game in after those young trees."

"Oh! Then you can't entertain Miss Innes." She glanced vaguely at the girl who stood by the oriel in the sunshine, which turned her burnished hair into a nimbus. Madam cleared her throat. "Do you think you can amuse yourself for a while, Miss Innes ? I am going to have my afternoon nap," she said with a silly little laugh.

"O please don't study me in any way; of course I don't want entertaining! Why, I've come here to be useful. Let me make you comfortable for your rest. Do you lie down in this room ?"

"Oh, no, upstairs in my own boudoir. I never sit down here in winter. Don't come up. I would rather you did not. I shall come down to tea at five."

Olwen begged so earnestly to be allowed to carry her book and shawl upstairs that this was conceded. At the door of her sitting-room, howe⁻ the lady shut out her companion with decision, and ⌐. en, not daring to face the arctic cold of her bedroom, returned with reluctance to the dining-room, where Ninian still sat, finishing his pipe.

There was a shabby old sofa and two or three comfortable chairs by the fire, and on a sunny day such as this the room seemed eminently habitable. The girl went again to the western oriel and surveyed the scene beneath her. The tower stood on the sheer verge of the precipitous hill, but beneath this window there was a very narrow path, from which steps led downward. The whole hillside was thickly covered with trees, and the tops of these, snow-laden, appeared from above like a mountain range in miniature. Among the woods in the vale below there was a wide stream, now blocked with ice and snow, but, as she imagined, lovely in summer-time.

"That is a river down there in the valley?" she asked after a time of silent contemplation.

"It is a river. So kind of you to throw the poor dog a bone—I mean a word."

She glanced at the book in his hand. "Which is French for saying that I interrupt your reading!"

He tossed the book aside, rose and came to the window. "That's the Guyseburn. It runs into the Irthing. It's a bad-tempered stream; the one thing it will not stand is a bridge. I've tried several times to make a way across, just down below here, but it was whisked away every winter, so I must wait until I can afford something different. Lower down, where the cliff comes nearer the water, we have got one of these chain bridges, which is safe but wobbly. You won't like it much when you first cross, especially if the water's high."

"This is a wonderful place," she said, surveying the barrel vault; "more like a cathedral crypt than a dining-room. Have you always lived here?"

"Oh, no. Only for the last ten years. In my father's

day it was used as a shooting-box, but when he died I had to come here and farm the little bit he had left us to keep the wolf from the door. He was a rare waster was my father, but a very fine gentleman. Would have suited you first rate."

"Oh! You think I like wasters?"

"I feel sure you like fine gentlemen."

"Do you? Well, I don't know myself. I never met one that I know of. My grandfather is very simple, you might say Spartan in his habits. My uncle, George Whitefield, is a successful manufacturer, loud and pushing. My own father was a Bohemian—a waster, too, perhaps you would call him. but I loved him best of all."

"Rum, that. Fancy your liking a man who didn't consider appearances! You, whose code is founded on prunes and prisms."

"Yes, I suppose I *am* very conventional. I am glad you have found it out so soon," she replied at once, declining provocation.

"My father used to say he was the fulfilment of the old saying in this country," went on Ninian—

> " 'No Guyse
> Is ever wise
> Until he dies.'

"Rather awful to be born with a name so easy to tack rhymes to. How do you like this?

> " 'Any Guyse
> With green eyes
> Will tell you lies.' "

Instinctively she raised her look to his. The strong sunlight was upon both their faces, emphasising her curious colouring—the warm skin too dark for the hair and the heavy lashes. She thought that his eyes were like those of a leopard, green and golden, flashing an unspoken menace.

"I should think that rhyme is founded on fact," she remarked.

"Thought you'd say that. The first time you have been obvious, I will admit that much. Well, I must be off, or it will be dark by the time we get to the farm. Think you can live without me till five?"

"I'll have a try. It's a thing I've often done before. What time, if any, does the post go out?"

"If the drifts are not too deep the postman will arrive here to-morrow morning about ten, and he will take your letter back with him. I hear he couldn't get through this morning, but we will hope for better luck next time. Anyway, your folk won't be anxious. You sent a message from Caryngston, didn't you?"

With these words he went out into the vestibule. She heard him whistling for his dog, and presently the sound of the oak door banging.

"If what I wanted was change, indeed it seems that I have found it," was her reflection, as she sat down by the warm hearth.

As she did not, so far, know where the library was, and had no idea of the sort of cataloguing required, she felt unable to make any move in the direction of commencing her new work. Madam had definitely sent her off duty until five, and she had therefore no scruple in sitting down to begin a letter to Aunt Ada. She made this letter a good deal more sanguine than her present frame of mind, for she did not wish to let them know how depressed she felt, nor how out of place and forlorn. She dwelt upon the surprising nature of her situation from the architectural standpoint, the piquant experience of being weather-bound at the country inn, and her first experience of a sleigh drive.

She wrote until the last red streak died in the western sky above the thick woods across the Guyseburn. Then she laid down her pen, wondering a little that she was not frightened at finding herself alone in this vaulted chamber. So wondering, her eyes closed, and she slipped into dreamland, only awakened by the entrance of a stout, middle-aged woman carrying a lighted lamp.

"Eh, but I've woke ye up!" said she, standing with her hands on her hips and contemplating the small girl in the large chair.

"Nobbut a bairn, so you are," she went on, "but ayah says you're a real beauty." She looked critical, as though her own judgment did not endorse that of the Hindu. "Happen ye're tired out, after sooch a long drive in t' snaw?" she suggested.

Olwen was tickled by the woman's honesty, and laughed out. "Perhaps I am," she admitted, "and you may be able to raise your opinion of my looks after a while in this good air. I'm a town-bred creature; all this wild moorland is like a fairy tale to me."

"Ah, ye'll soon get your fill o' that," said Mrs. Baxter calmly. "Dooll, that's what it is oop here. Woon day joost t' same as lasst, all the year roond."

"Why, it doesn't snow all the year round, surely! I just long to see this valley in summer-time."

"Oo, ay, it's fine soomer-time, I will say that," replied the north-country woman, taking a white cloth from a drawer and spreading it on one end of the table. As she laid tea she continued to talk, explaining that both she and her husband were born in that part of the world and were used to solitude, cold and monotony. In return, Olwen told her of her own town-life, and how she had never hitherto known what it was to live without taxi-cabs, telephones and typewriters.

Just as the deeply interested Mrs. Baxter had brought in the covered dishes of hot cake and the silver tea-pot, the front door was heard to bang, there was a sound of scraping and stamping feet, and with a wild scurry some big creature hurled itself against the door leading from the hall, which yielded, and a golden collie bounced in, rushed to the hearth, and stopped short at sight of a stranger there ensconced, backing, with shoulders hunched and a threatening growl.

"Eh, the brute!" cried Mrs. Baxter, catching him by the collar. "Muster Nin, here's Daffie showing his teeth at the yoong leddy."

Nin from without shouted some abuse, and the dog bounded back to his master. When they returned together soon after the man effected an introduction, made the dog shake a paw, and instructed Olwen to bestow a sweet cake upon him in token of alliance.

Madam now appeared, a shawl over her shoulders, entering, as Olwen had done, by way of the tapestry hangings.

What conversation there was at tea turned upon the broken fencing. Nin said the ground was as hard as iron, no repair was possible, but Ezra and he had done their best with some wire netting. Madam had evidently no conversation, apparently no ideas. Olwen remembered what her son had said of her, and felt a vague pity. She herself made little effort to talk, but what she did say fell flat, since the master of the house was apparently tongue-tied before his mother.

"Do you play billiards?" he suddenly asked.

"A very little. The Whitefields have a table, but I am much out of practice."

"Not much reach," said Nin, with another scornful

glance at her lack of inches. "Well, the one solitary thing that is good here is the billiard table."

"A billiard-room—here?" cried Olwen, hardly polite in her surprise.

"A billiard-room here!" he mimicked derisively. "Come upstairs and you shall see. Knocking the balls about helps to keep one from suicide during the long winter nights."

"Only I don't play," said Madam.

"Well, I shan't cut holes in your table. I do just know how to hold a cue," said Olwen. "If you have a great deal of skill and patience you may be able to teach me to play."

"Good notion. Plenty of chance for flirtation in teaching a girl to play billiards. Shall have to allow you to stand on the table for your long shots, I should think," said the young man with apparently no sense of his own ill-breeding.

Olwen made no reply to this, glancing at Madam to see how she took this kind of language to her new companion upon the first evening.

Nin nudged his mother. "Look at her! She simply can't stand my cheek!"

"I don't wonder," rapped out his mother with sudden emphasis. "Why do you behave so intolerably?"

Ninian looked somewhat taken aback. "Crushed again," he said. "What chance has one poor man against two ladies? Daff, come here and take my part. Shall I teach you to bite the nasty cross things—eh?" He caressed the dog as it stood between his knees. "Sorry I introduced you to the school-marm, Daff. She likes poodle dogs, trained to walk on their hind legs and show off. She's got no use for simple rustics like you and me— have you, Miss Innes?"

"But perhaps rustics can be educated?" she suggested

with a smile, unwilling to snub him too decidedly before his mother.

"Hallo!" with an instant change from bravado to soft insinuation. "Will the school-marm undertake our education?"

"That depends upon your wish to learn."

"I simply long,to learn! I'll be a model pupil. When shall we begin? A lesson in manners after tea, a lesson in deportment after supper, a lesson in charm before breakfast, and——"

"A lesson upon holding your tongue in between each, I should think," cut in his mother suddenly, and evidently to his surprise.

"The first lessons would have to be language lessons," remarked Olwen demurely. "I couldn't tell you anything until we could understand one another. At present we don't."

"Now what, precisely, do you mean by that?" sharply.

She smiled provokingly. "I can't explain in words you would understand."

He turned himself round in his chair, leaned his elbow on its back, his chin in his hand, and stared fixedly.

"It's a deal," he then said. "When does the first lesson come off?"

"That," she replied with a very small smile, "will depend upon what time I have to spare after my other duties are all done."

CHAPTER IX

INDIAN MAGIC

UPON entering her bedroom to change her dress for supper, Miss Innes found it bright with firelight. On the bed her frock was laid out, her shoes were warming in the fender. Upon the rug before the hearth, the red glow of the flames intensifying the colour of her crimson saree, sat the Indian woman, cross-legged, her chin supported on her hand, gazing intently at something on the ground, near the fire. There was a warm, seductive sweetness in the air, like the faint breath of flowers.

Olwen, who had crept in with muscles drawn together to withstand the biting cold, felt as if she had entered a conservatory unawares.

"Oh, what a lovely fire!" was her first impetuous cry. Then, reprovingly, "You must not spoil me like this. I came here to help you, not to make someone else to wait upon."

The ayah raised her soft eyes to the expressive little face of the girl, who had knelt upon the hearth beside her. "Missee must be served," she said in her curious, caressing voice. "I know it, first minute I see her. The stars tell me. Sunia know about stars, she what you call witch woman, you sahibs."

What girl of two-and-twenty is wholly destitute of curiosity concerning veiled destiny? Olwen's eyes grew big. "What do you mean," she asked, half laughing, half in earnest, "by saying that the stars told you things about me?"

The ayah rose to her feet with the lithe movement of a creature without bones. She held her hands to Olwen, raised her to her feet, and they stood a moment, eye to eye.

Olwen felt her hands tingle.

"Missee make bargain with ole ayah? Ole ayah never seen Missee, never know Missee, all up to this night. If she can tell Missee things gone by, things what happen to her long ago, will Missee believe she know what going to happen one day?"

There was something uncanny here. The Celtic blood ran warm in Olwen. Her voice shook a little. "Sunia, what *can* you know about me?" she challenged smilingly.

The little brown hands were softly impelling her, so that she sank into a well cushioned chair which stood beside the hearth. The Hindu crouched before her, her face in darkness, save when a wandering gleam from the blazing logs caught her eyes and made them flicker.

"My missee born upon the fells," she murmured. "Her folks carried her south—away south—but she came back. She born for the north, she never stay in London town. She come north, always north, farther north, where she belong, where she stay, in her own place."

There was a silence, during which the girl held her breath, her senses lulled into a kind of stupor. She noted for the first time that two tiny earthen pots stood in the ashes of the hearth. From one of these ascended a minute, twisting jet of smoke, evidently the cause of the subtle perfume which hung upon the air. The vapour seemed to be binding her senses in some kind of enchantment; but the words already spoken by the woman made her eager to hear more.

Bending forward, Sunia touched first one little pot, then the other, with her tiny brown hand; then, sitting back on her heels, she closed her eyes, holding her arms rigidly extended. They were covered with glass bangles,

and her movement caused these to ring or chime musi-
cally. The sound of them died away very gradually—as
it seemed to the excited imagination of the girl, rhyth-
mically—till all was still. The silence was intense when
the woman began to mutter:

"Two beside her when first she·set her feet to earth
. . . two who are divided by all but their love for her.
Now one goes . . . driven away . . . the one she love
most . . . a man. He look back all a time . . . but he
go. And now the other she go too. More slow. Much
more slow. She is alone. She is very much alone. I see
her in a room with many others . . . but quite alone;
always a-lone!"

The voice died away. Olwen was agitated far beyond
her expectations. It was, as far as she could tell, out
of the question that this woman could know the details
of which she spoke. She closed her eyes, leaning back
in her chair; and the soft chime of the bangles, as the
thin brown arms sank upon their owner's knees, sounded
like the last chord of some dim fantasia.

"Have I seen true, Missee?"

"Yes. Quite true. Oh, Sunia, tell me more, if you
can see! That one I loved—that one who went away—
is he still living, or is he dead?"

"Dead," was the soft answer. "Missee when I see her,
quite alone: till the north call and she have to come to
the Pele. Now look! I take Missee farther—only a
little. I not see very plain this night, because we only
begin. When Missee give me her thoughts more I see
better."

Leaning forward, she laid her hand again, quite gently,
upon the little earthen pots, which had ceased to smoke.
So far as Olwen could see, she put nothing into them,
applying merely the tips of her fingers; but at once there
ascended from each a thread of smoke, very distinct,

ascending spirally. As the upward draught took them, the two smokes mingled, and rose, passing out of sight as if entwined.

"This one Missee's, that mine," said the sorceress. "My fate and hers have touched and come together. Never come undone now. Can't do. Me Missee's woman always."

As she spoke, the smoke vanished, the little pots contained only a morsel of grey ash.

Olwen did not speak for some long moments. She sat fascinated, hypnotised by the perfume and the weird prophecy.

After a while, she rallied her senses, and spoke with a desperate effort to be normal. "That must be nonsense. I have only come here for a month. Most likely, at the end of that time, I shall go away, and you and I will never meet again."

"We may have to part," replied Sunia gravely. "I thought I saw a parting, and that is bad. But not for long. If you go, you come back again. I very well can see that."

"You speak as if you were really a witch! I think I am afraid of you."

"No need. I only show you I Missee's woman," was the simple answer, "so you let me do things for you. I do everything for my Missee, and that make ole ayah very happy."

As she spoke, she arose, went to the basin, and poured hot water into it.

Arising with resolution, Olwen passed her hand over her eyes as if to clear away cobwebs. It needed a real effort of will-power to wrench herself back to everyday life. Only the fear of being late for supper this first evening enabled her to unfasten her serge frock and slip out of it. Sunia had lit more candles, so that the room was now full of light. She stood a moment, gazing approvingly at the rounded outlines of the girl's form. Then, making her sit down, she folded a huge towel about her, brought the basin to a chair near, and bathed face, throat and arms with water which, like the air of the room, was subtly perfumed. As she wiped the wet skin with the softest damask, she muttered that there was no time to-night to make Missee really beautiful, but later on she would massage her properly. She let down her hair once more and rearranged it, this time with a trifling difference of effect which was most becoming. She changed shoes and stockings, and finally put on the simple little frock of dull green velveteen.

Wholly subdued by the woman's spell, whatever it was, the girl made no further objections. As she submitted passively to her ministrations, it was with a feeling that all this had happened before; that in some previous incarnation she had been thus attended. She did not rebel, even when the woman came to her holding in her hands a gauze scarf, curiously embroidered in dull gold.

"Cold, down them stone steps. Missee put this over her shoulders," she murmured.

"Oh, what a lovely scarf!"

"Belonged a Begum once. Just right for my Missee," said the woman, adjusting it over the girl's shoulders. The mirror was too small for Olwen to see the full effect; but the glimpse she did obtain was satisfactory. The gold of the scarf was the gold of her hair.

"I will wear this scarf if it pleases you," she softly said. "Only you know it's yours, not mine."

"All a same," said the woman simply. "I just glad my Missee like it."

As she spoke, the big clock over the gatehouse tolled eight in its deep, sad tones. The ayah collected the hot-water can and other things, and carried them off into the adjoining room.

"Is that where you sleep, Sunia?"

"Yes, Missee. You and me on this floor. My Sahib, he sleep next room to Madam, underneath."

Olwen felt glad to know that she had someone near her, although the woman made her half afraid.

"Missee better go down," said Sunia, reappearing. "Take a light."

She put a candle in a glass shade into the girl's hand, and, turning away with a last inhalation of the curious fragrance of her chamber, Miss Innes went down the twisting stair a little shakily, feeling overexcited and queer. Yesterday seemed cut off from to-day by some impassable barrier.

As she reached the floor below her, she came face to face with young Guyse, candle in hand, obeying the supper-bell like herself. He stopped short, a startled look on his face, which disappeared almost at once, to give place to his usual cocksure smile.

"I thought at first you were a fairy," he said. "You *are* turned out, upon my word! Determined not to leave me a single loophole of escape, aren't you?"

"Unfortunately, you are not speaking my language. I can't understand a single word you say," was the stiff retort.

"Ah, that reminds me! I'll have my first lesson after supper."

"It's very cold here. Will you go first, or shall I?"

"Let me lead the way," he replied, turning on his heel.

Madam awaited them in the dining-room. She had made no change in her attire. "Oh, dear," said she fretfully, as Olwen came in, "you *have* made yourself smart!"

Olwen laughed, glad to expend some of her bottled-up excitement.

"This is Sunia's doing, the scarf is hers. She begged
me to put it on. I thought it was her pretty way of telling me that my frock was a bit shabby for the occasion,
so I did as she asked."

"Well, you look very nice, I must own. You pay
for dressing, as they say. It is years since I have seen
anybody prettily dressed."

Ninian made a restless movement.

"In my husband's lifetime we had a house in town as
well as a big country place," went on his mother. "Ninian
doesn't realise at all how much I miss it."

Her son was very red. "Mother, what is the use of
talking so? You know I can't help it."

Madam sighed deeply, but as the ayah now entered,
with a silver entrée dish in her hand, they sat down to
table and the subject dropped. It had one good effect,
for it made Ninian exert himself to talk, so as to turn
the current of Madam's thoughts. Olwen was grateful
to him for making conversation, for her own fancy was
so full of the fortune-telling as to make it impossible for
her to fix her thoughts on anything else. Later, when
the ayah had left the room, she could no longer resist
speaking of what had occurred. "Is not your Sunia a
clairvoyante?" she asked. "She has been saying most
extraordinary things to me."

Madam stared in faint surprise. "What kind of
things?"

"About my childhood and early life. Things she could
not possibly have known. She spoke of my parents,
'divided in everything but their love for me.' That is,
unfortunately, true, but she could not have known it by
any ordinary means."

As she spoke, she caught Mr. Guyse's eye. There was
an expression in it which held her attention, but which
she could not analyse. It was rather like pity. As their

eyes met, he rose from table with a nervous laugh. "She's an old humbug," he said. "Don't listen to her, don't let her bore you. Shall I tell her to let you alone?"

"Oh, please don't tell tales of me! She has been so kind, she has done all she could for me. I—I didn't mind her saying that, only it seemed a bit uncanny."

He gave her another self-conscious look, then turned away and lit his pipe without replying.

"Let's go to the billiard-room," he said at length. "Come along, Ma."

Mrs. Guyse rose with evident unwillingness, and began to look for her shawl. Olwen found it, and put it over her shoulders. "The room will be as cold as a well," said she fretfully. "Understand, Nin, that I go off to bed in an hour's time."

"All right," replied her son shortly.

They mounted to the floor immediately above, and the puzzle as to where they kept the library was solved. This great apartment had evidently been the refectory or banqueting hall. It had been altered into a library by the Tudor Guyse, who had cut windows so recklessly; and Madam's dead husband had turned it into a billiard-room.

It covered the whole floor space of the tower, except for a small bit at the north end. On this side were three arched doors, enriched with ball-flower moulding, the easternmost leading to the chapel, the western to the priest's room, the central one to a small windowless space known as the dungeon.

Above the fine bookcases was oak panelling, on which hung a few inferior oil paintings of dead Guyses.

Near the south end of the west wall was a very large oriel, with a window seat and table and chairs. So large was the apartment that the full-sized billiard table looked quite small in it, and left plenty of space for settles and arm-chairs round about the Tudor fireplace, with the Guyse arms carved above.

The existence of this noble room delighted Olwen. It changed the whole character of the place. Here was an ideal spot for reading or writing. There were several fine screens in stamped leather, which would exclude draughts. The western oriel, commanding a view of the lovely Guyseburn Dale, would be utterly delightful in summer-time.

Ninian seemed pleased at her naïve admiration. He displayed to her the poor bare little chapel, destitute of all plenishing, and the two other apartments. Olwen wondered how the priest could close his eyes at night, if there were a prisoner in solitary confinement next door to him. Young Guyse laughed, and said that the Border folk, priests and laity alike, were a hard-bitten lot, and that in those days compassion was hardly counted as a virtue. It was as badly out of fashion as discipline and obedience are now.

"I must own that I believe my ancestors to have been a set of bloody-minded thieves," he remarked with candour.

"They're but little changed now," observed his mother, from her seat by the fire.

"Thanks, Ma, don't lose a chance," he flung back negligently, going to the rack to choose cues.

He found that Olwen had somewhat underrated her own skill. He gave her a big handicap, and she actually beat him. Mrs. Guyse, who at first sat languidly reading the paper, presently sat up, and at last even left her place to watch them. They all three became quite animated, and when Madam suddenly recollect herself and said she was going to bed at once, it was more than half-past ten.

Olwen, though the game was not finished, put away

her own cue, and began to collect the lady's workbag
and cushions.

"Oh, stay and finish your game! Don't let Ninian
be able to say that I took you off before the end," said
the hostess pettishly.

"But please I am very tired," said Olwen, "I am quite
ready to say good night."

She said it with so much firmness that Ninian, who
had flung down his cue and marched upon her with the
evident intention of sharp protest, said not a single word,
but allowed them both to disappear, through the narrow
door, with a candle to guide the steps of Madam on the
dark stairs.

When they reached the lady's own quarters, the girl
followed her into the sitting-room, and, setting down the
candle, asked modestly for a few directions.

"I'm very anxious, of course, to do exactly as you
wish," said she. "At what hour is breakfast, and should
you expect me to make the tea or coffee?"

Madam stood irresolutely by the table, twisting her
hands together as if worried almost beyond endurance.
Her face was set in obstinate lines. "To come down to
breakfast I absolutely decline," said she in a desperate
voice. "I haven't done such a thing for years, and it
can't be expected of me."

Olwen was so astonished that she stood with her mouth
open.

"I suppose you have no objection to breakfasting with
my son? You seem to be extremely particular," said
Madam after a pause.

"I am here to carry out your orders," was the girl's
reply. "I shall do as you wish, of course. At what hour
does Mr. Guyse breakfast?"

"At eight o'clock."

"And you would like me to be down and to breakfast with him ?"

"*He* would," was the surprising answer.

Olwen shrugged her shoulders. "Then," she went on, as steadily as she could, "at what time should I come to you ? Is there anything you would like me to do, or shall I begin at once upon the library books ?"

With a weary gesture, the lady dropped into a chair.

"Really, Miss Innes, I cannot be bothered like this. I am tired—I wish to sleep. Go to bed, for goodness' sake, and when I am up to-morrow perhaps I shall have some orders for you. I am usually dressed about eleven."

"Thank you," was the meek response. "That was all I wanted to know. I am sorry to be importunate, but I feel a little strange at first."

"Yes, yes, I know. Good night. I hope you will be comfortable. Sunia says your bed is soft, but comfort in this jail of a place seems a thing one can't even imagine." She turned, with a harsh laugh, upon the girl as she withdrew. "When I married Ninian's father I had never put on my own stockings in my life! I was a millionaire's daughter! And now—look at me! Look at my house! Look at my clothes! Even the sight of a girl from a town upsets me!"

CHAPTER X

EXTRACT from a letter to Miss Grace Holroyd, dated January 12:

"Since the first scrawl I sent you, telling you of my safe, though delayed, arrival, and trying to describe this extraordinary place, I have begun two letters and torn up both in despair. The truth is that ever since I got here my mind has been rushing round and round, mixing and curdling itself more like milk in a churn than anything I can think of. This is Friday. I arrived here on Tuesday, and I find myself just as bewildered, just as unable to give such an account of my environment as may sound sane and well considered, as I was the first day.

"I was always conscious of living, at Bramforth, in too deep a groove; but little did I guess how far I was sunk therein or how hard would be the process of readjustment.

"Having written that down, I pause to wonder whether it is true. Was my groove so deep? or is the eccentricity of the Guyses to blame for my mental confusion? Sometimes I incline to one view, sometimes to the other; but I am beginning to feel quite sure that, strange as this Pele-place is, the trio of persons who dwell therein are far, far more improbable.

"First, there is the Indian ayah, striking so bizarre a note of contrast to begin with, that it makes one quite giddy. She is the only one who took to me from the

100

first. Judging from what I hear, she is by no means agreeable to everybody, so I ought to consider myself lucky, I suppose.

"Her affection takes the form of waiting upon me hand and foot. One would fancy she had been languishing in a far country for years, buoyed up solely by the hope of being one day permitted to lace my boots! Picture me, Gracie, after such a youth as you know of, hardly allowed so much as to wash my own hands! I lie now under a carven canopy, in a nest of down so thoroughly warmed for me at night that I sleep a kind of charmed slumber from dusk to dawn. When I awake, it is to find my handmaid at my side with tea—such tea!—and cream —such cream! While I sip in luxury, she re-kindles the fire, which usually has not quite gone out all night, so cunningly does she bank it down.

"In front of this fire she prepares my bath, and—now I beg of you not to blush—she insists upon bathing me herself, rubbing me from head to foot with a kind of wondrous massage. She then dresses my hair, and I go down to breakfast all in a glow, ready for anything, even the Guyse ménage!

"I remember hearing your dear wise mother say that if you give your household staff thoroughly comfortable quarters and plenty of good food they would never grumble at work, however hard. Perhaps that is Sunia's idea about me. I am, indeed, well fed and lodged.

"I breakfast alone with the young man of whom I told you—the one who brought me here. He goes off to work on his farm immediately after. He works very hard, I think, for he has only Ezra Baxter, a man named Kay, and one or two farm labourers to help him.

"At about eleven o'clock, Madam, as Mrs. Guyse is called by everyone in the house, makes her appearance. When we reach her, we are at the thickest of the mys-

tery. I cannot understand her one bit. She is not merely
in no want of a companion, she even seems, quite unmis-
takably, to be bored by my presence, to look upon me as
an incubus, for whom occupation or amusement must
somehow be found.

"Is it not quaint? She wrote to me herself, she offered
me unusually high terms, she was apparently most anxious
for me to come at once. Now that I am here she does
not in the least know what to do with me. I have to make
work, for her main idea seems to be to contrive how
little of my company she need endure, to plan reasons
for keeping me out of her sight.

"The idea of her having a companion came, I suppose, from her son. Sometimes I think he suggested it
merely to give him somebody to tease. One could hardly
blame him; a winter here must be an ordeal. There is,
however, another possible reason. I have guessed that he
fears the isolation here is telling upon Madam's mental
faculties, and that she must be taken out of herself, even
if she doesn't like the remedy! They were apparently
very rich in former days, and the poor lady's fallen fortunes have no doubt preyed upon her mind.

"I can't flatter myself that I have made much head-
way yet. So far, I have merely made a preliminary ex-
amination of the library which, while anything but up
to date, seems valuable, and contains what even my ignorance knows to be rare editions.

"Let me give you an example of my difficulties.

"The day after my arrival, Mr. Guyse suggested a
sleigh drive. I assented, supposing, of course, that Madam
would go too. I found, however, when the time came,
that she had not the least intention of so doing. I therefore excused myself, pointing out to the young man that I
could not go out and leave her alone the whole afternoon.
Upon this, to my surprise, Madam lost her temper, turned

to me and asked what use I should be if I could not do as I was told? She expected me to take her place and accompany her son when she could not. She never went out when the snow was on the ground. Of course, I felt ashamed of having made a fuss, and I went obediently, but neither of us enjoyed it. He and I do not get on a bit. His idea of making himself agreeable is either to chaff or to flirt, and I hate both. This obliges me to be so grim and stony when I am with him that you would think I had never unbent in my life. I have the uncomfortable feeling that, if I so much as smile frankly at him, he will take advantage of it to make some personal remark about my dimple or some such folly. Well, to continue, I suppose that he brought some kind of pressure to bear upon his mother after that drive, for the following day she said she was coming with us, and come she did. Alas! My triumph was short-lived. Nemesis has overtaken me. She promptly took cold, and this morning we decided to send for the doctor. Young Guyse has some grudge against the doctor, so the matter has not endeared me in that quarter, as you may imagine. However, as I prefer him out of temper, that doesn't matter much.

"*Saturday.*—If I had dispatched this yesterday it would have ended with an emphatic declaration that I meant to look out for another post at once. Last night, however, something happened to shake my resolution.

"As poor Madam was too seedy to come downstairs, I went up to her after supper to see if I could do anything to amuse her. She had already informed me that if there is one thing she dislikes more than another it is having anyone read aloud to her! So I took my little patience cards. You know, a long experience with grandfather has made me quite a compendium of games.

"I had noticed a green baize writing-board down in the billiard-room, and I succeeded in arranging this across the arms of her chair, so that she could handle the cards conveniently. We started with an easy game, and before we had been going ten minutes I knew I had lighted upon something that took her fancy.

"She grew quite interested, displaying a childish eagerness. Then, just as she was beginning to chatter to me more naturally than she has ever done, that hateful young man must needs come pounding on the door to know if I wasn't coming down to play billiards with him.

"He marched in—nobody can shout through these oaken doors—and I saw her expression change and a nervous look creep into her face, as it does when she sees him. 'You had better go,' she said uncertainly.

"It came to me all in a minute that she needed a champion; and I got up and went to him, saying decidedly that I could not go, as he must see, for we were in the middle of a most interesting game.

" 'Oh, tosh!' he said easily, 'come along. I've had the room warmed on purpose for you.'

" 'I'm sorry you took the trouble,' I replied, 'but surely you understand that when your mother wants me I must be with her.'

"She was making little anxious sounds and coughing significantly. 'Go with him. I can spare you quite well,' she muttered; but my blood was up. I went to the door, and he, thinking he had gained his point, followed me out into the passage, or rather the tunnel. He had a candle in his hand, so he could see my face.

" 'Mr. Guyse,' I said, 'when you brought me here you told me that your mother was badly in need of distraction —that she suffered from ennui. Now that I have watched her for several days, I am sure that you did a right and necessary thing in persuading her to have somebody to live with her. She leads too solitary an existence, and it is telling on her health and spirits. To-night, for the first time, she has seemed glad of my company, and interested in what we are doing. You couldn't be so selfish as to want me to leave her to herself?'

"He flushed angrily. 'And what price me? Is it good for me to be everlastingly alone?' he began; and then quite suddenly he broke off and grinned at me as if it were a huge joke.

" 'Right as usual, teacher,' he said. 'Yes, it's true. I knew she ought to have somebody about. You go right on, and never mind me.'

"I was quite astonished and a little touched. 'I felt you were only thoughtless,' I said. He remarked that I was evidently born to be the mistress of a reformatory, but he evidently bore no malice and cleared off without further ado. As I went back I thought over the speech I had made, and it did sound horribly priggish! I never spoke so to anybody before. Isn't it astonishing how different one is with different people? I don't think I ever struck you as a sanctimonious little hypocrite; did I, Gracie, my beloved?

"Madam looked so surprised when I came back that I could not help laughing a little as I sat down by her.

" 'Please, Miss Innes,' said she faintly, 'go down and have a game with poor Nin; he is so lonely.'

" 'He may be lonely there, but you are lonely here,' said I. 'Was I engaged to look after him or you?'

" 'He'll be very angry,' she began, but I assured her that he was not—that he had said he thought me quite right.

" 'Oh, he may not show it to you, but it is I who will hear of this again,' said she.

" 'Nothing of the kind,' I said. 'I'll see to it that he shan't tease you.' (Rather cheek on my part!) 'He doesn't mean to be unkind, but men are inconsiderate. If I explain matters to him he will be more reasonable.'

"She looked unhappy and undecided, and then said, in a kind of burst, 'I am so anxious for you and him to get on together. I don't want you to go away.'

"Well, that was putting things in a new light. Apparently she thinks that if I don't make myself agreeable to the master of the house he will tell her to give me notice. The thought made me quite angry. The ingenuous speech had also shown me something else. I had not supposed that Madam liked me, and her unconscious admission bucked me to a surprising extent.

" 'Then you don't want me to go away?' I asked; and she replied hurriedly, 'No, indeed! I am most anxious, very anxious, that you should stay.'

*   *   *   *   *

"So that was settled, and just for the moment I mean to stay and to keep up, if I can, my new rôle of mistress of a reformatory! I worked it splendidly at breakfast, and was able to refuse a sleigh drive on the plea that I must not be out when the doctor calls. In spite of his rage that this said doctor, who is young and good-looking, should be coming at all, Mr. Guyse was fain to admit that this was a just excuse. He looked at me curiously, as if in wonder that anyone so severely proper as I could contrive to exist!

"So far, so good! The difficulty will be to keep it up if we see much of each other, for he is madly provoking, and, as you know, I *have* a tongue!

"Well, I must end this rigmarole, and go and brush my hair in preparation for receiving Dr. Balmayne, whose impending arrival is exciting me to an extent that I cannot expect you to understand until you have lived the best part of a week in a dark tower, cut off from all intercourse with the world outside.

"You see, we met the doctor on our way up here, and I thought he looked interesting. He stared at me as if he thought I was not quite proper, and, seeing what young Guyse is, I can hardly wonder. However, I hope to persuade him of my moral rectitude, and also (perhaps) of my rare personal charm, this afternoon! Best love and farewell.—Your chum-girl,   OLWEN."

CHAPTER XI

MISS LILY MARTIN

THE sight of Dr. Balmayne's little run-about car creeping slowly along the snowy road across the moor was indeed in the nature of an event. From Tuesday until Saturday only a few farm carts had dared the track. The doctor stopped at the outer gateway, crossing the causeway on foot, so his approach was not visible from the Pele itself. Olwen had, however, been out to feed the chickens, their mistress being actually in her bed; and Mrs. Baxter ran into the courtyard in some excitement to announce the arrival, descried by herself from the vantage ground of the Gatehouse.

Mr. Guyse being out, Olwen had no hesitation in going to the archway to greet the doctor. She stood, in fur cap and big coat, smiling and rosy, under the fangs of the rusty portcullis.

"Well," said Balmayne, drawing off his glove to greet her, "so you are still alive!"

She laughed gaily. "Did you expect to see my head fixed upon a spike outside the battlements?" she inquired.

"No; I find Castle Terribil strange enough, but possible."

"Good!" he answered. "Strange, but possible! You seem to have a fine taste in adjectives."

"I have felt like ransacking a dictionary for them since I came here, whenever I am wrestling with the difficulty of conveying to my wholly Philistine relations anything like the impression this place produces!"

He stopped midway as they strolled across the quad-

108

rangle, gazing up at the almost unbroken wall of the Pele, grim and grey, on that side pierced only by the loopholes which lighted the newel stair.

"It's still fine, you know," he said half grudgingly. "When it was first built it possessed, of course, the supreme attribute of architecture—that of complete fitness for its intended purpose. But even now that this is so no more—now that it is no praise of a dwelling that it shall also be a fortress—it is still wonderful, still dignified."

"Like some people one knows, it turns its most forbidding face to the approaching stranger," she replied. "On the other side, where it overlooks the valley, the Tudor Guyses opened out windows quite recklessly."

"They had no hesitation in adapting it to their needs. We are afraid to do that now, the spell of the past is too strong for us."

"Humph! Somebody or other, not so many generations back, perpetrated *that!*" observed the girl, pointing the finger of scorn to the low ugly kitchen huddled against the south wall, its chimney sulkily asmoke.

He laughed. "Well, that's not encouraging, I own. And so you are finding existence possible?"

"I am having an experience," was her reply, "and I was rather in search of that. However, it is early days yet—— I suppose the snow doesn't lie all the year round, even here. As regards Mrs. Guyse, I fear her bad cold is my fault. I urged her to go for a sleigh drive, and she is so unused to fresh air that it gave her cold, so I am feeling rather a failure just at present."

"Your theory was right, but in practice it went back on you," he replied amused. "A thing which does sometimes happen, even in these anything but tropical climes——"

"When a vessel is, so to speak, snarked," she concluded.

"Yes, you have helped me to a word. Mrs. Guyse is, so

to speak, snarked. Really she is a good deal like the
Bellman, in being courteous and grave, but the orders she
gave are enough to bewilder a crew—oh, I'm talking
nonsense, but really it is such a queer household! The
poor lady resented my coming, but, as a fact, she is in sad
need of a companion."

"Yes," he replied reflectively, laying his hat and gloves
on the hall table, for they had entered the Pele while they
talked, "but her last experience in that direction was a
bit shattering, wasn't it?"

She gave a startled glance. "Was it? I didn't know.
Tell me."

He coloured slightly. "I beg your pardon. I thought
you might have been told something of it by this time.
However, as the Guyses have said nothing, I have no
business to be discussing their affairs."

"Certainly, you are right," but she said it reluctantly.
She had the idea that this man might supply her with a
clue, tell her something which might form a key to the
characters of the strange people among whom she found
herself.

"Will you wait a moment while I let Mrs. Guyse
know?" she said, and vanished from his sight behind the
curtain which hid the stair-foot.

When she returned, he stood with his back to the
stove, contemplating the barrel vault. It was never anything like full daylight in the vestibule owing to the
primitive nature of the fenestration.

"Have you seen the well yet?" he asked.

"No," she replied with vivid interest. "Where is it?"

"Almost under your feet where you stand. Get Guyse
to show you. It's beautiful water, and was the sole source
of supply until they came to settle here, ten years ago,
when he brought water up the hillside into the courtyard."

"What a place!" she laughed.

"Have you ever thought to wonder how they conveyed any furniture to the upper floors?"

"I did, but never made inquiries. Now one thinks of it, how *could* they have got a billiard-table in?"

"Pulled out all the mullions of the big south window and hauled the table up with ropes outside the wall. That was Ninian's father all over."

"They must have done the same thing all over the house!"

"I believe they did, except for such things as had been carried up in pieces and put together on the spot. You know, in the old times when there was raiding on the border, the cattle were all driven in here, where we stand, the women and children being accommodated above. Sometimes there were too many beasts for this place, and on one occasion, at least, some of them were stabled in the Gatehouse with the garrison—but perhaps Guyse has told you all this?"

"No, indeed, we don't have very much to say to one another."

"Well, the legend is that the attacking enemy made a breach in the masonry of the Gatehouse tower, and that a bull jumped out through the hole and fell into the ravine. That is why they call the causeway the Bull-drop."

"I didn't know it was so called."

"Yes, it is; and the legend goes on to assert that when another bull shall drop into the ravine there shall occur the birth of a fair-haired Guyse, and the Guyses of Guyse-wyke shall come into their own again."

"Does that mean, get back their lands?"

"The folk hereabout think it means that title and all shall pass to the elder branch. The present Lord Caryngston, you know, belongs to the junior line, the title having been conferred on his great-grandfather."

"The present Mr. Guyse has quite black hair."

"You haven't seen his brother?"

"His brother? I didn't know he had one."

"Oh, yes, they are twins, and Wilfrid is as fair as he is dark. Well, I must not keep you here chattering but go and see my patient! Lead on, please."

They proceeded up the newel, Olwen's brain busy with the facts just learned.

Dr. Balmayne, while not recommending any more sleigh drives at present, urged his patient to as much change of air as the Pele could afford. He said the banqueting hall was the only really airy room in the house, and that she ought to spend the greater part of her time in it. Olwen eagerly said that she was quite sure that could be arranged; but as she marked the obstinate fold of the lady's pale lips, she guessed that, in face of the patient's opposition, no orders of the doctor could be carried out.

As they passed from the bedroom to the sitting-room, the doctor asked, "What has become of the ayah?"

"Oh, I don't expect she is far off; but she asked me to bring you upstairs, she is very anxious not to seem to be usurping any prerogative of mine."

"Dear me!" he said in a tone of great surprise. "She must have altered very much of late."

"Why, was she jealous of the last companion? But I forgot, I ought not to ask you that question."

They had reached the hall once more. "Oh," he said, "there can be no harm in my saying that the Hindu was very jealous of Miss Martin, and they never got on well."

"Why, she is kindness itself to me—almost too kind! She overwhelms me with devotion. She has some sort of superstitious idea that it is her destiny to serve me. Look here!" she held out her hands, the nails beautifully manicured; then, turning her back to display her head, "Are you a judge of hair-dressing? What do you think

of this for a winter's morning in the wilds of the Border?
Why do you look at me like that?"

In fact, his expression was that of consternation. "I—
I am surprised—what you tell me surprises me. What
can be the woman's object? For she does nothing without an object."

"To induce me to stay, I should think," laughed Olwen.
"She may have found that it is not easy to detain anybody
young in this weird spot."

"That may be," he said slowly, but not as if he were
convinced. "Are you an orphan?" he asked abruptly;
and her reply that she was caused him to furrow his brow.
He said nothing, however, picking up his hat and gloves
slowly from the table.

Looking up, he caught her anxious eyes, and a smile
kindled in his own. "Certainly the coiffure is tip-top,
but Sunia had fine material to work upon, if I may be
pardoned the remark." Tone and manner were alike just
right, and she laughed with a clear mind.

"Shall you be coming again?" she wished to know.

"Oh, yes. Mrs. Guyse must not leave her room until I
have seen her. It is a great thing for her to have your
society; but I—I feel"—he dropped his voice—"as if I
ought perhaps to utter one word of warning. The ayah
is not to be trusted; and——"

She smiled up at him with limpid eyes. "Are you
going to echo Mrs. Askwith's warning to 'keep Muster
Nin at a distance'?" she replied in the same undertone.
"Well, you needn't be uneasy. We are not hitting it off.
I have had to administer one or two snubs, and he now
says he thinks I was born to be the mistress of a reformatory."

They went out together into the frosty twilight. When
they had gone some steps she remarked: "The hall is
not a safe place in which to talk. You never know where

the ayah is. However, she is welcome to have overheard all that we have said to-day."

"Mrs. Askwith's advice was good; I am in a position to tell you that it was by no means unnecessary. But I think you are all right; you seem to have plenty of sense. Would it be an impertinence if I asked how you happened to come here?"

"Oh, very simply. I advertised, and Mrs. Guyse answered my advertisement. It wasn't quite what I wanted, but they pay well, and I thought it would be a beginning. I don't expect to be here very long, and if it grows in any way uncomfortable I shall leave."

"Good!" he said; and added after thought, "I wish you were not quite so isolated. You have literally no neighbours. There is nobody nearer than the vicarage at Lachanrigg, and Mr. and Mrs. Baines are both over seventy, so during the winter they might as well not exist as far as the Pele is concerned."

They strolled out across the Bull-drop. Just as they reached the outer gate Ninian Guyse rode up, mounted on Deloraine.

"Hallo!" said he, with a swift glance at the two. "Risked your precious Fordette on these roads, eh?"

"Don't you sneer at my tin-kettle! She's as game a little machine as ever hummed along these God-forsaken tracks," replied Balmayne. "Well, I've seen your mother, and she ought soon to be all right. Just a slightly relaxed throat which has sent up her temperature. I am telling Miss Innes to persuade her to pass more time in your billiard-room, or library, whatever you call it. It is spacious and airy, and while she goes out so little, she must take all the air she can get indoors."

"Yes, the doctor has put an idea into my head," chimed in Olwen, as the doctor shook hands, and hastened to where his chauffeur was cranking up the motor. "Good-bye, doctor, and thank you! I'll expect the medicine by the postman to-morrow and yourself the day after—and I'll remember all your directions!"

The car started. Ninian, after standing a moment as if in profound thought, took Deloraine's bridle, and Olwen and he walked across the causeway.

"Dr. Balmayne has been telling me that they call this the Bull-drop," said she conversationally.

"Oh, indeed! What more has he been telling you, I wonder?"

"Something extremely interesting—that there is a well under the floor of the hall. I do so want to see it!"

"There's nothing to see."

"Oh, if it's any trouble, it really doesn't matter in the least. Please forget that I mentioned it, and let me say a word about Madam. I have been wondering why she doesn't use the billiard-room more; it is much the nicest room in the house, and not a bit draughty, and I believe I have discovered the reason."

He turned his face to her, but the gathering night hid his expression. "You have noticed that my mother doesn't like the billiard-room?"

"Evidently she doesn't like being there."

"And you think you know why?"

"Yes. I think it is because she is not comfortable there. There is no sofa upon which she can lie down."

"I wonder if by any chance you are right," he mused, speaking for the first time since she had known him quite earnestly and naturally. "It might be worth trying."

"Exactly what I was going to suggest," she broke in eagerly. "Of course, I can see that no sofa could be carried upstairs. But I have been studying the catalogue from Barton's, the big Leeds people, and they have those canvas lounges which fold up. With the cushions off the dining-room sofa and some pillows we could make one of those quite comfy for her. The one I liked is only thirty shillings, carriage paid. We could move back the settle, put up the big leather screen, set a table close by, and she would be almost as cosy as she is upstairs."

He checked Deloraine in the courtyard and began to unsaddle him. "It's a rattling good idea. I'll write and order the thing to-night."

"Oh, thanks! I am glad you don't snub my poor little plan!"

"Why should I snub it?"

"Somehow I thought you would."

"You think you know all about me, don't you?"

"On the contrary, how can I know anything except what you have shown me?"

He made no answer, and in the dusk she escaped, hurrying upstairs to tell Sunia what the doctor had said and to prepare a fomentation for Madam's throat.

CHAPTER XII

MADAM lay nearly flat on her back under the canopy of her great fourpost bed. Her sunken eyes followed Miss Innes curiously as she measured a dose of medicine into a glass.

Approaching the bed the girl stopped, slipped an arm under the thin shoulder-blades and, lifting her patient, administered the draught.

"That's to lower your temperature," said she encouragingly. "You will feel much better when you are less feverish."

As she rearranged the bed and rinsed the glass, she gave news of the beloved fowls. Kitty, one of the buff Orpingtons, regardless of the time of year, had insisted upon "going broody," and Mrs. Baxter, having tried various cures in vain, had at last given her a "clutch" of eggs. Madam speculated sadly upon the problem of keeping the chickens alive when hatched.

Olwen hopefully suggested that the weather might be very different in six weeks' time.

"It won't. Not for months and months. You don't know this place. This accursed place," added Madam faintly under her breath.

"Oh, don't call it that! I find it extraordinarily fascinating. Nothing else like it anywhere, is there?"

"Let's hope not. Ah, it's all very fine for you to laugh. If you had been through all I have undergone——" She broke off, muttering to herself. Olwen could see that she

117

was under the influence of fever, and spoke soothingly.

"I'm sorry. I hardly know why I laughed. Laughter comes easily to me, I think."

"You're lucky. I never had a merry nature; and, if I could have seen into my future——"

She moved restlessly, while Olwen sat down near with her knitting.

Silence fell. How intense silence could be in that place! The thick walls shut off each room in a solitude of its own. No sounds of daily life arose to the listening ear; one might be isolated from everyone else in the world. As Olwen meditated on this the hush was broken by the voice of Madam, who began to speak in a low, monotonous narrative.

"I was born in a palace—a mansion on Streatham Hill, standing in a great park. My father rose from small beginnings to be one of the richest men in England. He was very ambitious for me, his only child. In the course of business he had come across Lord Caryngston, and had been able to oblige his lordship pretty substantially. It was arranged, in return, that her ladyship should present me at Court and invite me to her house to meet her friends. That was how I came to know Ninian Guyse. My father did not like the match, but he wanted me to be happy, and I was spoiled and wilful. I was head over ears in love. What a fool! Ah, what a fool! Ninian Guyse was as deep in debt as I in love, and only wanted my fortune."

"Oh, don't say that!" cried the girl.

The wistful eyes were turned upon her face. "It's true," she said defiantly. "Why should I not say it? Oh, I suppose you mean I ought not to say it to you! But that will be all right, as long as you don't tell Ninian." The drawn face assumed a look of deep cunning. "Not a word to my son, or to ayah. Understand? Why not our little secrets, you and me? . . . Where was I? Oh, yes, we were married, you know, and as long as my father lived he exercised some kind of control, but, to my deep misfortune, he died, and then there was nothing to hold my husband. He went from bad to worse. I would not live with him at last. The twins and I usually lived in London and he at Danley, our Yorkshire place. He was an excellent jockey, and he sometimes rode his own horses. That was how he caught his death . . . riding a race he felt certain of winning. He meant, if he pulled that off, to turn over a new leaf, or so he said. He just failed, and standing about afterwards he took a chill."

"And died?"

"Yes. It turned to pneumonia, and he made no sort of fight. Disappointment had beaten him down. I think he was sorry just at the end; but it was too late then, he had taken everything from me—my love, my fortune—and flung it all away. Until he was dead I had no idea how completely he had ruined us. It was the twins' last term at Rugby; they were going to Oxford that autumn. When he found out how things were, Ninian said we must sell all our other houses, and the yacht and the racing stables, and come and live here. I wanted to sell this horrible place too, but Ninian would not hear of it. So terribly masterful—just like his father. He always was a farmer at heart; he loves the land. Wilfrid is so different——"

At the mention of the name of this beloved son the whole tone of Madam's voice changed. Colour stole into her cheeks, a thrill into her voice. "Do you see that photo on the dressing-table, in the silver frame? Bring it to me."

Olwen brought the picture to the bedside. Unless it was flattered, Wilfrid Guyse was indeed a handsome man. There was a likeness—even a strong likeness—to his twin, especially in general outline; but his hair was evidently

fair and his expression wholly different. There was no
bravado, no sign of a sneer, in these clear, well-opened
eyes. The carriage of the head was fine, with the unconscious confidence of race.

"Do you like it?" The acme of maternal pride surged
beneath the quiet question.

Olwen started. The portrait had fascinated her.
"Like it? Oh, yes. There is a great likeness to his
brother, is there not?"

Mrs. Guyse laughed in pure scorn. "Wait until you
see them together," said she. "Nobody would look at poor
Nin while Wolf was present. Though I say it, he is all
the fondest mother could desire."

"Does he come home much?" asked Olwen, with a good
deal of curiosity as to the answer.

"Not so much as I could wish. He is secretary to Mr.
Borrowleigh, who is in the Cabinet, you know. London
is far from Guysewyke, and they work him terribly hard,
poor boy. He tried nobly to retrieve the family fortunes
when he left Oxford—went to Klondyke, starved and
toiled—you would never think it to look at him, would
you? My poor darling! It was too much for him. He
broke down and had to come home and begin all over
again. However, his health is now quite restored."

"This photo was taken recently?"

"He had it done for my Christmas present."

Olwen slowly replaced the frame upon the table.
When she turned round Mrs. Guyse had raised herself
erect, and her face was darkly flushed. There was a disturbed look in her eyes. "I've been talking—talking,"
she muttered. "Ninian said I should be sure to talk."

"Well, why not?" asked Olwen gently. "I am your
secretary, and your affairs are private to me. I am in
the same position as a doctor, you know. What you say

to me is a professional secret. But I think you have talked enough, and should lie down now."

The sick woman grasped her arm with hot fingers. "Have I said anything to set you against Ninian or—or the place ?" she asked uneasily.

Olwen was obliged to laugh. "Of course not; though it could not matter even if you had."

"You said, didn't you—you told me you found the Pele fascinating ?"

"It has a fascination, certainly."

"So have you," returned Madam most unexpectedly. Her eyes were fixed upon the girl's mirthful face and the pretty curve of her smiling mouth. "I consider you decidedly fascinating. I can't think where Ninian's eyes are."

"Tastes differ, you know," was the amused reply. "As you approve, that is all that matters, isn't it ? Perhaps Mr. Guyse will forgive me for being unattractive when he finds I am useful."

Mrs. Guyse lay silent for a while, during which time she was presumably thinking over her indiscretions. At last—

"Wolf won't be coming here for a long time," said she in a decided voice; "so don't build upon seeing him, will you ?"

"It's very disappointing, but I'll try to bear it," replied the girl demurely, dissembling her mirth.

After another pause—"I fear I was unwise to show you his picture. Are you susceptible, do you think ?"

"I believe not. You see, when one has to earn one's living, one has no time to be fanciful."

"I dare say"—with evident relief. "It was very different with me. I had been so spoilt, my father doted on me. I had everything I wanted; I had but to express a wish and it was gratified. That was what made the contrast, after marriage, so dreadful to me. I had been so flattered that I thought myself very attractive; and I was not. My husband told me so in plain words. He said I expected too much. You are not accustomed to flattery, are you? You would not expect too much?"

Olwen began to be alarmed at her high colour and rambling talk. "I want you to lie down and rest and not talk," said she coaxingly. "I think I will go and ask Sunia to bring your tea."

"Wait!" A thin hand was held up and beckoned. Olwen approached the bed. "Bend down. I want to whisper."

Olwen stooped, a queer access of pity in her heart.

"I have been imprudent. If you repeat what I have said you will get me into trouble; but, all the same, I am going to warn you. Ayah is his spy—Ninian's spy. Be careful, won't you?"

The colour flamed into the girl's face. This was her second warning that day not to trust Sunia. "I'll remember, and please to understand that I *don't talk*," said she, as impressively as she could.

She felt uncomfortable as she took up the Barton catalogue and carried it downstairs to point out to Mr. Guyse the lounge chair which she thought would be suitable.

He was standing upon the hearthrug as she entered the lamp-lit room; and, to her surprise, he met her with a scowl.

What does this portend? she asked herself, as she went to the tray and sat down to pour out his tea. The kettle sang on the hob, there was a fragrance of hot tea-cake, and the table looked tempting with its crystal glasses of preserve and old Jacobean silver. Ignoring his silence, she began to talk. "I have brought the catalogue to show you. How long will it be before we can get what we order, do you know? I am wondering how you manage to collect things sent by rail."

He was sitting at the side of the table, at right angles to her, and as he leaned forward his sulky face was close to hers.

"I wonder," he said, "if, on the occasion when I came to fetch you from Caryngston, I succeeded in impressing upon you the fact that I am anxious for you to have no dealings with Balmayne?"

Resenting his tone in every fibre of her, Olwen opened her mouth to say, "What concern is it of yours?" but, remembering in time her position in the household, she replied merely, "You impressed upon me the idea that you and he are not on good terms."

"So you thought you would have a nice, confidential talk with him, about me—eh?"

"Oh! What makes you think so?" she asked calmly.

He was ready for this question. "Mrs. Baxter told me what time the doctor arrived. I know what time he went. Sunia told me how long he was in the sick-room."

"Was that all that Sunia told you?" she asked innocently.

He reddened. Olwen summoned all her courage and, leaning back in her chair, she looked steadily into his eyes, which gleamed in a way which made her think absurdly of a panther lashing his tail.

"We had better have this out," she said quietly. "If, as I suppose, Sunia was listening, and if she has repeated to you all that passed between the doctor and me, you must know that nothing was said of which you could reasonably complain. Please understand that I did not come here to take my orders from you, and that I will not be bullied by you. If your mother has anything to complain of in my conduct she will tell me so. I know my place. I wish that you knew yours."

He sat upright, as if she had stung him, and gazed upon her as if he hardly knew how to take this.

"If you were not here," she went on, "Madam and I could get on very comfortably together; but ever since you saw me you have been trying to make things intolerable for me. After the way you have just spoken I shall, of course, leave at my month. But as long as I am here, perhaps you will let me alone."

He made a contemptuous sound. "That's just like a woman—flare up at a little thing like that! You give notice to leave just because I got a bit shirty over you and Balmayne——"

"Why, you made up your mind from the first that I shouldn't stay, didn't you? When you found that I am not pretty and that I won't flirt with you——"

"By Jove! how can you say that? Why, I tried with all my might to be friends, but you wouldn't touch me with the end of a barge pole."

"You knew quite well that you were behaving in a way no girl could stand."

He folded his arms, gazing down at the tablecloth. "I don't know any girls. At least, none like you."

Something in his tone made her feel a little sorry for him, but she hastened to improve the occasion a little farther.

"Why can't you understand that I only want to be let alone? What do you matter to me? From the way you talk, I suppose that Dr. Balmayne knows something to your discredit, and that you are afraid he might tell me. Well, what if he did? It is of no business of mine. It doesn't interest me. As for Madam—when I first came, I thought she disliked me as much as you do, but the last day or two she has seemed glad—pleased—to have me with her. She has begun to—to welcome me, to turn toward me, as if she—l-l-loved me. And now I must leave her, all because you—you——"

She could not finish. She was swallowing sobs, and, to her own vast mortification, was obliged to rise from the table and turn away to the fire so as to hide her quivering face.

She heard him push back his chair and rise too. He took a turn to the end of the room and back. Then he came near to where she stood.

"I'm a perfect brute," he said gruffly. "I say—can't we start all over again? Do let us. I can't think why things have gone so badly. You got up against me somehow. I thought you were so different. I can't explain. If I say that I'm fairly ashamed of myself, and beg your pardon with all my heart, won't you give me another chance?"

"I don't know what you mean," said she, furtively wiping away her tears. "Another chance? I never gave you a chance at all. You don't count. Why should you?"

"That's just what I mean. I want to count. Give me a chance."

She made no reply.

"I never had a sister, or perhaps I shouldn't be such a blundering fool with girls," adventured Nin. "Look here, can't you be great enough to hand me out a free pardon? I never guessed how much I was going to hurt your feelings just now, and if Madam is to lose you just because of my thundering folly—— Ah, well, you guessed quite right; Balmayne does think he knows something to my discredit, and I was anxious you should not hear it from him. I wanted to keep it dark altogether. But I suppose I'd better tell you about it myself."

"But I don't want to know. Will nothing make you see that it doesn't matter a bit to me——"

"You'd have listened to Balmayne——"

"He declined to say anything when he found I didn't know——"

"Ah, then he did mention it?"

"If we are talking of the same thing."

"Lily Martin, of course; the girl who was my mother's companion."

"Oh, yes, I remember. He said that your mother had rather a shattering experience."

"I suppose she had. Yes, it was a shock," he replied slowly. "Look here, dry your eyes and sit down to tea, and I'll tell you afterwards, if you'll promise not to go away at the end of your month. This place is quite jolly in fine weather."

She sat down to table and poured fresh tea. "I have no doubt it is," said she. "You will enjoy showing it to my successor. You should explain to her, however, when offering her the post, that she is to be your companion, and not Madam's."

"Now you're not playing fair. No good to say you forgive me and then stab me in the back."

"I don't think I have forgiven you. At least, I haven't said so."

He looked at her with puzzled eyes. "You try living here ten years, with never a soul to speak to, and see if you don't make an ass of yourself the first time you get the chance," he remarked presently.

She did not answer, but took up the catalogue and made a little talk about the folding chairs depicted in the illustrations.

He gave but a divided attention and ate hardly anything. At last he pushed back his chair with determination. "Now will you please listen?"

She rose with decision. "Once for all, Mr. Guyse, I will *not* listen. I have already told you that I don't

want to hear anything at all about it." As she spoke she
was moving as if to go out of the room. He rose, with
panther-like swiftness, and stood between her and the door.
"You've got to listen," he said.

CHAPTER XIII

NINIAN'S DEFENCE

OLWEN'S heart gave a throb, and for a moment she was afraid. Then she remembered how quickly Ninian had been disarmed by the sight of her distress. She lifted a beseeching face to him.

"Please, Mr. Guyse! Please believe what I say. I would rather know nothing of your private affairs. I am not likely to remain long at the Pele, and it is best that we remain strangers."

"We can't do that," he said with sharp decision. "Ask Sunia."

"Your spy!" she said, throwing into the words an amount of scorn which brought the colour to his face. He did not falter, however. Taking her arm, just above the elbow, he led her to the hearth, and pushed her gently into a chair. "This is the last time I am going to misbehave," said he. "After this you shall do as you like with me; but you have got to hear me now. Sorry, but really you've got to."

"But why? Why?" she cried.

"Because I insist."

She wavered. He was standing over her, and it seemed to her quite probable that, if she made as if to rise, he would push her back into her chair. She could see that he was putting all the force of his will into the affair, and, after all, was it worth fighting him about? She hardly cared, for herself, whether she heard him or no, and was chiefly conscious of a wish that he would leave off impor-

tuning her. With a shrug of the shoulders she resigned
herself, and Ninian, with a sigh of relief, seated himself
upon a big *pouffe* which stood on the rug facing her, Daff's
head between his knees.

Thus settled, he looked up with an impertinent grin.

"The Head of the Reformatory has given leave to the
latest arrival to explain to her how he first came to leave
the paths of virtuous rectitude," he said. "She faces
him, calmly judicial, and he proceeds to make a clean
breast of it."

She had some ado not to laugh. "Get on and don't
be silly," said she.

He drew a deep breath. "One black dark night a band
of robbers," he began. "No. That's the wrong gambit.
Ahem! 'I was not ever thus, believe, fair maid——' "

Olwen made to rise from her place, and he caught and
detained her.

"Oh, dash, how is it that I can't resist playing the
goat?" cried he. "Just one more chance, and that will be
the very last, but the mischief of it is I don't know where
to begin. Afraid I shall have to go back to our first coming to live here. I was about eighteen then, and it really
was the only thing to do, my father had left us in such a
tight place. Madam had been accustomed to something
very different, it was horribly rough on her, and I dare
say you'll think I was a selfish hound to bring her to such
a place. But I couldn't help myself. I'm Guyse,
through and through; and though I felt that I would give
up most things for her, I simply couldn't sell the last
Guyse stronghold and the last few poor acres. So there
it is. The first crime's off my chest."

"I can make every allowance for you there," said
Olwen with a rush of sudden sympathy.

He looked at her under his lashes. "That's something.
You see, by coming to live here I managed to send my

brother Wilfrid to Oxford. He's a credit to the family—brains and manners, and so on. The other reason was that I knew I could make a living out of the land, and also that, if I lived here, Madam need not lose all her friends, and I could get across a horse and carry a gun. If we had lived in a city I couldn't have earned bread and cheese, I've no commercial ability; and Madam would have suffered more, though she doesn't think so. Hallo! I'm sorry I'm boring you with what doesn't matter a bit. When we had been here a few years and Wolf had left the University, he was suddenly bitten with the notion of going to Klondyke. This upset my mother very much, made her so ill, in fact, that we thought she would go melancholy mad. Wolf and I talked it over, and he said she was moped to death and too much alone, and the best thing we could do was to hire a young lady to live with her, somebody young and jolly who would take her out of herself. We did as we did in your case, looked down a list of advertisers, and at last we chose Miss Lily Martin. She came, and she was a girl with high spirits, very good-natured, and used to make Madam laugh. She was here some time, more than a year, and we jogged along well enough, only Sunia never took to her."

"Do you know why that was?"

"Sunia said she was not 'pukka'—I expect you know what that means. Said also that she had something up her sleeve. Said she had a lover." He was speaking with his gaze fixed on Daff's silky head, but on that he raised his face, and his eyes were hard as jade in the lamp-light. "Of course, Balmayne thinks I was her lover," said he.

"Why does he think so?"

"I'll tell you. After about a year things began to go wrong. I expect Miss Martin got a bit fed up with this place and the monotony of the life. I couldn't even send

Madam away for a few weeks in the summer that year, for Wolf had got into difficulties and it took all I had to send him what he asked for. Miss Martin's temper changed. Sunia told us afterwards that when she first came she got letters constantly, always two or three a week, sometimes more. By degrees they had dropped off, until of late she had only one or two a month. I suppose this upset her; anyway, she became moody and had fits of temper. I didn't mind her working it off on me, but when it came to Madam I had to interfere, for she took to bullying her. One day she had a queer outburst. I had found Madam in hysterics, and I was obliged to call the girl over the coals about it. She flew out at me and said we were bloated aristocrats, but that she was as good as us any day, and that, if she only chose, she could make things hot for us. To this day I don't know what she meant by that. On my honour, I don't believe her change of manner had anything to do with me. I may have chaffed her a bit, but I never made love to her. However, the end of it was that I told her I thought she had better leave. She was evidently no longer happy with us, and, what was more, she didn't make Madam happy either. I couldn't have her upset—why, the only reason the silly fool was in the house at all was to keep Madam happy! . . . So I gave her notice. After that we had a treat. The first week she was furious, the second sulky, the third tearful—oh, my word! She wept at meals, she wept in her bedroom —so Sunia said—she wept all over poor Madam, and one day she—she wept on me. I couldn't stick it, and I am afraid I told her so, more hotly than I meant. Ah, I can see your sympathy for her showing in your eyes."

"You are quite mistaken. I was thinking that when you succeeded in making me cry this evening you must have been forcibly reminded of poor Miss Martin!"

He grinned. "After that it seemed to me that it would

be better if I kept out of the way until she took her departure. I was very busy at the time, as it happened, so I stayed down at Lachanrigg with the Kays, and had all my meals there next day. When I came home, late at night, Sunia and the Baxters were in a fearful state. Miss Martin had disappeared."

"You mean she had left?"

"Nobody knew. It seems she had spent the afternoon in the billiard-room by herself. Madam at that time used always to sit there, but she had got so fed up with the girl that, on that occasion, she went off to her own room and shut herself in. Sunia afterwards told us that Miss Martin, after an interval of five weeks, had got a letter that morning which had visibly upset her. She seems to have made a fire in the billiard-room and burned therein her whole collection of letters. Sunia took her a cup of tea, and found her kneeling on the hearth feeding the fire with torn letters, and noticed that she was in tears. Nobody saw her after that. She had not put on a hat, so they thought for a long time that she was concealed somewhere in the house, where there are a good many hiding-places. We began by searching pretty thoroughly, and when we proved unsuccessful, I thought I would go down to Lachanrigg by the short cut, down the hill, and get Kay to come and help me or advise me what to do."

"Did you know where she came from—who were her people?"

"She was living in rooms in London when we engaged her. She had no home. She came originally from Canada, I believe. We knew of no friends to whom she would be likely to go."

"Where did her letters come from?"

"Always London. We thought probably from a clerk in some bank, for the address was type-written. . . . Well, as I was telling you, I went out and down the hill.

It is almost precipitous down there, but there is a path of sorts, winding among the trees.   Just as I went crashing down the steepest bit I thought I heard a moan.   It was a very dark night, and I could see nothing.   I had a lantern with me, and I turned it this way and that.   The sound came several times, and it seemed to be behind me higher up the hill.   After questing all about I found it was always above me, over my head, and at last I had the wit to peer up into the branches of the trees.   There I found her.   She had flung herself out of the big oriel in the banqueting hall, intending to commit suicide, and had stuck in the branches of an ash."

"Alive, of course ?"

"Oh, yes, but she was badly injured.   I had to go and rouse Ezra, and between us we got her down and carried her to the Gatehouse, where we laid her in Mrs. Baxter's parlour.   It was not possible, with her broken bones, to get her upstairs at the Pele, so in the Baxters' parlour she stayed.   Balmayne had only just come here then, and he was immensely interested in the case.   Thought she was a poor martyred saint, victim of my heartless cruelty.   As for me, I was just about fed up with her, and I kept clear of her all the time she was ill.   She utterly declined to say why she had tried to kill herself, and only declared that she wished she had succeeded in her attempt.   At first she said that the moment she was strong enough to get about she would have another try; but Balmayne explained to her that, unless she took a solemn oath not to repeat it, he would have to inform a magistrate and get her bound over.   That frightened her a bit, but she remained in a queer state of mind; very unsatisfactory it was for all concerned."

"What did Madam say ?"

"Madam behaved very queerly.   I suppose Balmayne got at her, for she certainly believed that I was seriously

to blame. She said she pitied the poor girl from the
bottom of her heart, but for all that, she could not be per-
suaded to go and see her. I thought it would be a jolly
good thing if she did, as she might get something out of
her; but no. Never once did she see Miss Martin from
the day of the accident to the day of her departure."

"Departure? She went away then?"

"Yes. I was at my wits' end, wondering what on earth
was to become of the poor thing, and making up my mind
that I must screw myself to the point of making Madam
go and see her and ask what her plans were, when she got
a letter from the usual source. This letter seemed to buck
her up no end. She told Mrs. Baxter next day that she
was going to London as soon as the doctor would allow her
to travel. And she was as good as her word. When she
went off she informed me that I should see her again a
great deal sooner than I expected; and I was fully prepared for a letter from some firm of lawyers, threatening
an action of some kind. But from that day to this we
haven't any of us heard a word of her. The earth might
have opened and swallowed her. She was a queer one.
Sunia says she had a wedding-ring slung round her neck,
under her clothes, but I don't know if that is true. There!
Now you have heard the history of Miss Lily Martin and
myself to date. When Balmayne gives you his version,
you can put the two together and see what they amount to."

Olwen rested her elbows on her knees, her chin cupped
in her hands, and gazed thoughtfully at the glowing logs.
"And all that happened—when?"

"More than three years ago."

"I wonder what made you tell me?"

"It's pretty obvious. If you stay on you are bound to
hear it, and I wanted you to hear it from me."

"I—I think I am glad you told me." She was in fact
conscious of considerable relief. The story explained

many things. Deb's distrust of the young man, Balmayne's uneasiness that another girl should be placed in the same position as the unlucky Lily; Mrs. Guyse's reticence and anxiety, Sunia's careful spying, and, most of all, Ninian's self-consciousness and inability to be natural with her.

"Well, after hearing this pretty tale, shall you funk staying in the Dark Tower?" he asked, after a prolonged survey of her grave little face, lit by the flickering flame-light.

"I think I am safe enough," she replied, not turning her head to look at him. "I am not a bit a Lily-Martin kind of girl."

"Give a chap a chance! Can't I see that much? But you know there is another kind of girl just as bad, and when first I saw you I thought you were that kind."

"Indeed. What?"

"A prude."

"Well," the fire-light emphasised the dimple, "I think I *am* rather that kind. That is, I am apt to be thorny, except with——"

"People who speak your language?" The tone was soft and insinuating.

"That's it."

"Well," said Nin, laying his olive cheek down on Daff's yellow head, "I'm going to learn, if it takes me a year. As I just told you, I've misbehaved for the last time. I am now a reformed character, your word is my law. If you say, 'Detestable young man, leave the room,' hard as that command will be, I shall obey. I'll be like a lover out of Richardson or Mrs. Radcliffe——"

"Oh, but please! I don't want you to be like a lover of any kind."

"My mistake! I'm a pupil, am I not? And you're my teacher, if you'll take me on. Oh, do! 'I know it the only thing to save my yet young life in the wilds of time !' "

"With the poets at your finger-ends there is no excuse for you," she laughed. "Don't be so ridiculous."

"Oh, come, you'll have to let me be ridiculous! Prunes-prism was never my line."

"It need not be your line, or mine either, when once you have mastered the 'simple little rules and few' which lie at the root of the language you have to learn."

"Can't we begin now ?"

"Not now. Really I don't want to be crabby any more, but you do see that while Madam is so poorly I must look after her, don't you ?" She broke off and a wicked smile flashed at him, *"Why, all the silly fool is in the house for at all is to keep Madam happy!"*

"Jove, you're quick! I must mind my p's and q's with you !"

"Yes, they are rather important letters in your new alphabet !"

CHAPTER XIV

A FRESH START

WHEN Olwen came into her room that evening to prepare for supper, Sunia was curled up as usual upon the rug before the fire, mending some tiny rent in one of the young lady's garments. The room was now always warm and fragrant, a well-trimmed lamp on a bracket made a soft effulgence of light, candles were lit on the toilet table, and the carving on the ancient furniture shone with polish.

Olwen tried to shut her eyes to all this creature comfort. As she walked in, she left the door open behind her, and halting in the middle of the room, she pointed to the way out. "You may go, Sunia," said she coldly.

Sunia looked up. Evidently she was unprepared for this, but almost immediately she had herself completely in hand. She rose to her knees.

"My Missee not want me this night?"

"No, nor any other night. Go, please."

The woman's eyes dwelt as if in admiration on the determined little face. "What poor ole ayah done?" she asked.

"You don't need to be told that. You are a spy, and I won't have spies about me."

"Who say Sunia spy?"

"Your own sahib. He told me all about it. You come pretending to love me, and then go and make mischief. I have done with you. Please go."

The Hindu prostrated herself, laying her forehead upon the buckle of Olwen's shoe.

"Missee forgive her—forgive ole ayah this one time. She not do it again. Only because she frightened of pretty doctor, he look at Missee with too kind eyes, and Sunia seen pictures in the stars—pictures that say the doctor he come between Missee and my sahib. Ole ayah obliged to warn her sahib—and good thing too, very good thing she done it."

"Why is it a good thing? What are you talking about?"

It was very rarely that the ayah smiled, but the ghost of a smile crossed her lips as she replied, "My sahib angry, and Missee and him they have it out together, and now they friends. Good thing that, eh?"

"Then you were listening behind the curtain in the dining-room while we talked?"

"I was not. I tell you, no! How can I be leesten when I busy unpack all my Missee's things and put 'em away?"

Olwen gave an exclamation of surprise. She was not aware that her heavy luggage had arrived, but now she noticed that all her small possessions had been unpacked, and arranged with some taste about the room.

"Why, how did you unlock my trunk? Where is it? It could not come upstairs?"

The ayah laughed low. "All trunks got to stay in kitchen-house outside," said she. "Ole ayah find Missee key right enough, and carry things up in her arms. Missee tell her how she want 'em, eh?"

She rose from the ground, quivering with delight at having turned the subject, and her eyes were alight with eagerness.

Olwen shrugged her shoulders. "I am much obliged for all the trouble you have taken, and for putting away my things so carefully; but for all that, I cannot forget that

you are not to be trusted. You make believe to love me,
and then act treacherously."

"No, that wrong," said the woman earnestly. "Ole
ayah serve Missee and serve sahib too. Missee don't
really think ole ayah tell about her to anybody else? Only
to the sahib, because all Missee do is right for him to
know."

"How absurd!" cried Olwen; but she could catch a
glimpse, she thought, of the Hindu's logic. The house
of Guyse was what she served. She devoted herself to
Olwen only because the girl was for a time part of the
Guyse household. She suspected Balmayne of being
anxious to undermine Miss Innes's opinion of her beloved
sahib. To protect him, she went eavesdropping.

The girl gave a long sigh as she sank into her usual
chair, and felt in a moment the ayah's eager hands busy
with the fastenings of her dress.

"Missee trust ole ayah! She can trust her always, except Missee unkind to my sahib."

Olwen passed a hand across her eyes as if to clear away
mist. The face of Madam, as she eagerly urged her
not to place confidence in Sunia, was present to her fancy.
She knew that the past hour had materially altered her
opinion of Ninian. He had succeeded in diminishing, if
not in dispersing her dislike. She was sorry for him.
Yet something deep within her kept on uttering a
warning. . . .

She was like one upon whom a spell is being cast. It
was as though Sunia had prepared a deep bath and had
urged her to plunge therein, assuring her that it was what
she needed, that it would do her good and make her happy.
As yet she had barely dipped her foot into the flood, the
water was laving but her feet and ankles, but even so, she
knew that it was having some mysterious effect. She
foresaw that she would not emerge as she went in. Some-

thing within her was changing . . . and the feel of the
waters was delicious. . . .

Sunia's brush was slipping through her torrent of hair,
hypnotising as it passed. It seemed to thrill as it touched
the sentient scalp, engendering a feeling of perfect well-
being as though all life were just sensation.

She discerned danger, yet she yielded. When the ayah
had completed her coiffure, she brought a hand-glass that
her Missee might study the effect.

The subdued tints of her complexion were fitly framed
in the dusky gold of the hair. The eyes were clear, pale
in their dark setting. Was she really growing prettier,
or was it part of Sunia's magic, that she should think so?

Rebelliously she struggled against the feeling that she
was beautiful. She had always held herself to be one
of those lucky beings who can go through life quite unob-
served, without noticeable beauty or noticeable defect.
The reflection in the little mirror hardly bore out such an
idea. The charm it revealed was perhaps subtle, but it
was nevertheless apparent.

The thought of having supper alone with Ninian made
her self-conscious until she took herself to task for a weak-
minded fool.

She went in to see Madam on her way down. She found
her far more comfortable, and able to enjoy a cup full of
Mrs. Baxter's daintily made gruel. Olwen settled her
comfortably for the night before going down.

Ninian was awaiting her, but he greeted her with such
a change of manner as reassured her at once. No more
half-sneering compliments, no more of what she now supposed to have been *ballons d'essai,* designed to make her
show her hand. His manner was open, and almost pleasant. Was Sunia right after all? Was it a good thing
that they should have arrived at an understanding?

They talked about the procuring of the folding lounge

for Madam, and Ninian explained that there was a station much nearer than Picton Bars, but that it was practically useless to the dwellers in the Pele because the only road which approached their eyrie came from a totally different direction. They had to drive so far round to Raefell station, upon such bad roads, that it was easier as a rule for them to go via Caryngston.

Lachanrigg, his farm, whose tenant, John Kay, had married the Baxters' only daughter, was on the way, or not much off the road, to this other station. It was quite easy to fetch goods from Raefell to Lachanrigg, but from Lachanrigg to the Pele the only possible route was on foot.

Ninian was quite ready to carry the packed-up lounge from Lachanrigg up through the Guyseburn woods, and suggested that he should walk down to Lachanrigg next day, drive thence to Raefell, and telephone from the station to Leeds, ordering the couch to be sent at once.

She was eager in her thanks, and inquired whether he would have to go down the steep hill immediately underneath the windows.

He said yes, that was the only way; and added, "I suppose you would not care to come too? It's quite a pleasant walk to Lachanrigg and back, and would not keep you out too long."

"I'll go," she said, "if you are kind enough to take me, and if Madam will spare me. The doctor isn't coming to-morrow."

"You won't find it so dull, walking with me, now that I am beginning to talk the language," said Nin insinuatingly.

She laughed. "You have made strides in education to-day."

"Nothing like a Reformatory after all. Training seems harsh at first, but good results are soon perceptible."

"Sorry I was harsh. I never had a pupil before who required that kind of training."

"Indeed! One would have thought you had done it all your life! Your method was masterly!"

"What was my method?"

"Knocked him down, stamped on him, rolled him out quite flat, picked him up, dusted him, put him in the corner——"

"And here he is, sitting up and taking nourishment quite comfortably! In fact, the process has exhausted the teacher far more than the pupil! She hopes another application will never, never be necessary."

"It won't. I've sworn off, taken the pledge, and intend to wear the white flower of the Innes Brigade all my life!"

There were a few Christmas roses in a vase upon the table, and in a moment of impulse Olwen took out one and handed it to him.

"I found these in the garden to-day, and thought we might as well have the sight of them," said she. "The white flower of the Innes Brigade, conferred by the founder herself!"

Nin fastened the big white star in his coat.

Sunia, waiting silently upon them, seemed to notice nothing.

"Didn't you say you would like to look down the well?" asked Nin, as they strolled out into the hall together.

"Yes, I did, but, please, if it is a bother, don't think of troubling."

"Bother? Of course not. If you like this sort of stuff, there are heaps of things I can show you." He was rolling back one of the rugs as he spoke. "This is used every morning, we get our drinking water from it. The water I brought up the hill is all right for household purposes, but this is better."

He disclosed a circular hole, fitted with a flat cover.

They both knelt down, while he lifted the lid, and he held a lighted taper over the black abyss thus revealed.

"At one of the other Peles they have a tame electric light at the end of a rope," said he, "and they let it down till it hangs just above the water. You get a fine effect then; I wish we could do it."

For the first time in his company Olwen forgot herself and spoke as to a friend. "Oh, wouldn't it be grand! Fancy having electric light here, all up the corkscrew and in those fascinating little passages!"

He sat back upon his heels, looking at her oddly. "You like this old place, then?"

"Like is hardly the right word. It grips me. It is so unlike anything I ever saw——"

"You never could see anything just like it. It is unique."

"Are you not glad that it is yours?" she went on, carried away by the thought. "Guyses built it, Guyses dwelt in it, and still it stands, and still a Guyse holds it. Don't you wish another bull would jump down the Bull-drop and the luck come back to you?"

He shrugged his shoulders. "I hardly know. I don't want the humbugging title. There was no Lord Caryngston a hundred and fifty years ago; but there have been Guyses at Guysewyke since Domesday. My cousin, the present Baron, would give his eyes to own this place. He hopes that I shall be driven to sell it one day."

"Oh, *don't!*" cried Olwen so fervently that he laughed.

"You wouldn't sell, in my place?"

"In your place, I would live on a shilling a week, but I wouldn't sell."

He gave a sigh which was almost a groan. "God knows I think as you do," he answered, "but it's not so simple as that." He replaced the cover, and rose, with lips close set. "One day perhaps I may tell you about it," said he.

CHAPTER XV

THE sky was misty grey with a hint of blue just overhead. No wind stirred the snowladen trees, and the frost was intense.

Mrs. Guyse always slept after lunch, and seemed to think it an extremely good idea that her companion should have a short walk while she rested.

"Be sure to be back in time to pour out my tea," she stipulated. "It's rough going, down the hill; but I suppose young people like to scramble, and Nin says he has been since the snow fell, and knows it is passable."

Olwen was quite ready to brave a little snow; Ezra Baxter, by his master's order, had put nails into her thick boots, and she was anxious to shake off the reproach of being a town-bred miss who could not go out in bad weather.

Ninian at billiards the night before and at breakfast that morning had maintained the improvement in his demeanour. He seemed pleased to see Miss Innes when she appeared, and his attitude was now that of the courteous host, anxious that his visitor should feel at home and be entertained. Dr. Balmayne was not expected that day. Madam's condition was steadily improving. In spite of her statement that she disliked being read aloud to, Olwen had made an attempt that morning with the "Professional Aunt," and the result had been encouraging. The dull creature had been roused momentarily from her torpor, smiled several times, laughed once, and said she would like to hear more later on. This success, coupled with her expressed desire that her companion should pour out her tea, elated that young person considerably.

"Do you think," she asked as she joined Ninian in the hall, "that you could carry Madam down the one flight from her room to the banqueting hall ?"

He seemed in no doubt of his ability to perform this feat, even in the narrow limits of the newel stair.

"If so, we'll have her down the moment we get the couch," replied Miss Innes eagerly. "I am really quite keen upon shaking her out of her apathy and getting her to take an interest in things."

"Bravo!" he said. "Who would have thought such a scrap of a girl as you—— Holy Moses! I beg your pardon."

She made a little mock bow. "But what my friends may say and what strangers may say are so different!"

"Thanks. That's the best yet," was his reply, as he selected an iron-shod stick for her. "You ought to feel bucked," he added, as he opened the hall door. "Sunia licking your boots, Madam sitting up and taking notice already, and me wagging my tail like anything for a kind word."

"Good week's work do you think ?" demurely.

"Not to mention the doctor," he went on.

"Now *don't* spoil it!"

"Got to be jolly careful still," he laughed, leading the way to the quadrangle wall behind the kitchen, where, in the south-west corner, was a tiny postern door.

He stood a minute whistling Daff before opening it. She came bounding, golden and beautiful, from the kitchen door, which was opened by Sunia.

The Hindu stood in the opening, her face grave and soft, gazing at the two as Olwen waved her a farewell.

She raised her hand in a curious gesture as of benediction. The postern opened, and they passed through upon the narrow terrace which on this side edged the ravine below.

Standing there, Olwen raised her eyes to the oriel in the banqueting hall. The stone mullions were wide enough apart for a slim girl to push through; and as the window projected considerably, her fall would not be broken by the very narrow platform upon which they stood.

Below were the tips of the snow-encumbered trees.

"Mad sort of idea, wasn't it?" said Ninian, answering her unspoken thought. "Might have known she wouldn't get anything like a clean drop. Just a minute's temper probably."

"I can't think how people can do such a thing. I love life far too well. Think of cutting oneself off for ever from sunset and moonrise, from waterfalls and mountains, and hot weather in sunshine, from roses and lilies, firesides and interesting books, and—and—oh, all the things that make the world so fascinating!"

"The world seems grim enough to me sometimes," remarked the young man, kicking the steps free from piled-up snow which had slid from the battlements.

"Oh, there are moments when it seems grim to anybody; but you do understand the joy of living, don't you? I mean the pleasure of just being able to feel? The sight of almond blossom against blue sky, or of the evening mist in a river valley, or shallow water slipping over brown stones, or the smell of garden mould after warm rain?"

"Or the outline of a girl's face, pink against the grey stone of a tower wall. . . . Oh, you can't complain of that! It's all part of the subject . . . and I do know what you mean. George Eliot has something about it somewhere. I believe I could find it when we get home. . . . Yes, it is what makes the difference between people who can be happy in the country and people who can't.

Lily Martin was one who couldn't. This place fairly got
on her nerves, as it does on my poor mother's. I'm glad
it doesn't get on yours, for to bring you here in this
weather was trying you pretty high up. If you can see
beauty now, you could see it always."

As he spoke he preceded her down the steps and guided
her along an almost level bit of ground to the place where
the path plunged down among the trees. It was indeed
steep, but, in fact, easier with the snow upon it than when
it was bare trodden earth after a summer's drought.
Ninian helped her, but not officiously; and as she was
really active and strong, as well as light and small, she
got along well. A short way down he showed her the
tree upon which Lily Martin had fallen, and she was able
to appreciate the difficulty which Baxter and he had experienced in rescuing her.

The precipitous part of the descent was soon over, and
they went on more easily, plunging through the snow, and
still thridding woodlands, until by degrees they dropped
down almost to the level of the frozen river.

"Those woods," observed Guyse, waving a hand towards
the rising ground beyond the farther bank, "are full of
wild cherry. In April they are a sight to make one feel
that—what you were talking about just now."

Olwen could believe it. They turned to their right
and walked along, some thirty feet above the bed of the
stream, following a good wide path which ran under pines.
Then came some flat meadows, which they crossed, the
thin blue spiral from the farm chimneys encouraging them
onward.

The snow was very deep, but this mattered only inas-
much as it impeded progress. But once did she suffer
misfortune, and this was when she left the path to look
at a curious lichen upon a tree-trunk. There was a con-

cealed ditch, and instantly she was in the drift up to her waist.

There was much laughter as she was lifted out by Ninian and dusted down. He remarked that it would teach her to be careful, a saying so sensible and big-brotherly, and so unlike his former style, that she felt a very natural triumph.

Many dogs flew out baying as they approached Lachanrigg. Daff's joyous greeting seemed to set their minds at rest at once, and they were frisking round Ninian. Their noise brought Mrs. Kay to the door, her baby in her arms, all excitement to know who could be approaching the homestead on such a day by the woodland path.

Kay was out, but the sleigh and horse were in the stable, and Ninian soon had them harnessed, and asked Olwen whether she would rather come with him to the post office or stay and play with the baby. Anxious to show the reality of the truce, she chose the drive, and they started off, over a couple of miles of very exposed fell, down into another valley, at the foot of which the railway scored a sharp black track upon the blinding white. The telephone was working, and they rang up the Newcastle shop, gave their order, and received a promise that the folding lounge should be put upon the train that very afternoon, and would arrive at Raefell station next morning about eleven.

Ninian at once volunteered to come and fetch it, so that, in the event of Dr. Balmayne giving permission, Madam might be brought downstairs in the afternoon.

By the time the two walkers reached home in the January twilight, they were talking together quite easily.

By special invitation, Ninian had tea in his mother's room, so that they might all be together. Madam lay

among her pillows, watching them with her manner of
vague, faintly curious detachment.

One of the cakes upon the plate had been baked in a
droll resemblance to an old man's whithered face. Olwen
called the attention of Mr. Guyse to it, upon which he
stuck it on a hatpin, and together they proceeded to dress
it up with a paper collar and coat made of the little folded
damask napkin which held the cakes. Even Madam was
beguiled into amusement. She said little, but after a
while remarked to the girl, "You seem to find everything
amusing."

"Funny you should say that; it's the exact opposite of
what Mr. Guyse thinks. He calls me a school-marm, and
thinks I disapprove of everything."

"That was because you didn't like me," he cut in.

."Pardon, it was because you didn't like me."

"Have you changed your mind?"

"Have you changed yours?"

"I asked first."

"So you should be answered last."

"Ah, but it doesn't matter what I think; it is your
opinion that is the important thing."

"Utterly wrong. Madam is the only person whose
opinion counts. She will think I am too noisy and silly
if you go on like this. I shall now turn you out and read
to her a little."

"Why turn me out? I may have a pipe here, mayn't
I, Ma?"

"Oh, I never heard of such a thing!" cried Miss Innes
with indignation. "It's easy to see you've never been ill.
Out you go! You must amuse yourself till supper-time;
it was a huge treat your being allowed to have tea with
Madam, and if you don't behave nicely you won't get
another invitation."

She held the door open and he walked out, his eyes

twinkling. "What did I tell you?" he turned back to say to his mother. "School-marm!"

The girl, smiling, shut him out and turned to the bed, removing the empty cup and plate and restoring the order of the room with quick touches. She called Sunia, who apparently passed most of her time either in the stone passage or in the room next to Madam's, for she always appeared with the minimum of delay to carry out trays or do other behests.

Madam made no comment at all upon the little scene just enacted. She lay quite still, following the girl's movements with her eyes only. She had rather the air of one who watches a comedy, with a real though veiled anxiety as to what the dénouement is likely to be.

After the reading, when her secretary rose to go and prepare for supper, she remarked, "You read aloud well, and I like that book. I do not like all books."

"This is very light, but when one is ill one likes something light."

"What I do not like is a book where the people have a guilty secret."

Olwen laughed. "That's so untrue to life," said she.

"Do you think so?" The tone of the question surprised the girl. It was coldly ironic. "You've not had much experience of life, have you?"

"Well," said Olwen, "more than most girls of my age, perhaps. I have lost both parents. I have earned my living for three years."

Madam's lips curved in a slight smile. "Have you had many affairs of the heart? Have you ever had a lover?"

Olwen was near the bed measuring medicine into a glass as she put the question. The colour that flew into the girl's face answered her.

"You have?" The inflection was of surprise. "Well now, do you know, I should have guessed differently.

Would it be an impertinence on my part to ask whether you are engaged to be married?"

"Oh, no, certainly not," said Olwen confusedly. "I mean it is not an impertinence, and I am not engaged."

"Not? But you care for the—the gentleman?"

Olwen looked amused. "Don't you think I have all the aspect of a love-lorn damsel?"

The faded eyes watched her with close attention. "Your friends disapproved?"

"Oh dear, no! It is merely that—that the attachment was on the gentleman's side, not on mine," was the reply.

"I must beg your pardon for my inquisition. But perhaps it does concern me a little. I would not have selected a companion who was likely to leave me soon to get married."

"Quite so. I would have told you had there been any arrangement of the kind. You would have had a right to know."

"Do I understand that you definitely refused your suitor?"

"Perhaps," said Olwen after hesitation, "you may consider that I have said enough. An affair of this kind one should not talk of, in my opinion."

"And I have done little so far to earn your confidence," replied Madam, speaking likewise after some musing. She drank her draught and lay down. "Might I ask you, before going upstairs, to find my son and tell him I should like to speak with him for a few minutes?"

Olwen left the room and descended to the dining-room, where Ninian was seated before the fire, with pipe and newspaper. As she entered he pushed towards her two envelopes which lay upon the small table beside him. "Two letters for you," said he. "You seem to have letters every day. The postman feels there is something to climb the hill for now."

"Does he not come when there are none for the Pele?"

"Yes, that's the devil of it. The poor chap has to, because, as you know, he collects our post as well as delivering it, and he never knows until he gets here whether we have anything or not."

"That seems hard. Can't you arrange a signal?"

"Well, I have sometimes thought I would. Perhaps our united intelligence could devise something."

She took her envelopes from the table, glancing at them with pleasure—one from Aunt Maud, one from Grace Holroyd.

"Oh, I am forgetting. I came with a message to you from Madam. She wants to speak to you."

"Now?"

"Yes, now."

"Why, what about—do you know?"

"Haven't any idea unless she desires to complain of me. But I assure you I haven't been ill-using her."

He laughed, extending his long legs and rubbing Daff's hot back gently with one heel. "Best way to find out is to go and see, I suppose," he remarked, as he rose leisurely and with reluctance, stretched himself and left the room.

CHAPTER XVI

A LITTLE FRICTION

OLWEN lingered, after his departure, in the glowing warmth of the hearth. She curled herself up beside Daffodil on the rug, and gave herself the treat of reading Grace's letter.

"Two such contradictory accounts as you have given me in the last few days I never read," wrote her friend. "What a place this Pele must be! And what deplorable people for the likes of you to have to live with! The only point that gives me any hope at all is that you seem, even in your second letter, to have made up your mind not to stay. It is absurd that you should be wasting your talent and your technical training upon a post which any silly spinster could fill with ease. Even I could measure out an old lady's physic and feed her fowls! I could even go sleighing with the cheeky young man, who sounds rather attractive to me. Trust you to roll him out quite flat! I can see you a-doing of it! Anyway, you will have had your experience, and into the bargain a month's country air, which you really needed. I am not afraid that the place will conquer you, in spite of all you prate to me about the atmosphere of the past and the ayah's magic, which seems to consist merely of joss-sticks. You are too wholly a child of your age, and 'the need of a world of men' is as strong in you as it was in the young man who once landed at a farmhouse for a brief night's

153

love-making. You will come back all right where you belong, but in the meantime I hope you are not having too thin a time. Oh, my dearly beloved, having had your little adventure, *couldn't* you settle down to make poor old Ben happy? You know you could do just anything you like with him, strong-minded old thing that he is in most ways. Without you he will close like an oyster, never to open again—the process is beginning now; I watch it day by day. With you he would bloom like a dull-coloured bud in water, that may, when open, be a flaming cactus for all you know to the contrary. You did confess to me that he surprised you when it came to love-making. It is my impression that he could surprise you a great deal more if he got the chance. Am I a selfish little pig to talk like that? It is frankly one for Ben and two for myself. I want, want, want you for a sister; you make the world so different somehow. The taste goes out of things when you are not here. If I were a man I would make you marry me. You are a sort of 'porte-bonheur,' which I should insist upon annexing. Write again soon, your letters are absorbing, and I am discretion itself; I don't give away anything to Ben, though he looks at me like a hurt dog begging for water when he sees me sniggering over them. Good-bye, and God bless you.

"P.S.—I wonder if the Guyses know how lucky they are. I don't expect it. They think you are just an ordinary young female, glad of any job that prevents her eating the bread of dependence; instead of being (as you are) a pocket miracle!"

Olwen let the paper fall with a long sigh. She had the impression of hearing a voice which came from a vast distance. What was real and vivid at the moment was the snowy fell, the hoary Pele, wild weather, solitude, and the Hindu woman's spells. The High Street of Bram-

forth, with its electric trams, was becoming misty and
dream-like.

Grace's metaphor struck her—was all this just a night
of adventure?—something to be flung aside as soon as the
"need of a world of men" should once more grip her?

For a few minutes she sat on, chin in hand, staring into
the depths of the flames; then, with a suddenness for
which she could hardly account, she sprang to her feet and
flew upstairs—in the pitch dark, for she forgot to take
the indispensable candle. She knew the way by now, and
it was far too narrow for error to be possible. Without
a pause she sped on upward, until she reached the haven
of her own room, wherein Sunia and Sunia's care awaited
her. It was like coming into realities out of a nasty
glimpse of something ugly. She was too content to notice
the significance of her frame of mind.

When she went down to supper that evening, Mr.
Guyse's mood had completely changed. He was gloomy
and silent. He had the aspect of one who has received
bad news and is plunged in depression.

He quite failed to second her attempts at conversation,
and once or twice, when addressed, came with an effort
out of some apparently painful train of thought. His
eyes rested upon Olwen with a puzzled speculation, as if
either she or her actions had hurt and surprised him.

She became convinced that he was a moody man—
veering in his temper, altogether unreliable and uncertain.

As soon as supper was over he rose, went to the mantelpiece, lit his pipe, and muttered something about wanting
to speak to Baxter. Moving to the door he turned, his
fingers on the handle, and said, "I shall stay over there
with Baxter and smoke a pipe. Don't stay up later than
you care to."

With that he walked out, and she heard him bang the door.

A good deal relieved by his absence, she went up to Madam with a clear conscience.

She thought the invalid's eyes brightened at the sight of her, but she declined offers of reading or having her bed made, saying, "Nin will be lonely downstairs; you had better go to him."

"He has deserted me," said Olwen gaily. "He has gone to the Gatehouse to smoke a pipe with Baxter, so you and I can have a cosy evening. Very considerate of him, I call it."

Blank surprise seemed the predominant expression on Madam's face.

"Don't you mind?"

"Mind? Mind what? Being able to devote the evening to you? Dear lady, why did I come here but to be with you and do all I can?"

A fleeting smile crossed the faded lips. "I suppose you really did. I never mentioned Nin in my letter to you, did I?"

"No, you didn't. If you had, perhaps I shouldn't have come," was the mischievous reply, as Olwen went to the door and clapped her hands to summon the ayah.

Sunia came in, looking anything but pleased. She glanced at the girl's careful toilet and coiffure, and said sullenly that one did not make beds when dressed for the evening.

"Pukka mem-sahibs don't, but you see, I am quite different. I belong to the working classes, Sunia—see?" teased the girl.

"Ayah knows better," muttered the woman, with a glance of mingled affection and resentment. She condescended, however, to help her mistress from bed to the big chair by the fire. "Why you unkind my sahib? Why

send him away?" she whispered to Olwen, as they turned
the mattress together.

"I didn't do anything of the sort," replied the girl
aloud; "I went down quite prepared to be nice to him,
but he was as cross as two sticks, and hardly spoke all
dinner time. He's a spoilt, disagreeable thing, Sunia,
and it is you who have spoilt him."

This speech appeared to give quite remarkable pleasure
to Madam, who looked rather spitefully at the ayah.
"Hear what she says?"

"Yes, I hear," very sulkily.

"You shouldn't go telling tales about me, Sunia. You
have made mischief," went on Olwen gleefully.

"I told no tales—not since yesterday evening: Missis
here, my Madam, perhaps she tell tales this day," was the
vexed retort.

"I?" The colour flew hotly into Madam's face.
"Sunia! You forget yourself! Remember your place!
How dare you speak so?"

Olwen stood a minute, glancing from one woman to the
other. Her mind went seeking back over what had passed
that evening. Madam had asked her whether she had a
lover, and had seemed disturbed by her reply. She had
told her to send up Ninian, but not for a moment had she
connected this summons with herself. Yet his manner,
since he saw his mother, had completely changed. It
seemed too preposterous to imagine that he could be in
the sulks because his mother had told him that another
man wanted to marry Miss Innes. Yet Madam had all
the aspect of a guilty person, and Sunia was watching her
with angry eyes.

"It's all nonsense, I am only teasing Sunia, dear
Madam," she threw in quickly. "I am afraid I ought not
to speak so disrespectfully of your son. Forgive me."

The ayah, after a long searching glance, said no more,

and they devoted themselves to putting Madam back into bed, and bringing her supper, after which she submitted, with evident pleasure, to be read to sleep.

By the time she was soundly in slumber it was still early—about nine, and Olwen thought it too soon to go to bed. Taking her candle, she went down to the banqueting hall, in which each day since her arrival there had been a fire and lights in the evening. As she opened the door, a sudden gust blew out her candle, in spite of its protecting shade. She paused in the open doorway, fascinated by the spectacle of the great hall in moonlight.

The snow without made the effect singularly brilliant. Each mullion of the great south window lay in velvet blackness across the floor. One casement of the oriel was open, which was the cause of the draught which had put out her light. She closed the door noiselessly behind her, and stood enveloped in the complete silence of the vast empty place. To her right the closed door of the chapel seemed as though it might open at any moment and disclose the figure of the chaplain, turning from his prayers to seek his bed in the tiny stone chamber in the wall.

Picking up a shawl from some wraps on the settle, she folded it about her, and crept up to the oriel, seating herself upon the window seat. Outside the moonlit snow was so wonderful that she forgot all else in its contemplation. The tops of the trees were like snowy peaks of some distant range, upon which she looked down from an immeasurable height. As she leaned out, she could form some idea of the madness which had seized the unhappy girl who plunged into that underworld of mystery and gloom. There was an eerie fascination in it. It did look as though one might hurl oneself clean into eternity by merely letting go. . . .

There came the notion that all life is effort—is holding on, is resisting the temptation to fall. . . .

How simple, how curiously simple to cease that effort. Words of a hymn she had sung many times in church ran mockingly in her head—

> *Oh, could we but relinquish all*
> *Our earthly props, and simply fall*
> *In Thine Almighty Arms!*

The words had always formerly seemed most inappropriate for the singing of a general congregation, among whom scarce a dozen had any such aspiration. Perhaps Lily Martin had really felt it. Was it, after all, an aspiration, or was it a temptation of the devil? Simply to fall . . . simply fall. . . .

The snow without was hypnotising her—or perhaps some emanation from the soul of her who had agonised there, in that very spot, was exercising a malign spell. She was so absorbed, so utterly carried away by her fancies, that she did not hear the door open nor the low, choked cry which Ninian gave as he came in.

He crossed the floor in a dozen hurried strides. "My God!"

She heard that. She had been leaning out over the sill, but she drew back suddenly, and herself uttered an exclamation on realising the presence of someone in the dark behind her.

"Who is it?" she cried sharply, and a voice replied: "It's I—Ninian—who are you, in God's name?"

"Who should I be but myself," she said in common-place tones, the influence of the solitude and the entranc-ing night fading as she heard her own voice and his.

He laughed unsteadily. "Jove, but you gave me a fright! What in the name of all that's arctic are you doing there?"

"Is it cold? I believe it is," she replied, rising. "I

had forgotten all about it, because fairyland is outside the window."

"What on earth made you come here in the cold and the dark?"

"I wasn't thinking. I expected to find it warm and lighted as usual. I opened the door, and then it was so weird I had to come in. Isn't it?... but there is no word to paint it. I am going to enrich my language by a new adjective. I must find a word to express this Pele! But a word won't do it—you must have a long cumulative effect of built-up words, like the poem of 'Childe Roland to the Dark Tower came.'... I wonder if it was moonlight when he got there?... Nobody knows what he found, do they? But I know what I think."

She was talking at random, to give him time, because she could hear him breathing short, and knew that the sight of her leaning out there had been a shock. He had at first taken her for someone else.

He answered her a trifle jerkily. "What do you think he found?"

"I think it was all glorious within. There was nothing to do him any harm. The danger was all in the getting there. Once arrived he had a splendid welcome."

"I like that idea. But come away. Let us talk of it by the fire downstairs."

"I think I won't come down. It is almost bedtime, and I am tired after my walk. Good night."

As she took his hand she could feel his arm vibrate, as with some very strong emotion which he could hardly curb. "You have odd fancies," he said, half impatiently. "I say—I'm sorry I was such a bear at supper-time."

"Oh, you realise it, then?"

"Of course. I can't think how I could behave so when only yesterday I promised to reform."

"But you must sometimes be out of spirits," she reassured him, lighting her candle as she spoke. "If you and I are to be friends we must make allowances for each others' moods, must we not? You will have to make your peace with Sunia, though. I warn you she is much displeased with you. She seems determined that you and I should be friends, doesn't she?"

"Do you think it's possible we ever could?" he asked wistfully, almost humbly.

"Why not?"

"You're—you're so unexpected, somehow. I never know what you will do, how you will take things."

"Isn't that more stimulating than if you always knew beforehand what I should do or say?"

"Well, of course it is."

"Perhaps a little friction is what you need," she laughed, as she took up the candle and escaped.

CHAPTER XVII

In the market-place of Caryngston Dr. Balmayne met the vicar, a sturdy, rosy-faced man with a face like a jocund choir-boy.

"Hallo!" was the clerical greeting. "How have you been keeping all this awful weather? Going to thaw, though, now."

"Pretty well," replied Balmayne, who had stopped his car to purchase a keg of petrol at the local store. "Get in and I'll put you down at the vicarage."

Nothing loth, Mr. Lomas took his seat beside him. He was a sociable person, always eager for news, and with the exception of his vicarage full of nurslings, the doctor was his only associate, at least during the winter months.

One of the best and most simple-minded of men, he had nevertheless a curious taste for horrors, and found his keenest enjoyment in perusing the detailed reports of murder cases in the daily papers, or unravelling the tales of Arsène Lupin, Sherlock Holmes, and so on. A collection of true stories of celebrated *crimes passionels* related by a well-known author had lately delighted him, and he began to talk of it almost immediately.

"You know, Balmayne, it is positively unsettling to read a book like that," he said. "The thing it brings home to you is that people are hardly ever what they seem. Picture to yourself a young girl, living in her father's house, simple, dutiful, giving up an undesirable lover at

162

a word of parental entreaty, engaging herself most suitably, universally esteemed among even the strict Presbyterian circle she moved in, and she turns out to be——"

"Well, what does she turn out to be?"

"To have been secretly the mistress of the man she professed to have given up, and, furthermore, to be his murderess."

"It was never proved against her, was it?" asked the doctor.

"It was not; and there were many at the time in Edinburgh who believed her innocent; but she was convicted of enough, even without the murder. She was shown to have been without moral sense. Fancy a young girl who could engage herself to a good man, while all the time concealing that engagement from her paramour to whom she was continuing to send passionate letters! Isn't it inconceivable?"

"I should have thought to a priest, as to a doctor, there is very little that is inconceivable. This world is an odd place, and there are odd people in it."

"You're right there, and talking of odd people, Mrs. Askwith has just told me quite an exciting piece of news, though I expect you have heard it. She says that the Guyses have at last engaged another girl to go as companion up at the Pele!"

"Yes, your news is no news to me, Vicar. I was up there two days back, and am going again to-day, as Mrs. Guyse is not quite the thing."

"And you have seen the young lady?"

"And I have seen the young lady."

"Indeed! Indeed! And how does she impress you?"

"Very favourably. She seems all right so far. They have told her nothing about Miss Martin."

"Ah, um!" The vicar made little ruminating sounds as he turned this over in his mind. "Talk of mysteries," he remarked at length; "there, my dear Balmayne, is a thing to puzzle you! As queer as anything in this book, staggering though some of these undoubted facts are. Will that affair ever be explained, do you suppose?"

"I don't think there is much mystery there. What is it that strikes you as so mysterious?"

"My good fellow, we have discussed it a hundred times! The girl's departure, the way the thing was hushed up——"

"It seems fairly clear to me, as I have always told you. Young Guyse pays the girl to keep quiet."

"But why? Why should he do so?"

"Because he didn't want her to talk, of course."

"Then you really think——"

"Mrs. Baxter told me that all the time she was delirious she kept on repeating to herself, 'Lily Guyse, Mrs. Guyse.' There is no doubt that he had promised her marriage, there was a wedding-ring round her neck. All that story of the ayah's about her getting letters from London was concocted. They said she burnt the letters, and I never saw one, or heard of anybody except the ayah who saw one. If the thing had come into court the postman would have been called, and it would have been exposed, but, you see, it did *not* come into court. Of course, Sunia would swear that black was white in order to screen Guyse; an utterly untrustworthy witness. His mother knew, I am convinced of that."

"His mother knew?"

"Undoubtedly. She never liked Ninian, but she has hated him since then. I fancy she would have taken the girl back on her own terms—even as Ninian's acknowledged wife. She liked her well enough, and her life since she was alone has been anything but amusing. Guyse has the impudence to declare that he does not know where the girl is, and has never heard of her since

she left. But that is a bit too thin. No, in my opinion
it was a lucky thing for that young man that poor Miss
Martin didn't succeed in her attempt; an inquest would
have been embarrassing. But the hush money is evidently a drain upon him. He ought not to be so frightfully hard up as he evidently is. He makes a clear profit
on his farming, and they are not without means, though
they lost a big amount. Well, his dismal experience may
have taught him wisdom. He will be the less likely to
start philandering with Miss Innes."

"It seems to me an imprudent arrangement," remarked
the vicar in a troubled voice. "Here is a man who can't
afford to marry at all unless he marries a fortune. They
import into that lonely house a girl, young and presumably attractive, but so poor that she must work for her
living. What else is there for Guyse to do but flirt?
Shut up with her day after day, it must be hard to help
it!"

"But what can one do?" said Balmayne musingly.
"Would it be possible to warn her? I think she is a
girl of character—quite a different type from that other.
If she knew what sort Guyse is, she would be safe enough."

"Then I am inclined to think you ought to give her a
hint. I don't like it, Balmayne."

"It's so hard to say anything at all without saying
too much."

"It is. I see that—and you are a young man yourself. If Wilfrid were at home I could speak to him, but
Ninian is the kind of chap who thinks it clever to be
rude if you say anything he doesn't like."

"Wilfrid was a good deal cut up by that Lily Martin
episode."

"No wonder! A nice thing to come back from Klondyke—where he had really been risking his life to mend
the family fortunes—and to find out what had been going

on in his absence. Of course, they hoped that, as the girl got well and departed, nothing would come out. But it did—it did!"

"Inevitably, I suppose," replied Balmayne; "but I can honestly say it didn't get about through me."

"Who told the Kendalls?" said the little vicar shrewdly. "My wife is certain that Rose Kendall meant to marry Ninian. It was practically a settled thing, and Metcalfe told me she has thirty thousand pounds."

"I suppose Wolf is not likely to be coming home just yet?"

"Can't possibly come as long as Parliament is sitting. He took a few days' leave at Christmas, you know."

"Now if it were he with whom a girl was thrown every day and all day long, warnings would be fruitless," remarked Balmayne smiling. "Any girl alive would fall in love with Wolf if she got the chance."

"If I were to write to him," suggested the vicar tentatively. "Of course, I don't mean ostensibly. I do write to him from time to time. Say I am sending back the book he lent me, and am interested to hear that his mother has a new companion—that her presence will do much to wipe out unpleasant rumours or memories, eh?"

"Do you think that he doesn't know of the new arrangement, then?"

"I can't say."

"It was by his advice that they tried the plan before," said Balmayne thoughtfully. "He may have urged it afresh when he came home at Christmas and saw how depressed and unwell his mother was. A pity he didn't insist upon its being somebody middle-aged. But I suppose he thought that might be more depressing than nobody at all."

"Well, if you get a chance," concluded the vicar, as the car stopped at his gate, "I should put in a word; but be careful. The Guyses are a very old family, and this old blood does curious things. Generally a bit mad, these high-bred, thin-blooded chaps."

"You surely don't call Mrs. Guyse blue-blooded? She ought to have imported a good sane middle-class strain to replenish the old stock."

"Ah, true. Will you come in and see Ada?"

"No, thanks, I've got a pneumonia case, and I want to get up to the Pele this afternoon. Mrs. Lomas all right, I hope?"

"Yes, yes, capital. When I've finished 'Celebrated Murder Mysteries' I'll lend it to you," went on Mr. Lomas in a burst of friendship, "but I haven't read it all yet. However, bear in mind that nothing is really improbable. The young lady at the Pele can't be too careful. I don't know why exactly, but I shouldn't care for a daughter of mine to be there. I've heard it said that Mrs. Guyse is a bit queer in the head since their financial crash; and the foreign woman is almost the only servant they have. Safe or not, it can't be comfortable there for a young lady, it really can't."

"Miss Innes seemed all right when I saw her last. However, I will make particular inquiry to-day. When the weather breaks, you must make an effort and take Mrs. Lomas to call at the Pele. I'll motor you up. Poor old Reed (the vicar of Guysedale) won't be able to get there for months."

"A broken Reed, eh?" said Mr. Lomas, and the doctor glided away leaving him chuckling at his own joke. Like most people with no sense of humour, the vicar dearly loved a joke.

Upon reaching the Pele that afternoon the doctor was shown into the banqueting-hall.

The master of the house sat smoking by a good fire, and the furniture of the room was in some disorder, as if in process of rearranging. The greeting Balmayne received was less hostile than usual, though it could not be described as cordial.

"Thanks, my mother seems much better. Convalescent, in fact; I'll let Miss Innes know that you are here." He went to the door, opened it and clapped his hands. Then he was heard telling the ayah who had answered the summons to say that the doctor had arrived.

Miss Innes appeared at once and invited Balmayne to Madam's room. He was altogether satisfied with his patient, and quite willing that she should be brought downstairs if it could be managed.

When they had left the sick chamber and were passing through the adjoining sitting-room, he said to the girl, "I should like a few minutes talk with you."

She stopped. "It had better be here, then," said she in a low voice, "for on the stairs or in the hall we shall be overheard. The Hindu woman cannot be cured of listening behind the arras; I think she looks upon it as part of her duties. However, she can hear nothing through this door."

He hesitated. What he had to say would need some adroitness, in order that it might sound not too serious, yet important enough to be heeded. He felt it impossible to begin.

He smiled. "To blurt out what I want to say in cold blood is not easy, yet I think I may be sorry afterwards if I have failed to give you a hint——"

"Yes?" Her heart throbbed apprehensively.

"Have you heard anything—I think you told me that you had not—about Miss Martin?"

She flushed, but her answer came swiftly. "Thanks, Dr. Balmayne, but since I last saw you I have heard what I suppose to be the whole story; and—and shall you think me wrong if I say that I feel it a subject which does not concern me, and which I ought not to discuss?"

"I shall certainly think you wrong in the sense of being mistaken," he answered quietly. "In my opinion the matter does concern you. What young Guyse did once he may do again. Of course, that sad affair may have taught him caution; but it does not seem to me fair that you should not be put on your guard."

"You think Mr. Guyse was to blame?" she asked as indifferently as she could; but by the glance the doctor gave her she knew that he was disagreeably surprised.

"So you are already a partisan?" he asked with a smile, taking up his hat.

Olwen coloured, surprised herself at the desire to champion Nin of which she could not but be conscious. "You jump very swiftly to conclusions," said she steadily. "My point of view is, that as I do not mean to remain here, there is no need for me to pry too closely into the Guyse family records." She added with a smile, "Mr. Guyse recommended me to hear your side of the story. He said I was to put yours and his together and see what they came to. But, please, I think I would rather not. The knowledge of what befell my predecessor is enough warning, it seems to me——"

She broke off, for a sharp tapping at the door announced that Nin was outside. With a shrug of her shoulders and a backward glance of amusement she went and admitted him.

"Well, what's the verdict? May I bring her down? he demanded, entering.

"Oh!" Balmayne pulled himself together. "Mrs. Guyse? Yes, certainly I think so."

"Wait a minute, just let me give the finishing touches," cried Olwen, hastening back into the sick-room.

Mrs. Guyse was sitting well wrapped up in an arm-chair. Her eyes rested curiously upon the girl. "Been having a talk to the doctor ?" she asked expressionlessly.

"Yes, but Mr. Guyse is inconsiderate enough to interrupt! He is so impatient to get you downstairs that he has come up to fetch you! Now the comb for a minute! Your hair has got rumpled! There, now you are quite beautiful! If I just put on your shawl——"

Mrs. Guyse's features twisted themselves curiously. She was like one overcome by an access of remorse. "Don't let yourself be taken in," she mumbled under her breath; "what do you suppose Nin cares if I am up or down, alive or dead?"

Olwen paused. She was not certain of many things concerning Ninian, but she was convinced that he had a real affection for his mother, an affection daily wounded by her dislike of him.

"He doesn't like me to be upstairs because it takes you away from him," continued Madam with a spiteful smile. "You see, you take a different view of your duty from what Lily Martin did."

"Don't talk nonsense," laughed Olwen. She was so sure that Ninian was in no danger from her own attractions that she could afford to make light of the invalid's malice. "Now, Mr. Guyse," she went on, throwing open the door, "Madam is quite ready."

Ninian went in, lifted his mother carefully and brought her into the sitting-room where Dr. Balmayne was still standing. Some unamiable impulse caused the lady to give the doctor a cordial invitation to remain to tea. He accepted very readily, and Olwen saw Ninian's brows contract as he carefully edged out of the narrow doorway in such a way as not to inconvenience his burden.

Madam complained a little as he moved slowly and steadily down the spiral stair. He made no reply, but went on as though she had not spoken, finally setting her down, in the glow of the firelight, upon the couch which he had brought into the house not two hours previously, and which Olwen had just covered with mattress cushions from the dining-room, supplemented with pillows, of which Sunia had an unlimited supply.

"Now," said Olwen quite eagerly as they laid Madam down, "you must tell us just how you like to be; the back lets down or can be raised as you wish." Between them it was adjusted to her complete satisfaction, Ninian raising her in his arms while Olwen slipped the back rail into its appropriate niche. Balmayne stood watching the domestic intimacy of the scene, and his thoughts were grave.

Mrs. Guyse was evidently pleased with the new arrangement. As they had placed her, she could not see the oriel window at all. The high back of the settle screened it from her, and a little table stood conveniently beside her for her endless knitting.

Sunia now brought up tea, and Olwen poured it out.

"Fancy," said Madam to Balmayne, "Miss Innes reads aloud so well that I quite enjoy it. I always hated to be read to, but the story she is reading is so amusing that I am quite longing to hear the rest. I have been thinking about it all day, and it cheers me up."

"That's the very thing you want," said the doctor heartily. "Miss Innes will do you more good than my medicine."

"Yes, but I am afraid she is not going to stay," replied Madam with a wrinkle of her brows.

"Rubbish!" broke in Ninian; "she only said that because I ragged her and she got a bit riled. However, I'm a reformed character now, and I run her errands like Mary's lamb. Been to Raefell station and back to-day already for my lady."

"That's right, boast!" said Olwen scornfully. "Shall

I put an extra lump of sugar in your tea, a reward for a good boy?"

"Put it in my mouth instead—a reward for a good dog," he answered, grinning till the whole of his splendid row of sharp white teeth were displayed.

The demon of coquetry which sleeps in every woman prompted the girl to fall in with his mood just because of the presence of Dr. Balmayne. She laid the sugar on his sleek black head, her finger upheld. "Trust," said she absurdly. He sat immovable, his eyes long and eloquent under half-closed lids fixed steadily upon hers. "Paid for," she cried in a hurry, and he jerked his head, caught the sugar in his hands and ate it.

"The finger flavour," he remarked, "is excellent and very noticeable. What is that stuff which Sunia uses in her ministrations? Subtle but quite perceptible."

"You're atrocious," she said with a spurt of anger, swiftly neutralised as she caught his merry eye. "That is, I suppose you are behaving as well as you can, so we must make allowances."

He turned to the doctor. "Miss Innes is beginning my education," he said. "I feel sure it'll take longer than a month; don't you agree?"

CHAPTER XVIII

DURING a whole fortnight nothing particular happened, but many things took place; the first of which was the passing of the snow. By the end of January it was all gone, the trees in the ravine were black instead of white, and the roads, while the thaw lasted, almost impassable.

Madam speedily recovered her usual health, and Dr. Balmayne paid only one more visit, on which occasion Miss Innes was out, so he did not see her.

The state of the weather made farming impossible. Ninian went hunting once or twice, but was for a great part of the time short of occupation, and Olwen and he were much in each other's company.

Reading aloud became a recognised amusement. This took place usually in the interval between tea and supper. The rearrangement of the banqueting-hall, and the comfort of the new couch, had apparently reconciled Madam to the renewed use of the one stately apartment which she possessed. She reclined beside the fire, with her knitting, while Ninian sprawled upon the settle, smoking and netting a new tennis-net for next season. Olwen, between them, had a little reading-lamp all to herself.

Madam, like her son, was a creature of moods. She puzzled Olwen. At times it seemed as though she were on the eve of a burst of confidence. Sometimes, but very rarely, she permitted herself a spiteful sneer at Ninian's expense, as on the occasion of her first coming downstairs; but for far the greater part of the time, one

173

would have said that she tried, persistently, and at times quite openly, to throw her son and her companion into each other's society.

As for Ninian, his temper varied. Sometimes, for a whole day together, he would be perfectly delightful, saying and doing nothing which jarred—making fun, teasing, preserving the demeanour of a big, indulgent brother, who took increasing pleasure in the society of a small sister. After such a day, Olwen would drift upstairs to her night's rest, in a happy dream. She attempted no self analysis in these times. She was content with life as it was. Then would come a day when Mr. Guyse hardly spoke, when his brow lowered, and he either avoided her or seemed anxious to pick a quarrel. This did not often happen, and when it did it disturbed her a good deal. One morning she received a letter and a parcel, both from Ben Holroyd. His firm had just been experimenting with a new substance as an equivalent for silk, and as a result they were putting on the market some particularly charming sports coats in all shades. Ben said that he had given two of these dainty garments to Gracie, and that she had begged that Olwen might have the like. This gave him courage to venture upon sending them. "You are Gracie's friend—her almost sister," he wrote, "and you have no brother. You may find it impossible to be my wife, but don't be unkind enough to say I may not be your friend."

Olwen felt it would be ungracious to refuse the gift thus offered; in truth, it was very welcome, since one needed warm clothing at the Pele while the weather continued so severe. Grace's hand was clearly discernible in the choice, since both the coats sent harmonized with skirts in Olwen's possession. One was a dark, cold blue, not in the least what is known as "navy," but something like a starlit sky in summer. With a lawn collar, and a skirt to match, this looked extremely nice, and she went down to breakfast wearing it in high good humour.

It was damping to find Ninian plunged in a fit of the sulks, of which she could not trace the origin.

By next morning he had more or less got over it, but Olwen did not feel prepared to go back at once to the old footing. She was a little stiff, and he went off after breakfast in something of a huff, and did not as usual return to lunch.

Madam and her companion, now on most amicable terms, ate together. Then the lady was tucked up comfortably on her couch for her daily nap, and Olwen went upstairs to write letters. She was thus occupied—Ben's letter open before her, her own reply nearly complete—when Sunia came in, a little breathless and very eager.

"My Missee change her frock quick," said she; "people come a-calling."

"Why, Sunia, how marvellous! How unheard-of! I feel all of a tremble," laughed Olwen as she rose. "No wonder you're excited! Things like this mustn't happen too often, or they will upset my nerves!"

Sunia was swiftly taking from its drawer Olwen's prettiest frock, and one that she had never hitherto worn at the Pele, for want of a suitable occasion. The ayah admired it greatly—it had been purchased for a friend's wedding the preceding summer—and now she dressed her missee in it with great satisfaction, though in feverish haste.

"Missee go down quick; poor Madam not like having folks allylone."

"Well, I would have gone down at once, if you hadn't insisted upon dressing me up, you silly old thing," laughed the girl. "Who are the visitors?"

"Kendall folk," said Sunia in a slighting voice. "You never seen 'em, they never see you." She gave a little chuckle as if at some thought which pleased her. "They see you this day, certinly. Miss Rose Kendall she see you quite well. There now, here, my Missee, clean hanshif—run away, I must go and bring tea."

Olwen took the "hanshif," one of her best, and as she scuttled downstairs she inhaled its faint, exquisite perfume, described by Ninian as "subtle yet perceptible." She never gave a thought to the open letters on her blotter.

With Madam she found three strangers—an elderly lady and gentleman and a girl of about her own age. The gentleman was fierce and military, the lady nondescript and uncertain, the girl struck her rather unpleasantly. She was of the chinless type, with a salient nose, giving to her profile the look of a bird of prey. Her brown eyes were goggling, but she apparently considered herself a beauty, for she was extravagantly arrayed in ermine and velvet, with diamonds in her ears and at her collar.

Mrs. Guyse looked relieved when Olwen entered. "Ah, here is Miss Innes," she said; "let me introduce her— Miss Innes, General and Mrs. Kendall, Miss Kendall."

The attitude of all these three persons, when presented to Madam's companion, was stiff to the point of rudeness, but Olwen set to work bravely to do her duty and entertain them as well as she could. Mrs. Kendall turned her back, addressing herself pointedly to Madam, and the General followed her example; so Olwen gave her attention to the young lady.

"I expect you came in a car," said she; "it is the only way to get about in these parts. As we have not one, we are almost confined to the house, ·except when the snow is deep and hard enough for sleighing. How far have you come ?"

"About ten miles," said the heiress frigidly.

"Mrs. Guyse took cold sleighing," went on Miss Innes, unperturbed; "she was laid up for several days, and it was all that Dr. Balmayne could do to get to us. This place seems like the world's end, does it not?"

Miss Kendall stared forbiddingly. "It is one of the sights of the country," said she. "It is mentioned in Domesday Book."

"I was not criticising, but merely commenting," replied Olwen, amused. "As a matter of fact, I like the solitude, though I am surprised at myself for saying so. I came from Bramforth."

"Indeed!" was all the reply vouchsafed; and the speaker looked out above her furs, so curiously like a parrot that Olwen nearly laughed.

"Won't you take off your stole? This room is so warm; we are obliged to keep up the temperature for Madam."

"I am not too warm," replied Miss Kendall, with an indescribable arching of her skinny throat.

"No, it's not a parrot that she is like—it's a vulture," thought Olwen. "I can fancy her hopping sideways after a bit of carrion! I should like to see Nin deal with her!" Aloud she made one more effort.

"Do you live in the Caryngston direction?"

"No," replied the vulture, and made no further conversational attempt.

Olwen felt greatly inclined to say, "Oh, very well, sulk if you want to!" but at this painful instant the door opened and the master of the house walked in. She was so pleased to see him that she actually gave him what he would have called the "glad eye"—receiving in return a flash of green light which gave her a queer sensation of pleasure. They had had a tiff, and to both this exchange of looks seemed to say that all was right once more between them.

The looker-on thought she detected some embarrassment or self-consciousness in the cordiality of the greeting the young man received from the General and his wife; but Miss Kendall became a different creature at once. With much play of eyes and tossing of furs she made way for him upon the settle at her side. Olwen had risen at once upon his entrance, and the appearance of Sunia with the tea gave her occupation at some little distance, so that she could not hear what Nin was saying, only that he was making Miss Kendall laugh. Her high titter resounded through the lofty chamber. But when Olwen rose and began to hand round cups, he instantly rose also, took possession of the cake-stand, and did his duty as host in a manner which pleased Olwen enormously.

"Your ayah is wonderful," said Rose, accepting her cup. "I always think she is immortal, like 'She' in Rider Haggard's story. She never seems to grow any older, and she lends such a *bizarre* touch! The contrast of the feudal fortress and the Oriental servant!"

"What's *bizarre*, teacher?" asked Ninian of Olwen, with a wicked look.

"*Bizarre* is the word which describes the effect of Sunia in the Pele, as Miss Kendall has just told you," replied Olwen, rather saucily, perhaps, but she had been a little nettled by Miss Kendall's ill-breeding.

"Sunia is so devoted in her attendance on your mother that I should hardly have thought you required anybody else," went on Rose, her eyes fixed disparagingly upon Olwen.

"Oh, it isn't Miss Innes's job to wait on my mother," said Ninian quietly. It was curious that Olwen knew his voice inflections well enough to be aware that he was angry. "Sunia is all very well in her way, but she has her little tempers. She was getting a bit unbearable when Miss Innes arrived, but she has somehow contrived to

tame her entirely. Ayah is perfectly devoted—waits on
you hand and foot, doesn't she?" He spoke standing up,
with his cup in his hand, close to Olwen, determined
that she should be included in the conversation. She had
never liked him so well. His mother chimed in.

"Yes, as I hear Ninian telling your daughter, it is a
most remarkable thing the way my ayah has taken to Miss
Innes. It was almost instantaneous. She positively wor-
ships her. Miss Innes, tell General Kendall about the
table."

Olwen smiled as she related how she had wished to have
a writing-table in her room, and how, owing to the im-
possibility of carrying furniture upstairs, Sunia made
Baxter take off the legs of an unused table and transport
it to the top of the house, where it was put together again.

Rose Kendall made no comment, but after an insolent
stare at Olwen, turned her shoulder to her and said to
Mr. Guyse, "How strange that it never occurred to me
to wonder how the things were got into the rooms! This
fine billiard-table, for example."

"My father never went without anything he really
meant to have," replied Ninian. "This place had been
more or less uninhabited for a century, except by a farm-
hind, when he determined to use it as a shooting-box. He
took out all the mullions of that great window, and the
table was hauled up with ropes and pulleys."

"How glorious to own such a place!" said Miss Kendall
fervently. "How I should like to live in a historic tower!"

Ninian's grin over her head at Olwen showed that he
thought this attempt too clumsy even for Miss Kendall.
"Nicer to think about than to put in practice," he replied.
"Ask my mother."

"Oh, the Pele is a bit trying if you have to live in it in
winter, but it has its good points," said Madam. Her
voice had wholly lost the edge of bitterness with which

she had spoken of her home to Olwen as "this accursed spot."

"Miss Innes became acclimatised very quickly," went on Ninian to the young lady.

She acknowledged the remark with a smile that was almost a grimace, and changed the subject forthwith. "What news of your brother? He was looking so well when I saw him last."

"Oh, he's all right, but we haven't heard very lately. This is just the busy time for him, Parliament opening and so on." He sat down beside the visitor, and spoke with his eyes full upon her and an especially demon-like smile. "By the way, I heard a bit of news this morning. Came home hot-foot to tell Madam. What do you think, Mother? Noel Guyse is going to be married to Miss Leverett, of Leverett's Wash-White Slick-Soap!"

"Never, Nin!" cried Madam, with a little laugh. "His lordship has never given permission!"

"If he didn't, he'd be a raving lunatic. She's got money enough to buy the whole county. Now they'll have another try to get me to sell the Pele! See if they don't!"

"But you won't!" cried Miss Kendall in terrified accents, clasping her jewelled hands and gazing at him intensely. Certainly he looked wonderfully handsome as he sat there, so completely at his ease, with the impish smile flickering over his face.

"Depends on how much they offer," he said, with another glance at Olwen. For some reason which she could not fathom, he was evidently enjoying this conversation. "I suppose you had already heard of the engagement?" he went on, addressing the General point-blank.

The old gentleman cleared his throat, and admitted, a trifle nervously, that he *had* heard something of it. "Met his lordship on the bench on Monday."

"Did he seem pleased?" Ninian inquired.

"Oh, ah, yes, certainly. Very pleased. . . . Charming girl, so he said. Case of love at first sight on both sides."

"No doubt," said Madam, with her little nervous laugh. "Love of money on his side, love of a title on hers."

"Ha! ha! Good, my dear lady, good!" laughed the General. His daughter added:

"I've seen Amanda Leverett, she was at Danley Races last autumn, but I forget what she's like. Her clothes were all right. They were the thing you remembered about her."

"Well, no doubt Caryngston can do with the money. None of our family are what Nin would call coiny," said Madam.

"Ah, but you don't need it, you have something worth far more!" cried Rose, with a glance which she meant to be very expressive. Ninian acknowledged the compliment with a merry bow.

Mrs. Kendall rose. She had been looking decidedly ill at ease while the latest topic was discussed. "The days are so short," she murmured, "we must really say good-bye. Charmed to find you at home and looking so well, dear Mrs. Guyse. Now, I suppose it would be of no use to ask you to let Mr. Guyse bring you to lunch with us one day next week?" She bent over Madam's couch coaxingly.

"Oh, no thank you. I shall not go out until the weather turns really fine," was the quick response. "Miss Innes will have to do my social duties for me."

Mrs. Kendall ignored the hint entirely. "Mr. Guyse, you will have to take pity on us and come alone," said she playfully. "Shall we say Monday? Or would Tuesday suit you better? What with our having been abroad the two last winters, and in London during the season, we have seen nothing of you lately."

"Must be three years since I was at Copley, isn't it?"

"Oh, I can't believe that it is as long as that! How time flies! But do be—er—forgiving, and come over for an hour or two. The General is longing for a chat with you."

"Can't be done, thanks all the same. We're short-handed on the farm, and next week is going to be very busy. The long snow has made us all behindhand. You must realise that I'm a mere British workman, not fit to lunch with the quality."

Rose approached, laying her cheek down on her big white muff, and looking wistfully at him. He stuck to his refusal, however, in spite of entreaties. The discussion seemed to amuse Madam. She lay listening with one of her queer looks—looks which enabled one to glimpse a passing likeness between her and the son who was so unlike her.

The young man accompanied his guests downstairs, and as the sound of their footsteps and voices died away, his mother turned to Olwen.

"Dear! How funny!" said she.

"What in particular was funny?" inquired the girl, coming to relieve her of her empty cup.

"The Kendalls! Ha! ha! I can't altogether explain how funny it is, but I can tell you part. They tried hard, three years ago, to marry Rose to Ninian. She's got a nice little fortune, it wouldn't have done badly. Then suddenly something made them think that they might get hold of Noel Guyse, Caryngston's boy, and, of course, they thought that would be much better. They haven't been near us for ages, and when they walked in this afternoon, all gush, I couldn't make out what brought them. But, you see, Ninian knew! They had got wind of Noel's engagement, and hoped we shouldn't have heard about it! Hoped they wouldn't be seen through! But Nin wasn't

going to let them off! Did you see the General's face
when Nin made him own that he knew? Dear me, I
haven't been so amused for a long time!"

Nin was soon back again, and came into the room
laughing. "Well," he said, "aren't those people just about
the limit? Like their cheek, turning up here and coming
the long-lost brother over me, when they've boycotted me
for three years!"

"Oh, well, I think you scored," said his mother with
relish.

"What d'you think of 'em, eh, Teacher?" he continued,
dropping into a chair by her tea-table and stretching out
his long limbs.

"Sit down and have a proper tea," said she, instead of
replying. "You were behaving so beautifully that you
had not time to eat."

"Yes, wasn't he?" said Madam unexpectedly. "Your
manners are improving, Nin, did you know?"

The expression which crept into Nin's face touched
Olwen with a quick thrill of pity. His eye gathered
light, his lips curved, the colour mustered in his dark face.
Evidently his mother's praise was delightful to him.

Of course, however, he replied flippantly. "Ought to
be improving by now. Been living in a reformatory for
weeks."

"Oh," said the girl quickly, "has it been as bad as that?"

He gave her a sidelong glance, watching the effect of his
words. "It's been very painful." He sighed. "But all is
forgiven if the result seems to be worth the sacrifice. You
haven't answered the previous question, Teacher. What
do you think of the resident gentry, as exemplified in the
Kendall family?"

"Oh . . . I expect they improve on acquaintance, like
—like some other folks I know."

"Now what have I done for you to be nasty?"

"Said you'd been living in a reformatory," she snapped.

"Ah, but this one is run on the new lines—cure by kindness. I like being here so much that I'm going to stay as long as they let me have the same teacher."

"Doesn't he want shaking?" said Olwen to Madam.

"My dear, I think you _have_ shaken him—pretty thoroughly!"

CHAPTER XIX

OLWEN was very busy. For the last fortnight she had devoted herself to the library, and it had been a far more laborious business than she had anticipated. The books seemed to have been snatched from their places, thrown in a pile on the floor, and taken thence and thrust into shelves quite haphazard.

Not only was there no classification, but even the volumes of the different sets were divided, and had to be hunted for.

She had, by dint of steady work, made considerable progress, though still there were rows of books lying on the ground, carefully shielded from dust by newspapers.

This morning the sun was streaming blithely in through all the windows, and the sharp frost made one feel buoyant. Olwen was in vigorous health. Since she left the Palatine Bank she had improved very much in looks. The tints of her face were like a sun-warmed peach, her eyes were bright and clear, and the excellent feeding made her plump, though the exercise she took kept her from growing stout. She sang as she stood upon the library steps, garbed in a blue overall, with duster and feather brush. It seemed to her that all was right with the world.

The upper shelves were devoted to fiction, and she had just hunted out and found the last volume completing a set of Bulwer Lytton. She carried them up to their

destined shelf, and was carefully arranging them according to their numbers, when one dropped from her hand
into her lap. The leaves fell apart, and a photograph
slipped out from between them. Seated upon the top
step, she took up the portrait and studied it.

A young lady, with ebullient hair, teeth and a smile.
She wore a large feathered hat and a low—generously
low—evening dress, with a rose at her bosom and a di-
aphanous scarf over one shoulder.

"An actress," thought Olwen, and sighed a little pitifully; for the big bistred eyes were wistful, and the lips,
so evidently carmined, had a pathetic droop. She turned
over the cardboard and saw words scrawled across the
back in a thick, heavy hand:

"Ninian, from his Lily."

Beneath this, which was written in ink, the same hand
had added something else in pencil: *"Mrs. Ninian
Guyse."*

To her own surprise Olwen coloured hotly. She sat
down abruptly on the top step, studying the pictured face
intently.

"So that was the kind of girl he tried his hand upon
last! No wonder I puzzled him! No wonder that he
didn't exactly know where he was with me! . . . This
was Lily Martin! How could they engage such a person?
How could they have her in the house? No wonder Sunia
said she was not pukka!"

Sitting there, chin on hand, she caught sight of her own
reflection in the glass of the opposite cupboards. A small
person in a long plain overall, almost childish, nunnishly
garbed from throat to foot!

Then again her eyes sought the flamboyant image upon
the cardboard.

"From that to this!" she thought, with a curled lip.

Her puzzled eyes, staring out across the room, fell, as

they often did, upon the family motto, carved above the Tudor chimneypiece:

"Guyse ne sçait pas se déguyser."

Like many old mottoes, it seemed ambiguous. Did it mean that, once a Guyse you could not cease to be a Guyse, nor persuade anyone that you were anything else? Or did it mean that any Guyse would scorn to stoop to deception? Or did it mean (as Ninian vowed it did) that a Guyse was such a hopeless fool that any attempt to disguise or mask himself was sure to be found out?

She had herself inclined to the first interpretation. "Once a Guyse always a Guyse" would have been her paraphrase.

Now she looked upon it with a curl of the lip. She was recalling Ninian's telling of the story of Lily Martin, The recital had seemed to her to bear the stamp of truth. To-day her mind had received a nasty jolt.

She and Ninian had come far—very far—since their first meeting. Only last night the question of her remaining at the Pele had been practically decided. Ninian had expounded the rules to her. "If you wanted to leave at the month you should have given warning at the end of a fortnight, Miss. Now you have been here six weeks you will have to give a month's warning; after this month is over we shall engage you annually, as they used to do the farm-hands at Caryngston midsummer fair."

To this she returned that it seemed better that she should at least remain long enough to finish the library catalogue; and to celebrate that decision Ninian, at supper, had bade Sunia bring a bottle of champagne, in which they all drank each other's health.

Mrs. Guyse on this occasion looked more animated than Olwen had ever seen her; and Sunia, when putting her missee to bed later, had cooed over her like a triumphant mother over a new-born child.

Now this photo lay on her lap, and the sight of it was affecting her strangely.

For weeks past she had hardly given a thought to the warnings of Deb Askwith or Dr. Balmayne. She had *not* continued to keep Nin at a distance. In truth, this was a difficult feat, when Nin desired to approach; although, looking back, she realised how cautious the approach had been. . . .

. . . How, exactly, had they reached the stage at which now they stood—the point at which two people have a common stock of jokes, and memories, a common association of ideas—when they turn to each other with a certainty of response, an assurance of mutual understanding?

She could not tell. Ninian, the impertinent boor of the Seven Spears, had become her comrade, she might even say her intimate friend. It was almost like necromancy.

And now there lay before her this flimsy, out-of-date bit of pasteboard, with its costume of four seasons ago, so frail and worthless a thing, yet able to give the lie to her own opinion of Ninian. Here, if looks might be trusted, was a girl of the "cheap" variety, and yet, to judge from her expression, not a vicious girl, not a temptress. She had lived in the house with Ninian for more than a year. Some quality in her expression, in the appeal of the big round eyes, hurt the spirit of the girl who gazed.

He had told her to leave, and she had wept upon his shoulder! . . . How many times during her stay at the Pele might she have used his shoulder as a refuge without being repulsed? Olwen shuddered. There was an element of horror in her thoughts.

Was this man using her as a plaything? Did he still think of her as he had done of this predecessor of so different a type?

No wonder that his first impression, when he went to meet his mother's new companion, had been that of disappointment. She had not seemed to promise the kind of sport that he desired. Yet her very aloofness, her snappish, prudish ways, had acted as a lure. She had shown plainly that he did not please her, and he had determined that he would please her. Whether or no he found her attractive, he was resolved that she should so find him. She professed not to be interested, and he became determined to arouse her interest.

How long would it be before the pleasurable novelty of the situation wore off for him? Olwen clenched her small, ineffectual fists. She had been very arrogant, had believed herself so strong that such a man as Ninian Guyse could not matter. Now, all unaware, she found that she had reached a point at which he did matter, more than she cared to think.

Her wounded vanity found some comfort in the reflection that from first to last there had been no love-making. They had become friends upon her own terms. She had, as it were, made the rules. It was now up to her to see that he kept them. Surely she could do this. Yet the revulsion of feeling in her was so strong that she feared it must be apparent to him. She had believed his story of the "Lily Martin affair." In his mouth it seemed to her to bear the stamp of truth. Its disproof was in her hand. . . .

. . . She recalled Balmayne's curled lips as he said, "So! I see that you are a partisan already!"

The doctor had attended Miss Martin; he knew much more than Olwen could possibly know of the matter. She wished that she had allowed him to tell her his version.

It had not seemed to matter then. Now she would give much to have Ninian cleared.

If he and she were on bad terms, she felt that she could not stay at Guysewyke. This certainty gave her to some extent the measure of her own feeling. She caught a glimpse of the long road she had travelled, and saw for an instant the strength of the cobweb bonds which knitted her silently to this uncouth place and its inhabitants.

She sat on, the photo in her hand, lost in these uncomfortable speculations, humped up on the top of the steps, absorbed in gloomy thought.

The distant door swung back to let in a piercing sound of whistling. Nin and Daff precipitated themselves into the room with violence, and the young man shouted gladly:

"There you are, after all! Been looking everywhere for you! My word, you do seem busy!"

She did not change her posture, but turned her gaze down upon him as he stood below, smiling broadly up at her, his teeth gleaming, the sun catching the pale metallic gleam of his eyes, changing from green to shot gold where the iris touched the pupil, and making him look, as she often thought, like an animal. The same sun was shining richly through her own hair, so that she looked down upon him from a halo.

"Seeing that I told you at breakfast that I should be cataloguing all the morning, it's not very complimentary of you to forget it so soon," said she disagreeably.

"Hallo! Got the hump? I should think so, perched up there all these hours! You look like a saint and talk like a shrew! D'you know it's lunch-time?"

"No, I didn't. I've been so busy."

"You looked it as I walked in. You were sound asleep,

I believe. Now come along down to me! I'll jump you!"

He stood at the ladder's foot, his arms extended. But yesterday, and she would have jumped into them. To-day she felt that she would rather die.

"Oh, do get out of the way," said she; "you make me nervous. These steps are rickety. Stand aside, please."

"Oh, come, Teacher! Don't go back to last month in that discouraging way! I ain't done nothink fresh, 'ave I? Ain't 'ad the coppers arter me these three weeks, swelp me, I ain't, miss! Tell yer strite, I don't move from this 'ere till I gets yer! Come! Moight as well jump first as lawst!"

"Oh, please, Mr. Guyse"—in worried accents—"don't be silly. Stand on one side and let me come down."

He gave her a long, keen look, then moved aside and stood still, with heightened colour, while she replaced the photo in "The Last Days of Pompeii," rose upright, and deposited the volume in the shelf next its fellow. Then she descended slowly backwards, reached the ground, and shook the dust from her overall before unbuttoning it.

"Are you in earnest? Have I dropped a brick of any kind?" he asked in a totally changed voice, a voice which caused her to feel an insane desire to be friends.

"Oh, no, only one does get so tired of that everlasting ragging," she replied slightingly, moving towards the door.

He moved more quickly than she, and laid his hand upon the iron ring which raised the latch. His colour had faded, and he looked so white that she halted, a little frightened.

"D'you think it's fair?" he began, and broke off. "Sorry you're put out," he then said. "Don't know what it's about. Anyway, it's beastly disappointing. I had come to tell you such jolly good news. The ice is bearing, you know. . . . I've been over this morning to see."

Surprise stayed her retreat. "Ice? I didn't know there was any water—I mean, any water you could skate on—hereabouts."

"It's some miles away—Hotwells Lough," said he, pronouncing the word as they do in Northumbria—Loff. "Quite near the Roman Wall, you know. The ice is like glass."

Olwen drew a long breath. If she loved one thing it was to skate. From the time when her uncles taught her upon the ornamental water in Bramforth Park to the Christmas holidays when Ben Holroyd had taken her and Gracie some stations up the line to the Great Stang, it had been her greatest winter joy. Need she deprive herself of that joy simply because she had determined, after all, to "keep Muster Nin at a distance"? . . . There was not much skating in the neighbourhood, and there would be others there—perhaps Dr. Balmayne.

"Are you thinking of going over?" she asked.

"Not to-day; it's too far. If we go we ought to start to-morrow morning after an early breakfast, and take our lunch with us."

"Near the Roman Wall?" said she, waveringly.

"Quite near, really. Near the best bit of all."

"Well," said Olwen, half relenting, "we'll hear what Madam says. I must just run and wash my hands."

With these words she disappeared and hastened up the newel stair. Nin stood motionless for some seconds after her departure; then, softly closing the door, he ran up the ladder steps, passed his hand along the shelf, and took down "The Last Days of Pompeii."

The book fell open in his hand and he saw the photo. He stared at it as in a passion of disgust. Then he took it up hesitatingly and turned it over. His brows con-

tracted into a portentous frown as he saw the inscription.
His mouth puckered itself into a whistle, as if of sharp
surprise.

"The devil!" he said.   "Oh, the devil!"

CHAPTER XX

"Going to give myself a holiday to-morrow, Ma, and take Miss Innes skating on the Hotwells Lough," said Ninian when they were assembled at their midday dinner. "Isn't that a good plan?"

Madam looked furtively first at him then at the girl, as though trying to surprise the expression on both faces. "The question seems to me to be—does Miss Innes think it a good plan?" said she.

Olwen thus appealed to was in her usual difficulty. She had learned that Madam did not like her to say "No" to her son's invitations. On the other hand, she was always very careful not to seem anxious to forsake her duties and go off with the young man. It had lately become the rule for them to go out together of an afternoon, since Madam still kept to the house. The skating was, however, to be a whole day's expedition. Added to the girl's doubts as to the propriety of spending so much time in his society, was the distasteful memory of the thing she had found that morning. She was diligently telling herself that it did not matter. Why *should* it matter? She had never thought highly of Mr. Guyse. The knowledge that he had grossly slurred the truth, if he had not actually lied, in his account to her of what had passed between himself and Miss Martin was simply a conclusive proof that she had been from the first right to distrust him, and that she must revert with him to their former more distant terms, since he might and

194

almost certainly would misinterpret her present attitude of friendliness.

Friendliness! Of course it was nothing more. It could not be more.

The most cursory consideration of the facts sufficed to show how impossible a thing it was that the impoverished young master of the Pele should contemplate marriage with his mother's companion.

Rose Kendall had thirty thousand pounds. Though her first attempt at a reconciliation had been coldly received, it was not likely that it would be her last. She was probably glad that her discarded suitor had not been ready to jump down her throat; but she would not, for that reason, give up hope; and by degrees her efforts must be crowned with success. To put it plainly, the Guyse family could not afford to let thirty thousand pounds go a-begging.

This being understood, why should the knowledge of Ninian's treachery to one woman deprive another of a day's pleasure in a life which could not but be described as monotonous?

Rather did it insure her safety, since it must harden her heart against the young scamp's nonsense.

These considerations all passed through the mind of Madam's companion as she gently replied: "I think the expedition will take too long. We should be too many hours absent."

"How did you intend to go, Nin?" asked Madam. "There's nowhere to put up the horse."

"I know. But Miss Innes is some walker. My idea is to set out early with a package of sandwiches and drive there, taking Ezra with us to bring the horse back. We will skate for a couple of hours or so—I should think that would be long enough—and then eat our lunch and walk home. It is well inside ten miles, the roads are in

good condition, and if we start back about two we should
get home to supper."

"That sounds feasible," said Madam, "and I could
spare Miss Innes if she likes to go."

Ninian looked at Olwen, and seeing her hesitation, in-
sinuated what he knew would be an inducement. "The
Lough is only about half a mile from the Roman Wall,"
said he. "There's a mile-castle close by."

"Oh! I have always wanted so much to see the Roman
Wall!" cried Olwen impetuously.

"And, please, Teacher, you might continue my education by instructing me a little bit about it," put in the
incorrigible meekly.

"Well, my dear, the decision rests with you," said
Madam in an odd voice.

Sunia was standing just behind her mistress's chair.
As Olwen raised her eyes to answer she encountered the
soft gaze of the clear coffee-coloured eyes.

She felt inclined to say straight out: "It is of no use
your trying to hypnotise me." That being impossible,
she merely declared:

"I think I must stay at home and go on with my work
in the library."

"Tell you what it is," said Ninian confidentially to
Madam. "She's afraid. She thinks that if she spends
a whole day with me she'll succumb to my fascinations;
and from the bottom of her school-marm heart she dis-
approves of me."

"Everything is feudal here at the Pele," was Olwen's
instant retort. "We even keep a court jester."

Madam laughed. "She's a match for you, Ninian."

"Is she?" said Ninian, his bold eyes fixed fully upon
the girl.

Olwen did not change countenance, but she could not
meet his look. His previous words had had their intended

effect. She was not going to "funk," as she put it to
herself.

"You will have plenty of time for the library; but the
frost will not keep," observed Madam.

"Then if you approve, Madam, I should like to go."
Sunia let loose a soft sigh of relief.

When Miss Innes entered her room that night she knew
by the weird perfume that the ayah had been at her
divinations. The little pots stood in the ashes, and a
faint blue smoke, fragrant and making a troubling appeal
to the emotions, lingered on the air.

"Oh, Sunia, in mischief again!" said she, laughing, as
she came in.

Sunia rose, in her lithe, soundless fashion, and stood
gazing upon the girl. "Change coming," she murmured.
"Change in missee's life. A great change." Her wide
eyes were mournful, and she shook her head. "I not see
well this night," she remarked; a thing she usually said
when her incantations had not shown the desired result.
She fussed and petted the girl beyond her wont that night,
massaging her limbs, rubbing her feet in anticipation of
the next day's walk. She liked Olwen's little pink feet,
and often spoke in admiration of them. When at last
the girl was tucked up in bed, the ayah brought her a glass
containing a small draught of pale amber fluid.

"What's that?" said Olwen sharply.

"Something ole ayah want missee take," murmured
the woman coaxingly. She added that it was a tonic—
a strengthening draught which would invigorate her for
the morrow's walk. Olwen was very sleepy, and half-
hypnotised by her toilet and by the mystic fragrance of
the air. Yet the sight of that little draught gave a shock
to her pulses and put her on her guard.

It was as though something or some one quite near
whispered a word in her ear—*philtre!*

Sunia had not said a word about Ninian, but she had seemed depressed, as though she feared that things were not going right. That she should prepare a love potion was by no means unlikely.

Not for worlds—not for anything that life might have to offer, would Olwen drink it. Yet she felt that it would be wiser not to refuse it openly.

"Thanks, ayah dear. Put it there. I am going to read my chapter, and then I will drink it last thing before I go to sleep."

"Missee drink it now, I wash the glass."

"All right, I will. Get me a clean hanshif, please, out of my drawer—one of those at the back—underneath."

The moment the woman's back was turned, as she bent her head to search in the drawer, Olwen took up the glass resolutely. She felt afraid, but knew she had but an instant in which to act. With steady hand she poured the drug away into an earthen vase containing flowers which stood upon her bed table. When Sunia turned, she was holding the empty glass tilted against her lips. The single drop that passed them reminded her of Chartreuse liqueur, which Mr. Holroyd had made her taste one New Year's Eve. It was exquisite, but fiery.

When the woman had gone away she slipped out of bed and poured away the tainted water from the flowers.

Owing to the nature of the stairs and the difficulty of carrying pails up and down, each room had a kind of sink or semi-circular stone basin in the outer wall for the reception of waste water. This enabled her to dispose of the highly perfumed fluid, and to wash out the vase with disinfectant. This done she lay down in bed, trembling.

Why should Sunia wish her to love Ninian? The only answer that rose to her mind was too horrible for her to accept. The ayah had been invariably good to her, invariably respectful. That she should be seeking to compass her downfall was unthinkable. Yet what else could be her object?

Olwen knew well that Sunia had the most exalted ideas of the rank and station of her sahib, and of what was due to him in the way of a wife. That she could deliberately wish him to marry his mother's companion was preposterous. Then it must be true that she desired the girl to fall a victim.

There came a sense of insecurity—of suspicion—of terror even. There was something uncanny in this place, something unaccountable in these people. She ought not to have remained. She ought to leave. It was no place for her. Curled up in the downy softness of her bed, the firelight flickering upon the thick curtained walls, and on the courses of harsh, savage stone visible above them, she wondered how she dare sleep in such a place. Misgivings thronged upon her mind—the warnings she had received, the way in which Sunia spied upon her. The idea that she was a prisoner in the Pele stole over her —a premonition that, should she try to leave, they would prevent her.

After a while calmer thoughts succeeded. Such an idea as her captivity was merely silly. For what reason, what conceivable reason, should the Guyses have designs upon her, a young, harmless, powerless creature; but one, as she reflected with satisfaction, who had a home and relatives to back her.

Sunia was perhaps a little cracked, having been born with the traditions of the ayah, trained for generations to wait upon, almost to venerate, the conquering race. In her lonely, dull existence the coming of the young girl had been an event. It might have slightly disturbed her mental balance. Thinking back upon all Ninian's eccentricity, Olwen could not recall a single word, a single look of his which had suggested vicious desires. He had been impertinent, even rude—never offensive in that other sense. He merely laughed at Sunia. Madam also, odd as she was, had never seemed to her to be morally delinquent. Although the confidence between them which her short illness had begun had not continued since she was about again, still Olwen had the impression of friendliness, of some amusement. She thought she could say without conceit that Madam found her likeable.

By the time she fell asleep she was reproaching herself with folly. Sunia and Sunia's tricks might be ignored. Ninian had in fact offered to tell the woman to let her alone. She wished she had accepted the offer. Her refusal was based partly upon the feeling that things might be uncomfortable in the house were the ayah her enemy, and partly, she owned it with shame, upon her own pleasure in being waited upon hand and foot. Until this devoted service began she had no idea how much it would appeal to her. So Spartan had been her upbringing that the mere idea of personal attendance had a startling novelty. Now, after one short month, she was beginning to wonder how she would get on without Sunia's ministrations.

. . . Well, she had poured away the philtre ! . . .

. . . So that was all right ! . . .

She sank away into dreamland.

Next morning, when she and young Guyse met in the dining-room for breakfast, his breezy, early morning manner made her ashamed of her over-night panic. Something in Sunia's spells must, she thought, have been responsible for such horrible thoughts.

Admitted that Ninian had minimised his own blameworthiness where Lily Martin was concerned—what had that to do with Olwen Innes? She had assured him that it was no concern of hers.

In the days wherein Olwen looked back upon this phase in her life, she wondered that she could have quieted her fears thus easily. At the time there seemed so many other things to think about.

Ninian ground her skates beautifully, and as she was particular about this, she had to watch the process. Then there was lunch to pack into his rucksack, her own bad-weather coat to roll up and sling across her back, various small things to arrange, before walking through the court-yard and out across the Bull-drop, to where Ezra stood holding Deloraine's head beside the dogcart.

Ezra was told to get up behind, the two young people settled themselves comfortably, and off they spun, due south, striking after a couple of miles a good road leading right across the fells.

The gay morning had made them both a little wild. They hardly talked a word of sense all the way to the Lough.

Olwen had not expected to find this place so solitary. It was, she thought, the most desolate spot she had ever seen. It lay in the lee of a lofty, almost precipitous crag, standing up from the rolling fells in dark ferocity. No human habitation was in sight anywhere along to the horizon.

The road passed within a half-mile of the water, and at the nearest point they stopped, possessed themselves of their skates and their dinner, and dismissed Ezra.

The scramble over fawn-coloured tussocks of grass, with muddy ice between, proved enough to warm all their blood. At the Lough's edge Ninian adjusted first her skates, then his own. With a curt order to her to wait till he returned, he went coursing all around the surface of the ice, making sure of its trustworthiness. It was absolutely safe, and he came rushing back, his eyes spark-ling with the joy of the rapid motion.

"Simply great," he said, "come along!"

In a moment she was up, and they were off together, hands crossed, feet moving in unison, bodies swaying to the delight of it all. The ice was like black armour, as Olwen said, fantastically smooth, except where at the edges the withered reeds drooped their heads and made it lumpy here and there.

They were like a couple of children, playing all kinds of silly tricks. First they wrote each other's names with all kinds of flourishes. Then they did figures of eight, following each other's line of marks within an inch or two. Then rocking turns, and finally waltzing round and round.

They had brought sticks with a view to the walk home, and presently Ninian produced a little ball out of his pocket, and they played a kind of hockey.

It seemed impossible that the morning should have slipped away so imperceptibly. When Ninian proclaimed it to be lunch-time, Olwen could not believe it.

Both were glowing with health and enjoyment as at last they came reluctantly to the edge of the Lough, removed their skates, and looked about for a good place in which to eat their lunch.

CHAPTER XXI

THERE was nothing within reasonable distance better than the margin of the pool. Ninian spread his thick coat on the ground, and they sat down, glowing with heat, and with appetites sharpened by the keen air.

"I don't think I ever was so hungry in my life," said Olwen.

"You look twice as fit as you did when first you came to us," remarked Nin. "A little blue thing you were, with a red nose!"

"You're too complimentary!"

"And now you are what Mrs. Mountstewart Jenkinson would call 'a dainty rogue in porcelain.'"

"What! Have I ceased to be a school-marm and become a rogue?"

"I think you will, if we come skating often!"

"And meantime you have left off being a tavern clown and become a court jester!"

"That's a pretty thing to say!"

"No worse than you are always saying to me! It's mean to keep on attacking and not allow me to hit back."

"Don't you like to be a dainty rogue in porcelain?"

"I would far rather be a serviceable school-marm."

"You have been serviceable," he said, with a sudden change of tone. The change brought her heart unexpectedly into her throat. It sounded as though he were on the verge of becoming sentimental.

"Well, of course," said she hurriedly, "how could I earn

a living if I were not serviceable? By the way, you promised me a sight of the Roman Wall! Where is it? I can't see it anywhere! And what is a mile-castle? Is it so called because it is always a mile away from the place where you happen to be?"

"The Wall is up on the top of that black cliff," said he, "which latter is known in the neighbourhood as Duke's Crag; but that's supposed to be a corruption of Crag Dhu, the Black Crag. No connection between the Crag and any Duke can be traced."

"It wouldn't take us long, would it, to climb up there?" asked the girl. "Is the mile-castle behind?"

"The mile-castle is in that dip about a quarter of a mile to our right. But you mustn't expect to find either it or the Wall very high, you know. The highest bit of wall remaining isn't more than eight feet, I believe, and none of the mile-castle is much higher than my head."

"Do tell me what exactly is a mile-castle?"

"There was one every mile, that is, every Roman mile, along the wall. It was a little fort in which there was a garrison of about a dozen men. At each quarter of a mile there was a smaller one, big enough to hold two or three, so that they were always near enough to call up their mates in case of a surprise. The mile-castles were usually put just where the lie of the ground needed a little extra protection."

"Excellent! This is the young man who was asking for information about the Wall from his teacher!"

He chuckled gaily. "Well, I shall be delighted to hear anything you have to say."

"Do let us go up and look," said she impulsively. "This is the only chance I shall have——"

"Go to! Why the only chance?"

"Oh, because I shall be leaving. It is no use my stay-

ing here. There isn't enough to do. I shall give warning, as you call it, next time I get my wages."

"Then let us make hay, or—or anything else we want
to make, while the sun shines," he returned, rising his
lazy length, and stooping to help her to her feet.

"Can we go right up the rock?" she asked. "It seems
a tremendous way round."

"Yes, the steep direct way is the best, if you think you
can do it. We can use my stick by way of a rope for
you to hold on by. Are you likely to turn dizzy?"

"No, my head's all right."

"Then come on, and let's chance it. We must be pretty
quick, however, for we have not very much time to spare."

The sky was blue, the sun clear above their heads.
With their faces set to the northern wall of the cliff they
saw nothing of the black clouds behind them.

Olwen had never enjoyed anything as she enjoyed that
dizzy climb. Ninian left off fooling and became a guide
in all respects to be desired—steady, competent, and very
strong.

She followed his advice exactly, and in what seemed
quite a short time he had reached the top, swung himself into a sitting posture on the verge, and reached his
arms to raise her to his level.

Then, quite suddenly, when she had let go, as he held
her suspended at his mercy, he said in a strained voice,
unlike his own:

"Now say you believe me. Say you trust me! Do
you hear? If you don't say so, I am going to let you
drop."

She was used to him by now, and not at all frightened.
"Don't be an idiot," said she with the utmost calm; "put
me down."

"Not till you say you believe me. Say you are sure

that I told you the truth, *the real, whole truth,* when I told you about me and Lily Martin the other day."

His face was close to hers, his eyes looked right into hers. They were anxious, but perfectly clear and bold. She could not meet his glance and tell him that he lied. She tried to jest: "Any Guyse, with green eyes, will tell——"

In a moment he had caught her in his left arm, and with his right hand covered her mouth to prevent her completing the quotation.

"No, don't, for God's sake," he said in agitation which she knew to be real. "Answer me just once, quite straight. Do you think I would tell you a deliberate untruth?"

"Why should you? Please set me down——"

"In a moment. This is awfully important. Listen just a second. I have never told you anything yet that isn't—quite—true. Do you believe me?"

There was an appeal in his voice that shook her. She knew that the fact that he still held her in the crook of his arm shook her also.

"I'll—I'll be far likelier to believe if you set me down and don't bully," said she, still struggling for independence.

He set her down gently upon the rock at his side. "What a little feather-weight you are," he said absently; then caught himself up with a laugh and a glance of fun. "At it again! But you know you really are! You always remind me of the Duchess in the Browning poem—

> *'I have seen a white crane bigger,—*
> *She was the smallest lady alive!'*

I suppose it is your Welsh blood that makes you so small-boned, isn't it?"

"Welsh?" said Olwen in surprise. "How do you know that I am Welsh? I never told you!"

He coloured suddenly and deeply, and for a moment floundered. "Oh, but didn't you tell Madam? No? Then it must have been your name. Anyone would guess you to be Welsh with such a name as Olwen."

"It is rather a give-away," said she, wondering a little at his confusion, but attributing it to his realisation of the fact that his remark amounted to an admission of his having thought a good deal about her. "I'm not so very short," said she with dignity.

He had taken out a handkerchief, and was wiping her hands—those hands upon which Sunia bestowed such care —first one and then the other in an absorbed way, as if he disliked the least hint of earth upon them. "You haven't answered me," he said after a minute; "but you do believe me you know, only you don't like to say so."

"How many times am I to tell you that I don't have any opinion about you? You're outside my scheme of the universe altogether."

"That," said he, as he rose and helped her up, "is the merest piffle, as, of course, you know. Come along if you want to see the old mile-castle. It isn't much to look at. When the weather gets better we'll go to Housesteads, and I'll show you the stone sills of the gateway, worn away with the driving in and out of chariot wheels which were no more than a hoary legend to William the Conqueror's Normans."

"Oh, isn't it incredible?" she sighed. "The wonderful world!"

"Hallo!" said he, stopping abruptly, and shading his eyes with his hand. "Is this a snowstorm that I see before me? Gee whiz, we have got to be quick!"

"What do you mean? Oh, those clouds? Why, it will be ages before they get anywhere near us."

"Don't you be so cock-sure! What a fool I was not to look at the barometer this morning! If I know my weather, it is snowing like Billy-o at this moment in the Cheviots."

"Well, I don't know how Billy-o does snow, so I'm not impressed. I see a great broad worm wriggling up over the top of this height, and slithering off down the other side, and I believe, I do believe it is the Wall itself! My Wall!"

"Oh, Wall, oh, Wall, oh, sweet and lovely Wall!" echoed Nin with a shout of laughter. "Yes, there it is, right enough, and we can run along the top of it if you like."

In another few minutes they were both on the top, running fleetly along, and gazing down at the vast natural rampart upon which great Rome founded her artificial one.

"You'll have to do with the merest peep, my lady, and then I march you off home," cried Nin as they raced along. "What a goat I was to tell you anything about it! There's nothing to see."

"Just to set my foot within the threshold and feel like Macaulay's New Zealander on the ruins of London Bridge —'Rome shall perish! Write that word in the blood that she has spilt!'—and now Rome is gone, and we are here."

"Yes," he replied, "we're here, and thank God for that!"

They paused, for they had reached the small quadrangular enclosure which had once been a mile-castle. Here the proprietors had set up a bit of iron rail, designed probably to deter visitors from the favourite pursuit of walking upon the wall itself—a process leading to gradual disintegration. They let themselves down into the castle, and stood within its boundaries.

The site had been carefully excavated, and its dimensions and plan could be clearly seen. It had once been divided, like the upper floors of the Pele, into four small chambers, each about twelve feet square. Its northern face was built against the Wall itself, and there had been a gateway leading through, designed for foot passengers only. On the south side also there had been a doorway, not very wide. In the southwest corner the farmer who now owned it had built up a small shed or shelter, using stones collected from along the Wall, and roofing with corrugated iron.

Olwen was anxious to linger and make mind-pictures of the garrison seated round their charcoal brazier, throwing dice, as once they did in Palestine at the foot of the Cross. He began to describe to her the rows of wooden huts and booths which grew up in those old days under the sheltering Wall, forming as it were one long town from east to west.

"So that one could buy tooth-brushes and writing-paper and, I suppose, postage stamps, without travelling to Hexham or Newcastle," said she mirthfully.

Then he glanced once more at the menacing north, and urged her—

"Come! For us to-day as for the old legions then, trouble cometh out of the north. Let us get down from these dizzy heights and make our way across the fell to the road. I don't want to be caught by the snow up here."

He was turning in a different direction, but she cried out that they had better go down the short way. He hesitated: "It's a bit steep down there for you."

"But it's much, much shorter."

He admitted it.

"Then let us scramble down as fast as we can. You go first, and then you can find nice holes for my feet."

After a moment's doubt he gave in, and they retraced their steps to the place where they had made the ascent of Duke's Crag. For some way down all went well, though Ninian was a little anxious, having realised, by the slipping of a jutting bit of rock beneath his hand, how keenly the late tremendous frost had acted upon the somewhat loose and scaly surface.

"Look out, Teacher, it came off in me 'and," said he lightly; and it occurred to Olwen for the first time that she now understood that nervousness always made him flippant.

Perhaps her success so far had made the inexperienced girl a little reckless. She set her foot carelessly, the ledge upon which she dropped her weight gave, and she slipped, grasping with a sudden jerk at a projecting lump above her head. The lump detached itself with a crack like a pistol shot, and came down upon her, flinging her upon Ninian, who, just below, had fortunately braced himself firmly to withstand the shock.

The loosened rock rushed on, leaping down the slope, and he heard it crash dully upon the ice below.

"You clumsy little——" he began.

Olwen neither moved nor spoke. Her head was hanging over his shoulder, her limbs seemed to trail helplessly.

"Speak!" he said chokingly. There was no answer.

CHAPTER XXII

OLWEN opened her eyes. She was lying full length upon the ground, and it was very dark. She could smell damp earth, and for a minute she thought she was dead and buried. Her head swam and ached, but she could move her hands, and she began cautiously to feel about her. There was a coat under her, and some kind of pillow supported her head: but she was very cold. She shivered, and felt deadly sick. What had happened?

"Mr. Guyse!" she called sharply, and when nobody answered she cried out aloud in terror.

All was very still, she could not hear a sound. With a dreadful effort she sat upright, and putting up her hand to her head, found that it was bandaged. So dizzy did the exertion make her that she leaned sideways, unable to sit erect. Her sore head found itself in contact with rough stone. She gasped, in pain and fear—fear of the black, lonely silence. Leaning so, she wept a while, helplessly, then made an attempt to rise, but was forced to lie down again abruptly.

A hammer was beating in her brain, thump, thump, thump. It impeded thought. All attempt to remember how she came to be in her present plight failed. With the feeling that she was hopelessly defeated, that she could not struggle with pitiless circumstances, she lay down again and sobbed weakly, the tears rolling down undried, since she had searched her pockets in vain for the handkerchief which should have been there.

Just as she was wondering how much longer she could bear her misery, she heard a slight sound, like the lifting of a latch. Then came breathing and a footstep. "Ninian!" she cried, affrighted.

"All right, I'm here," was the reply, and her relief took the form of a new burst of blinding tears.

She heard him moving vaguely, cautiously, but could see nothing. He seemed to be putting something down on the ground. Then she felt him approach. Now he was crouching at her side. There came the scrape of a match, and its flicker showed her his haggard face.

"Well, you're alive," he said, "and that's something, you know."

She struggled to keep back the tears. "Where—where are we?" she managed to articulate. His grin somehow reassured her.

"Where you were so anxious to find yourself—in the mile-castle," he replied.

The match died away, and again utter darkness fell. She had glimpsed the narrow confines of the shelter which covered them.

"I expect you feel pretty bad?" His voice sounded anxiously beside her.

"Yes—no. Don't ask me," she sobbed. "I'm such a silly—fool—I can't help it. I'll—stop in a minute."

"Of course," he said, "I know. Never mind. We shall do fine. I'm sure I've done the right thing. We're safe inside the only shelter I know of within three miles; but the snow and the dark are both upon us. Poor little girl!"

"N-never mind. It can't be helped! I shall feel better presently."

"Sure thing. Meanwhile——" he had found her hand and held it. "You are as cold as a stone."

She shuddered as she answered "Yes."

"The trouble is that I can't light a fire. The silly blighter who designed this mansion built it without a chimney. I've been out in search of fuel. No wood to be found, nothing but dead grass, bracken and thorns. It's a bit damp and would smoke us out, I'm afraid, if I ventured to light it."

"Oh, but we can go on—soon. When I feel—able."

"Nothin' doin'. You could no more walk three miles against this storm than you could fly, in your present plight. And in spite of what I said about your feather-weight, I couldn't carry you—at least not till I've had a good rest. It was as much as I could do to get you up here. I don't know how I did it!"

"Tell me," she answered faintly; but he replied:

"Presently, when you're a bit more recovered. Now I've got a drop of comfort. Sunia put a thermos flask full of hot tea into my rucksack. I am going to give you a cup of that, which will warm you a bit. I have my electric torch in my pocket, but I fear it won't last long. I know it needs recharging. Let me give you a hot drink, cover you up as warmly as I can, and then I'll try and make Wade's road to the south. I might, perhaps, find the Twice-Brewed Inn with luck."

She cried out vehemently. "Oh, no, no! I don't think I could bear to be left. Don't go! Don't go! You would not be able to find your way in this storm, and—and if you were lost nobody would ever find me, or know where I am, would they?"

He was silent. He knew that for him to wander out into the now impenetrable darkness, with the storm rising every moment, would be a mad venture. He had suggested it half because he thought she might expect it of him, or at least, that she might feel more at ease if he were not there. It was an awkward situation, but fortunately for the man, she left him in no doubt as to her own feelings in the matter. Her hands were clutching his coat, he could feel the rigors that shook her slight body.

"Don't be angry with me, but you mustn't go! Oh, *please* don't go unless—unless you think it is horrid of me; do what you yourself think will be best! I don't want to be unrea-rea-reasonable."

He took the groping hands and held them firmly. "To tell you the truth," he said quietly, "I believe that the best chance for you and me to come through this night alive is for us to stay together. At least we are in shelter, and if the snow gets piled up around the walls we shall be more sheltered still. We have some wraps, and if two people huddle closely together they are twice as warm as one would be alone."

"You r-really think so? You are not s-saying so just to pacify me?"

"I really think so, you poor kiddie. Now I am going to give you that tea, and we will have a few minutes' light upon the subject."

He fixed his torch, and set it down upon the ground while he found his rucksack and took out a cup and the thermos flask. Olwen was so unnerved that he had to hold the cup to her lips; but when once she tasted the tea, its effect was almost instantaneous.

"Ah, how good! How good!" she murmured. "Now you have some, too."

"Oh, I don't want the muck," said he. "Tea's not my line, you know. I wish I had a brandy flask here, though."

However, she would not allow him to go without the hot drink he so urgently required. She would take no excuse, and he saw that to refuse would be to distress her cruelly. He made a bargain, however. He would drink if she would eat a sponge cake. To this she agreed, but found she had promised more than she could perform.

He was glad to finish a few sandwiches which they had
left from lunch, and found himself feeling a little less
fagged when he had done so.

Their refuge contained nothing except a few sheets of
corrugated iron standing up against the wall, one or two
hurdles, and a heap of sand in one corner. The sand was
dry and soft.

The snow without had already stopped the whistling
draught which had entered under the door. A hiatus between the walls and the roof let in plenty of air for venti-
lation. He put on his coat, which he had taken off to
cover Olwen when he went out to look for fuel. Then
he unrolled her own rain-coat, which had been pillowing
her head, and wrapped her in it, taking his own overcoat
up from the floor whereon he had spread it. Next he
arranged some of the sand as a sitting-place for himself,
with the main heap against his left elbow, to serve as a
support. On this heap he set his electric torch, within
hand's reach. Then he raised the exhausted girl from
the ground, and carefully sat down with her in his arms,
the arm which pillowed her head resting on the sandbank.
He covered her feet with the grass and bracken he had
brought in, and drew his own overcoat right over them
both. She lay as though in a cradle, and as his back was
supported against the wall behind, and he had arranged
the hurdles so that his drawn-up knees would not slip, he
felt that he could maintain his position for a long time
without too much discomfort.

She gave a little sighing gasp as he settled her gently
in his arms. She had closed her eyes, for her feelings
overwhelmed her. He thought her either asleep or unconscious.

With a premonition that, as the night wore on, he might
need light more than he needed it now, he switched off
his torch. The black stillness enfolded the two of them.

This time, however, it was not the horrible silence of desertion to Olwen, for she could feel the pumping of that vigorous and healthy organ which Ninian called his heart, very near her own ear.

For a considerable while they sat in silence, while by degrees a blessed warmth stole over the shivering girl. There was something most consoling in the close contact. Either the hot tea, or the wrappings, or the current of sympathy flowing between the two, was soothing the pain in her head, and making her feel more like herself. Her voice, coming from the engulfing darkness, made him start.

"I am remembering," she said. "A bit of rock came down . . . and I fell. But we are not down, but *up!*— I don't understand! How could you possibly get me up here?"

He laughed. "Ask me an easier one. I simply don't know. I clung there like a stuck pig for a time, which seemed like an hour to me, with you hanging across my shoulder like a sack of coals. You were completely unconscious, and I was so panic-stricken that I believe I laughed out loud and long. However, after a time it occurred to me that I had better get a move on, and my mind began to work in a funny, jerky fashion. First I thought it would be much easier to get down than up, and instinctively I acted on that belief, and went down a step or two, in order to do which I had to move a little to one side. Then I looked below, and caught a peep of the ice. The rock you sent down had broken it to shivers, just exactly at the place where I should have to step. I know the lake is forty feet deep there, and I thought if you and I dropped in, that would just about finish us. Then I began to calculate the chances of getting to any kind of shelter before it grew dark or the snow came. I couldn't think of any blessed plan. Hotwells Farm is the nearest, and it is three miles if it's a step. All at once I remembered this little cubby hole, and I thought 'If I can only get her there I can at least lay her down while I run and fetch help.' "

"Oh, I'm so sorry," wailed a sad little voice from the regions of his waistcoat.

"Why are you sorry? Because I thought of this place?"

"No, but because it was my fault we went down the cliff. You wanted to go round."

"Shucks! How could you know the perishing old rock would punch you on the head? Well, when I thought of this place I saw that it was my one chance; but it meant going up and not down. Then it dawned upon my fuddle brains that I was much nearer the top than the bottom; and looking up from where I then stood I could see, almost as though it had been made on purpose for me, a kind of a goat path, running up sideways. Providentially, you had draped yourself around me just in the handiest way, so I set out. . . . I tell you it was nasty. I shall be surprised if they give me anything much worse to do in hell than that journey. I had to stop and rearrange myself and you afresh after every step. I had to crawl on hands and knees. I had to keep wiping the perspiration out of my eyes; and the blood from your head kept dripping down on the stones as I crawled and crept, with one arm to steady you and one arm and two legs to haul with. Two or three times I said to myself, 'You're done in at last.' But I wasn't. I got to the top one day, I think it was about two months after I started, and I laid you down."

He stopped. His breath was coming very quickly, and the arms that held her under the big coat tightened their grip. "Forgive me," he stammered.

"Forgive you?" she whispered, faintly interrogative.

"I acted the fool," he muttered. "You see, I thought you were dead. You looked so absurdly young and—somehow pitiful. Your mouth was like a baby's mouth, and the blood was oozing and bubbling among that stunning hair of yours. Instead of setting to work there and then to bind it up, I——"

"Well?"

"Oh—er—it doesn't matter. Only I wasted time. By the time I came to my senses I knew that you were alive all right, and I found my hankie and your own and tied you up as best I could. Then I picked you up again, and just as I did so the snow began to fall. I was able to walk under the lee of the wall, but it—it seemed a long way; and gradually it got dark. I thought you must have concussion of the brain, at least; and there was nothing in this beastly place when we got here that would be any kind of help."

"I'm ever so much obliged to you," she said tremulously.

"You don't know what a relief it was to hear you talking sensibly when I came back to you."

"You don't know how awful it was to wake up and find myself all alone."

"Are you getting any warmer, do you think?"

"Oh, much. I'm quite comfy."

"And you've answered that question you wouldn't answer up on the cliff!"

"What question?"

"I asked you if you trusted me. And you do, don't you, you ripping little stunner?"

A gurgle of laughter came from the gloom. "Well," she said sleepily, "it ought to be a great satisfaction to you—after all the trouble I've taken with your education —to be able to repay me by just saving my life."

"Humph! Some people would say I had endangered

it. Odd, isn't it, and a bit awful to think about, how things happen all in a moment?"

"Yes, it is very queer, but I don't want to think. My head does throb so. Instead of that, I want you to amuse me. You said the other day that you could say a lot of Shakespeare by heart. I should like you to repeat some."

"But this is so sudden," he pleaded, with a twist in his voice which made her laugh in spite of all.

"But I want to hear you."

"Very well, Teacher."

"If I go to sleep in the middle, you won't mind?"

"No, Teacher."

"By the by, one thing I must ask you first. Will Madam be very anxious?"

"No, I don't think so. She will know we could not get home in this storm, and will think we have stayed the night at Hotwells Farm."

There was a long sigh. "I wish you hadn't tempted me to come to-day," she lamented.

"It's no use crying over spilt milk, my porcelain rogue."

"Ah, forgive me, I didn't want to seem to reproach you. You are being so good. No one could be kinder. Yes, Nin," with a sinking voice, "I do trust you—I do believe you in spite of—what they say."

She felt his arms once more tighten their hold, and he made an impetuous movement as if he stooped forward and down; then he straightened himself suddenly, and, after a tense silence, dashed into "Much Ado About Nothing."

CHAPTER XXIII

WHAT THE DAWN BROUGHT

WHEN our lives come to be written in their true proportion, it will be found that in some cases a year has passed like a watch in the night, while some nights have lasted for years. This is why the realistic novelists, who take pages to describe how a girl took a taper out of the sideboard drawer and lit the gas, are so pitifully mistaken. When a good cook takes a cabbage to cook for the pot, her first action is to strip and throw away the outer leaves, as of no value. The realist seems to deal only with these outer leaves. He does not hold that any cabbage is ever cooked, or, if it is, then it was not worth the cooking. Life, in his estimation, consists in the perpetual stripping of outer leaves.

The night in the mile-castle marked an extraordinary epoch to Olwen Innes. When she looked back to it she felt that had not her senses been so bemused there were certain deductions she must have drawn, certain conclusions at which she must have arrived.

As a matter of fact, all these things escaped her at the time, she being in no state to reason. Yet the impressions left by what then happened to her were so deep that afterwards she was able to think out the whole thing justly.

There were periods during that long waiting when her temperature rose, and she chattered a little deliriously. There were moments when she grew cold and sick, and shivering fits assailed her. Again there were merciful interludes, during which she slumbered heavily. In all these phases Ninian Guyse was close at hand to lay her down, to ease her posture, to chafe her cold hands, to hold her close in his efforts to keep life in her.

She did not know how, in course of those dreadful hours, he parted by degrees with quite half his clothing to reinforce her flickering vitality. She had longish periods of something that was half sleep, half stupor, and during these he rested. He dare not risk allowing their carefully cultivated warmth to escape by opening the door until the last moment, when they must make their final dash.

After what seemed to her an endless period of darkness and pain and ever-increasing discomfort, she felt that he was busily occupied in fitting on her squirrel cap over her bandaged head and wrapping her fur stole about her throat afresh.

"Are you awake? Can you hear what I say?" he was inquiring in a voice of dull patience.

"Oh, what do you want? Let me lie still."

"No, you must get up. See! I have a cup of tea for you, and when you have drunk it you must try to stand and to walk a little. We are going out."

She tried to resist these intentions on his part, feebly whimpering as she pushed away his hands. He held on steadily, repeating in a weary voice: "Sit up; I'll hold you. You *can* sit up if you try. There! Is that all right? Now you must eat this before I give you the tea. Come, be a brave girl! Pull yourself together. We're not dead yet!"

With a start she awoke to fuller consciousness. She was sitting on the ground, propped against Ninian, and his electric torch shed a light upon them both. She was past wondering whence came the tea or the bit of stale sponge-cake which he put into her mouth as though she were a young cuckoo. She wanted the tea so desperately that she ate as he commanded. Then came the drink. Having been kept all night it was barely lukewarm, but it was tea.

When she had finished, her guardian sat quite still for a few minutes, allowing her to recover. Presently her faltering voice uttered some pathetic little thanks.

"Come!" he said. "That's more like you. Now listen. It's six o'clock, and the sun rises before half-past seven. There's a hint of dawn now. The snow has quite stopped falling, and I think we can strike Wade's Road if we make for the south. Hotwells Farm is too far, but there should be a house of sorts within a mile or rather more from where we are in the opposite direction, and the lie of the ground is easier; it's down hill. Our only chance is to get there somehow. The movement will keep us warm. Are you game?"

"I'll do whatever you tell me," came faintly. "I'm sorry to be such—a pig."

A slight pressure of the arm which held her accepted her apology. "All right; then I'm going to lift you to your feet. It's just high enough in here for us to stand up."

He suited the action to the word. Two or three billiard balls, which had been floating about in her head all night, clashed together with a horrid shock. She hung limp against Ninian while she waited for the resulting tumult to subside. The perpendicular attitude seemed to restore her scattered wits. For the first time pride and a desire to make the best of things awoke within her. Up to that moment she had been too badly hurt to care.

"That's—better," said she clearly. "I—I think I can get along. I'll do my best. You are so good."

"Come on, then," he replied, pushing open the door.

He said nothing to Olwen of his struggle, half an hour earlier, with that same door.

It had taken him twenty minutes to force it wide enough for his arm and stick to operate upon the drift without: in fact, there had been a moment during which he had feared that the weight was too great for him to move alone. In the end, however, he had succeeded in cutting a path out through the doorway of the mile-castle, inside which the snow had piled itself.

Outside there was a more or less uniform depth of something more than a foot. Before them, as they faced south, the cliff, so precipitous on its northern face, sloped gently downwards to the level of the old coaching road that runs from Carlisle to Newcastle, and is, of late years, almost deserted.

Not only was there a glimmer of dawn in the east, but a belated moon hung over this white and lonely world. They could see quite well enough to make progress possible, but the distance was hidden. Ninian wanted to descry a house, that they might make a beeline for it, but they could see nothing in all the snowy wilderness. At last the girl spoke.

"Do you see that black little grove of trees to our right, lower down, not quite so far as the road, I should think?"

"Yes, I see where you mean."

"Isn't there something light against the black trees that looks like a line of smoke going up?"

"Jove, the porcelain rogue has done it! That's smoke right enough. They're astir early enough over there. Cheer-o, partner! We can hit that clump of trees without having to take such a very steady aim. Better keep along the top for a bit, in the lee of the wall; the snow is not half so thick there as it is just beyond."

They started off, and for the first few minutes the

stimulus of the tea and the sting of the high air revived Olwen surprisingly.

"What a blessing our coats hide some of the havoc!" observed Ninian, who upheld her by her arm. "I am nothing but rags underneath, and as to you the less said the better; you are in a ghastly mess, and I don't see how I can so much as wipe your face for you."

"Is it all over blood?" she asked, with such strong distaste that he began to turn over in his mind the possibility of wiping it for her. Their handkerchiefs had all been requisitioned for bandaging, and he would not allow her to cut up her clothes. After reflection, he found a convenient boulder, brushed the snow from it, and seated her thereon. Then, without announcing his intention, he cut away a bit of the sleeve of his flannel shirt. Having put a little snow into the tin cup, he thawed it by holding lighted matches under it.

Then he sat down, propped her head against his shoulder, and washed the poor soiled little face with the water thus obtained, teasing her softly the while with uncomplimentary remarks upon her features, such as a brother might have made.

"Oh, thank you, thank you," she sighed. "You really are a dear. You are good to me."

He made a queer little sound that was almost like a groan. Looking up quickly, she surprised in his face an expression of misery which was unlike any look he had worn before. His eyes met hers in a beseeching sort of way, and he put up his hand to her face as if to hold her head closer or to prevent her looking at him. Then he uttered this unlooked-for aspiration:

"I wish to God I had never seen you!"

At the time the words sounded incredible, but on thinking it over afterwards she was sure that he had used them. She felt too stupid, however, to ask him to explain. They sat silent for a minute, then arose and continued their difficult pilgrimage.

When they thought themselves close to the house they were stalking they had a disappointment. They came to one of those abrupt gaps in the cliff, up and down which the Roman builders carried their wall without flinching. This particular gap is extremely precipitous, and getting down was a long and difficult job. By the time it was accomplished, and they found themselves in a boulder-strewn field, they could see the house plainly.

"Oh, this is Hazel Crag, where old Abraham Bird lives," said Ninian hopefully. "He is the oldest inhabitant—must be ninety or more. He has a daughter, a sprightly young thing of seventy or so, who looks after him. The old girl gets up bright and early, doesn't she? Anyway, she has a good fire, and you can rest here and be warm till I bring the trap for you."

She smiled wanly, for she was sick with pain. "Do I look so very awful?" she asked with a truly feminine shrinking.

"I don't think old Mrs. Barcombe can see what you look like," he replied encouragingly; "but, in any case, I've washed your face for you. Now, a long pull and a strong pull, and we'll be in harbour in quite a few minutes. We shall beat the sun, I do declare!"

Slithering and wading through the loose snow, they reached the door of the farm-kitchen. The blind was drawn, and a glow of lamplight and firelight showed through it. As they stood awaiting an answer to their knock, the girl turned her pain-dimmed eyes upon the drear, inhospitable world wherein they had been so nearly lost.

A faint glimmer, premonition only of daylight, showed vague whiteness, mist, black trunks of trees that stood motionless at gaze in the now windless air.

It was like the vision of a clairvoyant, not a moment in actual existence. The girl's weariness and pain were interpenetrated by a strange new thrill, born perhaps of the contact of Ninian's closely folded arm.

"The call of the north," she said to herself, "Sunia is really a witch. This is where I belong."

The sound of a bolt being drawn from within made her turn quickly. The door was thrown widely open, and Dr. Balmayne confronted them.

The revulsion of feeling in Olwen, caused by his presence and his look, cannot be put into words. He had his usual aspect of well-groomed neatness. His blue eyes rested upon the couple outside, first with the blank stare of non-recognition, then with a depth of amazement which was in itself a condemnation.

"Well," said Ninian easily, "I do have the devil's own luck. Out of all the world you are the man we want at this moment, Balmayne. Miss Innes has had an accident."

"So I see," said Balmayne mechanically, speaking like a man overwhelmed.

"I've come to ask old Abe for hospitality while I go and fetch the sleigh and take her home," said Ninian, as he led the girl into the warm kitchen where the fire blazed gloriously, seated her in a cavernous chair and, kneeling before her, began swiftly to unlace her wet boots.

"Old Abe died about an hour ago," said Balmayne, standing aside with stony countenance.

Ninian stopped short with a start, then resumed his ordinary manner. "That so? I suppose you've been up all night?"

"I came last night and couldn't get back."

"The storm was sudden," said Ninian calmly. He rose to his feet, strode out of the room, and called up the stairs:

"Mrs. Barcombe! Mrs. Barcombe!"

"Why, who be you?" said a quavering voice from above.

"Guyse of the Pele. I got snowed up on the fell, and I've brought a young lady here. She had an accident. May I leave her in your kitchen while I go and get the sleigh to drive her home?"

"I'll be doon verra soon, Mr. Guyse. I'm joost a-putting the pennies upon his eyes. Poor old feyther, he do make a handsome corp, for sure he do."

"He was a fine man, Mrs. Barcombe. God rest his soul. Well, may the young lady stay?"

"Oo ay, she may bide if she will. She ain't your sweetheart, Mr. Guyse—eh?"

"Why, what makes you ask that?"

"You shouldna bring your sweetheart into the house wi' a corp in it or she'll never wed you."

"I'll have to risk it, old lady. You come down and get the doctor some hot water and clean rags, will you?"

During this colloquy Olwen had sat with eyes closed, and the doctor stood staring upon her as though he had been turned to stone. As the talk went on he saw the girl shrink and wince; and when Ninian came back into the room she was sitting up, holding the arms of her chair, shivering and shedding tears.

"What is it? You're not afraid to stay, are you?" cried he explosively, going to her side.

"Miss Innes has no alternative," put in the doctor curtly. "She is not in a condition to talk; in fact I doubt if she ought to be moved at all. I shall be able to judge better when I have examined her injury." He came a little nearer and stood looking at her. "How did it happen?"

"Just by accident—the frost——" she began, and Ninian cut in.

"Never mind how it happened; the thing is to get it

mended as soon as we can. I'm afraid it's pretty bad, but she's so plucky."

Balmayne's lip curled. "Mr. Guyse has singularly bad luck with the young ladies who come to stay at the Pele," said he, as if he could not resist the temptation to see Ninian writhe.

The culprit did no such thing. He stood there in the centre of the kitchen, as great a contrast to the other man as could be conceived.

He was so dark that to go one night unshorn made a ruffian of him; and his cut hands, torn clothes and tousled hair, joined to the fact that his cheek was green and blue with a severe bruise, and that there were flecks of blood about him, made him seem as unsuitable a companion for a night's adventure upon the fells as any poor girl could have been afflicted with.

He kept his self-possession, however. He had just caught sight of his reflection in the dim little mirror above the high chimney-piece, and he grinned as he sleeked his black head with both dirty hands.

"I'll leave her in your charge, doctor," said he easily. "Do all you can for her, and if the time hangs heavy before I get back, you can always amuse yourself by taking away the last shreds of my character."

For a moment he stooped over the girl. "Keep up your spirit," he murmured. "Think of home, and Sunia, and nice white bed-clothes."

She gave him a wan little smile; but the force she had put upon herself to enable her to reach the farm had left her spent. She was within measurable distance of complete collapse.

The moment the door closed behind Guyse, Balmayne went into the adjoining parlour and wheeled out a long horsehair couch. Giving rapid directions to old Mrs. Barcombe, who had come downstairs by this time, he secured enough pillows to enable him to lay the girl down easily. In a few minutes he had a hot-water bottle at her feet, and having warmed a little milk in a saucepan, added a tablespoonful of brandy and made her drink it before commencing his operations.

The removal of Nin's bandages revealed a more serious wound than he had anticipated. Investigation proved it to be superficial, but it was extensive enough to need a good many stitches. As a matter of fact, the fur cap which the girl wore had deflected the course of the descending rock, and probably saved her life by causing it to strike obliquely. A bit of the scalp had been torn quite away from the bone, which was itself slightly scratched, but not cracked, as he ascertained with relief.

She was so exhausted that she lay almost torpid under his handling, and he accomplished the painful business of sterilising and sewing up the wound with no greater sign of suffering than a few moans. It took him some time to unfasten her hair, and it was with real regret that he found himself obliged to cut away a long, thick tress to clear the ground for his operations.

When the job was done, and he had adjusted the lint, steeped in antiseptic lotion, with skilfully folded roller bandages, he gave her more milk and brandy. To his astonishment she had very little fever, but he expected considerable reaction that night when the effects of the shock became more manifest.

He covered her warmly and went away, leaving her to herself while he washed his implements in the scullery.

When he came back her eyes were open, and she murmured a few words of thanks.

"Is the pain in the head less?"

"Oh, much less."

"You must have fallen a considerable distance."

"I did not fall."

"No?"

"The frost had made the rock dangerous. We were climbing . . . Duke's Crag. A bit of rock broke loose and fell upon me."

"This, I conclude, happened yesterday?"

"Yes."

"Would it be impertinent to ask where you have passed the night?"

"In the mile-castle. There is a little hut there. I was unconscious, and the snow came on. We could not get home."

"It seems incredible that Guyse should take you to such a place on foot at such a time of year."

"We went to skate."

"Indeed! Does Guyse usually skate up the face of a cliff?"

She smiled a little. "It was my fault we went up. I wanted to see the Roman Wall."

He made no reply, gazing into the fire and wondering what he ought to say or refrain from saying.

Her voice was heard after a long pause. "It can hardly be necessary for me to assure you that our being out last night in such a way was sheer accident."

With a start he made some confused apologies. "I am perhaps intrusive in saying even so much," he concluded, "but I wish it had not happened—not with that man."

"I might have agreed with you . . . yesterday," she whispered faintly.

He flashed a keen look. "Yesterday?"

"But this morning I think . . . I am sure . . . there could not be a more perfect companion than Mr. Guyse for such an uncomfortable adventure."

To this he made no reply for some time, but at last, as if he could not withhold the comment, he remarked, "A man would have to be triply a brute had he been otherwise than considerate when you were so badly hurt."

She had no reply to make, and they sat on silently in the warm kitchen. Old Mrs. Barcombe trudged to and fro with deep sighs and some audible speculation as to the difficulty of getting the "corp" to the churchyard in such weather. She invited the girl to go upstairs and have a look at "feyther," an invitation which the doctor hastily explained that the young lady was far too ill to accept.

After an interval, when they had the kitchen to themselves, he said quietly, "Am I to conclude that you intend to remain at the Pele ?"

"Why not ?" she asked in sudden alarm. "What do you mean ?"

A sound without had taken him to the window, and he turned with a grave face and the news that Mr. Guyse had already returned with the sleigh.

"Oh, I expect he met Ezra come to fetch us," cried Olwen quite eagerly. "Is he—the man—there too ?"

"Yes, fortunately," replied Balmayne coldly, as he turned to her and began to wrap up her feet in a voluminous red flannel petticoat belonging to Mrs. Barcombe and to secure this swaddling with a bit of string.

By the time that Ninian entered the room he had wrapped her, head and all, in a huge plaid; and without a word he lifted her in his arms and stood looking at the other man across his burden.

"I conclude you will start for home at once ?" he said. "If so, I will put Miss Innes in the sleigh. Not a moment should be lost in getting her to bed. I have not written a prescription for her, because it is not possible for you to have it made up. I will come myself this evening and bring it with me. Meanwhile, ask Mrs. Guyse to give her some nitre, if she has any, to keep her warm, and

let her have hot milky food—nothing else until I see her
again."

So saying, he bore Olwen out of the room and the
house, leaving Guyse to take farewell of Mrs. Barcombe
and remunerate her for her services.

This was quickly done, and as Ninian was snatching
up his cap from the table to hurry out and see how the
patient was bestowed he saw lying across the table a
gleaming tress of hair. The bulk looked soft, misty
brown, but all the tips, which stood up and glittered in
the light, were burnished gold. He took it up, folded it
with care, and bestowed it in an inner pocket. Then he
walked out of the door with a devil-may-care smile, and
noted with a curl of the lip that Balmayne had laid
the patient right across the front seat, so that he would
have not only to sit behind with Ezra, but to drive from
that inconvenient position. However, he had the justice
to admit that if Miss Innes had to lie down this was the
only plan. His own, of holding her upon his knees,
would, in his mind, have been immensely preferable.

CHAPTER XXIV

But little recollection of the drive remained afterwards in Olwen's memory. She could recall only the moment when Ninian pulled back the folds of the enveloping plaid, lifted her and bore her into the Pele. The strait dimensions of the newel stair compelled him to carry her upright, and the pain of her head, thus unsupported, was severe.

There followed only a confused impression of Sunia's sympathetic hands, of being undressed, tended and laid in bed. After this nothing definite for several days.

The reaction, which Dr. Balmayne had anticipated, supervened. That night her temperature rose, and for some days she alternated between delirium and weakness. Her youthful strength, however, very soon triumphed. There was no symptom of pneumonia or any other bad result from her exposure. Her wound healed cleanly and rapidly, and on the morning of the fourth day after the accident she awoke to a normal state of things.

The room was warm with fire and gay with sunshine. Her head no longer ached, and her mind worked clearly. Sunia, as usual, squatted upon the hearth.

"Oh, Sunia," she said suddenly, "what trouble I have given!"

The Hindu rose and came to the bedside with a pleased face. "Come! Missee get back herself," said she cooingly. "All right, so long as she get well quick."

"I am well. I shall ask the doctor to let me get up to-day."

The ayah's face darkened a little at mention of the doctor. "Humph! First ting you speak of doctor sahib," said she. "He not care how long Missee stay in bed, he allowed come up and see her. English way—bad English way. My country, no let pretty doctor see mem-sahibs."

Olwen smiled at the old woman's talk. "There is so much news I want to hear," she said. "You must tell me all about everything. First, was Madam very vexed with us? Was she very anxious when we did not come home that night?"

The ayah glanced at her sidelong. "Um—yes. She wonder if you safe and warm. She think you stop in the farm all a night."

"We hoped she would think that. Now about Mr. Guyse. I hope he was not ill afterwards?" She spoke as unconcernedly as she could, turning away her head.

"He get shocking bad cold. Been two days in his bed. Better now," said Sunia, watching as keenly as a bird the colour that would flicker over the averted cheek at the mention of Ninian's name.

"I am sorry. He was very good to me all that night. I should have frozen to death if he had not kept me warm."

"With a clothes off his back," replied the ayah.

"Yes. Now about my own people. Did Madam write to my home, do you know, Sunia?"

"No, Madam not write. She not know what best to say. Think Missee better write her own self, Doctor say, don't frighten 'em, Missee all better in a little few days."

Olwen felt grateful. Now that memory was coming back she felt a keen desire that the whole of her adventure should not be known in Bramforth.

The intensity of this desire lit up the episode in an

ugly light. She knew full well that she ought not to
have set forth upon a day's lonely expedition with Ninian,
completely unchaperoned. She recalled the things she
had written concerning him to Gracie. Yet she had
accepted him as sole escort during the whole of a day, a
favour she would never have dreamed of according to
Ben, who was a dozen times more reliable. She was
greatly to blame, and had a lively consciousness that this
was so. The resulting disaster had been an accident; but
such an accident ought not to have been possible had she
been as circumspect as her grandfather and aunts would
expect of her.

And now, what came next?

Her mind held two distinct ideas, and they fronted
her like danger-boards. She heard Ninian's voice, saying, far more earnestly than she had ever heard him speak,
"I wish to God I had never seen you." . . . And she
saw Balmayne's grave, kind face, his anxious expression,
as he said, "I wish it had not happened—not with that
man!" . . . and woven into both these thoughts was a
wild thrill, a stir of the heart, a nameless sweetness which
she could not banish.

She was hovering once more in the tangle of doubt
and fear in which Sunia's attempt to administer the love
potion had cast her. She felt afraid to face Madam or
Ninian. Madam had not been to see her at all, and she
could not help knowing that most people in Madam's place
would feel considerable annoyance at such an escapade on
the part of a girl in her position.

With renewed force the conviction that the Pele was
no place for her asserted itself. But now she fought
against the conviction. She did not want to go—did not
want to leave . . . what or whom?

She glanced at the ayah, knowing full well that those
watchful eyes had discovered her secret.

"Poor Missee," said Sunia pityingly. "Ole Ayah saw it all that night—night before you go skating with the sahib—that you going to be hurt, going to hurt a head. She not say, no good frighten Missee. But ole Ayah never see wrong." She sighed deeply, lifting a little saucepan from the fire, and bringing to the girl a cup of such soup as Mrs. Baxter alone knew how to make.

Her gentleness, her sympathy, were so seductive that Olwen was almost ready to fling her arms round her neck and whisper that she loved the sahib—loved him and trusted him. Almost—not quite. The thought of the philtre stuck in her throat. What would have become of her in her extremity that night in the mile-castle had she swallowed the horrible brew? She shuddered as she thought of it.

She knew that Ayah was waiting there, pleadingly, hopefully, for her to speak again of the sahib—to give her some details of their adventure. This she was determined not to do. In her mind was stirring an uneasy wonder as to what she might have said when she was feverish. She knew that she had talked, for there had been glimpses of sanity during which she had heard her own tongue babbling, and wondered who that was who would go on chattering so disturbingly.

She longed for somebody in whom she might confide. But there was nobody; and she did not intend to write anything like the full story of her accident home to Bramforth.

She asked, presently, for pencil and paper, and wrote a line to Aunt Ada:

"I'm sorry it is so long since I wrote, but I have had a slight accident. It happened when I was skating. I cut my head against a bit of rock. As a result I have had to go to bed for a day or two, but am now well on the mend.

They are extremely kind, and I have a doctor in attendance. Ayah waits on me hand and foot. I am much vexed at being laid up, as you may imagine, and if I don't get well as fast as I hope to do, I shall come home for a week or two. Can write more fully after the doctor's next visit, but mind you don't worry. I am quite all right."

When the doctor arrived that day she was, for the first time, eager to talk.

He sat down at the bedside, and the ayah stood in the background with the air of being blind, deaf and dumb, but, as Olwen knew, alive to every word, every look, every smile that passed between them.

Balmayne was as conscious as she of this fact. He knew also that all the Hindu's ideas of propriety would be outraged were he left alone with his patient; but for all that he meant to have private speech with Miss Innes.

"Sorry to trouble you, Ayah," he said, "but I must ask you to prepare that hot lotion again for me."

The woman rose, looking malevolently at him, listened to his directions, and slipped out through the arras to her own room, where she kept a small cooking-stove.

He followed, and drew back the hangings, saying quietly, "Too much draught through these curtains. I will close the door." He did so, in spite of the gleam of hate in the old woman's eyes, returned to Olwen with a smile, and began his unrolling of the bandages about her head.

"Well, Miss Innes," he said, purposely lowering his voice, "it is strange how things settle themselves, as it were, accidentally. A while ago I was wondering how it would be possible to get you away from this place; and behold! You have decided to break your head and made departure inevitable."

She turned quite pale, as he noted with vexation. "Departure inevitable?" she repeated in a startled voice. "Why?"

"You won't be able to do any work for some time yet. I shall have to order you home, but I thought there was no need to tell the Guyses as much until we came within reasonable distance of the date at which I can allow you to travel."

"And that—when will that be?" she asked faintly.

"Well, let me see. To-day is Saturday. I ought to have these stitches out on Monday or Tuesday. You could travel the day after, or two days after. Yes, you might leave next Wednesday or Thursday."

"But—but I shall be quite well by then," she stammered.

"No. You will have to go quietly for some weeks. No careering on skates or in sleighs." He smiled. She returned no answer, she was most evidently perturbed. "Fresh air," he went on, "is necessary, and the Guyses keep no car. Now that the snow is gone, the only vehicle you could use is that dog-cart, which is most unsuitable."

She laughed a little bitterly. "Do you think my grandfather keeps a car? You don't seem to understand that I am out to earn my living."

"I am speaking," he said, "in the purest altruism," and he smiled a little ruefully. "Personally I shall be considerably the poorer when you go. But—well, I have sisters of my own, and I know a girl of the right kind when I see her. I tell you, I would not trust a sister of mine in the house with Guyse for a week."

"Yet I have been safely in the house with him for six weeks," she countered swiftly.

He glanced at the bandage on her hair, shrugged his shoulders, and said, "Safely? Perhaps safety is a matter of opinion."

"No, it is a matter of fact," said Olwen, with a shaking voice. "As a fact, I am convinced that Mr. Guyse would do nothing to harm me."

The doctor stood a moment silent, mechanically rolling a bandage between his skilful fingers.

"Well," he said slowly, "I must ask you to pardon my interference. This is the last time I shall speak to you on this subject. It is a very disagreeable duty, and will probably be useless; but I must clear my conscience. Were I in the place of your relatives, I should argue somewhat thus: 'She was young and inexperienced, and as innocent as all good girls. The only person who had a chance to warn her was the doctor. It was up to him to use his medical authority and give her a pretext to slip out of the net.'"

Olwen's colour was brilliant. "But," she expostulated, "if you mean—what you seem to mean—that Mr. Guyse has—bad designs—surely he knows that I am not without a family and friends——"

"He also knows that you are of age," put in the doctor quietly. "I should guess you to be a little over twenty-one——"

"I am twenty-three."

"Just so. Then what remedy has your family? None whatever. Anything they might do would merely make public what they would wish to hide. Abduction is a punishable offence. But this is another matter."

She was outraged. "Oh, Dr. Balmayne, won't you give me credit for *some* self-restraint, *some* modesty? Don't you realise that what you are hinting could never be?"

It was his turn to colour, and he did so. "I am aware that I am risking your friendship, even your toleration, by speaking," he replied steadily. "I do know, of course, that this could never be, except in the one case——"

"In the one case?"

"Of his having succeeded in making you care for him."

In the pulsating silence which followed this remark they heard the door unlatch, and Sunia brought in the bowl of hot lotion.

The doctor took it calmly from her hands, completed his treatment, and presently took his leave. As he wished Olwen good-bye, he added rapidly in French: "*Soyez calme. Je ne vous redirai jamais les choses que j'ai dit aujourd'hui.*"

Nothing at all passed between her and the ayah after the doctor left. All the rest of the day she was meditating upon what he had said. She could not but see that he honestly thought her in danger; and as she pictured to herself the next meeting between herself and the incorrigible Nin, she felt herself falter.

She was no fool. She knew that a girl does not think of a man day and night—even to be in a rage with him—unless he has made a deep impression.

She wondered a good deal that he sent her no written message. Each day Sunia brought an inquiry from Madam and the sahib as to the health and progress of the invalid. This was answered verbally. No note came from the young man. Was he her lover, or not? If he were not, she knew she could not stay. If he were, the doctor thought she ought not to stay.

On the following day, which was Sunday, she sent down a written message on an open morsel of paper: "Please send me up some light fiction."

Half a dozen books came up, but with no message. She would not ask Sunia how Mr. Guyse was, or what he was doing; but as the woman moved about the room, putting it to rights, she remarked: "First day my sahib gone out. He gone spend a day with Kendall-folk. They pleased, I thinking."

"Would not you be pleased, too, to have your sahib married?" asked Olwen boldly, hoping her colour did not change.

"I pray my gods all days for my sahib to marry," was the simple reply, "and that I hold his son in my arms before I die."

Olwen rolled over and pretended to hunt for a handkerchief under her pillow. "Well, I hope you will have your wish," said she tranquilly.

The Hindu woman paused a moment to contemplate the enigma of the European woman's coldness. Olwen nearly laughed, the woman's thoughts was so plainly written in her face. "You must be an inhuman she-creature," was the unspoken word. "I gave you the most potent philtre known to Hindu lore, and still you are unawakened. Still you can talk of his marriage with another woman quietly. I have been mistaken in you."

CHAPTER XXV

On Monday the doctor took out the stitches and gave permission for Olwen to sit up in a chair by the fire. Sunia having been sent away for an extra rug, he turned to his patient, and said abruptly:

"I was almost forgetting! Here is a letter for you. I went into the post office to get your new tonic made up, and Branson said: 'Here's a letter for the young lady at the Pele, and as it's a foreign one, she'll be glad to get it before to-morrow morning, if you're going up, sir."

"A foreign letter?" said Olwen wonderingly. "I wonder who is my correspondent abroad? I know of nobody."

"New York post-mark," said he, handing over the envelope. "Now I must go, for Mrs. Kay's baby is unwell, and I promised Ezra to drive on there. Good-bye."

He had made no reference of any kind to their talk of Saturday.

Olwen held the letter hesitatingly, wondering whether she should open it. Suddenly came a determination not to allow Sunia to know she had had a letter. Repeatedly she had been conscious of a suspicion that all her correspondence was overhauled by the woman—and she was Ninian's spy!

If she knew that Olwen had received a letter, she would probably search for it at the first opportunity. If, on the contrary, she was unaware of its arrival, she would not be anxious to learn its contents.

Although consumed with curiosity, the girl therefore

hid away the foreign envelope, with the name of a hotel in New York printed on the outside. A wonder was faintly stirring within her as to whether by any chance her correspondent could be Lily Martin? That young lady had originally come from America, so Ninian had informed her. She might have returned thither. Were she and he still in touch with one another? Had he mentioned Olwen, and had she determined to send the new love a chapter of the private history of the Guyses?

It was hard to wait in order to ascertain the truth of these exciting conjectures. Yet she forced herself to be patient until the hour at which the ayah went downstairs to wait at table, when she knew she would be undisturbed. Then she drew forth the mysterious missive from the place where she had concealed it, and prepared to satisfy her curiosity.

The first words upon the sheet of paper within brought the blood flowing to her face, and caused her to catch her breath with a low cry of amazement:

"Little daughter of mine, have they allowed you to remember that you have such a thing as a father? He doesn't feel worthy to be called anything so holy, but he exists, and the craving for you, which he has always kept stowed away in a dark corner of his heart, has been lately growing so large that he finds he has room in his life for little else.

"My child, I am actually that which I used to declare myself in church at the time when I didn't believe that I was anything of the kind—a miserable sinner. In my youth I must have been potentially so. For very many years I have been actually so. I have likewise suffered for it. Sometimes I have vague hopes that the suffering and the sin may perhaps, when God adds up the column, balance one against the other. That is probably because of my ignorance and my egoism. God, He knoweth.

"I have lived in such poverty and hardship that I have had to stifle the longing I always felt for you. Now, however, things are a little better. At the cost of health and a good many other things, I have scraped together enough money to bring me back to civilisation, and to prevent me from having to sponge upon the Wilsons.

"Has my daughter any memory of me, any love for me? Duty won't do. I want love for the few, very few remaining years—it may be only months that we might spend together. Knowing what I know of your training, your upbringing, I feel it very doubtful that you can judge of me otherwise than your poor mother was able to do. And yet, in the days when I had you with me—had you, and didn't know what it would be to feel the miss of you—I used to believe that you loved me, as she, poor soul, never did.

"When first I determined to write to you, it was my intention to wait here until I got an answer—until I knew whether there was strong enough reason for me to make the effort of the voyage to England. But last week an attack of illness decided me that there is no time to lose—that, if I want to hold my child in my arms, it is now or never.

"The doctors say I shall be ready to start in a fortnight from now. I have booked my passage on the *Stupendous,* and am due at Liverpool about the tenth of March. If you can give me a welcome, come to the docks. I shall look for you there, and if I do not see you, will drive to the Columbus Hotel. If you are not there, and have sent no message, I shall know that you repudiate the man who for so many years has grossly failed in his duty to you. Don't fear that I shall blame you. All the blame lies on my shoulders. I shall say, as once I said after the verdict in a Court House in the west of Canada, 'The sentence just passed upon me by the court is just.' God bless you.—Your prodigal father,

"MADOC INNES."

At the end of the letter appeared two spirited little sketches. The first, entitled, "My child as I remember her," showed a little girl in very short skirts, with thin black legs and long masses of flying hair. The second, "My child as she probably is now," showed an ultra-fashionable young lady, with hat of the newest tilt, carrying a parasol, yet with a something in her carriage and general aspect which did suggest Olwen.

These little pictures brought tears streaming from the girl's eyes. It was the first time she had sat up by the fire to eat her dinner, and she was still weak. For some time she could not check her weeping, although its cause was chiefly delight.

All unexpectedly Fate had come to the aid of Dr. Balmayne. She would have to leave the Pele now. Her father was to sail a fortnight after the date of his letter. Said letter had been through adventures. It had been sent to Gratfield, her grandfather's old parish, thence to Bramforth, thence to the Pele. He would set sail, as near as she could calculate, in three days' time. She could not reply to his letter, he would be gone long before her answer could reach him. He was due to arrive at Liverpool in about ten days' time. She could just manage it. If she left without notice, she would have to forfeit her second month's salary. No matter. One month's salary would take her to Liverpool and enable her to stay there a night or two until the boat came in.

She surrendered herself to the joy which the thought of her father brought. He had not forgotten her, he had not been heartless. She had often pictured him as settled in some new country, with a new wife, and other children on his knee. She had wronged him there. No one had supplanted her in his heart, ill-regulated though it might be. As soon as he had snatched out of the jaws of adversity enough to prevent his being a burden to her family, he was coming home to claim her. They would be together. Delight surged up in her.

Someone to stand by her, to advise her, to fight her battles! What would he think of Ninian Guyse?

It was curious that the whole affair seemed somehow different when she contemplated it with her father in the background. How little, as a fact, she knew of Ninian Guyse! Dr. Balmayne was a good adviser.

Ah! How splendid, yet how improbable it sounded, that in ten short days she would be in her own father's arms, his most serious object in life, recipient of his whole attention. Her future would be the one thing of all things in the world which would interest him. How glad he would be that she had not married Ben! She laughed out in her glee, and was so lost to all sense of time and place that she very nearly allowed the ayah to surprise her with the letter in her hand. A slight noise behind the arras was the only thing which saved her.

Sunia was in silent mood that night. She put the girl to bed almost grimly. Olwen longed to ask how the sahib had enjoyed himself with the "Kendall-folk," but refrained. Just as she was leaving her for the night the ayah remarked, "Don't be frightened if Daff bark in the night. Sahib not come in yet."

"I'm not likely to be frightened," said Olwen sleepily; and she gave a little laugh of childish exultation, at the thought of her news, her letter, her secret, which Sunia did not so much as suspect! . . . Yet, as she lay alone, after the woman had left her, she had a dull pain somewhere in her heart, for she believed that this day with the Kendalls showed that the night in the mile-castle had brought illumination to Ninian also. He had seen that he was following a will-o'-the-wisp—that nothing could come of the friendship between them, so oddly begun. "I wish to God I had never seen you!" . . .

So he was going to erect barriers. He was going to take Rose Kendall, to prevent him from making a fool of himself with Miss Innes.

Olwen was honest, and she knew that, had he been engaged to Rose, she would never have gone out for a day's skating with him. She had, then, hoped or expected something, in spite of all her denials.

What did it matter? She had her father now.

Next morning she sent a courteously worded note to Madam, asking her whether she could possibly exert herself to climb the top flight of stairs and pay her a visit, as the doctor would not let her go down, and she had something to say.

She rose, with the ayah's help, and dressed by about twelve o'clock. Soon after she was established by the fire Madam knocked at the door and entered. Her expression gave the girl a shock. Olwen had supposed, she hardly knew why, that her adventure with Ninian would not be likely to displease Madam very much. She had found her so *laissez-aller,* so languid in her views, that she had not anticipated severe condemnation: more especially as on certain occasions it had seemed as if their intimacy were being encouraged. Now she saw in a flash that she was seriously out of favour. Madam wore the look which Olwen had seen now and then on her face when Ninian had opposed her will, or she feared that he intended to do so. Her mouth was compressed, her eyes stony.

"I trust you are better," said she, standing just within the door.

Miss Innes sprang to her feet. "It is good of you to come," she began confusedly. "I have been wanting to see you. I don't know what you must think of—of my imprudence. I'm sorry—oh, I am very sorry that it—it happened."

Madam gloomed at her very stiffly. "That what happened?" she questioned.

Olwen crimsoned. "My—accident," she said mumblingly, sinking back into her chair. Madam's attitude had put everything in a new light. She felt like the veriest culprit. "Mr.—Mr. Guyse would have told you that it was altogether unintentional——"

There was a bitter little smile. "Mr. Guyse has not been too explicit. I had perhaps better hear your account of it."

Olwen's eyes filled. She felt most unequal to a scene. "Won't—won't you sit down? I can see, of course, that you are much displeased with me. I—I realise now that I ought not to have gone out with Mr. Guyse as I did; but it was with your approval, Madam—indeed it was with your approval, as you must remember."

Madam sat down, as it were, reluctantly upon the edge of a chair. She had somewhat the aspect of a most unwilling visitor in someone else's house. "Really, Miss Innes, you have been two months in this family. Surely you cannot pretend to be ignorant of the fact that I and my approval count for less than nothing with my son."

Olwen swallowed tears of extreme mortification. "Then you thought, all the time, that I ought not to go, but never said so! Yet I am in your care, and I am not very old or very experienced. However, perhaps, there is no need to go over the thing in great detail. It shows that I am not a suitable person for my position here, and I will relieve you of my presence as soon as the doctor gives me leave to travel. I think he said I might go on Thurs-

day, and this is Tuesday. I—of course I can only expect
one month's pay, as I leave you without notice. I am sure
it is what you would wish—that I should go at once. I
am grieved"—pride had upheld her so far, but here her
humiliation broke down her voice pitifully—"yes, indeed,
I am grieved to have been such a—such a failure. I
meant to do so well!"

Madam twisted her mouth up on one side as she re-
garded the drying of the tearful eyes. "I don't think my
son has found your society a failure," she remarked, with
meaning.

Olwen winced. Was this deserved? Had Madam all
along blamed her conduct, thought her too free, been cen-
suring beneath that apathetic manner? Nothing whips
and stings an innocent girl like the accusation of bold
conduct. "You think I deserve that?" she whispered
passionately.

"Do you deny that you have flirted with him?" asked
Madam, as if surprised.

"Yes!" cried the girl, flaming at the injustice of the
lady's attitude. "I have not flirted, I declare that I have
not!" . . . She meant to say more, but refrained. She
would not accuse Ninian. Had he had the baseness to
represent to his mother that the advances had been hers?

"Come, come, there is no need for so much tragedy.
What has happened is most unfortunate—I conclude, at
least, that you agree with me in thinking so? It was
a deplorable adventure, and the fact of your encounter
with the doctor at Hazel Crag made it a great deal worse.
But, fortunately, you have to deal with a young man
who, perverse as he is, has nevertheless a great deal of
good feeling. You need not be so apprehensive. I am
authorised to let you know that my son is quite ready to
marry you."

Olwen stared. Then she rose to her feet, choking. In her shame and terror she could hardly speak.

"You mean—you mean that I am compromised—that the only way out is for Mr. Guyse to sacrifice himself—to marry me?" she managed to bring out.

Madam's eyes surveyed her with a fish-like gaze. "What did you expect?" she asked.

"Expect? Nothing! What should I expect? I am here as your companion, and if I have been out with Mr. Guyse, I say frankly that his company has been thrust upon me—that you have actually thrown us together! If you have a spark of justice in you, you must admit this!"

"Well, but you bewilder me, Miss Innes. I was under the impression, as my son certainly was, that you had an affection for him, and were willing to marry him. Had I not supposed so, I should certainly not have allowed you to go out for the day together. I understood that he meant to ask you to be his wife in the course of that day. Did he not do so?"

"Certainly not. Nothing of the kind! He had no more idea of it than I had! I—I cannot think what you mean by talking like this! Your son and I, owing to a quite unforeseen accident, had to remain out all night. Nothing could be more scrupulous than the way he behaved—nothing could be more complete than Dr. Balmayne's understanding of the position! And even if he did not understand it—even if he did look upon me as compromised, what does that matter to me? I am leaving this place on Thursday, and I hope I may never see or hear anything of any of you again!"

"Thank you, that shows very good feeling!" said Madam icily. "I wonder at you, indeed I do, Miss Innes. I had supposed that I came to reassure you. I expected to find you in some mental anxiety, and was desirous to let you

know at the earliest moment that my son admitted his
responsibility and had no desire to shirk it. This will
be a blow to him."

"Oh, I think he will get over it. I can disappear, as
Miss Martin did, and you see this has only lasted such
a short time, it will not make any deep impression. As
a matter of fact, I should have had to leave in any case
owing to family reasons. I heard from home yesterday,
and find I am wanted at once."

Again Madam smiled. "Like the young man at a dull
house-party, you have received a telegram summoning
you away," said she. "I happen to be aware that the post
yesterday brought no letters for you."

"No, but Dr. Balmayne brought one. The chemist at
the post office asked him to take it with him when he
came."

Madam changed colour violently. She could not, for a
moment, control what seemed like extreme annoyance.
For quite an appreciable time she could not speak, and
Olwen sat contemplating the unexpected result of her
simple announcement, and saying over and over to herself, "I knew it! They have always overlooked my
correspondence! What a mercy the doctor happened to
bring this one!"

Madam rose from her seat and went to the window.
After a minute she faced round, and said steadily:

"As long as you are here you are in my charge. Before
allowing you to leave, I intend to write to your grandfather a full account of what has taken place. I could
not permit him to suppose me so careless of you as to
let you go out all day long with my son if I had not
believed that you were as good as engaged. Before receiving you back he shall be made acquainted with all the
facts."

Olwen half rose, but sank down again, and bit back

the plea that rose to her lips. She felt as if she were in a trap, running round and round, seeking a way out. But there was a last appeal she meant to try. She did not believe that Ninian would allow her to be bullied or coerced. She could take her stand upon his sense of justice and honour. . . . Ah, but could she? . . . Dr. Balmayne, who knew him far better than she did, thought otherwise. She trembled with a sense of her helplessness.

Madam saw that her last threat had hit the girl hard. She stood inflexibly awaiting a reply.

Olwen threw up her chin, and spoke bravely. "I shall appeal to Mr. Guyse," she said. "I will insist upon his telling you himself that no love-making has passed between us."

"Very good," replied Madam at once. "I, too, think that you should do as you suggest. I will not write to your grandfather until I know what the result of your interview will be. If you could exert yourself so far as to come down to tea in the banqueting-hall, it would save poor ayah some of the running up and down stairs which, during the past few days, has been almost too much for her."

This parting thrust brought the tears smarting to the girl's eyes.

Madam looked round the room with an appraising gaze, as she moved slowly towards the door. "I don't think," said she, with a very faint smile, "that you could truly say that you have not been comfortable here."

"Oh—I—you—what am I to say?" burst forth Olwen vehemently. "I was so happy, I was growing to love"— Madam turned swiftly—"to love the old Pele and the wild country, and my life here—and now you have spoilt it all! Nothing can ever be the same again." She grasped the arm of her chair, and leaned her brow upon her hands, almost disappearing beneath the overweight of her tumbling hair.

"Oh, come, things are not so bad as you think," replied Madam, in a different tone. "If you marry Nin you would stay here always."

"Marry him because I have lost my reputation!" cried the girl wildly, lifting her tear-stained face. "You must be mad to think I am that kind of a girl!"

Madam shrugged her thin shoulders. "Well, I shall expect to see you at tea time," she said, and went out.

CHAPTER XXVI

NINIAN'S TWIN

"MISSEE fancy chicken for her lunch?" asked Sunia softly.

Olwen shook her head miserably and mopped her eyes with her handkerchief. As the ayah saw the traces of grief, she uttered a pitying little sound and ran forward. Olwen made a brave attempt to speak and to control her weeping.

"Don't bring me any lunch, please. I have been working you to death, up and down stairs all day at my beck and call. Never mind, I shall be gone in a day or two, and then you can have a rest."

The Hindu took the kettle from the fire, poured out a little water, added violet salts and eau-de-Cologne, and came to her chair.

"Don't you talk no words like those words," said she under her breath. Her voice was rather like the very low growl of an angry animal. "Madam say things like that, she not pukka, Madam not. I sorry, for she mother to my sahib, but she not pukka. My dear lamb, let ole ayah bathe her eyes and not cry any more."

The girl yielded herself up to the soothing touch, telling herself that it was very likely for the last time. Ah, could she but have trusted this woman! . . .

Madam had left her with her uncomfortable feeling of doubt more accentuated than ever. She was unable to guess why the Guyses had determined that she should not leave the Pele. Perhaps it was merely for the con-

ventional reason that, if she did leave, there would be
another scandal tacked on to Ninian's shoulders. That
might be all. They might be desperately anxious to detain
her until things had blown over.

Yet for two reasons she felt that she could not stay.
Her father's impending arrival was quite enough, had it
stood alone. Added to it now was the situation between
herself and Ninian.

This she could have treated lightly but for her self-
distrust. Already, at the thought that she was to see
him in a few hours, her heart was turning over, her
pulses racing. She thought of his grave, preoccupied
face as he sat holding her head against his shoulder and
washing blood from her face with a bit of his shirt, as
though she had been his little sister; and how he had put
up his hand to her cheek, covering her eyes, holding her
a minute close pressed.

She felt absolutely convinced that it could not be he
who had sent the insolent message brought by his mother,
at the very memory of which her blood boiled. He was
ready to marry her, *he had no wish to shirk his obli-
gations!*

After that, even without her father's letter, nothing
would have induced her to stay.

Sunia fussed over her more than ever that afternoon,
as though in deliberate defiance of Madam's words. She
coaxed her to eat, to rest, to compose herself; and presently she set to work to dress her patient and to arrange
her hair properly for the first time since her accident.

She had been very angry when first she discovered
how big a tress had been cut away; as she stood to-day,
planning how best to conceal the ravage, she gave vent
to several remarks disparaging to Dr. Balmayne's sur-
gical skill, evidently hoping to make the girl's natural

vanity an ally against a man who had sacrificed her appearance.

However, she invented a new method of wrapping the hair about the little head—a method which hid the wound and proved very becoming. She arrayed her in the gown she had worn the day the Kendalls called; and had her ready a quarter of an hour too soon, that she might rest by the fire before the exertion of going downstairs.

"Ole ayah take dear Misset down now, 'cos she got to go and bring tea afterwards," said she at last.

As Olwen rose to obey, her heart sank and her knees trembled. She dreaded the impending meeting unspeakably; and yet, mixed with the dread, was the mysterious, flooding joy which would not be fought down.

She sought some motive for Madam's apparently senseless change of front. Had she, during that night of adventure, forfeited the respect of the owner of the Pele? Her whole mind rose to contradict the notion . . . but how could she, then, account for his mother's insolence? Something might have happened, must have happened, since they last met. She knew there was something between herself and Nin—and as she searched her mind she was aware of having known as much for days past. Otherwise he must have sent some message, some token of solicitude for her welfare.

The ayah preceded her carefully down the stairs with a candle to light her feet. She was weaker than she had foreseen, and came so slowly that Sunia, outstripping her, had opened the door of the banqueting-hall a few seconds before she reached it. Through the doorway there came clearly the sound of a laugh—Nin's laugh, but with something unfamiliar in the tone; and words followed—"of course, if it were possible to muff it, you would—just exactly the same kind of ass that you always have been."

The entrance of Miss Innes cut the speaker short.

She stood just within the door, feeling that the fireside was a long way off, steadying herself for a moment against the wall.

There were three people present. Madam sat on the settle, her face transformed with a radiance which made her almost handsome. Close at her side was Ninian, with an arm flung over her shoulders. . . . No, it was not Ninian. Never had Olwen seen anything resembling an endearment pass between those two. Ninian, with his pipe in his mouth, was leaning his back against the mantel, and behind his shoulders the two carved panthers upheld the Guyse coat, while the light flickered on the words of the motto: *"Guyse ne sçait' pas se déguyser."*

Upon the girl's appearance the young man who was seated sprang to his feet. Then she saw that his hair was fair and his eyes very blue. He was smiling—a smile which was Nin's and yet not Nin's. His teeth were as regular, but smaller. There was nothing in his manner which at all resembled the impudence of his twin.

"Is this Miss Innes?" he asked cordially, and moved forward so quickly as to intercept Nin, had the latter cherished any intention of going to meet the girl. Olwen gave her hand in mute wonder, found it taken, drawn under his arm, while he piloted her with care to a seat. "I'm Wolf," he said winningly, "as my people don't seem to think an introduction necessary. Have you ever heard tell of me?"

She stood, so taken aback that she could not at first speak. Her eyes rested in astonishment on his face. It seemed to her like the face of Nin translated into what it might have been but just was not. From it her look flitted to the silent brother, who had not moved from his post, and who stood with the queerest expression on his face. He had taken his pipe from his mouth, was holding it in his hand and staring at it. You would have declared that he was afraid to look up, afraid to meet her questioning eye.

"Yes," she said, when she regained her breath, "of course I have heard of you. You are Mr. Guyse's twin brother. I—I did not know you had come."

"I didn't know myself that I was coming until last night," he replied gaily. "My chief gave me a few hours' leave quite suddenly. This is a bad place to get at, but, fortunately, we have got rid of all that beastly snow that fell last week, and my brother was able to drive over and fetch me."

"And he can stay four or five days!" broke in Madam joyfully. Her very voice had changed. Gone was the forbidding, sullen woman who had so lacerated the girl's feelings that day. There was a flush on the faded cheeks, the eyes had light in them. She wore a handsome gown and a diamond brooch. Olwen wondered which was the real woman—this smiling mother or the dull, moping, vacant creature to whom she had grown accustomed.

"And so old Nin managed to let you down, skating, and gave you a bump on the head, I hear," went on Wolf lightly. He had thrown himself into the chair next hers, and was pulling Daff's ears with fine, white, well-shaped hands, which did not at all resemble those of his farmer twin. "But it can't have been as bad as my brother wants to make out—or, at least, I see no signs of it. How clever ladies are with their hair!"

His eyes, his smile, swept over her admiringly; his voice said, "How charming you are!" by its tone, not by its words.

"Oh, I am nearly well," she answered vaguely, for so many new ideas stormed at her brain that she could not at first think clearly. "I want to know how you are,

Mr. Guyse," she went on, addressing Ninian pointedly. "Ayah told me you had a shocking cold."

Still without looking at her, he laughed nervously. "Oh, there's nothing the matter with me," he, replied huskily.

"Oh, but there is," she answered quickly. "You are still very hoarse; and you look," she went on wistfully, "you look pulled down."

On that he gave her a queer glance, quite momentary, and, turning away, began to clean out his pipe, stooping for the purpose over the fire.

As Wolf had evidently not been given the true account of the accident—a circumstance for which she felt deeply grateful to Madam and Ninian—she could not allude to it, nor thank Ninian for his care of her. The new arrival had changed everything. Her anger against Madam must be choked down, she must smile and be polite to this handsome young man, must behave as though all were well and everyone on good terms.

"I've been quite eager to see you," went on Wolf confidingly. "You know, we had the greatest bother to get Madam to consent to ask a lady to come here, and we were so afraid she would bite your head off when you came! But no. Each letter she has written me has been full of news of you. She tells me you are settling down to be quite happy here."

"Everyone has been very kind," replied Olwen gravely; "but I fear I shall have to leave, at least temporarily, in a day or two. The doctor says I must lead quite an idle life for the present."

"Well, can't you do that here?" laughingly he demanded. "Our ancestral home seems to me an ideal spot for the purpose. We must suborn the doctor and get him to say so. However, at least we have you safe for a few days, as you can't travel without his permission, and the poor

chap is confined to his room with a sharp touch of 'flu,'
so we heard in Caryngston to-day."

Olwen's little "Oh!" of dismay was interrupted by the
entrance of Sunia with the tea. That the doctor should
have "flu" in such weather was a most likely thing to
happen; yet to her, after what she had gone through that
day, Wolf Guyse's unsuspicious words seemed like another
twist of the cord that bound her to the Pele.

Keenly the eyes of the ayah swept the room; keenly
they dwelt upon the faces of the four persons present.
She placed the little table where it always stood, and beside it the chair Olwen always used when she sat and
read aloud to the others. "Tea ready, missee-bibi," said
she softly.

Olwen rose, not without an effort, went to her chair,
sat down and dispensed tea. Ninian, who had only spoken
that once since her entrance, watched her movements,
brought hot water as she needed it, and handed cups
and cakes while Wolf engaged Miss Innes in conversation.

By the time tea was over the girl was almost exhausted.
This was her first venture from her room, and her head
still felt weak. She leaned back in her chair and her
replies became languid.

Ninian, who had hitherto been most unusually silent,
suddenly woke up and began to tell Wolf a long story
of the picturesque drunkenness of a certain farmer in
the district, and how his horses had brought him safely
home. His brother listened with what seemed like astonishment at his selection of a subject. When they had done
laughing the younger was approaching Olwen's chair.
Ninian stood up swiftly, and, going to the billiard-table,
began to pull off the cover.

"Play you fifty up before dinner," said he.

"Done," was the reply; and in a minute the two were

busy lighting the large lights over the billiard-table, leaving the convalescent free to rest.

Instinctively Olwen glanced at Madam to see if she wanted anything; but Madam had no eyes, no attention for anybody but Wilfrid. She made him move her chair so that she could watch them play, asking eager questions about what games Wolf had had lately, how hard he was worked, and so on.

Olwen had slipped into the large, low chair which usually was Ninian's property. She lay there with her eyes closed, trying to fix her thoughts coherently. She was vaguely terrified, because she did not understand. There seemed no reason in Madam's behaviour, while that of Ninian was so wholly unexpected as to be affrighting. It was some weeks now since they first dropped into the habit of teasing each other, chipping each other, behaving like brother and sister. And now—what? Was he ashamed of his mother's conduct? Was he apprehensive lest her coarseness might have scared the girl? Or did he not wish his brother to know on what terms they stood? He had the air of being embarrassed. Well, a man might well be embarrassed if he considered himself bound to marry a girl because of such an adventure as they had been through. . . . Was it true that Dr. Balmayne was laid up? It must be. Wolf could not be also in the plot, whatever it was, against her. He had said that the doctor had "flu," and had assumed that she could not leave the Pele until he had sanctioned the removal. She comforted herself with the thought that there were several days to spare before the *Stupendous* could reach Liverpool. It would really be better for her not to start upon her travels yet; she felt far from strong. If only Ninian were not in this curious mood she would feel quite different.

"Come, Miss Innes," said Wolf's delightful voice, "you

must back one of us. Here's my silly old mother putting her money on me. Won't you back Nin?"

"Why, yes, certainly," she replied, sitting up so that she could see the table. "What's the game now?"

Wolf gave the score, and informed her that if Nin won he would have to give her a pair of gloves. "Is he the kind of chap you would back to get anything he wants, in the usual way?" he asked mischievously.

Reflecting that Ninian might see a point in her answer which the questioner could not intend, she replied: "I think he is usually content with very little."

Wolf's laugh had perhaps an edge of malice. "By Jove! you've hit it," said he, chuckling; "and faint heart never won fair lady, eh?"

"Oh," laughed Olwen in sudden malice, longing to sting Nin into speech, "the fair lady seemed willing enough the day I saw her."

"Hallo! What's this? I am going to hear news," cried Wolf, approaching her chair, cue in hand.

Ninian spoke from where he stood, leaning over the table in the act of making his stroke. "If you don't lie back in that chair and keep quiet, Miss Innes, you shall go back upstairs to bed," he said calmly.

"Mr. Guyse, I must ask you not to talk while you are playing," cried she when his cannon failed. "Kindly remember that I am backing you."

"Backbiting me, I should say," he replied gloomily, chalking his cue.

"Well, I'm a generous foe. If our talking scandal put you off your stroke, little brother, we are dumb," was Wolf's amused comment. He looked from one to the other as though highly entertained.

"Come, that's better," said Olwen, lying back as admonished. "I assure you, Mr. Wilfrid, I often make him quite brilliant; but if he loses this game he knows what to expect," in tones of mock anger.

"What am I to expect?" demanded Nin, speaking from the far end of the table.

"Well, I shall never go skating with you again, for one thing."

"I shouldn't suppose you would do that, in any case," he replied, in what almost amounted to a return to his old manner.

"You want me to ask why, so I just won't," she flashed back. "I am not well, and my repartee department is all out of order."

"You always end with a jade's trick," said Ninian, as he once more took his turn.

"If you've got to the point of searching Shakespeare for your repartee, I fear you can't win," she told him sadly. It was not long before her foreboding was justified, and Wolf had to announce that her champion was defeated.

"It's my fault," said she. "He has had nobody but me to play against this winter, and of course it has spoilt his play." As she spoke the dressing-bell rang.

Olwen asked Madam if she might be allowed to dine with them as she was, without changing. Madam said she looked all right, and Wolf improved the occasion with a neat phrase, but Ninian said calmly:

"Miss Innes will not come down to dinner. She is already tired, and will go upstairs now."

"Oh, Mr. Guyse! Is this my punishment for back-biting?" she pleaded, standing up and looking beseechingly at him. Wolf happened to be the other side of the room, putting the cues into the rack, so that the reply was not audible to him.

"No, it's my own punishment for letting him beat me." As he spoke his eyes, for the first time that evening, met hers. Without a word said she understood that it cost him something to utter the sentence that would send her away—that consideration for her health had prompted his ungracious speech. She held her breath for a minute, her face full of a tender light. He lowered his own gaze, turned slowly from her, strolled down the room and opened the door. Sunia was waiting outside with a shawl. Olwen bade good night to the others, and passed out. Ninian held open the door, and did not seem to notice her outstretched hand.

CHAPTER XXVII

OLWEN came downstairs the following day between eleven and twelve o'clock.

It had been raining heavily since early morning, but was beginning to clear, and the temperature was much milder than it had been when first she arrived in that country.

From her window as she dressed she had noted that a soft purplish-brown tint was beginning to overspread the woods on the further side of the Guyseburn, and knew that this was a token of the budding of the leafless boughs. Somehow the fact that spring was on its way was consoling and made her feel more normal. She was schooling herself to believe that Madam's talk had been, as it often was, unbalanced, and that she ought not to take too much notice of it. Nothing could have been less presuming than Ninian's manner overnight. He certainly had not worn the air of one who knows that a girl is in his power.

As she descended the stairs she was considering the question of her own departure. She could not decide whether it would be wise to say openly that she was going to Liverpool to meet her father, and obtain permission to stay at the Pele until the boat was almost due, so that she could journey straight to Liverpool without returning to Bramforth.

She felt that this was far the best plan, if things could be so arranged. It would give her a longer convalescence and save money and travelling. If only the new and welcome addition to the party would remain to keep the peace it might be done!

She wished that Dr. Balmayne had not chosen this inopportune moment to fall ill. His advice would be invaluable, for, explain it away as she might, something held her back from putting complete confidence in the Guyse family. She knew that there was something odd in her position—that they opened her letters and spied on her movements. It was this which made her unwilling to divulge to them the contents of what she was fairly certain was the only letter which had reached her at the Pele uncensored.

She descended the stairs, and when she reached the hall, instead of emerging into it and opening the door which led to the dining-room, she continued along the passage, which, as has been said, was in the thickness of the wall, and gave access to the dining-room behind the tapestry. There was a door there, but it was most often open, as the tapestry curtains were thick enough to keep out draught, and the narrowness of the passage made it easier to move along, if the door were laid back flat against the wall and secured by a staple.

Thus once more, and quite without intention, she overheard something that was not meant for her ear. It was Ninian who was speaking, and he spoke like a man at bay.

"Well, then, I say straight out, on those terms I'm damned if I marry the child."

Wolf's voice replied almost immediately, "But you haven't got any alternative, old man; and if my mother is to be trusted, no more has Miss Innes."

Without a moment's pause, without reflecting an instant, with every passion at white heat, Olwen flung aside the curtain and came tempestuously into the room.

The brothers stood upon the hearth, side by side, almost the same height, almost the same build, so alike—so unlike.

Their faces, as they confronted her, were a curious study.

"I am not an eavesdropper," said she, fury steadying her voice. "You should not discuss me with the door open if you do not wish to be overheard. There is no need for Mr. Guyse to suffer damnation. I have not the slightest intention of marrying him, as he well knows. Now, Mr. Wilfrid Guyse, perhaps you will kindly explain what you mean by saying that I have no alternative but to marry your brother?"

Wilfrid and Ninian both stood for quite an appreciable moment dumb before this crisis. Then Wilfrid laid down his pipe upon the stone mantelpiece, turned to her, and said gently:

"I fear you have made some mistake, Miss Innes. What, if I may ask, did you think that we said?"

"I heard quite plainly what you said. Mr. Guyse said he would be damned if he would marry me, and you replied that you understood that neither he nor I had any alternative. I want to know what you meant by that?"

"Ought you not," he asked with a mischievous smile, "to attack my brother first? If he really said what you think you heard, it seems that it is he who ought to answer for such a preposterous——"

"Not at all. What he said was perfectly justifiable. He said he wasn't going to be pushed into marrying me. Well, that is just what I should wish him to say. I hope you know," she went on, with just a perceptible break in her voice as she turned to Ninian, "that I am completely in sympathy with you in this matter? I have nothing to complain of—from first to last you have acted just as you ought. Madam has made some dreadful kind of mistake, but we both have such clear consciences that we can afford to laugh at what people say. Oh, can't we? Can't we?"

The last words were a sudden appeal made with clasped hands; for as she spoke, Nin's face, upon which had appeared his usual demon-like smile at first, had slowly grown whiter and whiter. He was looking at her now as though she had hit him desperately hard.

"*You* can laugh, of course, at anything anybody may say; and I can knock them down for saying it," he replied slowly, his hoarseness making his voice sound a little strange to her.

"But, of course," she went on, too carried along by her subject to make any very special note of the extent of his agitation, "of course your brother is different. People who circulate lies can be knocked down; but he ought to be told exactly what happened. Mr. Wilfrid Guyse, will you let me speak to you? Will you let me tell you what has passed?"

"I shall be more than honoured," he replied, his eyes fixed in evident interest upon her. He wheeled an armchair forward, but she made a gesture of dissent, and remained standing, confronting him.

"It won't take long, there's not much to say, but you must be made to understand how we came to be out all night. If, after all that your brother went through, he were to be blamed . . . it would be dreadful. He has perhaps told you that I was stunned, knocked on the head by a bit of rock which fell upon me as we were descending Duke's Crag. If I had fallen I should have been killed, but Mr. Guyse was able to catch me. He not only upheld me, but actually succeeded in bringing me step by step back to the top, and it was a wonderful thing to do, for I was all the time a dead weight. By the time he had accomplished that feat, and we were in safety, you may guess that he was tired, but in spite of this he carried me the best part of half a mile, through the fast falling snow, to the only shelter there was for miles round. When we were once there, there was nothing for it but to stay. By that time it was dark. I was helpless—he had no brandy. He could not carry me further, the nearest house was so far off that he might have been lost in the snow before reaching it; and it was so cold that in case of his not returning I should have frozen to death. Now do you understand? Do you see that he had then most certainly—though it is not true to say so now—he had *then* no alternative but to stay with me and take care of me until the snow ceased to fall and we had some chance of finding our direction?"

Wolf's eyes rested upon the eager upturned face with sympathy and something which seemed like admiration. "My brother has an eloquent advocate," he said a little mischievously. "I own I am glad to hear your account of the affair."

"Mr. Guyse and I had Madam's full permission to go upon our skating expedition," she went on ardently. "Our being detained was sheer accident, and all my life I shall look back with gratitude upon that night and the thought of what your brother did for me—his patience and consideration were alike wonderful." She broke off. For a moment she thought that she had done. Neither of the two men, eyeing her silently, almost breathlessly, moved or spoke; and suddenly she resumed, "One thing more. I have heard—it has been hinted to me—that Mr. Guyse has been accused of—of different conduct in—the sad affair which happened here three years ago. I want to say," lifting her head proudly, "that, judging by his behaviour to me the other night, it would take a great deal to make me believe anything at all to his discredit in any other case. That is all."

Silence fell upon the room as she uttered those words, which seemed to be driven out of her by some inner force. She had not meant to say this, had not even known that she felt it. Yet it came from her like the cry of her inmost being. For a few instants the succeeding pause was full of possibilities. It was broken by Ninian, who turned, walked to the door, and went deliberately out, shutting it behind him with some force. In her zeal of championship Olwen hardly noted his going, except as it allowed her to speak more frankly to his brother.

"You cannot mean to tell me," she went on more quietly, "that you consider, after what I have told you, that I have compromised myself, or that any blame could be attributed to your brother?"

Wilfrid had turned rather suddenly to the fire and stood staring at the flaming logs. "You are right, of course," he said in a low voice. "Poor old Nin!"

There was a pause, during which he took up his discarded pipe, cleaned and refilled it. "You know," he continued presently, when he had it well alight, "I can't help being glad that you chanced to come in at that moment. The situation was puzzling me a bit, and now I think I have got the hang of it. Don't let anything my mother may have said worry you. She is really extremely attached to you. I have not heard her speak so warmly of anyone for some time. You and Ninian evidently understand one another; and I think this will all blow over very soon. It would be a pity, would it not, to let a—a sort of misunderstanding interfere with the fine work you are doing here?"

She answered: "You are very kind. I cannot stay, however. I shall have to leave in a few days' time."

"I hope you will reconsider that decision. After all,

we must call it careless of my brother to allow you to be scrambling up a cliff face in February, when the rock is all rotten with the frosts. The least we can do is to see that you are cured before leaving us. Wouldn't it be rather heartless of you to shake off the dust of your feet against us?"

She laughed a little. "Oh," she said, with traces of embarrassment, "it is not that. I—I have to go home in any case. I," she hesitated, wondering how to express it without mentioning her father, "I shall be changing— I mean, I intend to change my occupation—I shall not be free to take a post in future," she concluded stumblingly, not seeing at all that to her listener this could have but one meaning. He must suppose her to be contemplating marriage. His face fell.

"If that be so, we must make the most of your last few days," he answered gracefully. "I got the postman to telegraph for a motor this morning, and I propose to take you and my mother out for an airing this afternoon. She has been shut up indoors for some weeks, Ninian tells me, and it always makes her a bit capricious. Make allowances for her, Miss Innes. She has had some bad times."

"Oh, I know. I am so sorry to think how much I have added to her vexations, although most unintentionally."

He drew up a chair close to hers after this, and began to talk. By insensible degrees they slipped away from all sore subjects, and found themselves conversing on current topics, and comparing their taste in fiction and the drama. Wolf was like a whiff of civilisation in the savage solitude.

Neither Madam nor Ninian appeared until dinner-time, when the lady entered; but Sunia, with a very

272 THE LONELY STRONGHOLD

reproachful glance at Olwen, said the sahib had gone
to Lachanrigg and would not be back until tea-time.

They had a charming drive, for it was the end of February, the sun did not set until half-past five, and the
clouds had all rolled away, leaving the most brilliant sky
that Olwen remembered to have seen since her arrival.
The setting of the scarlet sun in purple mist was a thing
to remember.

Owing to Wolf's thoughtfulness, tea had been ordered
downstairs, to spare Olwen any unnecessary exercise.
After tea Madam went to her own sitting-room to lie
down; and after a while Wolf also sauntered off, leaving
Olwen alone by the fire. Ninian had not come in, and her
whole mind was racked with speculation as to the why
and wherefore of his mysterious behaviour.

"I'm damned if I'll marry the child."

All the afternoon the words had rung in her head.
Could he really have thought that she meant to catch
him? The mere idea made her writhe. Anyway, she had
spoken out at last. He knew that she was not the Lily
Martin brand.

"I am glad," she reflected. "I wonder if I realise
how glad I am about father. Even if he is very trying,
even if he still runs into debt, even if people look down
their noses at him, still he is somebody to belong to.
I shall not stand alone as I have stood, with everyone saying, 'Poor child! She must earn her own living, for she
has nobody to do it for her!' Aunt Ethel won't speculate
as to whether a really eligible young man would overlook
my having been a clerk in a bank. Fred Holroyd will no
longer feel moved by compassion to protect me. Dr. Balmayne will no longer debate within himself as to the
degree to which he may push remonstrance!"

She would have a place in the world. It would be at her
father's side. She would also have a refuge from thought

and memory, both of which were scourging her cruelly just now.

She could not help remembering how happy she had been upon the fine frosty morning when she and Ninian had driven together to the Crag Lough. Now everything was changed.

The sound of Daff's barking outside made her prick up her ears. The outer door banged, there was a scuffle of feet, some words in a deep voice, and Ninian opened the door.

She sent him a welcoming glance from her chimney corner. "You are late!" said she reproachfully.

He looked as if half inclined to bolt; Daffie, rushing against his legs from behind, settled the question for him. He entered with a laugh and a reckless swing, closing the door.

"If I'd remembered that teacher was about again, I should have hurried more," said he, in almost his usual style.

Olwen's heart leapt.

"For a punishment only three lumps of sugar in the first cup," said she, rising and going to the table; the tea-pot, which had been keeping hot before the fire, in her hand.

He took a seat, not his usual place, at right angles to her, but at the further end of the table, pushing aside Wolf's cup and plate in order to sit there, so that she knew it to be intentional.

"How's the broken head?" he asked in a brazen sort of tone.

"Mending fast."

"That's right. Easier healed than a broken heart, isn't it?"

"Well, I don't think I ever tried."

"No, and I don't think you're likely to," he replied,

eyeing her as it were by stealth. "I wonder what kind of love-making *would* melt you down? Not sending you silk coats by post, I'll go bail."

The hot colour flamed to her face. She was at that moment wearing the rose-coloured coat which Ben had sent.

"Ha!" cried Nin with glee. "Look at her cheeks, Daff! Some stray shots go straight to the goal! It *was* a man, then?"

"I don't understand. You are speaking that unknown tongue which you used when I first came."

"Yes. One can't always be on the high-brow tack, you know. I've chucked it. I express myself far more easily in my own language," with the one-sided smile and green light in the eyes which still made her think of Mephistopheles.

She looked steadily at him for a moment, and then said, "Very well. It would be a pity to bore you."

"Yes," he replied, helping himself to a piled spoonful of jam. "It is a bore to tell lies; and I've told more since you came than ever in my life before."

"Then the sooner I go the better," she swiftly cried; to which the retort was instantaneous.

"Sure thing."

She sprang to her feet, snatched her shawl from the back of a chair and put it on. "You won't mind pouring out your second cup?" said she.

"No, that'll be right enough, but before you go off in a naughty temper, there is a little ceremony we ought to go through, isn't there?"

"I don't think so."

"But I do, and we may as well get it over." He leaned his two elbows on the table, with his cup of tea supported in front of his lips in both his hands. "Miss Innes, will you marry me?" he asked, and took a drink immediately.

She stood looking at him for a long minute without speech, hardly knowing whether to go on jesting or to let her anger have its way. At last:

"I've a great mind—oh, I really *have* a great mind to say 'Yes,' and be revenged! Just to see what you would do! You go too far! You rely too utterly upon my good manners. What *would* you do, now, if I were to say 'Yes'?"

He got to his feet, his eyes gleaming. "I should think, if you're not an idiot, you know pretty well what I should do," he replied; and took a step towards her.

She winced, as if her hurt had been physical. In her passion of self-despising she could almost have shrieked. This was the man she had championed, this the man who had, so she told him that morning only, *from first to last acted just as he ought!*

She got to the door somehow. When she actually had the iron ring of it in her hand she felt strength to speak. "I stood up for you," she said gaspingly. "I—I don't think I have deserved that you should treat me—like this!"

He turned an odd colour, but she was too absorbed in her own outraged feelings to remark that. His voice was steady enough as he answered: "Now you know what sort I am. Like nothing on earth, eh? But you haven't answered. I've asked you to marry me, and you've almost accepted me, you know."

"Accepted you? . . . Accepted *you?*"

"Come! That's more like. Miserable caitiff, avaunt! Soil not the ear of Vere de Vere with thy pernicious twaddle! But, I say, if I've guessed right, and you are turning me down in a manner which might perhaps be described as unmitigated, at least you'll let Madam and my brother know that I did come up to the scratch, won't you? As for Balmayne, I'll tell him myself that I asked you, but you wouldn't have me."

She could not resist a last thrust. "Did you expect me to take your damnation upon my hands?"

"You've come pretty near it. I'm more than half-way to hell at this minute—put out your finger and I'll come the rest of the way!"

As he stood, his green eyes flickering like light upon steel, the idea that he was the worse for drink flashed upon her for the first time. Had that been the explanation of his devilry upon the occasion of their first meeting? It was from the bar parlour of a tavern that he had appeared upon her horizon. Was this—*this*—perhaps the real meaning of Dr. Balmayne's hints?

As she fled from the room upstairs to her chamber she had but one intention in her mind.

It was the intention to escape. She must leave this house, leave this man with his unholy fascination, put all this degradation behind her, and run to her father's arms as to a city of refuge.

CHAPTER XXVIII

ESCAPE

Sunia awaited her—Sunia, with eyes that seemed to entreat, to expect—to listen breathless for some tidings.

For the first few minutes Olwen sat where she had flung herself, in her chair beside the hearth, fighting for the control she knew to be so necessary if she were to carry out the purpose taking shape within her.

First she was inclined to announce that she would not go down to supper. On reflection she thought it would look better if she were to dress quietly, as though nothing had happened, allow Sunia to leave her, and then be, as it were, suddenly obliged to undress and go to bed.

She owned, in a low voice, that she was not feeling well, and the ayah, in consequence, tended her with extra gentleness and no words. When she had hastened away upon her other duties the girl began to consider possibilities.

It was of no use to ask to be driven to Caryngston, because they would say she was not well enough to travel. She could not post a letter, ordering a fly to be sent, until to-morrow, which meant that she could not set out until the day following. It seemed clear that her only practicable course would be to descend the mount, walk through the woods and go to Lachanrigg, where Mrs. Kay would no doubt have her driven to Raefell station, and her homeward journey would be more simple than by way of Picton Bars.

So she sat cogitating, planning by the fireside until, as

277

she had expected, the ayah returned to know why she had not come down to supper. She said she had been suddenly taken faint and must lie down, begging that no food might be brought to her.

Sunia had her disrobed and between the sheets in a very short time. She then departed, returning, as well the girl had expected, with a tray of appetising fare. Upon the plate lay a note, addressed merely to O. I.

Hoping that Madam had chosen this manner of giving her notice, she opened it. Then her colour changed. Whatever she had expected, she had not been prepared for what she read:

"I can't stand this. I give in. I must tell you every-thing. That's what I've been trying to avoid. I made an attempt to write it down, but in black and white it makes me seem too great a blackguard. How can I see you alone? Could you come down to the banqueting-hall at six o'clock to-morrow morning? It won't take long, for I shan't try to make excuses. You shall know me for what I am, and then I suppose it will be 'Good-bye' for always.   "NIN."

Half stupidly she sat up in bed, staring at the tapestried walls, holding the paper in her shaking hand.

Her trust had been misplaced. Ninian had evidently lied to her when he professed his innocence with regard to Lily Martin. Just now, in the dining-room, he said he had told more lies since her coming than in his life before. Yet on the summit of Duke's Crag he had sworn that he had told her nothing but the truth. She could not reconcile it. The only saving clause was that he had de-termined to confess—at last!

Tumultuous thoughts chased each other through her mind.

Did he really care for her? In her heart she believed that he did. She had trusted him, and that trust, which he knew to be undeserved, had melted him at last. He would not marry her, with this hateful thing between them. He meant to tell her . . . what?

Strong shuddering seized her. She felt her whole self yearning with longing unutterable for him—for the merest chance to believe in him. She knew that if he showed her his sweet side she must believe anything he told her. Yet, ah! How could she pardon it, if the girl who attempted suicide were—it must be put in plain language—if she were, as Dr. Balmayne evidently thought, Ninian Guyse's discarded mistress?

She must not, would not love such an one as he must be, if this were the atrocious truth.

How her words of defence, her assertion of faith in him, must have cut him to the heart! He had left the room and the house precipitately. He had wandered about, trying to make up his mind; he had been suddenly confronted with the sight of her—alone—and had intended flight. That not being practicable, he had turned to his usual weapon, derisive flippancy.

Having hurt her more deeply than he intended, he had at last come to a decision to make a clean breast of it.

Such was the situation as she saw it. How to grapple with it was the point upon which all her energies were directed.

It came to her soon, as with a flash of illumination, that at no cost must she allow Ninian to give her the explanation he desired. Her weakness where he was concerned was too abject. She was in his hands. The one thing she craved was to be in his arms. If he dropped his rude flippancy, if he pleaded, she well knew there was in her no force to resist him. . . .

In the extremity of her mental distress she loathed herself for her weakness, yet acknowledged the man's power.

She wondered whether, after all, Madam was the best judge of her own son, and whether this knowledge was the cause of her anxiety to get him married, even to so poor a match as Olwen Innes. She must know, or suspect, the worst. Her opinion of Ninian, as the girl had seen from the first, was anything but high—was, in fact, what it must be, granted the truth of this ugly story.

. . . And she, little fool, wanted him, loved him, longed for him with every pulse she possessed. So strong was the rush of her feeling that she felt she dare not see him. dare not meet him, even in the presence of others, for a single moment more. If she decided to renounce him, it must be done forthwith; and her better self had so decided.

How to accomplish her flight was now the question.

As has been said, the top floor of the Pele, like the others, was divided into rooms. Of these there were three, the remaining quarter, entered from the stairs, being a receptacle for spare articles, a kind of landing. This landing formed the south-east quarter, Olwen's room opening from it, being the south-west. Sunia's room was the north-west, next Olwen's; and from the way she would emerge thence, bearing trays of tea and so on, the girl had always suspected that on that side of the tower there was another newel stair. This reflection now gave her an idea. Knowing herself to be safe from observation for the moment, she sprang out of bed and went to reconnoitre. It was as she had supposed. In the corner of the ayah's room was a little door, set slanting, and within was a stair not quite like the one in general use, for it was enclosed in a circular corner turret, and she knew it must go straight down to the ground floor, and no doubt communicated with the kitchen by a passage in the thickness of the wall.

By this stair she could go, so she believed, right out upon the narrow walk which edged the tower upon its precipitous side. The door below was not likely to be locked from without. The key would almost certainly be in it. If she waited until all were in bed she might thus get away with ease. The difficulty was that she could not enter Sunia's room when its owner was there without being heard.

With the thought that there might be some small chamber in the wall where she might lurk until the woman came up to bed, she slipped down the dark corkscrew, descended past the next landing, and reached the first floor. Here were two doors, one leading into a passage and one into the Priest's Room.

This was the place. She must dress herself warmly, creep down the stairs, leaving her own room locked behind her, hide in the Priest's Room, wait until the house was quiet, and then simply let herself out.

Hurriedly reascending, she set about her preparations, putting what little money she had into a small handbag, with one or two necessaries. In order completely to reassure Sunia, she wrote a note to Ninian, put it in an envelope, and sealed it elaborately. It contained only these words:

"I will come to-morrow morning if I can.—O. I."

When Sunia came to take away her supper tray Miss Innes gave her this note, impressing upon her the necessity of delivering it quite unseen by anybody else. The ayah undertook the commission with beaming smiles. Was not this intrigue—the very air in which she flourished? She would, in return, have done anything that Olwen chose to

command; and when ordered not to come in again, but
to leave the invalid undisturbed until morning, she cheerfully consented.

It seemed to the over-excited girl a long time before
everything was arranged finally for the night—a supply
of bed-candles near at hand, Brand's extract and Horlick
lozenges in case of hunger in the dark hours, the fire built
up as only Sunia could build it, a kettle full of hot water
in case her bottle needed replenishment.

Was not any girl a fool to leave such luxury? Was
she going to flee when Ninian's love awaited her? Just
because he had behaved badly to another girl, who, if her
portrait were to be trusted, was distinctly a minx?

Yet words would ring in her head, words learned when
a child in the schoolroom—"Haste, for thy life escape,
nor look behind!"

As soon as she felt sure that Sunia had gone down to
her own supper she arose and dressed herself with the
greatest haste, all but her thick boots. These she carried
in her hand, wearing her felt bedroom slippers that she
might make no noise upon the stone steps.

Warmly wrapped, she crept out into Sunia's room,
locking her door behind her and taking away the key.
Very softly she descended two floors, opened the little door
and emerged into the Priest's Room.

In the pitch darkness a very narrow thread of light was
visible below the door which opened into the banqueting-
hall. She sat down, hardly daring at first to breathe,
upon an old arm-chair which she and Ninian had stored
away there when rearranging the room. She began to
wonder how she would know when the ayah came up to
bed; for it was quite possible that she might not come up
this way at all, since she could reach her own quarters
through the third room upon the top landing, a room in-

tended for another servant should the dwellers in the Pele employ one.

There was a youngish moon near its setting. Olwen gazed from the window and noted a curious fact. The light from the Pele windows was flung right across the valley, and made little squares of radiance upon the black trees on which it fell. There was the pattern of the oriel, quite big and bright. There, too, was the dining-room below it, extinguished even as she gazed. Presently, about half an hour after the beginning of her vigil, the little glimmer at the very top. That was Sunia. Yes, there was another patch, which was Madam's window. To watch them become dark was amusing.

But, although these darkened most satisfactorily, the oriel in the banqueting-hall remained lit up. This was awkward. Somebody was still awake, still sitting up in the Pele. If she began to move about, would not she be heard? Could she leave the Priest's Room, close the door behind her, descend the stairs, unlock the door below and shut it again without some unwonted stir penetrating to the ear of the watcher?

If it was Ninian, as she thought most likely, Daff would be with him, and she dare not risk attracting Daff's atten-tion.

Her eyes, fixed upon the far-flung square of light, saw a shadow flit slowly from side to side. It must be Ninian, and he was pacing restlessly to and fro. The longing to push open the door of her hiding-place and emerge,—to run to him and forget everything in the stronghold of his arms, was hard to master. She closed her eyes that she might not see the weary pacing.

There was nothing for it but to wait until he went upstairs. She was very sleepy, the arm-chair was com-fortable, the night not very cold. She slipped into slumber.

When she awoke it was with a start. She was cramped and chilly, and at first wondered where she was and what had happened. It was not altogether reassuring when she recollected that she was in the Priest's Room. She gazed from the window. The light was extinguished in the oriel, and everywhere else. The moon had also set, which made it a very dark night for her expedition. She had hidden a box of matches in her bag, and she ventured to strike one. To her horror she found that it was a quarter to four. However, it could not be helped. Having got so far, she meant to carry out her plan, and she hastened downstairs, laced her boots, and before long found herself out in the cold dark hour before the dawn. Instantly she made the disagreeable discovery that it had again begun to rain. She had no umbrella, but was warmly clad, and as soon as she was under the trees she was sheltered. It was wet and not at all easy going, but she held on, knowing that the descent was not really very long, and that as soon as she was in the larger path to which it led down she would make much easier progress.

She would hardly have credited the difficulty of threading one's way along a path among trees in the pitch dark. If once she left the track she felt that she would never regain it. When at last she stood upon the wet, dark leaves which thickly carpeted the main path along which she must turn to her right, she felt that the worst was over.

The rain was to be regretted, for she was not yet quite well. However, she comforted herself by reflecting that Dr. Balmayne had said she might go home on Thursday, and this was almost Thursday. She struggled along pretty boldly for some time, listening to the rush of the unseen river below her on her left hand. It had been fast bound in frost when first she came. Now its song was loud and clear; and when at last she reached the lower level of the meadows she found that her path was under water.

This was quite unlooked for. She dare not risk stepping through water of unknown depth in the dark, so she struck up the hill-side to her right. After going up some distance she found a track which seemed to go in the right direction, and this she followed until she was extremely tired. In her remembrance of the way, the woods ended after about two miles, and you crossed open meadows to the farm. She felt sure she had walked considerably more than two miles, and the woods were still thick about her. In one way this was good, for it kept her dry. But she began to think that she had better not go on too far without knowing where she was. She had little choice, however. To sit down and rest in the wet, wild woods was a risk she dare not take. Usually untiring on her feet, she felt the power to go on for a long while yet.

Another half-hour's walking, on ground which still ascended, brought her to a gate leading out of the woods upon a high road. Here she felt sure that she must turn to the left, since she had not crossed the river, and Lachanrigg lay upon its bank. But when, still farther on, she came once more to cross-roads, she had no idea whether she ought to go on or to turn again. She had now been at least two hours upon her feet, and the first dim light of dawn was beginning to make the line of the roads more apparent, the hedgerows blacker.

As she stood, bewildered, wondering what to do, she heard a sound of cheery whistling along the road she was deciding to follow. Could this be a human being, some-one who would direct her? She felt a rush of hope, and stood waiting until out of the gloom ahead came the figure of a sturdy boy, wearing the cap of a telegraph messenger.

His whistling, probably executed in order to keep up his own spirits upon his lonely tramp, was suddenly checked and his feet halted. In her mist-coloured coat and veil the apparition in the road might easily have been something of the kind which raises the hair.

To reassure him she called out at once: "Oh, please, can you tell me how far am I from Raefell Station?"

The boy stopped. After the manner of his kind, he said nothing of his startled surprise, though his chest rose and fell rapidly.

"It's all of five miles," he replied stolidly. "Want to get there?"

"Yes, but I did not mean to walk all the way. How far am I from Lachanrigg Farm?"

"Lachanrigg? Oo, thaat's a canny way baack. Six mile happen."

"Oh!" she cried. "Am I really nearer the railway than I am to Lachanrigg?"

It appeared that this was so.

"I came through the Guyseburn woods," she said, "and the path was flooded, so I went up the hill and lost my way."

"D'ye coom from t' Pele?" asked the boy with sudden interest.

"Yes," she replied, not desiring to risk a lie which might be quite unnecessary.

He gave her a long, speculative look, his hand fumbling doubtfully with the leather pouch containing the dispatch he carried. An inquiry after her name was trembling on his tongue, but to deliver a cablegram to an unknown woman in the dark was too risky. It would save him some miles of unpleasant walking, but, on the other hand, it might cost him his job. It did not occur to Olwen that he was bound for the place she had come from, for she believed she had come far out of the way. Her preoccupation was to obtain directions for reaching the station, and these he gave her. It did not sound a difficult route, and it would be dawn before long. With hearty thanks she bade him good morning and set off. Beyond a headache she did not feel over-tired. She thought she could manage five miles, and she had several malted milk lozenges with her. She took her way, and the boy took his, bearing the message which contained such important news for herself.

CHAPTER XXIX

BRAMFORTH AGAIN

SOME time later Olwen sat down by the roadside upon a very wet tree trunk, and wondered if she could get any farther.

Things might have been worse, for the rain had ceased at dawn and the weather was not so very cold. But her head ached excruciatingly, and she was conscious at the moment of hardly any desire, except to find herself back in her room in the Pele with Sunia in attendance.

A winter's morning and an empty stomach, taken together, do not make for heroism. She was wondering vaguely why she had acted thus—what had induced her to pass the night in such an ill-regulated fashion, and what she should say to the Vicarage circle at Bramforth when she got there.

The sound of an approaching motor upon the road gave her a faint hope of a lift. It caused her no apprehension, for she was not aware that the car which Wolf had chartered had been hired for the time of his stay and was stabled at the Pele. According to her calculation, there was not yet time for any pursuit to catch up with her even if they knew which way she had gone. Thus, as the car swung round the corner, she had no foreboding, and she stood up by the roadside, her arm outstretched to attract the attention of the occupants. But for this they might have passed her without notice, for they were travelling fast, and daylight was not fully come.

There was an exclamation, a sudden jamming on of

brakes, they drew to a standstill, and she found herself caught. Both the Guyse twins had come in search of her. Ninian was driving, Wilfrid beside him.

In a moment the whole frame of Olwen's mind changed. The weakness of her spirit passed. She was almost free, and they had pursued.

They did not mean her to escape.

In her terror and distress, a cry broke from her. She held up her hands, like one at bay, and her voice was strangled as it is in nightmare as she gasped:

"Go away! Go away! I will not come with you!"

Wolf was at her side. He held his cap in his hand, and his expression was that of pitying kindness.

"Thank God we have found you!" he said. "What can have happened? Did you walk out of the house in your sleep?"

She put up her hands to her throat as if she were choking. "No! no! I have escaped," she panted. "I will not go back, I tell you! I will not go back!"

"Oh, but I think you must," was the gentle, regretful answer. "You could not be so unkind as to cast this slur upon our hospitality? We know that there have been difficulties, but I do most earnestly assure you that my mother has always wanted to do her very best to make you happy and comfortable. Surely—surely things were not so bad yesterday that nothing would do but a midnight flight? Come, come!" He took her helpless hands. "Try to quiet yourself. Try to reflect. You are feverish and overwrought—not fit to travel. Let me——"

He was drawing her gently towards the car where it waited. Ninian had kept his seat at the driving-wheel, his face hard set, looking straight in front of him as though he had turned into a chauffeur.

In her extremity, resisting the compulsion of Wilfrid's hands, the unspoken reproof of his eyes, she appealed passionately to the elder twin. "Ninian," she cried, "help me! Don't let me be taken back! I won't go back! I can't! . . . You know I can't!"

Ninian flung himself into the road and approached.

"Why," Wolf was saying, half playfully, "if Ninian knows why you cannot stay with us another hour, he knows more than I do. Come, come, when the doctor has been and your temperature goes down, you will be grateful to us for having saved you from the consequences of a little temporary delirium—indeed you will!"

Ninian spoke suddenly. "She isn't going back if she doesn't want to," he announced.

"But, my dear chap, what can she do?" cried Wolf aghast.

"What do you want to do?" asked Ninian, standing over her.

She lifted her white face to his. Her knees were shaking under her, she was within an ace of sheer breakdown, but his unimpassioned coldness steadied her a little. "I want to go—home—to Bramforth!" she brought out. "Oh, please, please!"

"Miss Innes, anybody would tell you that you are not fit for a long cold journey," began Wolf, but Ninian pushed him aside.

"You really mean it?" he demanded of her. "You are determined not to go back to the Pele? You insist on leaving us?"

His voice sounded lifeless and weary.

"Yes, yes," she faltered, bringing out her handkerchief and wiping the two drops which had overflowed her eyelids and lay on her white cheeks. "I must go. Can't you see I must?"

He stared along the dim road as though he stared into the future.

"This is the end then?"

She assented dumbly.

"All right. I'll take you to Raefell and see you into the train. There's a through carriage on the 8.20, and you can get to Newcastle without changing." He turned to open the door of the car, adding, as she hesitated, "You can't trust me even to do this?"

She yielded at that touch. She was wax in his hands. If he had caught her up in his arms, told her not to be silly, but to come back with him, she would have done it. Perhaps Wolf saw, and it may have been the reason why his fine lip curled as he looked at his brother rather contemptuously.

Miss Innes got into the car obediently. Ninian opened a bag which stood on the seat, and produced a thermos and a package of sandwiches. He poured out hot coffee and made her drink it. Then, wrapping the fur carriage rug warmly about her, he shut her in, took his place, with Wolf beside him, and they made best pace for Raefell.

She hardly knew what were her thoughts as they sped on. Probably she did not wholly trust Ninian, and was watchful to see whether he really would do as he promised. When they arrived in the pretty village, set among woods sloping to the river, they stopped before the inn, and Wolf dismounted, as it seemed to her, unwillingly.

"I will leave my brother to see you into the train," he said, coming to the window. "Good-bye. I am regretting every minute that your visit should have such a termination. It was doing my mother no end of good. Don't you think, even now——"

Nin started the motor, and he was obliged to stand back.

They crossed the river, and doubled back to the station on the further side. There was not much time to spare. Ninian opened the door and helped her out, with her handbag, leaving her a minute in the waiting-room while he went to get her ticket. The train drew in to the station as he returned. He put her into a first-class carriage, and covered her knees with the fur rug from the car. She began to object, both to the class and to the loan of the rug.

"You can send it back by post," he replied, tucking it about her. "There is your ticket. You have an hour at Newcastle, plenty of time for a good lunch. You are due at Bramforth at a quarter to three. Good-bye!"

"Good-bye!" The rush of feeling was overpowering. This was the end, and by her own act, her own wish! All the fervent life, the keen emotion of the last few weeks was over, and there was nothing to be said—nothing! She joined her hands, as if to hold herself back from stretching them out to him. For a moment her tear-dimmed eyes caught a green ray from his. "I leave you as I came," cried she with a gulp, "a little blue thing with a red nose!"

He nodded, speechless, and, to her mortification, shut the door upon her and departed there and then, though it was a long minute after before the train began to move. She gazed from the closed window upon the waiting car, but could not see its driver. He had not remained for so much as a parting glance.

With all her heart she then wished that she had consented to let him do as he asked, and "make a clean breast of it."

For some miles her mind held but one idea. There was a place on the line where, upon looking from the window of the train, one could see Guysewyke Pele square against the sky-line. Upon catching this last glimpse she set her whole attention. In vain. The mist was too thick. No distances were visible. She began to cry then, miserably and persistently. It was over. She was going back. It was an ignominious return. Had she felt less ill it is possible that she might, when she reached Newcastle, have

taken a train for Liverpool instead of Bramforth. She
dare not, however, risk such a proceeding to-day.

With her own hand she had pushed away a temptation
whose strength appalled her. She had done her duty, but
the thought brought no drop of consolation. She felt as
if her very heart had been torn out of her and as though
the gaping wound so left would never heal.

At Newcastle she was much too depressed to go to the
restaurant, and she crept into the ladies' waiting-room,
where she nursed her grief in a corner. Presently a boy
came in, carrying a tea-basket. "Lady in here ordered a
tea-basket?" he piped. All the dismal occupants of the
place shook their heads. He advanced, doubtfully.

"Well, that's funny. I've been all over the station. It
was a lady with a grey coat and veil," he went on, placing
himself before Olwen.

"I did not order it, but I shall be very glad to take it,"
she replied. It was a fortunate blunder for her, as the
hot tea was just what she needed; her thoughts winced
away from the idea of dinner. This seemed an extra nice
tea, with buttered toast and brown bread and butter.

As she emerged from the waiting room, a polite porter
just outside relieved her of her bag and rug, putting her
into a comfortable compartment, with a label "Ladies
only" on the window.

Her night of wandering had tired her so much that,
being able to lie down, she presently dropped asleep and
forgot her misery for a time.

As she neared her journey's end, she reflected with vexation that she might have sent a telegram from Newcastle
to tell the Vicarage to expect her. Even an obvious precaution such as this had not once occurred to a mind
entirely preoccupied with its own distress.

However, when the train at last drew in to the dirty,
noisy, clamorous platform, she had hardly opened the door

of her compartment before she descried Aunt Maud's yellow mackintosh.

She almost fell into her aunt's hungry arms. "Oh!" she cried, "how did you happen to be here?"

"Why, I came to meet you, of course. You telegraphed this morning."

"Oh—did they?—that was kind," said the girl falteringly. "I—I thought I had better come home. I was ill. They didn't want me to travel, and I expect they were right, for I—I've left all my luggage behind."

Her aunt was looking at her with much concern and some consternation. She suggested an immediate visit to the lost property office, but Olwen said that she had seen to that—her things would be sent on.

"I'm afraid we must drive," she faltered, "I feel too crocky to walk. I can afford it, for they paid my railway fare."

They found a taxi and got in, Miss Wilson full of anxiety to hear fuller details of the circumstances, and her niece realising (and wondering why she had not sooner done so) that it was wholly out of the question for her to reveal what had actually happened.

"The doctor was taken ill," she explained slowly, "and he said it would be a long business; and I was at the top of the tower, having to be waited upon. I did not like to feel that I was being a trouble."

As she spoke, they were passing, having been held up by the stream of traffic, out into the main road from the station approach. Her eyes, fixed vaguely upon the passing show, suddenly dilated. A tall man, coming from the station, had just gained the island in the centre of the thoroughfare, and was detained by the passage of a huge motor lorry from moving on immediately. He had his back to her, but had she not known the figure, the clothes were familiar to her. It was Ninian Guysc.

An instant and the fast-running taxi had carried them away.

"This sumptuous fur rug," Aunt Maud was saying. "It will cost something to send back!"

She did not notice the sudden pallor, the stifled silence of her niece; or, if she did, ascribed it to exhaustion. Olwen's emotions were turbulent. Ninian must have come in her train all the way. It was to him, doubtless, that she owed the persistence of the boy with the super-tea-basket; also the courtesy of the porter. During those hours of anguish, when she had been imagining them parted for ever, he had actually been within a few yards of her—perhaps in the next compartment!

The force of the shock of joy was enough to show her her own heart. She could hardly say a word for some minutes.

Miss Wilson gathered the impression that Olwen was more ill than she was willing to admit. She thought the best thing to do was to put her to bed at once, and leave her unquestioned until she had had a long rest. On receipt of the telegram, her room had been prepared by her aunt's own hands before she set out for the station. Olwen was very grateful.

Aunt Ada, no less than Aunt Maud, was quite evidently glad to see her on any terms, although she detected behind their affection a jealous hope that their darling had not been a failure—that she was not in any sense of the word coming home in disgrace.

She could hardly give as emphatic a denial to the suspicion as she could have wished, for she dreaded very much what Madam might say should she take it into her head to write to her grandfather.

She remembered the threat held over her, and knew that her flight would cause deep displeasure. It seemed almost certain that Mrs. Guyse would indulge her anger to the extent of a severe letter.

. . . But Ninian was in Bramforth ! . . .

Nothing could take from the joy of that. For what had he come ?

The answer which her heart returned was that he had come to make to her, under the shelter of her home roof, the confession which he had not been able to make at the Pele.

Her bedroom was very cold, and her bed very hard. She thought of Sunia with a yearning which made her wonder whether she had been induced by the ayah to swallow some nostrum, unawares, which should produce acute craving for the Pele the moment she left it.

She fought, however, with such thoughts. She must pull herself together, rest, be ready for the morrow. He would know her to be too tired to-day for him to venture upon a call.

She passed, however, a disturbed night, awakening with bad dreams every time she went to sleep. They most kindly insisted upon bringing some breakfast up-stairs to her. After she had eaten it, she slipped out of bed, and started to rummage among her things, to find a clean blouse which she might put on.

Before she was dressed she heard the familiar click of the gate latch, and from behind her muslin blind saw Ninian stalking up the gravel path.

The door-bell pealed, and with a small giggle of delight she hugged the thought of keeping my lord waiting, chafing, cooling his heels in the ugly, cold drawing-room.

He was shown in; of that she was certain. But no message came up to her. After waiting a while, during which she completed her toilette—not without an ill-tempered struggle over the arrangement of her hair to conceal the scar—she crept out upon the landing. The cook was sweeping the hall, and a cautious signal brought her half-way upstairs.

"Cook, is there a gentleman here?"

"Yes, miss," said the woman, who was a new arrival since Olwen's departure.

"Did you let him in?"

"Yes, miss."

"For whom did he ask?"

"For the vicar, miss."

"For the vicar?"

"Yes, miss. He asked how you was, and I said you wasn't downstairs yet. Then he asked for the vicar, and they're talking together now, in the study."

Olwen crept back, shaking with anxiety. What was Ninian doing? Why did he want to see her grandfather? Was he assuring him that she had left without their desire? Was he giving that full account of their nocturnal adventure on the Fell of which Madam had warned her? He was taking time enough over it, anyway.

Restlessly she wandered about, up and down her room, every moment expecting a summons, and every moment growing more excited, more apprehensive. The hands of the old tin alarum clock upon her mantelpiece moved on; yet still the visitor was closeted with Mr. Wilson.

At last she heard a noise—the sound of an opening door. Softly she crept to the balustrade, and saw the top of Nin's black head as he came out into the hall. Her grandfather accompanied him to the entrance. There they shook hands. In a moment, as it seemed to her, the door had opened and closed upon him. He was gone. He had left the house without seeing her, without—or so she must suppose—even asking to see her.

Almost at once she told herself that he would return. He had been asked to lunch, doubtless—or he was coming back after dinner. . . . So far had pride sunk that she wished she had been out in the hall to waylay him—just to look into his face and judge what he was feeling.

Her grandfather stood in the empty hall, his hands clasped behind his back, as if plunged in deepest thought. At last he lifted his head.

"Cook! Is Miss Innes dressed?"

"Yes, sir, I believe she is."

"Kindly tell her that I wish to speak with her at once upon matters of grave importance."

CHAPTER XXX

It did not take long for Olwen to reach the study. Her whole self was nothing but one huge mark of interrogation as she went into her grandfather's presence. Her eagerness was even enhanced by her desperate dread. She felt that she might be going to receive the wigging of her life. What tales had Ninian told of her or himself?

The old man was not seated, but pacing his room in evidently great perturbation. As he turned to face her, she saw that his usually parchment-coloured face was quite red. He eyed her with a peculiar stare which struck terror to her heart.

"But he can't do anything to me," she said to herself. "I have got father now—somebody to stand up for me!"

"My dear, how are you?" was the vicar's pacific opening. "I was sorry to be out when you arrived yesterday, but, when I came in, your aunt said she thought you had better not be disturbed."

"I don't feel very well yet, thank you, Grandfather, but I am well enough to hear what you have to say."

He eyed her apprehensively. "I—I wonder," said he, shuffling across the room once more. Then, turning, he sat down at his desk as though resolved upon controlling his nerves. He cleared his throat. "Be seated, my dear," he said quite solicitously. His faded eyes dwelt upon her as she obeyed his behest. "I have—er—just had a visitor."

"Yes. Mr. Guyse. I saw him come," she replied as naturally as she could.

"Yes. H'm! You and he have seen a good deal of each other?"

"We have. It was winter, and the Pele is not at all a large house."

"How did he strike you, I wonder? But perhaps such a question is merely futile. We must come to the main point—the surprising, I may say the extraordinary information which this young man has just given me. My dear, you must prepare yourself for—for something in the nature of a shock."

"Oh, Grandfather, please, please tell me! Is it about —about Mr. Guyse?"

"Well, in part—in part it is. Very painful, very distressing, of course . . . but in the main it concerns you, my dear, you and your father, my poor son-in-law, Madoc Innes."

She sat like a stone. "My father!" she whispered. "He—he is worse. Ah, don't say he is—dead?"

The vicar bowed his head. His hands were playing with a cablegram which lay upon the table before him.

"He is dead," he said. "This message arrived for you after you had left the Pele yesterday morning. Mr. Guyse brought it to me, because he feared, in the state of your health, he ought not to give it to you under the circumstances. He thought you should be safe at home when the news was broken. Er—your aunt forwarded you a letter from New York, which she thought was from your father, some days ago?"

She found her voice with a sob. "Yes! He said he was coming—sailing in the *Stupendous*. I was to go to Liverpool to meet him. That was partly why I hurried home. Oh, don't say he is dead; don't say I shall never see him!"

"My dear, you must calm yourself sufficiently to allow me to proceed. The most surprising part of the story is still to be told. I have seldom been so completely taken aback as by the news Mr. Guyse has just given me."

"Mr. Guyse! What does he know about father?"

"Ah, my dear, that is the point. That—is—the point. He did not know poor Madoc himself, but it seems that his twin brother knew him very well indeed."

"Wolf!" cried the girl bewildered. "Wolf knew my father!"

"Intimately. They were in Alaska together. They went to Klondyke together. Your father had the most astonishing good fortune. He struck an oil well when he was looking for gold. It was in the very place where it was most wanted. He managed to keep it quiet until he had bought up all the land he required, and then turned it into a company. He died—your father died—a millionaire, my dear."

He handed over the cablegram, and she took it in her shaking hands.

"Regret Madoc Innes died yesterday. Wire at once permanent address to Ware and Shuckton, solicitors, 536 West Forty-ninth Street, New York City."

Olwen faced the old man with a blank stare. She had thus far drawn no inference at all.

"The—er—the Guyse family is, I gather, greatly impoverished?" went on the vicar presently. She assented, still bewildered.

"Yes. The brother in London was in regular correspondence with your father, and knew he was desperately ill. In fact, he knew that he could not live long. While he was staying at the Pele for a few days' vacation at Christmas, they saw quite by chance your advertisement in the daily paper. The name of Innes struck the young man, for he knew well of your existence, having heard your father speak of you. He knew that poor Madoc had not been in communication with you for years—that he had willed all his fortune to you, that he meant to claim you when he returned to England, but that his state of health made it unlikely that he would ever reach this country. Your first letter, in which you signed your name in full, made him certain that he was right. The name of Olwen was so uncommon. He suggested to his brother that they should offer you a post in the family, that the elder Mr. Guyse should—er—secure your affections, and that you should become engaged under the impression that nothing was known of your fortune."

The girl to whom he spoke uttered a choked cry. She rose from her seat, made for the window as if to open it, stopped half-way, dropping on her knees before a big chair, on which her head fell, while she shook with helpless sobbing.

So this—*this* was the truth, the incredible, undreamed-of truth!

She had been picturing one kind of infamy for Ninian, when all the time it was something different, but just as contemptible. He was nothing more exalted than a fortune-hunter—a mean, hypocritical fortune-hunter.

There had been a deliberate plot, to which, of course, both Madam and the ayah had been parties. To get her there, to pet her and make much of her, and later, when she proved harder to manage than they had anticipated, and time was running short, to entrap her, to persuade her that she had no choice but to make the marriage which had all along been planned. . . .

"Oh!" she thought, "I shall go mad! This is more than I can endure!"

Her grandfather, in much distress, vainly begged her to be calm.

"I must ring for one of your aunts," he said at last; and this threat enabled her to control herself.

"No, no, don't do that," she gasped, swallowing her tears. "I am going to be sensible, I will try and face it. You see, it is so dreadful, so wild, so mad—and it is all coming at once!"

"It is most natural that you should feel emotion, dear child. I myself hardly know what to say or to think," replied the old man, wiping away a tear. "Such a change of fortune is enough to stagger the strongest head."

"Clever plan of theirs, wasn't it?" she muttered, with an irony whose effect was marred by tears. "Seems quite a pity they just did not bring it off." (Oh, Ninian, Ninian, why did you confess? Why must you roll yourself in the mire like this?)

"It was, as you may imagine, with great difficulty that the young man brought himself to speak to me on such a subject. He did so because he said you had refused to hear him, and he wished me to inform you of the facts. He seems to have had scruples from the first. But there were heavy pecuniary liabilities, concerning which he was not very explicit. However, I gather that as the days passed his natural good feeling began to get the upper hand. You were so unsuspecting, you were being cajoled and hoodwinked. . . . In short, he came by degrees to feel that he could not bear it, and that the dishonourable plot ought to be made known to you——"

"It was probably more policy than honour that suggested that course," she sneered. "If my father came over, he knew he would be found out."

"Well, there is that view of the subject," said the vicar doubtfully. "They did know, of course, that it must come out sooner or later. Had you been actually married, I suppose there would have been no help for it. I think," he added with hesitation, "yes, I do really think that the young man was heartily ashamed of himself."

"I trust he was," said Olwen with trembling lips. "Think, Grandfather, suppose he had succeeded! I am young and inexperienced. Suppose he had made me care desperately—what then?"

He looked at her with solicitude.

"That, of course, would have been most regrettable. However, all's well that ends well, and he will never trouble you again."

Standing in the window, her face turned from him, she repeated the words blankly. "He will never trouble me again? . . . I suppose not. Oh, how I wish that he had been caught in his own net! If I had been a different girl, tall and beautiful and fascinating! If I could have made him wild for me, and then—then found out this, so that I could punish him, make him suffer, as I am suffering now!"

This outburst was beyond the scope of the old cleric, who sat peering with weak eyes upon a passion that passed him by.

"Is—is Mr. Guyse still in Bramforth?" she asked at length.

"No. I understand that he made his visit to me so early because he had to catch a train. He has gone back to Guysewyke."

Over! It was indeed over. In all her thoughts of Ninian she had not suspected him of playing the hypocrite with her. Now she saw it all, in the fierce light of her grandfather's bald words. He had played a part with her—pretended he liked her, pretended he was eager for her society. . . . As time went on, he must have seen that what was all jest to him was earnest to her. He had begun to feel some stirring of remorse. "I wish to God

I had never seen you! . . . I'm damned if I marry the child!"

How easy of interpretation now were those words which had been so puzzling!

How nearly she had fallen a prey!

It seemed as if Providence had intervened to save her, as if some power greater than herself had nerved her to that midnight flight, and spared her the humiliation of hearing from the lips of the man she loved the cruel fact that he had meant to marry her for her money.

He had gone back to Guysewyke.

And Wilfrid, handsome, debonair Wilfrid, had been privy to all this. He, who knew her father well, had kept silence on that head. Together he and Ninian had planned to net a fortune. How very nearly they had succeeded!

She summoned up a picture of Wolf, standing in the damp, tree-shaded road, coaxing her so gently back to the car, luring her so plausibly to return to her prison.

He had not succeeded. Ah, God be praised for that! She was here, at Bramforth, bruised, half killed, but safe! Oddly enough she had at the moment a glimpse into the soul of Madam—the other heiress who had been lured into a loveless marriage by a former Ninian Guyse! She pictured herself, dull, faded, embittered, listless, while the man who did not love her passed lightly on his way.

From that she was saved—at least she was saved from that!

"He was as deep in debt as I in love; he only wanted my fortune. . . . He said I expected too much." . . . She seemed to hear the very tones of the dry, lifeless voice.

"I think," said the vicar's quavering voice, "that you should try to turn your thoughts a little from this young man to the startling news he brought. It seems—though it is hard, indeed, to realise—that you are not only wealthy, my child, but enormously wealthy. It"—he broke off with a nervous little laugh. "Such a thing has not happened before in our family. I will confess that it has shaken me."

Olwen came out from her own trouble and faced, as it were, suddenly her fortune from a new standpoint. She saw it no longer as the devilish thing which had tempted Nin to pretend that he loved her, but as a weapon of power, something that should enable her to repay to the family who had mothered her for so long some part of their unselfish performance of duty.

"Oh, Grandfather!" she cried, springing to her feet. She ran to him, flung her arms about him, and broke down into laughing and tears. "To be able to make you comfortable, to give you all you want . . . and the aunts! Those wonderful aunts! They shall come out into the sunshine; the people who have patronised them shall come begging favours! Oh, Grandfather, it is true, you are sure it is true? We are not making any terrible mistake?"

"I feel sure that it is true. Mr. Guyse brought me this paper to read."

He laid before her an American newspaper, containing a long paragraph upon "The Glen Olwen Oil-King, Madoc Innes."

"Madoc returns a millionaire to the old country. Left home without a fiver. Left something that cost him more. His only daughter, Miss Olwen Innes. Romance of the gold-seeker. Miss Olwen knows nothing of the pile that awaits her."

So it ran.

"It appears that Mr. Guyse's brother wrote recently to your father telling him that you were staying with his mother at the Pele—speaking as though your coming there had been accidental.   That accounts, so Mr. Guyse thinks, for the fact that the New York lawyers sent the cable to the Pele direct."

"Oh, they planned it well, didn't they?   But somehow I escaped the snare," said the girl a little wildly.   She sprang to her feet, ran to the door, opened it, and cried aloud for her aunts.   They came in, their faces expressing consternation in every line.

"Olwen, you ought to be in bed, you look half crazy, child; let me take your temperature!"

The heiress flew upon undemonstrative Aunt Ada, locking her vigorous young arms about her.   "Take anything you like!" she cried, "for I owe you everything I have or am!   Oh, Aunt Maud, Aunt Maud!   Do you remember how we played at fancying we were rich, chose our house in Gainsley Park, furnished it with our favourite things out of the best shops, chose our Daimler or our Rolls-Royce, and went off together for a tour in Italy?   Well, we'll do it!   We'll do it all!   We'll do more than ever our poor little starved imaginations dared to think of!   You shall do just exactly as you like, my dears, from this moment for the rest of your lives!"

"Is she crazy?   In a high fever," cried Aunt Maud apprehensively, lifting the burnished locks to gaze anxiously upon the wound beneath.

The vicar got to his feet.   He trembled, as his gnarled hands rested upon the sheet of soiled blotting-paper on his desk.

"It's true, my dears, she is not crazy.   Madoc Innes is dead and has left her more money than she will know what to do with."

CHAPTER XXXI

THE CHANGED WORLD

OLWEN INNES stood in the hall of her house in Chelsea, bidding good-bye to her guests. It was a charming hall, for the wall of a room had been removed to make space for it, and the result was excellent, creating an effect quite unlike a London house.

Though years had elapsed since she acquired No. 2 Orchard Row, this was her house-warming; and the guests who were departing were all of them friends in more than name, since they had become acquainted under stress of the most terrible period of modern history.

Hardly had Olwen decided where she would make her home, hardly had the decorators completed their dainty work upon it, when the European War broke out. No furniture was as yet in the house, and Olwen and Aunt Maud promptly turned it into a hospital for wounded officers.

The expenses of its working were borne entirely by the mistress of the house, and Aunt Maud personally superintended all the catering. During the grim summers and winters when the fortunes of the Allies ebbed and flowed, the new heiress worked as hard as ever she had done in the Palatine Bank, with short and very occasional holidays.

Now that peace had returned and the war-worn nation was settling down once more, the hospital emptied gradually, the nurses departed, and the owner found herself at last able to indulge her taste for beauty and to remodel the place which for so many months had been a refuge for some of the bravest of all the splendid men who served their country.

Languidly, and like a patient who has undergone a severe operation, England opened her eyes upon Peace once more. It seemed incredible, and for long its unreal aspect was increased by the fact that the officers and men of the vast new armies returned only tardily and in small numbers from their regiments.

Crippled limbs, crippled incomes, crippled businesses were the order of the day; everywhere a brave attempt to hide financial wounds, to triumph over personal sorrow, to set the face steadfastly to the England of the future, wherein so much was changed, so much was gone, never to be replaced; so much, one felt, was in store, but not as yet near fruition.

A good many of the officer patients who had passed through what came to be known as the Orchard Row Hospital had been anxious to persuade Miss Innes to join them in founding at least one family for the future of England. But in vain. Aunt Maud said the war had changed Olwen. It had sobered her. Or was it, perhaps, her illness?

A somewhat severe breakdown followed her foolhardy midnight flight from the Pele. For a long time she was too ill even to write to Mrs. Guyse to thank her for her kindness during her stay. As soon as she was well enough to travel Aunt Maud took her abroad. They had returned to England in the June before war was declared. Since that time so much water had rushed under the bridges of life that one could hardly keep pace with the swift flow of events. Everything personal sank into the background and was lost. The war and the war only had been the preoccupation of existence ever since Olwen became rich. Except in the one direction of helping those she loved, she had not tasted the sweets of wealth.

One of her first acts was to make her grandfather resign his living. He now resided, as had always been his ambition, in a pretty and comfortable house at Harrogate in company with Aunt Ada, and was happier than ever in his life.

His departure from Bramforth made intercourse with the Holroyds less easy. Grace became a V.A.D. worker as soon as war broke out, and she longed to come to London and help Olwen with her hospital. But there was too much to be done in Bramforth, and her mother disliked the idea of her going so far. Thus the girls had seen nothing of each other until Gracie came to town for her first taste of pleasure, since the V.A.D. work became a thing of the past.

She now stood beside the young hostess and watched the leave-taking with interest.

"What a lot of people you know!" she remarked, when the final guest had departed and they turned and went up the wide staircase to the drawing-room.

"A good many," said Olwen; "though when I took this house I knew nobody in London. These are almost all the families of our various patients or clergy with whom we have been brought in touch—doctors, visitors, or helpers of some kind. I feel rather like the upstart ladies who cut their steps to the abode of the upper ten by dint of big subscriptions to charity or the secret party funds. Really, I haven't tried to advertise myself, but the people with whom I have found myself thrown are mostly nice, and I don't believe they realise how rich I am." They passed into the drawing-room, and she sank down upon a low chair with a little lazy yawn and stretch. "We are getting deluged with invitations," said she. "You'll have

to come with us to two or three houses to-morrow afternoon.   What time does your brother's train arrive?"

"Somewhere about half-past four, at King's Cross."

"The small motor had better meet him," said the mistress thoughtfully.   "He won't have very bulky luggage."

Ben Holroyd had not been to the war.   Government
had taken over his mills, and he was indispensable to
their management.   Olwen had given but little thought to
him during the stress of the past years.   Now she was
idly reflecting that he was the only man she knew, of whose
disinterestedness she could ever henceforth be sure as long
as she lived.   He had loved her honestly and with no
thought of money.   He was to arrive on the morrow to
spend a couple of nights and take his sister home.   Olwen
and he had not met since the outbreak of war.

The change wrought in both girls by the pasage of
those years, packed with destiny, was noticeably great.
Gracie, who had been threatened, even at the time when
Olwen went to Guysewyke, with a repetition of her
mother's unwieldy embonpoint, was now almost slender,
fined down to a muscular trimness, the result of unremit-
ting work.   She was happily betrothed to a north country
"Temporary Captain," who in peace time was a solicitor,
and was now busily employed gathering up the threads of
his interrupted practice in preparation for marriage.

Olwen bore more plainly still the traces of what she had
gone through.   Her face had acquired, as it were, new
meanings.   Her beauty, which had always been largely
a matter of expression, was now much more evident than
formerly.   Those who met her for the first time never
failed to be struck by her, to remember her voice, her
look—"What a *memorable* face Miss Innes has!" said old
Lady Cumberdale when she came to visit her nephew, one
of those officers who had implored Olwen to marry him.

"I never remember to have seen an English girl with quite so much distinction; but she looks sad."

The remark was repeated to Olwen. She sighed, remembering who had once described her as a "dainty rogue in porcelain." Not much of the rogue was now left. Everyone always added that little conclusion to any criticism of her appearance. "She looks sad."

The sadness had been there throughout the weary months of war; but as long as the necessity of the moment kept her at work, it had been an undercurrent, far below the surface. Like the hopelessly estranged husband in "A Confession," she might have said:

> *"Therefore I kept my memory down, by stress*
> *Of work."*

But memory, howsoever held down, arose the moment the grip slackened, and stood upon her feet. Each day that passed seemed now to bring the heiress back a step, across the dim gulf of separation, to the re-living of the old days at the Pele.

Since the moment when, overlooking the balusters at Bramforth, she had seen the top of Ninian's sleek black head, a little bent, as he moved to the door, no word of him had ever reached her. He might have stepped from the vicarage threshold clean over the rim of the world, for all she ever knew to the contrary.

Her own severe illness had almost immediately supervened. Everyone thought it natural enough, not only that she should return post-haste from Guysewyke on receiving the news of her fortune and her father's death, but also that she should succumb to the double shock. There was no need for her to say anything to anybody in explanation of her proceedings. The Holroyds knew that she had hurt her head when skating, and had thought it

best to come home in consequence; but no suspicion of the
true state of affairs ever leaked out. Old Mr. Wilson kept
his granddaughter's counsel faithfully. The plot revealed
by Ninian remained in his own memory alone.

By the time she was well again, enough of the business
resulting from her father's death had been completed for
her to be in possession of ample funds; and she only craved
to utilise this unlooked-for aid, to transport her out of the
old groove, to enable her to go where she might find the
means to turn her thoughts from contemplation of her
tortured aching heart.

For a while, the two powerful agents, wealth and change
of scene, were more successful than she had dared to hope.
In the crowding of new impressions, she let the thought of
her humiliation sleep.

Steadily she set herself to face the world as it was, to
consider the position fairly.

Ninian had indeed trampled her maiden pride in the
dust. He owned that he had meant to marry her for her
money. He gave, as the reason why he had not fulfilled
this intention, his own consciousness that he was playing
a base part. This was, this must be, only a courteous way
of saying that it seemed to him a shame to marry this girl,
a nice little thing enough, for her money—that is, without
caring about her.

In other words, her attraction had proved insufficient
to hold him to his purpose.

In the light shed by this atrocious thought, she went
over endlessly all that had passed between them from the
time of their first meeting. She remembered the disappointment which had been plainly observable in Ninian
when he met her first in the inn; his subsequent changes
of mood. Sometimes he had seemed as though he really
liked her. Then he had veered, as though he felt he could
never keep it up. His unreal, jeering manner was quite

accounted for. From the first he had felt unable to be
natural with her. Then, as time went on, he had realised
that as a chum, as a little sister, he could have liked her
well enough; and it had seemed cruel to cheat her any
longer. She saw it all with horrible clearness; and the
worst pang was occasioned by the knowledge that he must
have seen and known that she was taking his sham atten-
tions for the real thing—in short, that he had been quite
aware that the girl he could not bring himself to marry
was in love with him all the time.

As she recalled scenes that had passed between them
she felt able to trace each alternation of his feeling, between determination to take advantage of her folly and
carry out his purpose, and the fits of self-contempt and
shame which had from time to time overswept him.

Sunia, too! Olwen had even been led by her vanity
to think that the Hindu woman really liked her. Nothing
of the kind. The ayah was merely helping to catch the
golden goose for the use of her sahib and his family.

These were racking thoughts. Her only consolation
was the remembrance that, after all, she had had strength
to tear herself away. Sometimes she wondered whether
her dead father had known of her danger and had exerted
some unseen influence to snatch her from the brink of the
gulf which threatened her, and which she herself had so
dimly perceived.

When war broke out she at first failed to realise that all
the young manhood of England would volunteer. She did
not begin to study the *Gazette* until three months or thereabouts after the beginning of the campaign; and not once
had her perseverance been rewarded by the discovery of
any mention of the Guyse brothers. Not that her search
had been exhaustive. There had been days let slip, under
stress of a new flood of cases coming into hospital. She
knew she had hoped that some day the unlikely might

happen, and that one of those maimed heroes, so carefully carried on their stretchers into the quiet rooms, and tenderly laid upon the soft beds, might turn out to be one of the Pele twins.

Nothing of the kind had happened. As the war went on, patients were more and more methodically distributed, north to north, and south to south. Chelsea received none of the casualties among men born north of the Humber.

One result there had, however, been from the ayah's boasted incantations. The call of the north was for ever sounding in Olwen's ears.

Whether or no the woman had ever succeeded in administering the love philtre, Olwen felt fairly certain that she had found means to give her some unhallowed drug; for not poppy nor mandragora, nor the far more potent influences of money and the power that money gives, had availed to still the craving she felt to return to Guyseburndale.

No day had passed, since fighting began, during which she had not prayed for Ninian's safety. Now that all was over, the stress and strain a thing of the past, she began to feel more and more certain that he was dead.

She knew enough of him to be certain that he would be reckless. His love for the Pele and for the land on which the feet of his forefathers had trod for centuries was the main motive of his life. For this he had been ready to sacrifice himself and her, until his own nobler nature had risen and forbidden the banns. Deprived of this last chance of reinstating himself in the country, what would he do?

There was but one course open to him before the war broke out, and that was to marry Rose Kendall. He might have done this; but if he had not, then at the outbreak of war she felt he would have flung himself into the breach. Most likely he had been killed upon the

Marne. She could fancy him going into battle with a jest upon his lips:

No Guyse
Is ever wise
Until he dies.

It seemed certain that he was dead and that Wolf was master of the Pele. If it were so, then she felt sure that he had sold the place and that his mother had come to live in London to be near him.

Was that really so? Could it be so? The image of the Pele and of all that was in it was clearly before her mind's eye, and the picture had all the qualities of permanence. She felt that it literally could not change.

Then she tried to imagine Rose Kendall as its mistress. That seemed equally impossible.

The craving to know the truth was growing to such dimensions within her that she began to revolve wild plans for leaving town and going to stay somewhere in the neighbourhood—so that she might obtain news without seeming to ask for it.

"Are you frightfully tired, Ollie?" asked Grace wistfully, having spoken twice without receiving an answer.

Miss Innes came out of her reverie with a start. "Pardon, old girl, I was just thinking," said she, laughing, as she sat more upright and gazed about her with eyes still introspective.

"I was saying that those people who went almost last—I think you said it was Lady Cumberdale—seemed very nice. I liked the girl."

"Lilla Penrith? Yes, she is a dear," replied Olwen. "I told you we nursed the brother here, Captain Penrith. He made a very good recovery, much to the surprise of the doctors, since he developed enteric in addition to his wound. We are going there to-morrow afternoon. If you had not gone and got engaged so precipitately to James Heslop, I would have introduced you to the Captain; he isn't half bad."

"The Honourable Miss Penrith took my fancy very much. We had a long talk. She was doing V.A.D. work, too."

"She did it very well. But we leave out the Honourable, you know, my dear, except upon envelopes."

"Do you? Is she just plain Miss Penrith?"

"Only that. Did you suppose she wore her Honourable like a coronet?" teased Olwen. She talked at random, for she was tired, and her thoughts had been switched completely away from her house-warming by the unaccountable rush of memory which was assailing her.

Aunt Maud came in smiling. "Well, I do think it went nicely," said she. "Of course it ought, because everything came from the best places, and our staff is efficient. But this new idea of simplicity in entertaining, and not having any programme, made me afraid it might be dull. However, it wasn't!"

"Before the war, I should have paid a hundred guineas to a few second-rate singers to perform good music to an audience that couldn't understand it, and only longed to talk," said the mistress of the house. "By the way, Lady Cumberdale said, quite apologetically, that she is having a programme to-morrow afternoon, as she wants people to hear some very fine singing from some poor girl whose career was interrupted by the war."

"I'm glad," said Gracie, with true Yorkshire fervour for music. "I can never hear too much."

Aunt Maud launched into the usual kind of talk for such an occasion—a repetition of what people had said, and how they had looked; much comment having passed with reference to the different appearance of the house since it ceased to be a hospital.

Both girls were yawning before she had half done, and she broke off, with a laugh, to order them both to bed.

Miss Maud Wilson looked ten years younger than she had done in her niece's earliest memory. She had regained much of the fair beauty which had been hers in girlhood; and Olwen privately confided to Gracie that night, during hair-brushing, that it was Aunt Maud really, and not she herself, who required a chaperon!

Next day, Orchard Row had recovered its normal appearance; and the two girls, having breakfasted in bed, just by way of contrast to the strenuous fashion of the past few years, passed a lazy morning, lunched in luxury, and then dressed and started for Lady Cumberdale's afternoon party. They looked in at another house *en route,* but at about five the car set them down in Chester Square, and they heard, as they mounted the stairs, the strains of the singing of the protégés, as Olwen called them.

They entered as softly as they could, and greeted their hostess silently. The men who were on the watch to see Miss Innes could not approach until the song was done. There were some minutes during which Olwen stood still, near the door, glancing round for friendly faces.

Someone who had been standing in talk with a girl moved, so that the face of the girl over whom he had been bending was suddenly visible to Olwen. It was a face which oddly succeeded in being pretty, in spite of a somewhat hatchet-like outline and green eyes. Those eyes were subtly expressive, the curve of the lip showed a row of good teeth, slightly pointed. The whole face reminded her of Ninian, and her heart gave a great throb.

"Lilla," whispered she to Miss Penrith, who was beside her, as soon as the music ceased, "who is the girl with the white plume in her hat, there, against the curtain?"

"That? Oh, that's Elma Guyse, Lord Caryngston's

daughter, you know. Her only brother was killed at Neuve Chapelle."

"Her brother? What, the one who married——"

"Who was to have married Wash-white Slick-Soap? Yes, but it didn't quite come off. He went to the Front, and never came back. Shall I introduce Elma to you?"

"Oh, presently—when you get a suitable chance."

No more was possible, for others were pressing forward to greet Miss Innes, and she had to talk about things of no interest, while all her thoughts were centred upon Elma Guyse. She began, half unconsciously, to move nearer by degrees to where the girl stood, and was absurdly disappointed to see her leave the room with a man in search of ices.

"Miss Innes," said a voice at her elbow, "here is someone who wants to be presented. He says he has a slight acquaintance with you—Colonel Guyse."

CHAPTER XXXII

ONE TWIN RETURNS

FOR a moment Olwen's very heart flagged in its beat. She was so taken by surprise that until she had had a moment in which to recover, she could not look up. It had, then, been premonitory—the fashion in which her thoughts had persistently strayed in the direction of Guysedyke during the preceding twenty-four hours.

Colonel Guyse! Promotion had, of course, been rapid during the war; but that he should have risen to the command of a battalion!

She kept her head turned away as long as she dared, pretending to be occupied in giving greeting to an elderly club man, Mr. Berkeley, who had been very good to her hospital in the way of presents of game, fish and poultry from his country estate. Then, with a feeling as though she stood, her back against the wall, facing the rifles of a firing party, she turned slowly round. . . .

. . . And found herself looking into the deep blue eyes of Wolf. He was older, more bronzed, but his appearance was, if anything, more attractive than ever. The whimsical smile which he shared with his twin was curving the mouth under his golden moustache.

. . . But, of course! She had foreseen this. She had known that it must be so. Wolf would be a colonel and Ninian would be—dead.

"Well, Miss Innes, this is pleasant," said Wolf genially. "I wonder if you remember as vividly as I do the circumstances under which we parted—on the Raefell Road, in the early morning?"

"Why, Olwen, I had no idea you were acquainted with my cousin," said Lady Cumberdale pleasantly, "my maternal great-grandfather married a Guyse."

"I'm afraid I didn't know it," smiled Olwen, as she shook hands with Wolf, "but you ought to be aware by this time that Debrett had little or no share in my education, dear lady."

"It is the greatest relief to me to see Miss Innes safe and well," went on Wolf, addressing her ladyship. "She came to stay with us at the Pele the winter before the war, and poor old Nin took her out skating and allowed her to fall and cut her head open. The blow made her delirious, and in the absence of her attendant she got out of the Pele at night and went wandering over the country. We had to race after her with a motor, and found her, wet and half starved, by the roadside."

Olwen listened to this account of her proceedings with interest. So this was how things appeared to Wilfrid! Well, it was natural enough! She laughed a little, but did not reply.

"My dear!" said Lady Cumberdale, in much surprise, "what an adventure! Did it not make you very ill?"

"Of course it did," Wolf answered for her. "I knew she ought to be bundled back and popped between the blankets in double quick time. But poor old Nin thought she ought to be humoured, and it was her humour to travel back to Yorkshire, so he let her do so, in her wet things. She had a bad time afterwards, so I heard; and it did not surprise me."

"Yes, I had a bad time," replied the girl with lowered eyes. "I lost my father just then, and it was a shock. However, I recovered completely."

"Greatly to the advantage of the nation," said Wolf courteously, "if what I hear be true—you have been turning your house into a hospital, have you not?"

"I have. But I am glad to see that you, apparently, have been in no need of hospital treatment," said she brightly. "You look very well."

"Yes, the army has got me for keeps, as they say. I used to be a Territorial captain before the war, you know, so I was not quite as new to my job as most of our poor chaps were. But won't you let me take you to have something to eat, or at least a cup of tea?"

She went with him out of the room and down the stairs to the tea buffet. A particularly interesting item on the programme was just about to begin, so this room was comparatively empty. They found chairs, and sat down together.

"Well," he said, after a prolonged scrutiny from beneath his thick lashes. "So the country mouse has become a town mouse."

"But remains a mouse, as you see. Mice can't turn into —well, into gazelles, for example, or swans, or birds of paradise."

"Now what, I wonder, is the exact significance of that remark?" pondered Wolf aloud. She smiled.

"Oh, there was a time when the mouse longed exceedingly to turn into something more striking," she answered lightly, "but that was long ago. Now tell me some news, please. How is your mother?"

"I'm sorry to say that she is anything but well," replied Wolf, his face clouding. "In fact, I'm afraid she is very ill. Of course, the loss of poor old Nin was a great blow to her."

Olwen felt the blood drain from her cheeks, and saw that Wolf was noting her ghastly whiteness. "Indeed," she managed to falter, "I—I had not heard. I am so sorry." . . . The lifeless words fell from her mouth, while her heart seethed within her. "I wish I had said I would marry him," she was fiercely thinking, "I wish I had let him kiss me, as he would have done, that last evening. It would be something to look back upon—something snatched out of the dreary wreck of everything." Aloud she went on, "Poor Madam must be very lonely."

"She is. You know she never liked the Pele."

"Is Sunia still with her?"

"Yes, oh, yes, Sunia is there."

She longed to ask for details—to inquire when, how and where, but found to her vexation that she could not do so with a steady voice.

While she was struggling for composure, Wolf began to speak. He told her how deeply disappointing it had been to him to be unable to continue the acquaintance begun at the Pele before the war. What he said was quite light and not too pointed, but he managed to convey the idea that he had been interested in her from the first, and had wished to see more of her.

She listened, and replied as in a dream. All the time she was wondering how much Wolf knew. That he had been in the plot to secure her fortune was certain, from what Ninian had told her grandfather. But did he know —had he ever known—that Ninian had confessed?

From his tranquil self-assurance she felt almost sure that, although he must know that his brother travelled to Bramforth that day, he yet had no idea of his having given away the secret cause of her invitation to the Pele.

As she thought it over, she felt it most likely that Ninian had said nothing about it at home. Wolf probably thought his twin's intention had been merely to see that she reached home safely and to give the cable to her grandfather.

So often and so closely had she pondered over the whole question as to render it remarkable that at this precise moment a certain thought dawned on her mind for the first time.

She perceived clearly that Ninian's confession had been quite gratuitous—that, if it had never been made, nobody would ever have known of the discreditable little plot.

Had Madoc Innes still been living, the damaging fact of Wolf's acquaintance with him and knowledge of his affairs must have come out. But Madoc Innes was dead; and *at the time of making his confession Ninian Guyse, having read the cable, knew that he was dead.*

Thus the secret was safe; yet he had chosen to make a clean breast—why?

She could see no answer except that he was a man whose integrity demanded such a course, whose conscience would not be satisfied without it.

Examined in the light thrown by this thought, his conduct showed up gallantly. Ah, suppose she had all along been wrong—suppose that he had loved her, after all, and that he had felt unable to take his happiness without first frankly admitting the sorry part he had set out to play?

That longing for his physical presence which had beset her when she was at the Pele, which had tortured her many times since, now surged over her until she could have wept with the pain of it.

She no longer judged him, she just wanted him, with a craving now to be for ever unsatisfied.

The presence of Wolf was half agony, half joy. He spoke in a voice which recalled another. The expression of his face, the very turn of his head, was so like that of his twin that she could not achieve any sort of composure. The news she had just heard, the sound and sight of a Guyse, agitated her so deeply that she hardly knew what she did or said. She only knew that they talked for more than an hour, and that when she left Chester Square he had promised to dine with her at Orchard Row the following day.

Going home in the car, she had to brace her shaken

nerves to the knowledge that Ben Holroyd had arrived, and
would be awaiting them.   The minutes between Belgravia
and Chelsea had never seemed so few.   She was on the
rack.

Nin—who had seemed the incarnation of health and
nerve and sinew—whose indomitable soul had resisted the
depressing influence of poverty, of his sick mother, of his
joyless existence at the Pele—Nin's life-blood was among
that poured out that England might live.   At the moment,
she felt that his twin brother was the only man in the
world whose society she could endure.

By to-morrow she would have recaptured her serenity,
and be able to ask the questions that trembled on her
tongue, but which her voice refused to carry.   She would
learn when, where, how, that buoyant spirit had been resigned, those muscles of tempered steel had become dust.

They arrived at Orchard Row to find that the guest was
in his room, changing for dinner.   Olwen was able to go
to hers, where her maid awaited her, a clever but unre-
sponsive person, who was not likely to notice signs of
mental perturbation.   As she skilfully but coldly performed her duties, the heiress thought, as almost every
day, morning and night she thought, of Sunia's soft hands
and cooing voice.

Oh, for the days beyond recall!   Oh, for the sound of
a teasing laugh, the provocative gleam of dancing eyes, the
challenge of Nin's utterly masculine personality!

She had had it all and lost it.

Had she yielded, had she loved him, he would have gone
to the war and laid down his life just the same.   Yes, but
he would have been hers—hers, as in spite of reason, in
spite of scruples and fears, she had known him to be, ever
since the night when he had kept life in her, out upon the
wild snowy fells.

She wanted to be alone, to cast herself down upon the

floor and give herself up to her desolation. Nothing of
the kind was, however, possible. She went downstairs at
last, and entering the drawing-room, found Ben in awed
contemplation of the last note in modern interiors.

He was very pale as he advanced to meet his hostess.
She thought he had improved, as almost everybody was
improved—since the war. She knew he had made a considerable sum of money, and that the Holroyd Mills would
be henceforth quite on a par with those of her uncle, Mr.
Whitefield, whose particular branch of industry had not
been much in requisition during the struggle. Ben, like
Gracie, had fined down; yet he struck a discordant note
when set in the midst of the subtly restrained, costly elements which composed the general effect of the room.

"Oh, Ben," said Miss Innes sweetly, "I am glad to see
you. But I have grown so old—so very old! Should you
have recognised me?"

He laughed uncomfortably. "You're not speaking seriously, Miss Innes," he replied, rather ceremoniously. "I
would recognise you anywhere—and however changed.
But you are not changed, except for the better."

She turned to Aunt Maud and Gracie. "Isn't that
beautiful?" she asked. "Could it have been better said?
Well, and so here we are at last, and the black barrier
which was stretched over the whole future of the world is
broken and gone. We are free once more to think and
talk of ourselves a little."

It was on her tongue to tell him that she had met
Wilfrid Guyse only that afternoon; but when she approached the subject such a lump swelled in her throat that
she could not proceed. To speak of any of the family
naturally was beyond her strength; and she was sure that,
should anybody bring in the name of Ninian, she must
break down obviously. Therefore she said no word,
though she knew that Wolf was coming to dinner the fol-

lowing night, and that she must collect her forces by that
time; must even be prepared to hear his brother's death
discussed as if it were just the death of an ordinary person.

The preoccupation caused by these considerations was
so great that she forgot to be awkward or tongue-tied before Ben, with whom she had exchanged but a very few
words since the occasion when she refused his offer of marriage. The evening passed off quite agreeably in an attempt on the part of the three ladies to teach their visitor
auction bridge. Aunt Maud, through constant playing
with convalescent officers, had become a really good player;
and Ben's intelligence was of the calibre which quickly
seizes the drift of anything which can be accomplished by
the aid of common sense. At the end of it all, Olwen felt
that things had gone better than she had anticipated. She
had got through without self-betrayal, and found herself
at last alone, in a world which no longer contained Ninian;
and then her misery rolled over her head indeed.

Morning found her sleepless, red-eyed, wretched.
Gracie exclaimed when she appeared, asking hurriedly if
she were ill. Ben, whose own sleep had been of a very
broken and scanty description, wondered if he dared to
hope that the bad night to which she was fain to confess
had been in any way connected with the thought of himself.

The day was filled in with lunch at one of the big
restaurants, a matinée, and tea at a fashionable lounge.
This programme inevitably recalled to her mind, as well
as to Ben's, the occasion of the expedition to Leeds. Little
had he then thought to see the girl typist seated in her
fine car, entertaining him with a careless generosity that
had no need to count cost. His love had, indeed, been
disinterested.

As Miss Innes dressed for dinner that night, even the
detached Parkinson remarked that she looked very white.

A few friends had been invited to dine at Orchard Row. She had achieved with creditable composure the imparting to Aunt Maud of the news that Colonel Guyse was to be one of the number. Aunt Maud, who had always had her suspicions, was very careful not to betray them.

As for poor Ben, when the magnificent Colonel walked in, he felt that his own chances were gone for ever. Nobody had made any explanation, he concluded that this was the Guyse in whose society Olwen had spent those weeks at the Pele. That these two would marry seemed the predestined end.

Wolf's manners were really extremely nice. He devoted himself to handsome Aunt Maud with a deference and desire to please which most triumphantly accomplished their object. At dinner he sat upon Olwen's right hand, Ben being upon her left. She explained to both gentlemen her own pleasure in the fact that, as she and Aunt Maud were of the same sex, and each took one end of the table, the difficulty which exists in houses where this is not so, when the number dining is eight or twelve, did not exist.

After dinner there was music, and one of the guests sang charmingly. There was no chance at all for Wolf to have any private talk with his hostess.

The following day the Holroyds departed, and Olwen reaped one benefit from the meeting between Wolf and Ben, namely, that Ben went away without attempting to resume a more intimate footing, without the plea which she had more than half expected, and for which she was not yet ready.

The dread of her life was lest she should marry a fortune-hunter, and Ben was the only man in the world of whom such a thing could never be said. Now that Ninian was no longer in question, she dimly thought that it might —some day—be Ben.

A day or two after his departure she was at home, by herself, listless and dissatisfied. Aunt Maud had thrown herself heart and soul into the question of training partially disabled soldiers for various trades. In this question a certain General Grey was much interested, and Olwen thought that the half of his interest not monopolised by the soldiers was most evidently given to Aunt Maud. At the dinner aforesaid, he had sat next to Miss Wilson, his absorption having suggested to her niece that before long she would be left without a chaperon. She was, above all things, desirous to see her aunt happy—to feel that life might at last offer her something in return for those long years of rigid self-sacrifice at the vicarage.

It began to seem that Olwen's only happiness in the future would be gained in this way—by playing providence to those she loved.

She was ready to feel her wealth as dust and ashes, to wish that it were gone, and she under the necessity of earning her bread once more. Night and day she thought of Ninian, until the craving to find out what his exact fate had been became so strong that she hesitated between the desire to question his brother and the determination to apply to the War Office or some official place where complete lists had been compiled.

Her inward suffering was so intense that it seemed to her that she could hardly look anybody in the face without discovery—that her despair must be written so plainly that none who saw it could fail to say, "she has lost her lover!"

She had had tea, and was sitting in a corner of the Chesterfield, doing absolutely nothing, her capable hands listless before her, her eyes fixed on vacancy, her thoughts gnawing incessantly at the one subject which occupied them—when Colonel Guyse was announced.

CHAPTER XXXIII

THE BULL-DROP

She went to meet him with the feeling that now—now was her chance. He must not go until she had inquired as to the exact facts, which he seemed to suppose that she knew already.

He came to invite herself and Miss Wilson to go down to the docks the following day to inspect one of the great captured enemy ships which was lying there for the inspection of visitors. She accepted the invitation, and they drifted into talk, which grew by degrees more and more absorbing. He told her some of his more poignant experiences at the front, and she gave him a sympathy which he appeared to find most gratifying. Though he never said a word that could be called love-making, she yet felt increasingly that he was wooing her; and the fact that he was doing so with Nin's voice and Nin's smile, and every now and then with Nin's very expression, filled her with sensations that she could not analyse. She was half fascinated, half revolted, and she had a feeling that if it went on—if she should be much in his society—she would succumb to the curious attraction.

A dozen times she tried to lead round the talk so that she could touch upon the one subject without too great effort.

In vain. As soon as she found herself within measurable distance of the words "your brother," her throat began to swell, her heart quickened its beat. He had risen to take leave before she was aware. . . . He had gone, and her chance was over for the present.

He called the following day, and they motored down to the docks, after which he gave them lunch at the great new Anzac restaurant.

It was as he was putting them into the car afterwards, and stood laughing and animated on the kerbstone making his farewells, that her eyes, straying past his in order not to meet their challenge, fell upon a lady whose face seemed familiar to her. The lady in question was young and handsome in a showy way, and as she strolled slowly past Olwen thought her eyes rested upon their party with a look of special interest. The impression was momentary, the stranger had moved on and was lost in the crowd surging thickly on the pavement.

As they drove home her mind held the picture of the backward glance and the expression; but sub-consciously, and all mixed up with Wolf's charm and the magnetism of his personality.

She felt that the hours she and he had passed together that day had made a great, a real difference.

If matters were to advance at this rate, she must face the situation which might ensue. She reached home in restless mood, wondering how to pick up once more the thread of a life which seemed to have broken off short. The war and its resulting activities had filled in at first the blank which lay void after her departure from Guyse-wyke. Now even that palliative was taken away. It showed itself as the mere stopgap that it had always been. In truth, though peace had returned, life was exciting enough, had she felt that politics and social economy were things that could absorb her. She did not so feel. Hers was, life her father's, a nature which craved love as its starting-point. The fabric of her life must be built on love, so she felt, or go to pieces.

The Colonel had taken care not to part without an arrangement for another meeting before long. He was to lunch the following day at Orchard Row, and take the two ladies to see over one of the great new institutions prepared for the reception of those permanently disabled in the war.

He came accordingly, and the time passed charmingly. Aunt Maud thought him the most fascinating man she had ever seen. The situation piqued her curiosity. Not a word of confidence had Olwen given her, not a sentence had she ever let fall concerning this man's twin brother with whom she had spent so many hours at the Pele. Miss Wilson's conviction that some reason other than what appeared had all along existed for the girl's sudden departure from her post gained strength every minute.

As for Olwen, she felt that she was skating on very thin ice. Easily though Wolf talked, he avoided any mention of his home or his family. He seemed to assume that Olwen knew of his brother's fate, and he did not allude to it. Their talk was always superficial, gliding lightly over a surface beneath which were unknown depths.

That day Wolf asked permission to bring his cousin, Lady Caryngston, to call upon Miss Wilson and Miss Innes. The plan was carried out very soon afterwards, and with her ladyship came that Elma Guyse who so strongly resembled her cousin Ninian that it was agony to Olwen to be in the same room with her.

Every minute some tone in her voice, some curve of her mouth, some gleam in her mischievous eye, recalled Nin in his most captivating mood. Olwen's emotion increased every moment. She felt that she could no longer endure the strain of going on in her present ignorance. She would ask Wolf all about Ninian, even though in the attempt she found herself compelled to betray her own feeling.

Her chance came, for the Colonel did not depart when the other visitors left. Aunt Maud had a committee at half-past five, and so made her escape from the drawing-

room, going out of it with the two ladies. Wolf and
Olwen found themselves left together; and this was obviously the moment for which she had waited so long. He
went to the window, glancing out to see if it rained. Now
or never.

She moistened her dry lips, and was just opening them
to pronounce the fatal words, when the Colonel swung
round, saying carelessly:

"By the way, I heard from my brother this morning."

Silence fell. She hardly breathed for a few moments.
Something within her rose up in tumult, and she had to
beat it down. For the second time, upon the mention of
Nin, she showed Wolf an ashen face.

"Your . . . brother?" she said at last, feeling that at
all costs she must not betray the extent of her stupefaction.

"Yes. I think you said you knew what a horrible fate
befell him?"

Weakly she shook her head; she could not speak.

He seemed surprised. "But I thought, the day we first
met, you said you knew——"

"No, I don't know anything. I beseech you to tell
me."

"Well, but at least you knew he was a prisoner of
war?"

"Not—even—that."

"Yes; he got taken, poor chap, the very first time he
went into action—right at the beginning, before we turned
them on the Marne. He was badly hit, and they picked
him up and took him to Griesslauen, the most remote of
all the military camps—a place where unheard-of things
went on. . . . We didn't know for nearly a year whether
he was alive or dead. He was reported missing, you know.
Rough luck, wasn't it?"

"Ye-es. *Rough luck.* . . . Is he at home now?"

"Oh, yes; he's been back more than six months now, and

his native air has done a good bit for him; but he's very
much changed."

"Is he—maimed, do you mean—or disfigured?"

"Oh, no, not as bad as that. He had a horrible sup-
purating wound in his leg, the result of neglect and semi-
starvation; but the Guysewyke air healed that in a couple
of months. Of course, things are very depressing for him;
in fact, he's just had another bad blow, poor chap, and
I'm afraid he's taking it frightfully hard."

"Tell me . . . if you think you might? I . . . want
to hear."

He came and sat down opposite, fixing his eyes upon
her quivering face. She was so rapt that she had ceased
to heed what he might be thinking. Ninian was not
dead. *He was not dead.* He lived. She heard, but
could not realise; she felt as though a blow had stunned
her.

"I don't know whether I ought to tell you," said Wolf
thoughtfully. "Nin might give me socks if he knew.
But you seem to take some interest in the poor old chap,
after all."

She made a sound which she meant for a laugh, but
which was merely a sob. "Perhaps I do."

"I don't suppose he ever conversed with you on the subject of finance," went on Wolf softly; "but you may perhaps have gathered during your stay with us that he was
pretty hard up?"

He was narrowly watching her face, but she replied
frankly enough:

"Of course I knew it. I knew he was fighting as hard
as he could so as not to—not to have to sell the Pele."

"Oh, you knew that? You knew how set he was upon
the old place?"

"Indeed, yes, I knew."

"Well, when the war came, there was no way out of

it. He was bound to raise such a sum of money as should make my mother independent in case of his death. He went to our cousin, Caryngston, and offered to sell to him, upon conditions." .

"Conditions ?"

"Yes. Caryngston was to give an undertaking not to sell again, and to allow my mother to remain in possession for the duration of the war."

"Then—then it is actually sold ?"

"Yes. At that time Caryngston was fearfully keen, for his son was just engaged to Miss Leverett, daughter of an American millionaire——"

"Wash-white Slick-Soap," she murmured.

"Just so. Her father found the purchase money, because he fancied his daughter in a feudal pile; and the deal went through. Since that time, however, the whole situation has changed. Poor Noel went to the front three months later, and was to be married as soon as he got his first leave. Well, he never got any leave. He was shot before he had been out a month. Miss Leverett never became Mrs. Guyse, and the old man wants his money back. Caryngston can't repay him unless he sells the Pele, and he has written to Nin to say that he will be reluctantly compelled to do so."

"Oh, what a shame! What an utter shame!" burst forth Miss Innes, springing to her feet in her vehemence.

"I'm afraid, from what he says, that it has just about broken poor old Nin. The last straw, you know."

Olwen sat down again as suddenly as she had uprisen. Her very knees were shaking. Perhaps Wolf saw that she could not speak, for he filled in the pause glibly.

"I wonder whether, when you were at the Pele, you ever heard the odd story—legend, I should say—of the Bull-drop ?"

She brought back her mind with an effort. "The Bull-drop?"

"Yes; the causeway leading to the Pele. There was a tale of a bull having jumped out of the keep through a breach made by the besiegers, and they prophesied that if such a thing ever happened again there would be a fair Guyse, and the family would recover its old importance."

"Of course I remember. Why, of course!"

"Well, a curious thing happened just about the time you left us. Do you remember meeting a messenger-boy on your way to Raefell? As a matter of fact, he had a cablegram for you in his pocket, and he told us where to look for you. We questioned him and found that he had seen you on the road."

"I remember well."

"Like all boys, he was fascinated by the desire to walk on the parapet of the causeway. It was in a bad state, for the long frost had caked the old snow upon it so thickly that the rains had not removed all of it. He slipped and fell into the ravine."

"Was he killed?"

"Not a bit of it. He fell quite near the farther end, among the underbrush on the slope. However, he broke a rib or two and was pretty bad. But the funny part of the story is, that when we put the chap to bed and sent for the doctor, we discovered that his name was Tommy Bull."

As he hoped, this story diverted her attention from the consideration of Ninian's tragedy.

"Bull? It seems like the fulfilment of the prophecy! Oh, what did Sunia say?"

"She was perfectly certain that it was, as you say, the fulfilment of prophecy. She was so completely reassured by it that she was able to bear up under the sale of the

Pele and the departure of her sahib for the war. She said that things must come right; it was merely a question of waiting. But I think she has lost heart at last. This latest blow is too heavy."

"You say—did you tell me—that the tower is actually sold? I mean that Lord Caryngston has actually sold it?"

"I believe not. He wrote to warn Ninian that it was to be sold, and he mentioned that he had already had an offer of more than he gave. Of course, he is breaking his contract, but he knows Nin has no money to fight him."

"No, but Mr. Guyse is in the Pele, and possession is nine points of the law," cried Olwen passionately. "If I were he I would decline to turn out, and surely the Courts would support him if anybody tried to evict him."

He shrugged his shoulders. "Maybe. Maybe not. I don't believe the conditions made are legally binding. He trusted to Caryngston's honour."

She sat, hands locked together, mind so busy that it seemed to whirl.

"Does Mr. Guyse know that—that you and I have met?" she asked at length.

"No. I didn't say anything about it. It's a sore subject, you see. He has never got over your turning him down." As the colour flew to her cheeks, he added, "I beg pardon. I had no right to say that."

"It is hardly accurate, moreover. Mr. Guyse only offered to marry me in order to satisfy a somewhat fantastic sense of honour. He would have been much surprised had I taken advantage of his proposal."

Wolf's most expressive glance was upon her. "I wonder if you expect me to believe that?" he asked mischievously.

Olwen drew herself up. "Whether you believe it or not hardly concerns me, Colonel Guyse."

He shrugged his shoulders. "Well, you are a person of importance now," said he, "and can take your pick of the fortune-hunters. I can tell you one thing, however. You will never find a man among them fit to tie up old Nin's shoe-string. But I had better say 'Good-bye,' before I offend past forgiveness!"

He rose and held out his hand. "Then we meet at eleven to-morrow morning?" he said.

She let him go, scarcely heeding what she did. The world was upside down, and she wanted time in which to readjust her ideas. When he had left the room, she went towards the door almost as though she were blind, groping for the handle. Just as she emerged upon the landing the parlourmaid came up from the hall, bearing a note upon a salver.

It had been delivered by hand, and was marked "Urgent."

She carried it up with her to her room, locked herself in, flung down the envelope on her toilet-table and herself upon the bed.

Floods of tears came to her relief, and for a while she lay there helpless, overswept by a torrent of feeling, while a host of plans, hopes, wishes, fears, thrills careered madly through her mind.

Not until the first bell reminded her that Parkinson would be arriving almost immediately to dress her for dinner did she arise; and going to the glass to survey the ravages of the past hour's emotion, remark the note lying on the jewel tray.

It did not look at all important. She expected one of the appeals which reached her with distressing frequency from some impecunious person who had "heard she was celebrated for her kind and feeling heart." The contents were surprising. It was dated from an address at Finchley, and written in a pretty, ladylike hand.

"DEAR MADAM,—Pardon my troubling you, but as Colonel Guyse seems to be very often at your house, I am writing to inform you of what you may not know—namely, that he is a married man. I saw you talking to him in Regent Street the other day, and I have watched him since. If you need proof, I can show you my marriage lines, but if you show him this letter he won't deny it. We were married in Canada years ago, and I adored him so that I fell in with his idea that to have his marriage with me known would spoil his whole future. Now I feel that I have had enough of it. He has a Colonel's pay, and he ought to acknowledge me, instead of which he says he is going to reduce my allowance. I have come up to London unknown to him, for when he said he was going to cut me short I guessed there was something going on. I feel I must put a spoke in his wheel before it is too late. I have borne a great deal, but if he thinks he is going to deceive a nice young girl like you, who has done good all through the war, he is mistaken. My cousin from Canada was one of the boys you nursed, and I don't forget it. Write to me if you like, but if you are the girl I take you for this letter ought to do the trick.—Yours truly, LILY GUYSE."

Lily Guyse! There was but little need to inquire what the lady's maiden name had been. She was Lily Martin, and the face which Olwen had noticed as Wolf took leave of her in Regent Street was the face she had seen between the leaves of a book in the Pele library.

Wolf's wife!

CHAPTER XXXIV

MESSRS. GREEN, SON & WILKINSON, who had the care of Miss Innes's legal affairs, were much inclined to advise her to think more than twice before purchasing a Border Pele. In like manner they had striven to persuade her not to face the tremendous expenditure of running a private hospital. The result was the same in both cases. Miss Innes, as she gently pointed out, was no longer a child. She was now well on in her twenties, and when she had made up her mind to do a thing she did it. She did not come to them for advice, but to have her orders carried out.

They told her that the land to be sold with the tower was inconsiderable and of poor quality. The Pele itself needed to have a large sum laid out upon it in order to make it fit for residence. The country was exposed, the distance from the railway great, the difficulties of water supply and electric light alike formidable.

She listened, smiled, said she knew the place well, and had set her heart upon it. She declined to entertain the idea of a lease, would buy only the freehold; and stipulated that the present tenant, Mr. Guyse, should not be told the name of the purchaser.

She was perfectly willing to agree to the somewhat stiff terms of sale, namely, that she undertook, under heavy penalties, not to divide the land, not to pull down the Tower, not to build cheap houses on the property, and a dozen other restrictions which seemed to her very absurd, but which were, none the less, insisted upon.

There actually was another would-be buyer in the market, besides herself—an American; and she gave instructions that whatever this gentleman offered, her own representatives should offer more. The result was that, although she came off victorious, she had to pay more than Messrs. Green, Son & Wilkinson thought a fair price.

Little cared she!

It seemed to her that never had she really grasped the happiness of being rich, until she actually held in her hands the bulky title-deeds, the precious documents which made her the owner of the Peele, which gave Ninian's future, so to speak, into her tyrant hands.

It was not until this transaction was accomplished that she realised how completely she had burnt her boats. The capital sum paid down must appreciably cripple her own income. Suppose that her worst fears were true—that Ninian had never loved her, and did not want her—what was she to do?

What would the rest of life be like, after she had made over the Pele to him?

She shut her ears to all such maddening thoughts. She was going to see him, or die in the attempt.

"He has never got over your turning him down." So Wolf had said. That might, however, easily be true, even though he had no spark of love for her. Had she accepted him, his home need never have been sold. Here was matter enough for regret from his point of view. It must be the loss of the fortune and not the woman that he lamented. Wolf's lip had curled as he said, "You can have your pick of the fortune-hunters now. You'll not find a man among them fit to tie up old Nin's shoe-string." In her heart she admitted the exact truth of this.

As soon as she received Lily Guyse's letter she deter-

mined not to see Wolf again for the present. She coaxed
Aunt Maud to leave town, and they went to a hotel a few
miles out, whence she could easily motor in and interview
her lawyers. During the time that the negotiations were
pending, she was in a state of mind so unlike herself
that Miss Wilson confided to General Grey her wish that
Olwen would take a fancy to somebody and marry soon.
"If she doesn't, she will be quite soured," said she with a
sigh.

"Is there anybody?" he asked.

"Not that I know of. I always had an idea that there
was something or somebody, but it was while she was
staying away. There was a young doctor—it is possible she is fretting for him. I thought that very irresistible
Colonel Guyse might have a chance, but somehow I don't
fancy he has made much impression. I suppose the poor
child feels that everybody must be after her money."

"Oh, but she is attractive. She need not feel that. She
is a girl who would always have had lovers."

"Yes, indeed, Mr. Holroyd would have married her
long before anybody dreamed she would be rich. But I
am glad she did not care for him. He is not the husband
for her; she wants a more dominant person, for she is
very wilful and impetuous."

The wilfulness and impetuosity of her niece were more
clearly demonstrated in the course of a very few days.
Miss Innes announced her intention of starting upon a
tour in the north of England.

Miss Wilson was seriously annoyed. She was wrapped
up in her own affairs at the time, very busy, every moment
occupied, London full, plenty of interest, the General
just in the stage when a man may or may not go further
according to opportunity.

"What has made you all of a sudden turn against Lon-

don ?" she asked with natural vexation. "You were wild
to come here at first."

"I know. One has to find out one's mistakes, and I have
found out mine. There are disadvantages that I never
foresaw. One is the way in which men keep on asking me
to marry them without caring one bit for me, and expect
me to take their devotion for granted."

"Nonsense, Olwen!"

"It isn't nonsense. I wish they wouldn't do it. I said
to Mr. Lambert only the other day, 'You don't know what
love means, you haven't any idea! I am younger than
you, but I know and you don't.' He took me up very
quickly. 'Do you know by personal experience?' he
wanted to know, and I asked him what he meant. 'Has
a man made violent love to you—has he kissed you?' he
asked. I told him nobody ever had done that; though five
men, counting Ben Holroyd, have asked me to marry them.
So he said I couldn't know. But I do, so what's the good
of arguing? Heigh-ho! One man is just the same as
another to me, and I'm sure they all go to the same
tailor."

"Don't get bitter, child."

"If any of them looked different, or—weather-stained,
or—even did things at a different time from anybody else,
like the Snark you know—breakfasted at five o'clock tea
and dined on the following day. But in London people
are not like that. We are just like the carpet-bedding
in the parks, we look all right in the mass, but if you
examine any one of us individually, it is a poor little
specimen, and if we grew too tall or too big, the gar-
dener would snip us and trim us to make us match the
others."

Miss Wilson had no reply to make to this, and the
heiress continued after a minute.

"Have you ever heard that if a man brings the girl

he loves into a house where a corpse is lying he will never marry her?"

"Really, Ollie, what unpleasant things you sometimes say! No, I never heard of such a thing."

"Well, I did. I believe it's true, too. Superstitions often are. They grow out of wild nature. In some parts of the world wild nature is still alive, and strong enough to hurt. The elements—cold and wind and snow—might kill you there. They have power! But for all that you would be free; ever so much more free than we are here, where everybody's thoughts are coloured by the latest novel that everybody else is reading, too."

"I'm really not sure what you are talking about."

"Oh, I'm not talking, merely thinking aloud. You have got to bear that now and then. If you knew how often I brood over things like this, and how seldom I bore you with them, you would think yourself lucky. I have just now got a craving for solitude and savagery. I want to see a black crag with a frozen lake at its base, and a low grey sky, a flurry of snow, the mist blotting out all the rest of the world—and in the midst of it all just one little place of refuge. . . ."

"At the end of June, I'm afraid, even in the wildest parts of this country, you won't be able to indulge your desire," said Aunt Maud with irony. "Do you want to go abroad?"

"N-no. Only to the north."

"Well, I am afraid I really can't leave town for another fortnight at least."

"Then you mustn't think me a beast if I go off without you. You can join me, wherever I happen to be, can't you? You had better let me go, for I shall be poor company. I have nothing to do, I am at a loose end, and I think if I go somewhere where I can walk and walk and walk till I am so tired that I drop off to sleep the moment

I have eaten my supper, I shall regain a more normal
view of life. I'll go in the car. Aunt Ethel's in town
this week, and she would love it if I were to motor her and
Marjorie back to Leeds with me, and drop them at Mount
Prospect on my way."

"My child! Go travelling alone! Grandpapa would
not like that."

Olwen smiled serenely. "He won't be asked, bless him!
Dear aunt, consider my advanced age! Chaperons and
dodos now occupy the same glass case in most museums.
I'll take Parkinson, and then Heaven knows I shall be
respectable enough!"

The plans thus made were duly carried through, as plans
made by Olwen had a habit of being.

Mrs. Whitefield, since her niece's accession to wealth,
had varied in her feelings between envy and a desire
to stand well with the heiress. She accepted all favours
offered, but could not forbear disparaging criticism. She
was pleased to travel north in the fine Rolls-Royce, but
vexed because she could not understand why Ollie should
continue her tour alone, instead of taking Marjorie with
her. Marjorie had grown stout, and was stolid and un-
interesting. Olwen was kindly disposed to her, but just
now she felt that her continual company wuold be quite
unbearable, and breathed a sigh of relief, when, after
spending a night in the overpowering magnificence of
Mount Prospect, she was free to pursue her journey un-
hindered.

She passed by way of Watling Street, up to the Tyne,
pausing when she reached Corbridge, to wander down
to the river's edge, and trace the old line of the great
highway, through Corstopitum. She slept that night at
the Wheatsheaf, and early next morning passed through
Hexham and Fourstones, to Bardon Mill, and thence
over the shoulder of Barcombe. The hedgerows as they

passed were crimson with the glow of such brier-roses as seem to grow only in Northumbria; but when they had passed Vindolana and the Roman milestone, and come out upon Wade's Road, they had reached the end of the hedge-rows.

At the Twice-Brewed Inn they stopped, and she left the car with Parkinson and Goddard, the chauffeur, to do as they liked until her return. She was going off by herself to slake her desire to behold once more Duke's Crag and the Hotwells Lough.

Over her head was a sky of cloudless blue, in which larks sang and curlews wheeled, with their mewing cry, over the lonely land. She had a map with her, and was able to make straight for the mile-castle.

She had hardly left the road, and set her face northward, before she was out of sight of all habitations. Before her, on the ridge, lay the long line of the outer vallum, and beyond it the swell of the height which carried the Wall itself, and was precipitous upon its northern face.

After she had climbed some way she could, shading her eyes from the glare, descry, far away to her left, the smoke from the chimney of Hazel Crag, drifting idly on the warm breeze; and she lived again the moment of the opening door, and the face of Balmayne as he recognised the night wanderers.

The cry of sheep, straying on the moor, came to her ears like a far away lament.

> *Silence and passion, joy and peace,*
> *An everlasting wash of air*
> *Rome's ghost since her decease! . . .*

This was Ninian's native land. Its freedom, its loneliness, were alike typical of him in her mind. The short turf on which she trod was enamelled with the purple and gold of wild pansies. "There's pansies, that's for thoughts," she found herself whispering; and thoughts were thronging almost unbearably.

In the long, awful months and years of his captivity, how must his wild heart have turned with sick longing to those broad spaces, that galloping wind, that fullness of liberty, that crowded solitude of his native north! She had a fantastic notion that for every time he or she had visited the place in spirit, one little thought-flower had sprung to bear witness of the dream!

She was making for the Gap, like a mountain pass in miniature, which brings one through, close to the dark Lough. The water to-day looked temptingly cool and clear. Somewhere in its depths lay the stone which had struck her head. She did not descend to the plain beyond her, but turned westward and made her way along the ridge to the mile-castle.

To her active feet the distance seemed very short in the fair weather. It was hard even to picture the drifting snow, like cold foam about clogged feet—the keenness of the driving blast, the furious opposition of the elements.

Her imagination brought Ninian so near that she stopped and faced quickly about, with some idea of being followed. There was no one, only the memory-laden landscape looked her in the face, whispered in her ear. . . . How he had suffered since then! . . . She used to read in the papers of the horrors of Griesslauen, harrowing details of typhoid, of bad water, of half rations, of torture. . . . Had she known what he was enduring she never could have borne it. The very memory forced drops from her eyes as she dwelt upon it.

She reached the mile-castle, where it lay open to the sun. Over its broken wall she could descry the corrugated

iron roof of the shed which had sheltered them. Her feet
were noiseless on the grass, and her approach was unseen,
unheard by the man who sat within, upon a remnant of
inner wall.

He was seated sideways, so that she saw his profile.
His head was downbent, his elbows rested on his knees.
In his hands he held something which at first she took to
be a skein of silk, which he was idly pulling through his
fingers. His hat lay on the ground beside him, and Olwen
saw his hair, thickly sprinkled with grey.

What was it which his fingers ceaselessly caressed?
The sun glinted upon it, and it fell in a shower of gold.
It was a tress of hair.

A mixture of amazement, joy, and wicked triumph
so flooded her that she could hardly see. Hair! It was
her own hair! It was the big tress which, to Sunia's rage,
Dr. Balmayne had been obliged to cut away in order to
sew the wound on her head.

There is no word to describe what she felt, as she fought
for composure, schooled the trembling of her limbs and
the muscles of her mouth.

His gaze was fixed upon something which lay on the
ground between his knees; something too small for her
to see. Having made herself ready for the encounter, she
let a bit of stone fall, with a rattling noise. He looked
up.

Nin it was, but the change in him was at first sight
awful.

His face was lined and parchment-like. There were
puckers about his eyes, which looked sunken. He might
have passed for ten years older than Wolf. For a long instant his look met hers as though he did not see her. Then
suddenly there awoke, in his bewildered stare, something
that resembled the Ninian she had known. With a swift
movement he thrust the tress of hair into his breast pocket,

snatched up what lay upon the grass, and with a flicker, a characteristic glance, he opened fire.

"Ah, well, you haven't succeeded in growing any taller, you know, in spite of all your new dignities." His manner, at least, was unchanged, though his voice sounded forced and unnatural.

His words pulled Olwen together wonderfully. She had been on the very verge of self-betrayal—of a burst of silly tears. The familiar mocking seemed to put them back at once, just at the place where they left off, and she summoned her strength to fence with him as of old. "Yes," she replied, with a conventional smile, not moving forward, but speaking from her post in the entrance. "I am still a mouse, as your brother reminded me the other day; only the country mouse has become a town mouse."

A quiver crossed his face as her voice was heard. "Oh," he said, "so you really are, are you? I've once or twice thought I saw you before to-day—slipping round a corner or peeping over a wall; but never face to face like this. How did you get here?"

"My car is waiting at Twice-Brewed. I have walked from there, and am very hot. I didn't expect to find you here."

"Obviously not," he replied, with a grin which showed his teeth to be as good as ever. "You looked as if you had found a black-beetle in the sugar-basin. However, I'm not a fixture, you know." As he spoke, he laid down the thing he held in his hand, as it were furtively, on the stone at the farther side of him, out of sight.

Determined to know what this was, she came suddenly forward and sank on the grass at his feet with a flutter of white skirts. The manœuvre found him unprepared. Quickly he covered the little square bit of card with his hand; but her eyes were very keen, and she had seen that it was her own photo. She remembered that she had extracted it from a drawer while at the Pele, with the intention of sending it to her father, and had placed it on the mantelshelf in her room. She had never noticed the fact that it was not among the things so carefully packed and returned after her departure.

Now, it told her all! She found him here, in this place, sacred to a memory which she alone could share; and with him he brought her picture and a tress of hair!

Her courage rose with one bound, for all doubt was solved. Her lips curved with mischief as she looked up at him provocatively, bold in the delightful knowledge that she was prettier than she used to be, and that her clothes set her off to the best advantage.

"Since you don't ask me to be seated, I do so without ceremony!"

"My manners have gone to pieces since I saw you last. Pretty annoying, isn't it, to think how you wasted time and instruction on me?"

"Oh," was her retort, "I'm not surprised. I remember you had decided that you could not keep it up! You prepared me for a lapse."

"It's worse than a lapse. It's what you might describe as a *débâcle* if you knew as much French as I do."

She was below him, facing him, and she looked up steadily at him as she replied:

"Ah, well, I suppose I shall have to begin all over again."

That moved him. "No, by God you don't—not again," he answered defiantly.

"Do you suppose that you can stop me, if my mind is made up?"

"Upon my word, you have the cheek of the——"

"Cheek! I should think I have. Don't be under the impression that you can browbeat me."

"If you'll take my advice, you'll run away to that car of yours as fast as your expensively shod feet will take you. I'm not good company to-day for the wealthy and frivolous."

"I know, you always did find me a bore. But you can't get rid of me so easily as all that. I had the intention of coming to the Pele to call upon Madam, but as we have met here, perhaps you will take this as a call—like the two ladies in *Punch,* who met while bathing? Now let us begin to talk properly, and remember as much as you can of the nice manners I once taught you. How is your mother, Mr. Guyse?"

His face, which had changed a dozen times as she teased him, settled into a scowl. "She is very ill," he said gruffly, "and she is getting worse. That's a topic I can't joke about."

"I don't ask you to joke. I think you ought to consider it very seriously. Madam needs change of air and scene. Why don't you take her away somewhere—say to the Riviera?"

He looked at her as if he could box her ears with pleasure. "Oh, just because I don't choose," he answered savagely. "I like to thwart her, just for the sake of thwarting her, as you ought to know by this time."

"I do know, but I like to force you to admit it," said she with a demure smile. "I am wondering whether I could not do something to help cheer her up. I often think with regret of the fact that I refused to do what she wanted me to do so badly. I—I wonder whether it would do any good now. . . . Or whether it is too late."

She pulled a blade of grass from beside her, and twisted it round her fingers, carefully keeping her eyes fixed upon it.

"Afraid I can't help you to a decision," he said harshly.

"Oh, yes, you can. In fact, it all depends on you," she replied, in a very small voice. "Do you remember our last talk at the Pele—when you came in to tea and I was so kind, I had kept yours hot for you, and I stayed to pour it out? And do you remember that on that occasion, in the intervals of drinking your tea, you did me the honour to ask me to marry you?"

"Did I? I must have been an ass."

"Well, perhaps you were. But I really am not sure. Perhaps I was the ass for saying NO. Anyway, it has been in my mind that I ought to have said Yes, on account of Madam. Don't you agree?"

He sprang to his feet. "Not in the humour to-day for any more twaddle," he said, laughing, with a catch in his breath. "I—I know I've been a beast and—and drawn this on myself, but have a little pity for me. This morning I've heard that the last blow has fallen. I'm now not merely a beggar but an outcast. I can't sit bandying words with you, I tell you I can't stand it."

She did not move, but answered with a quiet which disarmed him. "Well, I won't keep you long, but as we have met, I wish you would just put up with me for a few minutes longer. You have roused all my curiosity and I think you ought to satisfy it. What do you mean by saying that you are not merely a beggar but an outcast?"

"Just what I say. When I did the one thing I shall regret all my life, and asked you to marry me, I did think I had something to offer a woman. Now I've nothing. It is sold over my head—the Pele I mean—and I shall have to take Madam on my back and tramp the country, asking the charitable for shelter."

He had sunk down in his place again, and sat there, eyes fiercely fixed on the contemplation of his troubles.

"Oh, Nin," she said softly, "don't you think even having to marry me might be better than that? It *does* sound so uncomfortable for poor Madam."

He looked at her, marvelling at her cruelty, and made a shrinking movement, as if hurt. "Out there," he said, after a pause, "out in Griesslauen I used to think I had endured everything a man could, and that hereafter I might reckon myself immune to pain. But I—I expect you have the right. If you get any satisfaction out of baiting me, go on. It's up to me to take what you give."

She rose deliberately from where she had been sitting, and went away a few paces. He raised his head. She had gone to the door of the shed in which they had sheltered and stood staring in. After a while she turned slowly and caught his look fixed upon her. The colour flowed warm over her face.

"Perhaps," said she in a low voice, "perhaps your mother was right. It—it *was* very unconventional, wasn't it? Do you think—perhaps—on those grounds—I was wrong to say 'No'?"

He stood up, and his face was rigidly set. "I think you had better go," was all he said.

She turned to him, looking not into his face but somewhere about his second waistcoat button. "So you won't marry me on Madam's account—nor because it would be more *comme il faut*. Would you marry me—now tell the truth—if by doing so you could get back the Pele?"

"No!" he shouted wrathfully. "No, no, and yet again no! I wouldn't marry you if you were hung all over with silver and gold—not if you were Venus and Diana rolled into one——"

"Well, well, well, you needn't make such a noise about it. I'm not a bit deaf——"

He broke off, seeming to swallow rage in gulps. For a moment he surveyed her critically, as if he sneered at her fine clothes, then he turned abruptly on his heel. "Good-bye," he said shortly, making for the entrance.

CHAPTER XXXV

'TWIXT CUP AND LIP

"OH, please wait a minute," said his tormentor; "I have a great deal more to say before we part."

He halted, though chafing against himself for displaying such weakness, and stood, his hands in his pockets, glowering at her small figure, instinct with energy, erect in the sunny enclosure, framed by the grey stones.

She smiled at him, a rapt kind of smile, seeming more occupied with her own thoughts than with him.

"Oh, doesn't it all look different?" she asked.

"I don't know quite what you mean, but everything is different—the whole world is changed since you and I were last here."

"Yes. Utterly changed. The only thing that remains the same is just the very thing I thought would have changed most."

"And that is?"

"You."

"Ah, well, if you think so, that only shows what a little duffer you must be," he snapped.

"All right. I'm a duffer now. That is a change, since you used to look up to me, or pretend you did! However, it doesn't much matter. I want you to do me a very small favour. Walk back with me to Twice-Brewed."

"No fear. What for?"

"I'll explain. I am doing a little tour up in the north—nobody is with me but my maid. I was intending to call at the Pele to-morrow, to leave something there—a little

355

present for Madam and—and you. You were very kind to me when I was with you, and I was so ill afterwards that you never got properly thanked. Now it occurs to me that as we have met I can motor you home, going on afterwards to Caryngston, where I am to stay the night. I have written to the Seven Spears, and Mrs. Askwith expects me. By the way, how were you going to get home if I had not met you?"

"On my feet, of course."

"Well, you may as well come in the car instead."

He considered her, half angry, half amused. "You and your car!"

She laughed out gaily. "It does seem absurd, doesn't it? But you might come and look at it. It's such a nice one. Don't be disagreeable."

"I never need make any effort in that direction. It comes natural."

"It doesn't. You cultivate it because you think it's clever, but you are completely mistaken. Now come along, and be thankful I can go on my own feet to-day instead of having to make use of yours."

"I'm not sure there's any cause for thankfulness in that."

"Oh, you *are* perverse! You must have got out of bed the wrong side this morning. I wonder how I put up with you; but, you see, I feel a little responsible. Having begun your education and then allowed it to lapse, the least I can do is to be patient with you."

"I have frequently met with assurance," he remarked, "but for sheer brazen impudence, I certainly never met your equal."

"And I don't think you ever will," she replied, as though highly complimented.

Her feet went dancing over the heathery grass, mauve with harebells. Her heart was beating so wildly that she wondered if it could be audible. She had to fight her impulse to turn and cling to him as he strode beside her, gaunt and bony, the marks of suffering plainly on him, but Nin still—the same Nin. She refrained, however. There was something delicious in the present moment. She wanted to prolong it—wanted to know what he would do when he found out that the Pele was his.

Suddenly he spoke. "Well, it will, as a matter of fact, be a convenience to me to get back home quickly," said he, "for I have to put myself inside a tail coat and go and dine with the Kendalls."

"The Kendalls!" she cried . . . and, in the extremity of her surprise, the next words came out without her own consent, "Why, what in the world do they want with you now?"

He grinned in the way she knew so well. "You may well ask. Perhaps you haven't heard of poor Noel's death. That leaves me heir to the rotten title, worse luck!"

"Nin," said a low, changed voice from under her hat, "tell me the truth. Are you engaged to her?"

There was a long, dreadful pause. "Yes," he said at last, "I think I am. That is, her father has given his consent. That's what I am going over about to-night."

"And you—and you—you could bear—to come up here —with *that* in your mind?"

"I came up here," he answered heavily, "to say goodbye to a dream."

They went on for some way in silence. She told herself that no well-conducted young woman could venture farther than she had done in the direction of encouragement. The light went out of the skies, her step flagged, she could have cast herself upon the grass and wept. Yet for very pride she could not say, "Jilt her, marry me!" Had he

not sworn with energy that nothing would induce him
to marry her?

"Well," said she at last, primly. "I can but hope you
will be very happy."

"Happy?" he said with a fierce little snort.

"There's one drawback, Sunia doesn't like her. Sunia
does like me. You don't know how many times I have
longed for her; my present maid is a kind of fish, she
never entertains me with spells or mesmerising or fortune-
telling or any of the devices to make time pass agreeably,
of which Sunia is mistress. I wonder whether I could
tempt her with very high wages to come to me and desert
Madam?"

"She won't desert me, even when Miss Kendall is her
mistress."

"I don't think you need build on that. Miss Kendall
won't keep her a month."

"Jove! I never thought of that!"

"Well, I hope you will, under the circumstances,
excuse my having proposed marriage to you this afternoon. I can only say in extenuation that I had no idea
your affections were already engaged, or I would have
been more discreet. Why, here we are already within
sight of the inn. What a little way down it really is!
A couple more fields and we are on the road! Goddard
must have seen us coming down; he has brought the
car along, I see."

They spoke only trivialities until they reached the gate
which the chauffeur held open..

Olwen came out in a kind of dream. She felt as if she
had been to a function which she imagined was a wedding
and it had turned out, as sometimes in nightmare, to be
a funeral after all.

She addressed Ninian with a self-possessed smile,
asking him to sit by Goddard and direct him. Then she

got into the car with Parkinson, who proceeded to remove her mistress's wide-brimmed hat and tie her up in her motor-bonnet as they sped along.

It was past five by the time they reached the little road that branched off to the Pele. Olwen stopped the car.

"It is getting so late that, as you have to dress, Mr. Guyse, I will not call upon Madam this afternoon," said she. "I shall hope to give myself that pleasure another time, if I ever come back to this neighbourhood, which, perhaps, is not very likely. Meanwhile, may I trouble you to carry this parcel to her? It is really a present for you, but I think she may share in its enjoyment. Give her my kind remembrances. Good-bye."

Tongue-tied before the two servants, he made his adieux. Now it was he whose eyes eagerly sought for a glance from hers, but in vain. She felt as if one look would break down her pride, and that she would show some inkling of what she was enduring. As on the day when he had put her into the train at Raefell, they parted with barely a farewell. In a couple of minutes the car had become a dark speck upon the moor road to Caryngston.

. . . She had but just glimpsed the grey tower—had hardly ventured even a glance, so sorely did she fear to give herself away. Now she leaned back in her corner, drawing down her veil to hide the drops that swam in her eyes, yet not daring to give way or to relieve her feelings by any sign of what she was going through.

Caryngston in summer-time was quite an attractive village. Over the porch of the Seven Spears clambered a Gloire de Dijon rose. On the long benches outside the doors sat the hard-bitten northern farmers, enjoying the restful moment. Deb stood in the porch, and her eyes lit up as she recognised the little lady who had come in

the snow upon an evening now far back in the mists of
that antique period usually alluded to as "before the
war."

As they entered the passage, whose very wall-paper
was unchanged, each moment, each event of the former
occasion revived with poignant freshness.

Deb had plenty to say, the whole war news of the
village to give. Her young daughter had married the
bootmaker's son the first time ever he came home on
leave. She pointed out the house now inhabited by the
reunited couple. "And she's a deal luckier than the most
of 'em. Her man's only short of one foot, and that's
no matter for the boot trade." It was a comfort to find
her so absorbed in what she had to impart, as not to be
very inquisitive concerning Olwen's own affairs, after
once she had expatiated upon the wonderful fate that had
befallen the "yoong lass" in having all that "brass" be-
queathed to her.

Supper was presently partaken of, and removed. At
last, about half-past eight, Olwen was left alone, in the
depths of that armchair where once she had sat swelling
with resentment at Nin's impertinence. She had told
Parkinson to go to bed, and was therefore free to indulge
unnoticed in the luxury of red eyes. Her tears flowed
fast.

What folly had been hers! She had spent such a sum
of money as, following on her large disbursements
throughout the war, would make a real difference to her
—and this in order to bestow the Pele upon Rose Kendall,
the odious girl who had treated Mrs. Guyse's companion
with studied insolence. Yet she gave thanks that she
had given it. In the first passionate tumult of mortification, upon hearing of his engagement, she had been
tempted to withhold the gift. She had put that temptation by. Having started to right a wrong, she could give

Nin the one thing he wished to have, even though her own happiness proved to have been permanently lost. She had misjudged him, she had been ungenerous, undiscriminating, and for this she desired to make amends. Ninian, at a time when he knew her father to be dead and his own discreditable secret safe, had yet confessed. She in return, at a time when she knew him to be about to marry another woman, and her own happiness to be lost, yet held to her resolution to make him once more master of the Pele.

By this deed she felt that she proved herself worthy of him.

Though they would never see each other again, yet there would lie between them the memory of high things. It would make a sanctuary of life in the future—that future which loomed before her so long and so dark. As the slow minutes dragged on she fancied Ninian and his betrothed sitting together—left alone, no doubt, by considerate parents, so that they might make love.

Such are the torments of jealousy that Miss Innes was quite exhausted by their keenness.

He had never made love to her. He had never kissed her!

If ever she had hated anyone she hated Rose Kendall at that moment.

She felt as if ages had passed when she began to hear the stir which indicated the closing of the inn for the night: the sound of the kitchen fire being raked out, benches pushed back, voices raised and dying in the distance, the opening and shutting of doors. The hoofs of a horse clattered on the paved market stones, and ceased abruptly. Deb rattled some crockery in a cupboard, and her husband on the other side of the house turned a great key in a lock.

Olwen must go to bed. She lifted a drenched hand-

kerchief and wiped away the drops which still fell fast.
She had extinguished the lamp, and was sitting in the
dark.   Thus she might slip past Deb without exciting
remark.

The door opened. She spoke, trying to use a natural
voice: "It's all right, Mrs. Askwith; I am not gone to
bed, but I am just—going."

The door shut as softly, as swiftly as it had opened.
The person who had entered moved round the table in
the gloom and came close, standing over her as she
cowered back into the depths of the big old porter's chair.

CHAPTER XXXVI

SHE heard the breathing of one who has ridden hard and far, and right through her there shuddered a thrill so exquisite that for a moment she could not move. She was on the point of springing up, flinging herself into those unseen arms, when she heard his voice, low and mocking.

"You little wretch—you treacherous minx! Don't you think you are the limit?"

As in the mile-castle, she had but the time it took him to deliver himself of this courteous address in which to meet the challenge. She did it, however. If she died for it he should not know that she had been sitting there crying for the moon until her eyes were all swelled and her "hanshif" drenched.

"You must have left your dinner engagement very early, Mr. Guyse. It is barely ten o'clock. However, as I have been travelling all day I am very tired, and I will ask you to excuse me."

"You may ask, but you won't get excused," he said rapidly. "What the dickens are you sitting in the dark for? I want to see your wicked face—to see the conscious guilt steal over it! How dare you? Oh, how *dare* you insult me as you have insulted me to-day?" With a sudden change of tone he added, after a moment's breathless silence: "How could you plan such a fiendish vengeance?"

"Vengeance! How fatiguing you are!" said she

languidly. "What vengeance should I want? I am giving you what you love most in the world. You always have wanted it—don't deny it! You would even almost, have married me in order to secure it! Only I bored you so utterly! However, if you are talking about insults, I don't think I can beat the one you have offered me. You couldn't bring yourself to marry me, but you can bring yourself to marry a poll parrot like that Kendall thing! Oh, *do* go away; I wonder I have the patience to talk to you at all!"

"I wonder I have the patience not to shake you! . . . Do you happen to know where there are some matches?"

"I'll call Deb and ask for some." . . .

She rose from the depths of the chair, and found her hands held.

"Why, you're as cold as a stone! Sitting alone in the dark and the cold—you're actually shivering——"

"That's with rage, not cold. Good night, Mr. Guyse. Sorry I can't stop and talk to you, but you pay your calls at unseemly hours."

"Olwen!" It seemed he was in earnest at last. He had never before called her by her name. "Could you really be so stupid, so utterly unlike yourself, as to imagine that I should accept that deed of gift?"

She gave a little low chuckle. "You can't help accepting it, silly."

"Haven't you got the sense to see that it must be all or nothing between me and you?"

"Well, the choice lies with you, I suppose."

"You suppose nothing of the kind," he cried in exasperation. "You know that all is out of the question, so it must be nothing from you to me—Miss Innes!"

He was so near her that the warmth and energy of him seemed to enfold her. His breath still came fast—and no wonder. The distance between Caryngston and the

Pele, though easy in a motor, was a long, hard ride. She knew that he could not have been at the Kendalls at all. She felt that he was within an ace of sheer explosion, yet still he resisted. Would *nothing* break down his pride?

"Nin"—she threw all the appeal she could into her voice—"Nin, what do you mean? Why do you say that it is out of the question for me to give you—all?"

"Because you don't love me."

"Indeed? And what about you? You don't love me, either."

He gave a rough sort of laugh as if of utter scorn. "You unprincipled woman! Here, I have had enough of this bo-peep, I am going to make a light."

He let go her hands to feel in his pocket for matches; and instantly she made a dart to get past him. He gave an exclamation.

"No, you don't!" dropped the match-box and caught her as she fled—caught her in both arms, held her a breathless moment in silence, breathing hard. Then, with a muttered ejaculation which sounded like "That's done it!" he bent his head down to where he supposed the top of her head to be. She had flung back her throat, and instead of the hair he meant to kiss, he found her lips. . . .

*   *   *   *   *

"Well, it's your fault. You shouldn't have said I didn't love you! Such an obvious lie, now wasn't it?"

The dark still enfolded them. She lay in his arms; but she could not answer. Life had gone past speech.

"What is it?" he whispered. "Are you angry? Have I hurt you?"

He had to bend very close to catch what she said:

"At last!"

"At last!" he echoed; "but girls are the very queerest! Why on earth, if you felt like this, did you treat me in the old days as though you wouldn't have anything to do with me?"

"Oh, Nin, it would take such ages to explain. I—I couldn't even begin yet. I'm—I'm too completely muddled. . . . Hadn't you better put me down now?"

His hold did not slacken. "You are such a will-o'-the-wisp that I dread letting you go, in case you slip away into the dark, as you used to do when I dreamed of you at Griesslauen. Let me sit in the big chair and hold you as I did in the mile-castle—my little white-crane lady!" His odd voice held the tenderest, shyest note—both tones so new to her that they caused delicious shivers to pass through her, as if at a caressing touch. He sat down as he had suggested, cradling her head against him, and added with a choky laugh, "Gad, perhaps it's as well it happened in the dark, so that you could forget the kind of scarecrow I have turned into. You saw to-day, though, up on the moor. You once told me that I looked like a demon. An elderly demon isn't at all a charming sight, I should suppose."

She slipped an arm about his neck. "You have altered, I won't deny it. But you are going to get back all your looks. Wait till you have had a six months' honeymoon! Even Sunia won't know you at the end!" And there her control gave way and she began to sob. "When I think—when I think—what you have gone through——"

"It was bad. But it's over. Yes, it was pretty bad. We won't talk of it now. You see, I was only a private. I went and enlisted in the Gordons because I had no previous military experience. There wasn't a hope of my getting a commission; and I wanted to get out there quick. So I did; I was out of England into France, and out of France into Germany before you could say 'Knife.' . . . Well, if Germany is going to receive retribution at

the hands of Providence for all her misdeeds, it's likely
to be a good while before she's through."

"You are not to think of such things now, but to listen
to me. There is one thing I simply must know. When
you looked up to-day and saw me standing there in the
mile-castle, what did you think? Now don't tease, boy,
tell me really."

"I would if I could, but I can't. I felt as if I couldn't
feel anything. The only idea left was a determination to
keep my end up."

"And I was just as determined to break you down."

"Much you know about it! Break me down with
your flippant Leap-Year proposals, which merely shocked
me! . . . That was what made me run over my whole
list of ammunition and hit upon Rose Kendall!"

"Nin!" Two hands, which small though they may
have been were still decidedly vigorous, went round his
throat. "Were you having me on? Tell the truth now!"

"I can't, if you choke me! Well, yes and no. I was
and I wasn't. It is not true that I am engaged to her, but
they have been letting me see that they would be pleased
enough if it came about. I was thinking that by going
there this evening I was perhaps committing myself.
Anyway, I thought it just possible that if I threw that
stone it might hit you and hurt you, and I wanted to hurt
you as much as I possibly could, because I knew I could
never ask you, and you had shown such incredible effrontery in asking me! You really did deserve——"

"But, Nin, you are a perfect owl! If you thought I
should mind being told you were engaged to the poll-
parrot, how can you say you thought I didn't care for
you?"

"Oh, I don't know! Weren't you sticking pins into
me all over?"

She laid her cheek close against his. "Effrontery!"

she echoed, with a gleeful chuckle. "Yes, I was rather outrageous, wasn't I? Your prunes-prism school-marm asking you right out to marry her! But, you see, you had given yourself away completely. I saw you some minutes before you knew I was there . . . *and I saw what you had in your hand.*"

She boldly plunged her hand into his coat pocket, but found nothing.

He laughed. "Not there, not there, my child. I can't show it you without pulling off my coat and rolling up my sleeve. I've got a 'bracelet of bright hair about the bone' like the chap in Donne's verses . . . it went to Griesslauen with me. . . . Kiddie, this is too good to be true. How nice and soft your cheek is against mine! Just like a peach. Does mine feel scratchy? Rum, isn't it, that it should be such bliss to rub them against each other! Oh, Jove! Here's Mother Deb!"

They had but a moment to regain their feet before the sleepy landlady was upon them, bearing a candle in her hand.

"All in the dark! Then he must have gone," she began, and broke off to continue, in a shocked voice, "Muster Nin, it's time you was a-going."

"You'll have to put me up here to-night, Deb, and to-morrow, yoong lass'll be away oop to t' Pele with me. We're going to get wed, yoong lass and me! What d'you think o' that?"

CHAPTER XXXVII

In the gay morning air the car rushed over the high plain, carrying two lovers to the grim Pele.

Olwen had informed Parkinson that she was going to stay a few days with Mrs. Guyse, but that she must leave her behind, as she was not sure of there being the necessary accommodation. She therefore wished her to remain at the Seven Spears until further orders. As a fact, she felt most uncertain of the treatment her maid would be likely to receive at the hands of the ayah.

Parkinson listened grimly, with an offended air that made Miss Innes feel that a month's notice must be impending. She hoped it was, for she knew that this woman could never be an inmate of her future home.

Early that morning Ezra had ridden into Caryngston upon one of the farm horses. He came to bring news of the sudden grave increase of Madam's illness, and to fetch Dr. Balmayne.

Olwen's experience of sickness, gained so recently, caused her to be very prompt in action. She telegraphed to Newcastle for a nurse, begged Dr. Balmayne to send his car to Picton Bars to bring her up when she arrived, and offered to take him now to the Pele in her own fast car, and to send him back by the same means.

She also insisted that Ninian should telegraph to Wolf the news of his mother's condition before leaving the town.

There was embarrassment on both sides at the first meeting between Miss Innes and the doctor, especially

369

when Ninian, at her special request, announced to him
the fact of their engagement.

He warmly congratulated the bridegroom elect, but
was unable to feel that the lady was to be congratulated.
However, he concealed his opinion as best he could. Having regard as much to his feeling as to their own, Olwen
placed him beside Goddard on the journey, so that Nin
and she might sit together. The night seemed to have
worked a miracle in her lover. The light had come back
to his eye, the glow to his cheek; he looked ten years
younger already, as she assured him when she came down
to breakfast and found him hungrily in wait for her. He
commenced the day's amenities by the · remark that he
hardly knew which he wanted most, his girl or his breakfast.

"I object to being lifted up like a baby," said she reprovingly, as she smoothed her rumpled hair after his
fervent greeting.

"I always did think what fun it would be to carry you
about," was the unabashed reply. "I very nearly tried,
that last evening at the Pele, when you declared you had
a great mind to say 'Yes.' "

"If you had, Nin, I should never have run away,"
she whispered. "You could have held me with one hand,
with a word, a look. You knew that, didn't you?"

"No, I didn't. I only knew that I couldn't, somehow.
I had to let you go. But in my heart I thought—if you
did care—and Sunia kept on telling me you did—that you
would forgive me. Oh, my aunt, if you knew how I
hoped and craved and expected day after day. It never
dawned on me that you would drop me utterly. I don't
know what I expected, but not that!"

"If you had known beforehand that I should drop you
utterly, would you still have told Grandpapa?"

"Oh, I had to tell him in any case," he answered simply.

She then described how her grandfather had received from him the impression that he felt no attachment to her, but had been tempted only by her fortune. She made him understand something of her own agony of humiliation, and of what she had gone through before her impulsive flight.

He had no idea that Madam had told her of her own loveless marriage—of how another Ninian Guyse had wedded her for her fortune. "It was always running in my head," the girl confessed, "I could never forget the exact words she used—*"He was as deep in debt as I in love.'* You can understand how exactly it seemed to apply."

"The thing I thought you would find it hardest to forgive," said he, "if you ever found it out, was our tampering with your correspondence. I loathed the necessity, but having once started on the beastly plot, it had to be done thoroughly, for we knew we had very little time —you must hear before long that you were an heiress, which would shut my mouth—and, after all our care, the one letter which gave the show away came straight to your hands through Dr. Balmayne! I think the knowledge of that was what made me throw up the dirty game. I said, 'Providence is taking care of this little girl. Am I such a hound as to interfere?'"

"It was too late then," was her low reply. "You had done the mischief."

"I somehow felt that it was so, wild as it sounded. It seemed impossible to believe that you were not feeling something of the storm that was shaking me. I thought if I could take you and hold you tight, I might make you believe in me, even when I had told you the truth. But you were too wise——"

"Too cowardly!"

"Too well protected by guardian angels!"

So they talked; and by the time they reached the tower they had talked out all remnants of misunderstanding.

Mrs. Baxter had been on the watch for the doctor's car, and came out into the courtyard. Her face, as she saw who sat with the master, was a curious study.

"Why, if it isn't oor yoong leddy!" said she, staring.

Olwen, lifted out like a doll by Ninian, and set down upon the stones, ran to the good woman and gave her gay greeting.

"Oh, I am glad to see you! How's poor Madam?"

"A little easier-like this morning," was the answer. Nin went off at once to take the doctor upstairs, after asking Mrs. Baxter to show Goddard where to keep the car, and to provide for his sleeping accommodation.

"Where's ayah?" asked Olwen eagerly.

"She was upstairs with Madam," said Mrs. Baxter. Olwen guessed that Nin would send her down, but without telling her who was awaiting her. In fact this was just what he did.

"You're wanted below, ayah," he said to her, when Balmayne had been ushered into the sick room.

Olwen stood in the hall, talking softly to Mrs. Baxter, and noiselessly the curtains parted and the little brown face, framed in its saree, made its appearance.

The Hindu stopped short. For a moment the surprise was overwhelming. She had wondered what had come to her sahib, dashing off on horseback quite late in the evening, and not returning all night—a thing he had not done since she could remember. Just now as he spoke to her upstairs, the light in his eyes, the thrill in his voice had moved her as she had not been moved since first he had come home from his German prison, broken, changed, despairing.

Here stood the answer to the puzzle, and in a swift moment Sunia was on her knees, holding Olwen's hands, kissing them repeatedly, murmuring soft Hindustani words of caressing.

"Ah, Sunia, you have been at your wicked spells," laughed the girl, "all the time I have been away! I have heard you calling, calling, never ceasing. I have struggled hard, but I am here at last—and I am never, never going away again!"

The woman threw up her hands with a wild gesture. "Oh, Missee, my Missee, if only one little week—few days ago! You come too late! My sahib lost his castle! He never be really happy now, even with you!"

"I'm so vain that I think he *would* be really happy, even without the castle, as long as he had me! But never mind, dear, it isn't too late! He has got back his old tower all right! I *was* in time, only just in time!"

For the first time she saw Sunia overpowered. Sinking to the floor, the woman wrapped herself in the folds of her saree and her thin form shook with the intensity of her feeling.

"Sunia," softly said Olwen presently, "do you feel better? Can you listen?"

The woman raised her face, all quivering. "And I ask my gods to curse my Missee!" she cried in anguish.

"Well, but they knew I didn't deserve to be cursed, so they took no notice," cried Olwen playfully. "Here I am, alive and well, and all the rest of my life I am just going to try and make your sahib happy. Now you must wipe your eyes and get up, because I have brought my luggage with me, and I am going to stay here."

Sunia bounded to her feet. "Ayah dear," laughed the soft little voice, "I am rich now, very rich, and I have a maid who waits on me. May I send for her to come and be my maid here?"

Violent rage transformed Sunia's face. "She not come

here," muttered she; "I see to my Missee, I dress my Missee for her wedding."

"You shall, I promise you," replied the girl, fairly hugging the little woman.

It was a busy day. They had the nurse installed by soon after midday, and at about three Olwen was admitted to kiss and smile at her future mother-in-law.

Mrs. Guyse was looking terribly ill and thin, but she was fully conscious and evidently took great pleasure in the sight of the girl.

Olwen told her that she must make haste and get strong enough to be moved, so that she could go away to the south of Europe and grow quite well. Would she not like that? Wolf could take her, while Nin and she went for their wedding journey.

Madam seemed quite pleased, and smiled; but there was a curious expression in her eyes as she turned them on the girl. She pressed the hand that held hers. "You are good and kind, my child. We treated you very badly. You have returned good for evil, and I could not bear for you to be—unhappy."

"Unhappy, dear? I hope there is little chance of that. Nobody in the world was ever so happy as I."

"I have been very ill," said Madam faintly, "and that makes one think. I have lain here and thought . . . and there is something . . . something you ought to know. Will you send Nin to me, my dear?"

"Don't you think," urged Olwen, "that you should wait until you are stronger? It is very likely that Nin will tell me the thing you have in mind. We have had so little time as yet to talk things over. Try not to worry."

Madam hesitated. "Well, perhaps. But I think he will not tell you. He has never told me, often as I have

begged him to. However, you can ask him. Ask him
—as a message from me—tell him that I adjure him,
before marrying you, to tell you the truth about—about
Lily Martin."

Lily Martin! Her name had vanished from Olwen's
very thoughts. That story, which had so occupied her
mind formerly as to blot out any other idea, had now
receded into the dim background. However, she hastened
to reassure Madam. "Dear, he told me all about that,
long, long ago, while I was here."

Madam smiled. "I think not."

Olwen's heart beat. To Madam in her weak state she
dare not say anything of what she knew. The patient lay
still for a few minutes, then in a weak voice, gave some
directions. Olwen was to find a key, unlock the bureau
in Madam's sitting-room, take thence a dispatch-box, open
that, and bring the envelope it contained to her.

Carefully carrying out instructions, the girl easily
found the required paper, and brought it to the bedside.

"Open it—look," whispered Madam.

Olwen drew from the envelope another, which had been
partially burned. This was the remains of a letter which
had been through the post. It was thus addressed:

> Mrs. Ninian Guyse,
> 3, Lockerbie Terra
> Southamp

The remains of the address had been burned away. She
looked at it in some bewilderment.

"The day that Miss Martin tried to kill herself, she
burnt a lot of old letters in the billiard-room grate,"
whispered the sick woman. "I came in and found this,
which had fallen out of the fire. I picked it up, thinking
that some day—some day—I would have the truth from

Ninian. I hid it carefully, and was thankful it was I who found it. If there had been an inquest, it would have been terribly strong evidence. As it was, it all passed off. I suppose he has been keeping her ever since, and that is how he gets rid of so much money; but I have never spoken to him of it."

"Is it his writing?" asked the girl.

"Yes."

"I will talk to him about it," said Olwen quietly; "but I think you may be certain that he is not to blame."

"If I could be! In other ways, he has been a good son, in spite of his odd manner. You really love him, in spite of his manners, my dear?"

"Because of them, I believe," laughed the girl, bending to kiss her and to hide the colour in her cheeks. "I wouldn't change him."

She said nothing to Ninian of what had passed until after tea that evening. They had it in the dining-room, and grew very foolish over their memories of the last time they had shared the function.

Afterwards, resisting the lure of his desire to play and be silly like two children, she told him there was something she must speak about, of a not particularly pleasant character; and that she demanded his full attention.

"Madam surprised me to-day," she went on, "by speaking on a subject which I would far rather were not mentioned between us; but what she said makes it necessary that the whole matter should be cleared up. She and you have never understood each other. You think she loves you less than Wolf, because she has a feeling of resentment against you, for making her live here, contrary to her inclination. But that's only partly true. She has something else to charge you with; and she has told me what it is."

He was evidently surprised, and asked for an explanation with all the seriousness that she could desire.

"Before I say anything of what Madam showed me to-day," she continued, "I want you to read a letter which reached me in London some days ago. Its contents may not be news to you. I am inclined to suppose that they are not. The affair had faded from my mind, for the thought of you drives out everything else; but after what your mother said, I am sure you ought to know the whole truth."

So saying, she put into his hands the letter she had received from the *ci-devant* Lily Martin.

She watched his face with acute curiosity as he read, and she could see that he was unprepared for what he found.

"*Wolf's wife!* . . . That girl!" was all he said; but his voice expressed extreme distaste.

Laying down the letter he propped his chin on his hands, and puckered his mouth into a soundless whistle; then, flinging himself back in his chair, "This is a facer for me," he muttered.

Leaning forward, she laid a hand caressingly on his forehead, stroking back the hair. "Nin, did you know nothing of it?"

He shrugged his shoulders. "Honestly, no, I didn't. I don't say that I didn't know he was in some matrimonial scrape, for I did. If it hadn't been that he was not free he wouldn't have allowed me to have the first innings with you. He was awfully fed up about that. He has drained me of every penny I could spare, and most of those I couldn't spare, in order to continue her allowance. He always said she was consumptive, and that it was only an affair of a few years. I never knew it was Lily Martin. Why, she must have been married to him when she first came to us! Help!"

There was consternation in his accents. Olwen looked into the depths of his eyes, so limpid and boyish. How could she ever have thought this man untrustworthy?

After a while she produced the burnt envelope, telling him where his mother had found it.

To her relief, he seemed to attach small importance to it.

"If she is really Wolf's wife," he said absently, "that explains things. She wrote Mrs. Ninian Guyse on the back of a photo which she must have left by accident in the pages of a book. I thought when I found it that it was just her confounded cheek; but she had right on her side. You know that Ninian is the typical Guyse name in our senior branch of the family. Thus my father named his twin sons Ninian Wilfrid and Wilfrid Ninian respectively, so that if one of us got knocked out the survivor might still be a Ninian Guyse. Wolf's wife might almost as well call herself Mrs. Ninian Guyse as you might. As he wanted the thing kept dark, he would be very likely to use his other name. It was an obvious precaution. As to the writing, Wolf and I write so alike that our hands are often mistaken for one another. There is, however, one letter that we make quite differently, and that is our initial N. I always write it plain like a printed N, and Wolf writes it as on this address. My, mother might not notice that, because I am always with her and she doesn't often see my signature. But I think I could easily convince any impartial person that I didn't write that address." He felt in his pocket, brought out some letters from his brother addressed to himself, and showed the initial N exactly as it appeared on the letter. Then he went to the bureau and fetched out a letter which he had just written to a local correspondent. The N at the foot, where his signature appeared, was, as he had said, quite different. "Rather tiresome, isn't it, that I

an only clear myself in Madam's eyes by incriminating
Wolf? She thinks a hundred times more of him than
she does of me. I can't tell tales of him."

She contemplated his serious, absorbed face, and
laughed out aloud in the completeness of her relief. "Oh,
Nin," said she, "you *are* a darling!"

His expression changed like lightning to its most
wicked twinkle.

"Come," he said, "we're getting on. That's the very
first pretty name you ever called me—are you aware of
that, my porcelain rogue?"

"I prefer being a school-marm and a white crane and
a blue thing with a red nose to any amount of darlings,"
was her contented reply.

Madam's condition changed for the better that evening.
The following afternoon, when the Colonel arrived, he
found her much improved.

He had been a good deal mystified, upon his arrival
at Picton Bars, to find Miss Innes's Rolls-Royce and
chauffeur awaiting him.

Goddard told him that the young lady was staying
at the Pele, and thus he was more or less prepared for
the state of affairs which he found upon arrival.

Ninian and Olwen were having tea in the banqueting-
hall. They were sitting in the oriel, and at the moment
of his entry, Ninian was wholly absorbed in demon-
strating that he could fold his fiancée's hand within his
own, so that it was completely concealed, and could be
withdrawn without his unlocking a single finger.

Olwen received her future brother-in-law graciously
enough, but with a new reserve in her manner which he
felt uncomfortably.

Ninian explained to him their plan, which was to be
married at once without any kind of pomp, so that he

might take his bride to Italy or the Pyrenees until his health was thoroughly re-established.

"I shall invite nobody but my grandfather and my two unmarried aunts," said Olwen; "but there is one person whose presence I particularly desire, and that is your wife, Wilfrid."

"My wife!" he said, with first a flash of anger, and then a hesitation, a dark look at his twin. There was a pause, which they left it to him to break.

"I had no idea that my brother knew," he said at last, very coldly.

"He did not until I told him," replied Miss Innes. "Your wife wrote to me. I feel sure that she wrote for my sake, not for her own. It happened that I had been kind to some cousin of hers, and she thought she ought to warn me that you were not free."

His eyes flashed. "If I had been free, what price Ninian's chance?" he asked, with a sneer.

"No human creature has a chance as long as Nin is above ground," was her tender reply. "I only liked talking to you because every now and then you are so astonishingly like him—superficially."

"Well, Nin, I congratulate you, from the bottom of my heart," said Wolf, in a softer tone.

"I feel as if, seeing that I am going to be one of the family, I ought to scold you, Wolf," said Olwen. "But somehow I can't. I feel too happy to scold. However, there is one thing I must do, and that is, to set you a penance. I want you to go upstairs to Madam—she is much better this evening—and tell her, quite quietly and simply, that Lily is your wife. You owe this to Ninian, for she is quite sure that it is he who has done what you have done. I must tell you frankly that, until you do this, and acknowledge your wife, you and I won't be friends."

Ninian interposed, in a bashful, muttering fashion. "Don't ask him to tell her! She loves him best, and it doesn't hurt her half as much to think I have done a shabby thing as it would to think that he had."

Olwen lifted her gaze to the Colonel's moody, handsome face. Her eyes were alight with joy and pride in her lover. "You hear that, Wolf?" she asked a little chokily. "That's your brother—your twin; won't you show yourself worthy of him? Must all the generosity be his to the very end?"

His look dwelt upon her, half resentment, half admiration. "By jove, Ninian, you and I are going to be shown our places now, aren't we?" he sneered.

"Always told her she was a school-marm," replied Nin, his mouth curved sideways into his most crooked grin.

Wolf turned away, with an envious look under his eyelashes. He walked the length of the room, came slowly back half-way, wavered a minute, then went out, closing the door behind him.

"It won't hurt her, Nin," said Olwen gently; "she likes Lily, and she has brooded for so long over what she imagined to be your deceit. It is best to tell her the truth, and then I can write to Lily to-night and invite her to the wedding."

"Trust you to manage it all," remarked he, with a chuckle of intense satisfaction.

THE END